KU-270-579

DISCLAIMER

ISBN: 978 0 992 95701 8

Acknowledgments

It was my medicine when I got sick, my friend when I got lonely; my precious **Fur Coat No Knickers** couldn't have come this far without:

Editor: Teena Lyons. Thank you for believing in me.

Proofreaders/Copy Editors: Sandra Martin, Domenico Marsala, Francesca Marsala, Ellie Baldwin.

Cover Illustrator: Alex Furley of AF Designs.

I'd like to thank my mum, dad and my beautiful sisters whom I love very much.

To my sisters, you both mean the world to me. I couldn't have got through this without your continuous love, support and daily encouragement.

To my partner, SI, Thank you for your patience and still loving me while I lived in an atrocious, fluffy red dressing gown for years when writing this, my first novel. And thanks for your patience when I screamed in temper if things didn't go my way.

To my utterly bonkers best friends; don't ever change - I love you all. You know who you are.

To my dear friend, JM, without you, Franc (pronounced 'Fronk') would have never existed. I miss you.

Lastly, to my three, perfect children. I'm so glad you got the beauty *and* the intelligence genes. Thank you for wiping my tears when my short-term memory blew its fuse. I couldn't be more proud of you all.

And if I have missed anyone out here, my apologies, but I fully intend to blame my (bastard of an) under-active thyroid.

To Mum, the kindest and bravest woman I have ever known.

The following story is based on true events...

CHAPTER ONE

I glanced up at the tinsel-covered clock; it was nearly closing time at Glamma-Puss.

Just Siobhan's hair to blow-dry, a quick change of clothes and I would be off to the airport to spend no doubt another crazy Christmas with my family in Dublin. I couldn't wait. This break had been a long time coming.

As I counted down the hours to my big getaway, I could hardly believe Glamma-Puss was about to go into its second year of business. I'd loved setting up the Hair and Beauty Salon, but every aspect of it had been really hard work. I'd thought carefully about every decorative detail; I had mixed contemporary with boudoir, soft mushroom and cream walls, with dark oak wooden floors. I had really gone to town with all the accessories; mixing rich French lavish curtains in shimmering taffeta with dramatic, swooping tails in a mix of silver and pale gold. The walls were covered in large baroque silver mirrors and to add to the grandeur and opulence to the Salon, for the complete 'wow' factor, I invested heavily in a pale gold leather chaise longue for the reception area.

I'd been lucky enough to find a great team that complimented the feel of the Salon perfectly. Jackie, my beauty therapist, was in her early fifties; quite tiny in height and kept sharp, short, copper-coloured hairstyles. She was bubbly and always smiled. She was great for business too and was constantly stacked out with clients from opening to close.

As for my drama-queen nail technician, James, aged 23, he simply minced in like he owned the place.

'I am your right-hand man,' James declared, with a dramatic curtsey when he first came for an interview. I instantly loved him; although, to this day, I still don't recall advertising for a nail technician. He arrived on opening day, white blonde hair waxed a mile high, clad head-to-toe in a neon pink boiler-suit and fluttered around like Miss World. He simply set up a portable nail bar with every colour of polish and acrylic you could think of... and promptly hired himself. I just couldn't say no.

Then there was Jayde. Aged 20, she was short, curvy, blue-eyed and blonde. She was the definition of a rough diamond. A pure, out-and-out Londoner. Despite this, from the moment I met her, I could see she was passionate about hairdressing; she just needed those rough edges smoothing down a little. She needed someone to believe in her. So, whilst she came across as bit crass, I nonetheless felt compelled to nurture her and give her a chance.

Jayde's mum had died of cancer when she was just three years old and she never knew her dad, not even his name. Jayde had spent most of her life being fostered out. Luckily, her last set of carers had generously put her through college to learn the art of Hairdressing.

I remember the day of the interview; Jayde arrived an hour early, wide-eyed and eager to show me what she was made of. With crumpled shopping bags, she asked if she could use the staff toilets to change. She emerged in a jacket and trousers combo that in no way formed a matching suit. Worse still, the price tags were dangling for all to see.

'If I don't get the job, let me know, cos I've still got the receipt for me outfit see. Otherwise I'll just bring it straight back to New Look,' she said unashamedly, fiddling with one of her many gold hooped earrings.

I couldn't help but enquire about Jayde's background. After her answering my 21 questions, I simply couldn't get over her resilience and happy-go-lucky attitude, despite having such a harsh start in life. Jayde considered herself to be one of the lucky ones, which humbled me. I just wanted to take her under my wing, so I offered her a few trial days at the Salon.

Jayde displayed such a fresh, artistic approach and incredible creations in such a short space of time, I made her permanent on day two of her trial. She burst into tears, squeezing me so tight I thought my silicones were going to rupture.

I was on a roll and was thrilled to be hiring another valuable member of staff. Sheila, an aesthetic nurse practitioner joined us for one day a month to perform a range of cosmetic skin treatments and non-surgical procedures. She was a 1940's screen goddess if ever there was one. Her signature retro hairstyles, siren red lipstick and hourglass figure were admired by all who met her. She was the perfect candidate for my expanding business; adding another exciting string to my fledgling enterprise.

Of course, this diverse mix of staff meant there was never a dull moment at Glamma-Puss, and once you threw my best friend Siobhan into the mix, you'd never know what might happen.

'Howerya everyone…? Meeeeerrrrrryyyy [hic] Christmas!' slurred Siobhan as she stumbled through the Salon door as if on cue. That's Siobhan; she always likes to make an entrance.

'Hi Siobhan! Been on the sauce already I see? You lucky thing you. I'll be with you in five. James, take Siobhan's coat. Jayde, shampoo her for me, please?'

I walked into the staffroom with Jackie to go over the running of the Salon while I was away. As I crossed the floor, I could hear the usual rapid-fire banter begin.

'Hi [hic] James,' said Siobhan with a lop-sided grin, 'howerya?'

'Oh my! That's a rather gorgeous coat. Is it from the new Dior collection?' James asked, stroking it as he hung it up. He stepped back, a hand planted firmly on each of his slim hips and gave it a fuller inspection.

'What? That old thing?' Siobhan enquired with a dismissive swipe of her hand. 'No, it's a Primani special! Does it look like the [hic]... the new Dior coat?'

'Eww... *actually*, on closer inspection, it certainly does not,' retorted James, instantly dismissing it. He then promptly turned on his neatly polished slip-ons and pointedly distanced himself from the offending garment.

'Ha ha!' cackled Jayde. 'The poof got it wrong!'

'Get on and do your job, you filthy little scrubber,' James shot back sharply.

'So someone's a bit grumpy today...' Siobhan whispered to Jayde.

'Ignore him - he's been a whiney bitch all day,' answered Jayde deliberately loud enough so James could hear her.

'Jayde!' pointed out James furiously, 'had *you* not made such a catastrophe of my crowning glory, I would not be so upset. You've completely annihilated my asymmetrical fringe for the party season!'

'Ah, come on now James, your hair is... well... it's lovely,' said Siobhan, leaning her head back into the washbasin.

'That's just it Siobhan... I *don't* do *lovely*... I do *fabuliscious* or *magnificent!*' protested James. 'How can I do my blonde-with-strategically-placed-violet-tips hair flick and pout now that my fringe no longer rests on my high cheekbones? That is *sooo* the point of asymmertricalness. It's a good job I have a diamante headband to cover this abomination on my head!' ranted James. 'It's simple; it *all* has to be perfect - something you don't know the meaning of, Jayde. It's all about tight-arsed glory!' He barely paused to breathe as he swung around, wiggled his toosh and threw his tall but tiny frame into a 'slut drop' for good measure (this being one of his best party tricks. The clients loved it).

'*This*,' James added dramatically, lowering his arm theatrically down his body, 'has to resemble a piece of *art*. Do you think this all comes naturally? *No*, no, it does not! For example... *if* I may continue?' glared James, as Jayde began to mimic him. 'These freckles, or, as I prefer to call them, *"clustered beauty spots"*, have been cleverly blended by one of my bestest friends. *No*, not you Jayde - the sun bed! Artfully amalgamating them through years of baking and frying one's self has giveth *moi* a sexy tan, and viola!' James lifted his Jean Paul Gaultier floral shirt, revealing a toned, tanned and boyish body. His freckles had indeed formed together to give the illusion of an even tan.

It had to be said; he *was* such a pretty boy. His feline features accentuated his continual purr of pride as he performed to his captive audience. In fact, I'm sure some clients booked in just to watch 'The James Show', rather than for a particular treatment. The James Show nearly always included dramas about his latest love conquest; or the highs and lows of whichever 'rubber-arsed bastard' had broken his heart this time. The gossip of his constant sexual onslaughts was complicated, dramatic and thoroughly entertaining to say the least.

Having such strong personalities in our den of madness inevitably meant there were sometimes clashes amongst the ranks. However, I could never figure out why there was *so much* tension between James and Jayde. James' barrage of bitchy comments had a real barbed edge when it came to Jayde. It was as though he *really* meant it; whereas with everyone else, it was clearly a part of his carefully crafted diva personality. I often wondered what he saw in her that no one else did. He certainly wasn't swayed by any pity for her tough upbringing.

Jayde, for her part, was used to fighting her own battles. She'd made it clear from the start she wasn't going to tolerate any flack and so gave as good as she got.

The resulting battles were highly entertaining, as long as you didn't listen too closely. Now and again though, they made you catch your breath in wonder how they could say this stuff.

Of course, Siobhan loved to disturb the peace so lobbed in the odd verbal grenade if she ever sensed hostilities were flagging.

'So James, come here till I ask you... have you been in receipt of any *swollen* goods [hic]... lately?' Siobhan asked, her voice full of innuendo.

'Hmmm... it's a sore subject,' James quietly said, pouting, 'I'd rather not talk about it now. Well, certainly not in front of *her* anyway,' he added, narrowing his intense stare in Jayde's direction.

'Might dat subject be your arse, you dirty fecker?' Siobhan chuckled whilst Jayde continued to massage shampoo into her hair.

'Na, the only thing what's been down his designer fong lately is Jackie with a wax strip, innit!' howled Jayde, cackling like a hyena on speed.

'Ooow, go and cram another tray of mince pies in that hole in your face before I fill it full of acrylic!' James spat back in fury. 'And by the way… I saw the state of those scissors after you had been hacking away at your pubic jungle!'

'Arrghh! Shut up, you fudge packer!' Jayde hollowed back. 'You know damn well it was Mrs. Johnson's Afro barnet what done that!'

'Ah g'wan! Get him in the crown jewels, Jayde!' squealed Siobhan in childish excitement.

'Siobhan, please keep your head back!' insisted Jayde. 'I can't wash ya locks while you're windmillin' like an ape.'

'Sorry, but this is even better than the Jerry feckin' Springer show!' shrieked Siobhan.

She was right. The Salon was always pretty entertaining, but when Siobhan came in, it always had that extra edge. Everything just seemed crazier somehow.

Siobhan and I had only known each other a year, but already she was like family to me; except, she never judged me - unlike my biological sisters.

Watching her staggering around the Salon bantering with Jayde and James, I was reminded of the day we met last December. Siobhan burst into the Salon wearing a shocking peach bridesmaid dress and covered her face up with a bouquet of plastic flowers, demanding a pot of wax. I'd had a hard time understanding her through the flowers, but in a broad Irish accent she was mumbling something about being 'mortified'; with a few 'feckers' and 'gobshites' thrown in. Seeing my look of puzzlement, she had whisked the bouquet from her face and slurred a fuller explanation:

'I didn't want to go to the poxy wedding anyway… I was only going for the free bar!' she ranted, as though I should know what the hell she was talking about. Suddenly however, the floodgates were open and I didn't have a chance to interrupt.

'(Sobbing)… There we were, me and me fella, all ready to go to this *stupid* wedding, when the gobshite started eyeballing me,' she cried. 'He turns around to me and says: "you've a moustache when the sunlight hits your face". Then he says, "I don't know whether to fight you or fuck you." He thought it was hysterical! He's a feckin' *gobshite*! That's not funny, sure it's not?'

Even now, the thought of that moment makes me smile. At the time, I had to turn around, as I couldn't suppress the grin on my face. I managed to say that Jackie would be able to sort her out, but when I saw Siobhan pawing at her top lip and imitating a male voice, I couldn't hold back any longer and burst out laughing. Luckily, she cracked too and soon enough the tears were rolling down our faces. And that was it; our friendship was made from that single moment of madness.

Despite the entertainment value, I did often have to bring everyone back down to earth and remind them that this *was* a professional and high-end establishment. It was my business after all.

'Oh c'mon you guys - it's Christmas Eve! Where's your sense of forgiveness?' I asked the battling pair in frustration, as I signalled Siobhan to come and take a seat so I could blow-dry her hair. 'Let's call a truce.'

'Hmm. You'd be alright if ya stopped snorting that acrylic,' whispered Jayde under her breath, shooting a look of daggers at James.

'I heard that - you uneducated bitch!' responded James furiously. In an instant, hostilities had resumed.

'I am a designer nail technician - getting high off the fumes is part of my job!' he said in mock indignation.

'It's gone to your 'ed,' Jayde chortled. 'I'm telling ya! I mean, you could totally do with sorting out that tan of yours. You look like a malnourished Oompa-Loompa.'

'As much as I'd like to thank you for my malnourishment compliment, Jayde, I'd also like to point out that your pores are so diabolically huge they should be paying council tax!'

'Ho-ho-ho!' belted Siobhan like a referee Santa Claus, 'round two: DING-DING-DING!'

'James, Jayde!' I pleaded, 'drop your weapons, now! I'm not in the mood for hair and beauty tools at dawn!'

'Ah come on now,' pouted Siobhan, 'there's only me here, we're all only playing.'

'Stop now, that's enough!' I commanded. 'Siobhan, *please* don't encourage them.' I rolled my eyes to the heavens, turned my back on the pair of them and switched on the hair-dryer to drown out their bickering.

Is this what I have really signed up for? A life of keeping this lot in place?

I began to daydream. *I should have a rock-solid, perfect, gob-smackingly gorgeous husband by now; who dotes completely on me and our perfectly behaved, impeccable children. We would call them Hugo, Tommy and Mercedes. They'd attend the finest of schools. Hubby would be here with* *me right now, keeping <u>this lot</u> in order, but only after he's finished preparing the three-course Michelin style meal that would be waiting for me when I got home. Yes, he'd be a top chef,* I mused to myself. *Not one who screams and shouts and loses his temper, although I have to admit: Gordon Ramsey telling me to 'get my fucking head down' on him would be nothing other than an absolute pleasure.*

Now, where was I? Ah yes, my husband would be so successful that he didn't have to work over Christmas. He could even have retired very young. *Actually, scrap that, idle minds equal idle hands, we don't want them wandering...* No, wait... we would have a nanny. Yes, a live-in nanny. A butt-ugly one though, that's very important. She would have warts - not genital warts, or anything like that - just enough warts with a few sprigs of pubic-like hair darting around. A Nanny McFee type. Yes, that would be perfect.

We would remain in London - perhaps in a penthouse apartment - around Hyde Park. Actually, make that a mansion in Hampstead. It would have to be huge, because it would need to house, amongst other things, a humungous Christmas tree - a real one. It would be decorated in traditional-style, with fairy lights, all white and twinkly; with huge red velvet bows.

We would decorate it together as a family. I could almost see my gorgeous husband lifting our eldest, Tommy, to put the angel on top. No wait, Hugo would be our eldest, Tommy can turn the Christmas tree lights on. But then Mercedes may feel left out. *Gosh, being a parent is difficult.* I'd need to find her something to do. *Oh, I know, I will have to put her to bed because she's tired... Or perhaps I should just have two children? I've got it! Even better, I'm pregnant with Mercedes!* I would be a vision of fertile loveliness for the festive season.

So, back to the child lifting. My handsome man will be lifting our son up effortlessly in his muscular arms while we all watched together in admiration, revelling in a perfect Christmas.

'OUCH - that's hot! Don't be scolding the head off me you loon!' irked Siobhan.

'Oh... sorry! I was miles away.'

As I was adding the final touches to Siobhan's hair, Jackie was getting ready to leave. Fortunately, Jackie had been with me since the opening of the Salon and was a very skilled beauty therapist. She was however a lot quieter than the others and often seemed bemused by their incessant jokes, but she was always good company. Indeed, out of all of them, I would often go to Jackie for wise counsel. I'd noticed she seemed withdrawn in the last few days and I had been waiting for a good opportunity for a word in private. Luckily, she paused next to me as she readied herself to go.

'Jackie... you look a little worried, are you alright?' I asked quietly as I switched off the hair-dryer.

'Hmm. I'm not sure,' whispered Jackie, looking around her in a secretive manner, 'have a look at this; I got a text earlier from the old man and it's confused me.'

[Text from Pete]

'Hi sexy, can't wait to see u tonight. And wear that new underwear I got u ;-) xxxxx'

'Oowh lucky you,' I said playfully, handing back the phone, 'looks like you're on a promise tonight!'

'No,' replied Jackie, shaking her head, 'you don't understand... Pete hasn't bought me any underwear... and he said he was going out for a few drinks with the boys tonight.'

My heart sank a little. I deliberately tried to avoid eye contact with Siobhan, because I knew she'd been eavesdropping and this didn't sound good.

'I'm sure there's a reasonable explanation,' I said as brightly as I could. 'It must be one of his friends messing about with his phone or something, don't worry yourself, sweetheart.'

Reaching into the drawer of the reception desk, I pulled out the Salon spare keys and handed them to Jackie, along with her Christmas bonus.

'Here's your Christmas bonus. Thanks for all your hard work this year. Now, you get yourself home and I'll lock up. Merry Christmas and thanks again for taking over while I'm in Dublin,' I said while giving her a big, reassuring hug.

'No problem,' she said, forcing a smile. 'Enjoy your family Christmas. Bye everybody, merry Christmas,' she said, unconvincingly as she left the Salon.

'There's no way he is playing away. He wouldn't, would he?' I asked Siobhan, as I started spraying her hair into place.

'Well,' slurred Siobhan, swaying slightly in her chair and clearly making an effort to focus on her reflection in the mirror, 'he *is* in his 50's… and didn't you tell me that he just bought himself a mid-life crisis, penis extending set of wheels?'

'Siobhan!' I chided, tapping her on the head with the brush. 'There's no way! And it's just a car.'

Quietly though, I did concede to myself; she did have a point. It *was* a Subaru; a huge statement in itself. I had to push the thought to the back of my head. Any hint of marital impropriety really didn't fit in with my own fantasy of a 'perfect' family life; with three kids, a mansion in Hampstead and an index-linked pension.

'But they have been married for like… forever,' I eventually stammered out, 'they are the perfect couple… aren't they?'

'Ah Tara, c'mon now, she has five kids! She must have a fanjita like a clowns pocket!' scoffed Siobhan.

'Do you have to be so crude?' I tutted, handing her back her coat.

I was just about to launch into a lecture on the sanctity of family life when James, who never knowingly missed out on any potentially hot gossip, interrupted us.

'So… I couldn't help overhearing,' said James inquisitively, as he slithered over with a raised eyebrow. 'What's all this about Jackie? Go on, do tell!'

'*James*,' I said cutting him short and raising one hand in the air like some sort of helpless traffic cop, '*nothing* is going on.'

'Pete's feckin' cheating on Jackie,' piped up Siobhan. 'I'm [hic] telling you!'

'Siobhan, shoooosh!' I snapped, whirling around to face her while adopting my best headmistress-in-a-temper look.

'Reeeally… ooooh, the naughty bugger!' said James, in obvious delight. He couldn't have been that excited by the news though, because he immediately turned the conversation around to himself. 'And talking of naughty buggers - no pun intended – my new hot piece of man-candy seems to have fallen off the 'gaydar' system and gone icy-cold on my little behind. It's put me in such a foul mood! I keep texting him and he's not replying. It could have something to do with what he said about being 'confused' - but I've told him, his undercarriage is for men only! It's just ridiculous!'

Siobhan was all ears. She loved all this stuff. '[Hic]… So [hic]… so James [hic]…' she persisted, seemingly to encourage him into more revelations.

'I mean, how could *anybody* be confused after a night like that with *moi?*' James continued bluntly, raising his manicured hand to his chest, evidently flabbergasted. 'I might need to give him the silent treatment so he realises what he's missing. I mean, what more could he wish for?'

James, momentarily upset, re-adjusted the fluffy halo he'd been resolutely wearing in the Salon throughout the run-up to Christmas. 'How do you give a man the silent treatment when he's the one being silent? It's *so* hard.'

'How *hard*?' Siobhan asked, one eyebrow suggestively raised as she predictably zoned-in on the word *'hard.'*

'He's so sexical, you know. Sex on a stick. And don't get me started on what he keeps in those tighty-whities. I could ride his disco-stick *all-night-long.*' With that, James threw back his head and laughed uproariously, while treating his audience to a little wiggle of his leather-clad bum.

'Wow [hic]… so wait… back the feck up. You said he was confused?' queried Siobhan, who had clearly not been keeping up well in her befuddled state.

'Yes, well he has only recently discovered that 'gay is the way' after I showed him the night of his life! But he has since *wrongly* decided that he wasn't so sure!' said James impatiently.

'NO!… so he goes both ways…? He's bi-di-bi-di-bi,' roared Siobhan.

'I'm talking 5' 10" of toned perfection,' James continued, ignoring Siobhan's hopeful conclusion.

'How many marks out of ten would you give him?' pressed Siobhan. 'How young is he? Is he ripe for the picking? Oh feck it… I'm getting myself all worked up now!'

'Oh Siobhan, let me tell you, he was off the Richter scale,' said James with a long, loved-up sigh.

'Mmm [hic]… well James, because I love you sooo much, I'm gonna do you a favour and test-drive him with me fanjita for you, just to see what genitalia he likes best. That way you'll know for sure,' said Siobhan conspiratorially. 'Now I can't be any fairer than that, now can I?'

'Thank you for offering the use of your… err… 'lady-garden' Siobhan, however I plan to keep him on the dark side,' sniggered James, 'but, Happy Christmas, darling.'

James and Siobhan were both clearly pleased with the exchange and finished the performance with an elaborate display of air kissing on one another's cheeks.

'Happy Christmas to my best friend,' said Siobhan, turning and throwing her arms around me, locking me into a bear hug. 'I'm going to miss you so much. Be good. And if you can't be good, be damn good at it!'

'Aww - and happy Christmas to you too!' I replied, returning the hug.

'See you on New Year's Eve! And James…' shouted Siobhan, 'if you change your mind and want me to take lover-boy round the block for you… do let me know,' she said with a wink.

With that, Siobhan sailed out of the Salon, grabbing her 'fanjita' and thrusting her hips as she left. For a moment, the Salon fell silent. It was always like that with Siobhan. She was such a ball of life and energy that when she left the room it felt like a vacuum.

'James, Jayde… c'mon… it's pressie time,' I said, recovering the festive feeling by choosing this moment to hand them their Christmas bonus envelopes.

'Thanks, Tara!' They both chorused, then shot each other evil stares after they realized they'd chanted in unison.

Jayde broke the tension, 'I weren't gonna give you a crimbo pressie, James; but it is the season of giving to the unfortunate,' began Jayde, looking genuinely contrite.

'Oh goody… I got you one too!' James replied, clapping his hands together with delight. He obviously completely missed Jayde's dig.

'Gimme, gimme!' jumped Jayde excitedly.

'Here you go…' James said, passing her a beautifully gift-wrapped box; complete with tag, bow and curled ribbon. Jayde then passed James an Aldi carrier bag with his present inside, before unceremoniously ripping her Christmas gift open.

'Err… you're so kind,' he said with a downward curl of his mouth, taking it with his fingertips as though it contained toxic waste. 'I'll bring mine at home and put it under the tree (outside).'

'Wow, James! Ya got me a shell suit! An' it's all checkered an' shit,' shrieked Jayde, holding up a brown and white outfit and smoothing it out with one hand.

'It's called Burberry, you uncouth beast! I got you the matching scrunchie to scrape your greasy hair back to stop it falling in your trough when you're eating,' James sneered.

'I'm gunna look like… OMG… just sooo cool!' exclaimed Jayde, excitedly ignoring James.

'Wow, what a generous gift,' I remarked, smiling.

James whispered in my ear, 'It's okay... it's fake. I acquired it from ChavLand.com.'

Having said our goodbyes, I switched off the never-ending, looped Christmas CD, blew out the mulled wine scented candles and pulled out the plug from the Christmas tree lights.

I went into the staffroom, which was still littered with mince pies and plastic cups containing the remnants of a bottle of Cava, got changed and ordered a taxi to take me to the airport. As I made a halfhearted attempt to tidy up, I mused on what lay ahead for my Christmas holidays.

In what seemed to be an increasingly common habit of mine, I circled and rubbed my tummy longingly. The desire to have a baby was growing ever stronger. I was becoming obsessed, wishing that I could go back to my younger self. However hard I tried, I had *still* not found my Mr. Right. *Perhaps I should settle on a Mr. Nearly Right?* Who was I kidding... I'd have leapt at a *Mr. Slightly Right* given half the chance.

Even though I joked about my hopeless situation with my friends, I did feel incredibly sad that yet another year had flown by and there was still no husband and still no baby. It's true what they say: youth is wasted on the young. I stared at my reflection in the staffroom mirror. Sure, we can Botox to the hilt, have facelifts, stretch and inject every conceivable part of our body, yet, we cannot stop our ticking biological clock. Each minute, each hour, each day, youth was slipping from my fingertips, from the inside out. I couldn't do anything about it. It was and is impossible to stop that ageing process inside-me.

I didn't want to go down the road of having my eggs frozen and stored like a frozen Petit-Poi. My baby would get frostbite and if he/she was anything like me - they would hate being cold. And what if something happened to me whist it was in the deep freezer? Would it be left there for eternity? Could they accidentally defrost my petit-poi and plant it in some other mummy? It wasn't that I had anything against others who took this route. In fact, I was almost envious that they had the courage to do it. I just wanted a fresh one, straight from him, my Mr. Right; planted in my own lady-garden, where I would protect it, house it and keep it warm and safe.

No, the answer is most definitely to continue my search to find Mr. Right. Surely this coming year would bring me the happiness I deserve?'

I was stirred from my daydream when the taxi beeped outside.

I lugged my suitcase from the staffroom, locked the door behind me and breathed a huge sigh of relief.

CHAPTER TWO

Feeling exhausted, I scooched over to my window seat and flopped down. I couldn't help noticing a gorgeous ride coming down the aisle. *Phwar! Please let him be sitting next to me,* I thought. He could most definitely be a candidate to be my Mr. Right. My heart sank a little as I watched him walk past. He didn't even give me a second glance, the gobshite.

It was then I noticed a commotion further up the plane. I could see a rather large businessman trying to make his way down the aisle. He looked like he was heavily pregnant. Everyone had to clear a path for him as he squeezed through the seats; tatty briefcase in one hand and a half eaten pasty in the other. *Sweet Jesus,* I thought, *can he not stop eating just for a few minutes while he gets on the plane?* Obviously not, it turned out. I watched him take a huge bite; with only half of the gigantic mouthful managing the journey to his mouth, the rest was in free fall, rolling off his belly and into the aisle.

I breathed a sigh of relief as he trampled his way passed me. Then, all of a sudden, he stopped and then began to perform a three-point-turn in order to maneuver himself round... and into the seat next to me. *Oh for the love of God,* I thought, shuffling in my chair uncomfortably and trying to get as far over as possible whilst grabbing my possessions at the speed of light. I couldn't help but watch this enormous mass coming towards me. Oh God... *beep... beep... beep.* This man seriously should have been equipped with warning hazard lights and a 'WIDE LOAD' sticker.

He finally managed to align himself in order to come in for landing. Mission impossible had been accomplished. But, as wide loads inevitably do, he clearly required two lanes. In a matter of seconds his bulk had started to spread over into my space. His *I've-had-all-the-pies* belly could have taken up a seat all on its own (and the person's in front, I might I add).

By then, I was fuming. *Why should I have to pay extra for going over 15 kilos in my luggage, when this colossal vehicle can get on the plane for the same price as me?* His elbow and chubby leg had already launched a full-scale invasion of what was left of my personal space, despite the fact that I was leaning so far the other way. All I was left with was a few centimeters of space, leaving me precariously balancing on one bum cheek. He gave me a cheery smile.

'Howerya? Sure, the weather's shocking, is it not?'

I gave a dismissive nod. *Yuck*, I thought. Half the pasty was still sitting in his moustache. It grossed me out so much that I shuddered. He had more hair sprouting from his ears than he did on his head.

I knew exactly what was coming next. The compulsory, boring aeroplane chat, which, of course, my portly new seatmate followed to a tee;

'So, are you heading off home for the holidays?' he predictably began as the plane taxied down the runway.

'Yes, I'm spending Christmas with my family,' I answered through gritted teeth. I already knew what was coming next. A pound to a penny he's going to ask where my family is from next.

'So, where in Ireland are your family from?'

Bingo! I just wanted him to shut the feck up and let me close my eyes so I could snooze during the flight.

'Rathmines in Dublin,' I answered. (He will of course know it well and his uncle and three times removed cousins will also be living there). He'll be asking the family name next.

'Oh, I know those parts very well, what's the family name?' he boomed.

'Ryan.' I answered shortly.

'Ah sure, I know the Ryans well,' he said, 'fine upstanding members of the community.'

I knew then that he definitely had the wrong set of Ryans. Even though my family's story had started romantically, the middle and end of that story was far from a fairytale.

My parents had met and married in Mills & Boon-like circumstances. My dad, Michael (back then, a fine young whippersnapper), only had eyes for my mum, Josephine. He spotted her sunbathing on Greystones beach in County Wicklow, Ireland, back in the sixties.

'A thunderbolt,' dad used to say, eyes brimming with tears. 'It was love at first sight, so it was,' he added with intense pride. 'There she was, in her navy blue and white polka-dot swimsuit, dancing around, kicking the sand about without a care in the world. I heard shrieks of laughter as she dipped in and out of the cold sea. I could have watched her for hours so I could; her long, dark, glossy hair catching in the summer breeze, floating across her lightly tanned skin. She was a vision.'

Mum, however, having a very strict upbringing (yet a playful edge to her personality) declined my dad's incessant offers of courtship.

'You'll have to ask me daddy,' she teased nonchalantly. 'He'll probably have you hung, drawn and quartered, though,' she continued, unwittingly setting a daring challenge that my dad would never refuse. And quite the challenge it was.

'Not in your wildest dreams would I allow you to date my daughter - sure what do you have to offer her?' my grandfather bellowed brutally as my dad sought permission to take my mother out.

'But I'm a qualified bricklayer, Mr. O'Leary,' dad added with pride, offering his chapped hands up as proof.

'No scaffer's dating any daughter of mine, I can tell you that for nothing!' shot back my grandfather. 'Goodbye, on your way so. Good luck son, but the answer is still no.'

'I play the guitar and sing as well sir, sure, I may even become a musician - even a rock star,' my poor dad stammered in a last-ditch attempt before being escorted out of the house.

'Not in a million! Go-way with you, shoo… a rock star, never heard anything so re-dic-lous in all me life.'

For weeks during that summer, mum secretly revisited Greystones beach every day at the same time in the hope of bumping into dad. Unbeknown to mum though, dad was still sulking over his encounter with her dad.

Instead of going to Greystones beach to swim or sunbathe, after he finished work on the building site, he headed down to another area of Greystones beach called the 'The Mens'. Back then, women, girls and children were forbidden by law to enter this part of the beach. It was, as you may have guessed, for 'men only'.

The Mens had dangerously high, ragged rocks covered in slimy algae where only the bravest men would perform acrobatic dives into the sea, risking life and limb. Many had died attempting to out-do each other, performing twists and turns as the ante was raised to execute the perfect dive.

Dad was always a great sportsman and swam and dived like a dolphin; effortlessly performing complex dives with ease and grace. What no one knew was that when he climbed high on the rocks in preparation for his dive, he could see over to Greystones and steal glances at mum.

On one particular afternoon, the blue, clear skies began changing. A raging storm formed from nowhere.

Mum, unaware, was suddenly swimming far of her depth. Dad could see she was getting dragged further away from land and further out to sea. Without a second thought, he dived from the rocks and began to swim rapidly in her direction. He tore his body to shreds on the reef as he struggled to reach her, fighting currents, winds and huge, crashing waves. Finally, with supreme effort, he reached her and managed to drag her back to safety. They lay together on the beach, exhausted. Entwined in each other, they kissed for the first time.

'Son,' said my relieved grandfather, 'I will be forever in your debt! You have my blessing to date my daughter.'

My parents were soon married and, in search of a better life, crossed the waters over to England where they had heard the streets were paved with gold.

Dad immediately got work as a bricklayer and mum fell pregnant with Laura, with me soon to follow. Dad had to work harder than ever to keep a roof over our heads, as times were tough. He was building by day and singing in a band at night, gigging around London. Adding to his already long list of genius attributes, dad was also painting, sculpting and writing music. His dream was to perform live the love song to mum he had written when he very first laid eyes on her. Life was good for them; they were young and very much in love.

It could so easily have been the perfect story. They could have made their fortune and returned to their native land, happy and prosperous in later life. But, it all came crashing down around their ears.

The catalyst was dad's beloved love song he'd written about mum. He'd taken it to a music producer who said it was 'extremely marketable'. This producer made all the right noises about dad becoming a star and vividly described how he would be playing gigs to thousands of adoring fans. Then, inexplicably, the producer went cold and stopped answering dad's calls. Having had a taste of potential success, dad became increasingly desperate and his behavior became more and more erratic.

He often skipped days on his building jobs, claiming he was too exhausted to get up. It left poor mum struggling with her two young children and, even though she was pregnant with her third, she had to take every odd job coming to support us all.

Around a year after dad first met with the music producer, a great new rock group hit the scene. They were an overnight success; with their slick outfits, perfect good looks and romantic melodies. And their first number one hit? Yeah, you've got it; my dad's love song, written about my mum.

The betrayal destroyed my dad. He was utterly devastated and never recovered. Sure, he consulted lawyers about the theft of his song, but they said it would cost thousands to sue and the chances were he'd never win against the powerful music moguls.

By then, mum and dad didn't have a penny to rub together. Any money dad did get he spent on booze - or, worse still, drugs - but nothing could numb his pain. He swung between abject depression, sheer anger and bouts of shouting, crying and throwing things. Try as she might, mum couldn't pull dad out of his spiralling depression.

'Please, Michael,' mum would beg, 'please take your tablets. We love you, we need you. You can write another song!' But nothing could penetrate the hatred and despair dad was experiencing.

Dad began disappearing for days on end on drunken benders, and when he did return, he became violent with uncontrollable rages. But then he would switch without warning and start praying, reciting the rosary and attending church.

We would often hear him talking to himself, conversing with someone who wasn't there. You couldn't engage him in direct conversation for fear of him overreacting and turning aggressive. He began accusing us all of plotting against him. His ability to discern between reality and his hallucinations had become non-existent.

This cycling torrent of abuse and neglect went on for over a decade, getting worse and worse. Mum, the bravest woman I had ever known, had to leave. She had no choice. Her once-beloved husband - her hero, our dad - had changed beyond any recognition.

With her marriage in tatters, mum fled England with my two sisters, Laura and Katie, and moved back to Ireland. Of course, as the middle child, that automatically entitled me to self-diagnosed stroppy middle-child-syndrome. And strop I did. There was no way I was leaving London having already started a hairdressing apprenticeship. So, I stayed and tried to help sort my dad's alcoholism and schizophrenic behavior with the help of mental health advisors.

Back in Dublin, Lickarse Laura (as she was known to me and Katie), the eldest sister and the *Einstein* of the family, decided to become a career girl and studied for a doctorate in Psychology. When Laura graduated, it was mum's "proudest moment". In my secret opinion though, Laura shared one too many of our dad's schizophrenic traits beneath all that professionalism and condescension to the human race. Laura could be the life and soul of any party and everyone was her best friend; however get one too many drinks in her and she would revert into a female version of our dad; patronizing, intimidating and erratic.

Katie, my youngest sister at just 22 years young, was currently residing in rehab. She was however allowed home for just a few days at Christmas. She was in rehab due to her newfound hobby: shoving every which substance up her nose that she could get her hands on. To top it off, her homegrown cannabis plant had been lovingly tendered and watered by none other than our poor, unsuspecting mum. Bless her, mum was as clueless as she was penniless.

'I ought to get shares in Kleenex!' Mum used to sob down the phone to me on our weekly phone calls. 'Katie goes 'trew a box in a day. I can't keep up with the child. And she has a constant sinus infection. Her poor nose is collapsing with all the congestion.'

Katie and her tree-hugging, weirdo mates went too far one night a couple of months back. She had been found wandering the streets, totally out of her 'hippie-dippy trolley', sobbing; claiming that she had committed a murder and would never forgive herself.

She was picked up by the local priest and confessed all to him. The account was a bit garbled by the time the poor guy got hold of my dear old mum. He was clearly suffering from some sort of post-traumatic stress, but this is pretty much what Katie confessed to (in her continuous motor-mouth style):

'I had a few friends around, Father, while mammy was at mass. We had a few jars and, you know, well, I looked at poor Moses (that's mammy's budgie). I felt sorry for him, sure he's always locked up; so I thought I would give Moses a little treat. I only put a little bit of me lager in his birdcage, but then I accidentally left his door open. Before I knew it, he was whizzing around and around mammy's lounge like a fighter pilot at a hundred miles an hour. It was just so cool to watch him. He looked so happy, so free. But then Moses kinda crashed into the glass patio door. That was it, Father, he dropped to the floor like a bomb. He was flat on his back, legs bolt upright up and stiff. I had to do something and fast... so I panicked and ran up to mammy's bedroom. She has one of those ceiling fans, so I kept throwing Moses up into it, you know Father, just to try and get some wind beneath his wings. I begged him to start flapping his little bird arms, but his feathers just dropped off all over mammy's bed. He was ice cold, so I wrapped him in cling-film, not over his face now, Father - I'm not that stupid! Anyway, I popped him in the microwave because he was so cold, Father, so I did. I thought I had put him on defrost... but instead... I think I nuked him. I mean, there were a few of us alright that had polluted the air with, err... let's say, "plant fumes", Father, but sure, I'm confessing and you don't need to know every detail of the murder, do you?'

That was it for Katie. Off to rehab she went. I don't think Father Murphy was ever the same after that.

I felt a gentle tapping on my arm. The huge man sitting next to me informed me that we'd touched down. I must have dozed off.

Feeling drowsy, I collected my luggage and was relieved to find that Laura was already at the airport entrance waiting to give me a lift to mum's. *Here we go,* I thought.

On Christmas morning in Rathmines, Dublin, I woke up to my phone beeping from my handbag.

[Text from (Unrecognised)]

Ur not gunna feckin believe this. Danny #2 found out about Danny #1 and tried 2 go thru me phone... so I swallowed my sim card! My throat is feckin' killin me! Luv ya babe, Siobhan Xxxx (ps. this my new number). PPS... MERRY PISSEDMAS!!! xxxx

[Text to Siobhan]

Omg! I've only been gone 1 day and you are in trouble already! I'll call you later. But if you were able to swallow it, you should be able to pass it. Just keep your eyes peeled for a shiny shite coming down your chimney! Merry Xmas Xx

I shook my head. Siobhan was crazy. Only *she* would do something like that.

I stretched out in my cosy bed, basking in the feeling of having nothing to do; no bickering to breakup (well, apart from my sisters), just a few days of eating and drinking in front of me.

Mum's house was so warm and inviting. I loved being there. You could lose yourself in the big, soft, brown velour sofas whilst your feet sank deep into the shagpile carpet. The house was a medley of beiges, browns and oranges. Nothing matched, but it all worked somehow. There were little multi-coloured trinkets dotted around the place, but the one that tickled me the most was in the bathroom, in the form of a legless plastic doll, who's meringue-esque, pale blue frilly skirt concealed the toilet roll beneath it.

At this time of year, mum has her usual plethora of brightly coloured, gaudy Christmas decorations up. And of course, there was always a real Christmas tree; overloaded to the point of collapsing, with ill-matched, yet strangely aesthetically pleasing bits and bobs. Mum had hung Katie's embroidered stocking on the mantel above the roaring log fire and surrounded it with tinsel. I'd always have to duck here and there whilst walking around the house, in fear of being strangled by mum's hanging pullout paper chains. And, of course, there was the wave of two thousand or so cards, supported by cotton string and thumbtacks.

Santa's grotto had nothing on our over-illuminated beacon of Christmas trash.

By the time I wandered downstairs at the blissful hour of 11am most of the hard work had already been done. The table was beautifully set for Christmas dinner, with wine glasses all placed accordingly. There was a brand new carafe filled with red wine on the table; Laura saw me and instantly poured us both a glass.

'Slante,' we both chorused and took a gulp.

'Eww… what the hell is *that*? Is that… *RIBENA?!*' Laura and I spluttered at the same time.

Mum waltzed in on cue, 'the doctor said your sister isn't allowed to be near anything 'mind altering' while she's on release from rehab. She could end up with one of those corse-diction things.'

'I think you mean *cross-addiction,* mum,' Laura corrected spitting out the remains of the offending Ribena back into her wine glass.

'She's such a pet, sure she is,' said mum, ignoring Laura and wrinkling her nose at Katie with pride and affection.

I watched Katie smirking behind mum's back and then sticking her pierced tongue out at me. I did love my youngest sister; it was just so infuriating that, even when she'd done something horrendously bad, she still got praise.

'My arse she's a pet,' I growled under my breath, unable to hold back, as I laid out the Christmas crackers. 'She's had more chemicals in her than a lab rat!' I snapped, throwing a look at her that could kill.

'Well, *you* would know about chemicals more than anyone else, Tara,' Katie barked back. 'You have your road-mapped face injected every week!'

'I DO NOT!' I shrieked. 'It's… it's… only every once in a while!'

I enviously looked at the beautiful, olive, clear, wrinkle-free complexion of both my sisters. I was the only one in the family that had naturally milky, winter-white skin. My artificial glow came courtesy of St. Tropez's finest spray-tan and the tanning booth, while both of my sisters had been lucky enough to inherit mum's beautiful skin. Even more unfairly, that was the case in the old breast department as well. The memory still smarted from the time when I'd spent hours as a teenager gently picking out the stitching from mum's 'Dynasty style' jacket and borrowing the shoulder pads for my bra fillers without her knowing. Of course, I got caught putting them back one day while Katie was (apparently) on guard. I was grounded for a month. It was back to stuffing socks down my 28AA bra for me. A few years later, with help from a plastic surgeon, I got the coveted chin-hitting breasts I so desperately wanted. I deliberately went twice as big as my sisters to make a point.

'Lord preserve us, where's the turkey gone?' mum screeched at full volume from the kitchen. The cooked bird was now utterly pathetic in size. It was like one of those little ones the cat brings in. 'I couldn't close the feckin' door when it first went into the oven! Sweet Jesus… I know I cooked it as it said on the instructions (*may God forgive my blasphemy*).'

We all rushed into the kitchen. By now mum was sobbing, flapping her apron up and down and blessing herself all at the same time.

'Oh mum… don't get upset,' Laura hushed reassuringly, 'there's enough veg, stuffing and Yorkshire puddings to feed a small army.'

It took mum a few minutes to calm down, but she was a trooper. With us girls rallying around her, she soon recovered her composure and resolved the 'show must go on'.

'Right, girls, that's it - my New Year's resolution is to attend a cooking class,' mum said, pulling it back together in an instant. 'It's never too late. I will be purchasing a brand-new oven - one of those ones that them celebrity chefs have. In fact…' she added, kicking the oven door closed with her Santa slippered foot in mock temper, 'I want a new kitchen altogether. *I'll have to get saving…* Right! Dinner - or should I say, *rations* - in five minutes.'

While we were waiting for mum to put the finishing touches on the dinner, I walked over to the couch where *Saint Katie* was lying. I handed her a Christmas cracker as a sort of olive branch because I hadn't shown her much support over our temperance lunchtime drink of poxy Ribena. If I was honest though, I really *really* wanted what was inside that cracker, whatever plastic shite it turned out to be. I guess you never really get over that competitive sibling rivalry thing. Plus, I had never quite forgiven Katie for poking out the eyes of my much-loved Tiny Tears doll when I was young. She'd cut off all the hair too, the bitch. I only allowed her to play with it because mum had made me.

We both heaved and pulled at the shiny cracker, my hand carefully placed near the middle to try and guarantee me victory. But, as it went *bang*, I felt the body of the cracker slip from my hand. I had lost. Katie had won the prize. It was a novelty key ring, in the form of mini handcuffs.

'That's a sign from the Big-Man upstairs.' I said malevolently. I couldn't help it, I had to throw *something* in. 'He's reminding you to stay on the right side of the law.' Inexplicably, the usually robust Katie seemed to crumble at my words. Her face dropped and she looked teary. Maybe I *had* gone a little too far this time?

Feeling a rush of guilt and sisterly love (and relief that it was only a pair of poxy plastic handcuffs which were of no use to me anyway), I sat down and hugged her.

'We all just want the best for you,' I said, sympathetically. 'I would love to see you complete your Music diploma; dad would've been so proud of you. And then, maybe a year or so down the line, you could get yourself a nice, steady boyfriend. You are very beautiful you know, Katie,' I stated with a forced smile. As much as I admired her floral hair garlands, tie-dye gypsy skirts and hand-made Aztec jewelry, I hated to say it. It really smarted that it was all so natural and effortless for Katie. She never wore makeup - she didn't need to.

'Tara…' Katie startled me as she suddenly sat up and looked straight at me, 'I've something to tell you.' Her eyes were lit up now and she had a beaming smile on her face.

'Dinner!' interrupted mum, who still hadn't quite got over the shrinking bird problem. 'I thought that butcher had a shifty looking face,' she continued muttering. 'He couldn't even look me in the eye when he sold me that bird, so he couldn't. Mind you, he had only one eye, so he did. Strange looking fella all the same.'

'I'll tell you after dinner,' Katie whispered with a firm shake of her head, indicating that she didn't want mum to hear.

'Okay,' I answered, as we both shot up and ran for the dinner table, both trying to get the closest seat to mum.

'Who wants to carve the bird then?' mum asked, looking directly either side of her at Laura and Katie. The budgie-sized turkey was placed on a platter that took up half the table, dwarfing it even further.

'Err…' we all stammered, avoiding eye contact with mum.

'You're the head of the family, mum. *You* carve the budg… err… turkey,' broke in Laura with a smile. She *still* is (and always was) such a complete lickarse.

Mum, armed and dangerous with an electric carving knife the size of a hedge trimmer, proceeded to try and carve. But, as soon as the enormous blade made contact with the minuscule turkey, it flew off the platter, hitting the wall at breakneck speed. Then it fell to the floor with a soggy thud.

'Oh my God… the fecker flew away, mammy!' exclaimed Katie with glee.

'Saints preserve us!' mum said in shock, shaking her head staring at the mess it had made.

After exchanging glances, we couldn't help but all burst out laughing as we continued to dish up the rest of the (now turkey-free) Christmas dinner. Even mum started to see the funny side.

We toasted with our Ribena and pulled the rest of the Christmas crackers as the atmosphere settled down. By the time we were finished, I was full to the brim with veg and Yorkshires, but still couldn't help myself enquiring about dessert. Mum always made *the* best Christmas pudding.

'So what's for after's, mum?' I asked, feeling the need for something sweet. 'You know how much we love your Christmas pudding. Are we going to set it alight?'

'Sure they're laced with alcohol, so no, I've gone for something else this year,' said mum, briskly tidying away the plates.

'Oooh,' I said excitedly, 'what is it? Trifle?' I loved mum's trifle. She shook her head once again.

'Sure, that's full of sherry,' she said, nodding in Katie's direction.

'Tiramisu?' I asked hopefully, my mouth watering. It slowly dawned on me this dish also contained alcohol. I felt an all-too-familiar surge of resentment towards Katie. 'I take it there's no chocolate liqueurs for after either?'

'Well, I thought I'd go with something a little more modern, given our fragile family situation,' began mum.

I waited with baited breath.

'We're having angel fairy cakes for desert and toffee-filled Rolos with our coffee!' exclaimed mum proudly.

I shot my eyes in Laura's direction, but she was deliberately avoiding my gaze. I looked back at Katie who was sitting all prim and proper, like butter wouldn't melt in her mouth.

'How thoughtful of you to think of Katie *again*, mum,' I said sarcastically, while continuing to shoot death stares in Katie's direction. Katie (rightly so) put her head down and started fiddling with her Christmas paper hat.

'Oh, I forgot,' mum added, completely unaware of my sarcasm, 'I've made mince pies!' They did look very yummy, generously sprinkled with copious amounts of icing sugar. They were polished off instantly.

'I bagsy licking the plate!' screeched Katie, at the speed of lightning.

'Ugh! I was going to bagsy that!' I said, as I deliberately sprayed some spit on the plate while I passed it down to her.

'Ah, you're getting a bit *slooooow* in your old age, Tara. Maybe Santa should've put some TENA-ladies in your stocking,' teased Katie in a singsong voice.

'Oh come on now,' I spat scornfully, 'I could throw one in about needing extra large nappies and how long you wet the bed for, but I won't... because it's Christmas!'

With Katie and I at level pegging in the insult league, we all moved into the lounge to watch the Queen's speech on the TV. It was the same every year (the subsequent routine, not the speech). We'd all wait for mum to fall asleep (which didn't take long, usually 30 seconds were enough). Then the silent but deadly fight for the remote control would start between the three of us. This time, as Katie and I fought (perhaps not for the remote, but more probably because we just wanted to knock the shite out of each other), Lickarse Laura dived in to take charge of what we were about to watch... a boring documentary about penguins. I mean, *really*?

Not in the mood for penguins (unless they were of the chocolate variety), I remembered that I had some unfinished gossip to unearth from Katie.

'So, what was it you were going to tell me before dinner?' I probed; resolving to put Katie's last cutting comment behind me, as I fell down beside her, still exhausted from our scrap.

'Well... I'm in love,' she whispered in my ear, while cupping her hand around her mouth, 'I've met this fine, fit ting you see...'

'Hang on... how could you have possibly met somebody while you've been in rehab?!' I asked with frowning concern, still trying to catch my breath and poking in one of my hair extensions that she had nearly pulled out.

'Listen till I tell you,' she said speaking quietly, yet rapidly and with obvious pleasure. 'He had come into visit his brother in the clinic and we got chatting about caravans, don't ask me how, but we did. It may have something to do with the fact that he lives in one.'

'WHAT?!' I yelled. 'Don't tell me you're seeing a PIKEY?'

'Shhhh!' she implored, putting a hand over my mouth. 'Don't be saying that in front of me mam!'

'Jesus, Katie!' I said, struggling to keep my voice down. 'Will you *ever* learn? They are not allowed to date outside their community. They have to stick to their own; and so should you! Surely you must have watched *My Big Fat Gypsy Wedding*?'

I shook my head with utter disgust and then set upon her again (well, I was on a roll. Why stop now?)

'You were told *no relationships* for a *year*, then you start one up the *minute* you go to a *rehab* centre? ... You are NOT to have anything to do with him again. And I MEAN IT. Or I will tell mum and Laura!'

Nervously, Katie started fidgeting and fingering the icing sugar around the mince pie plate which she'd brought with her to the sofa.

'Ah sure, I'm better now… and he's up for the craic [pronounced "crack"; roughly translating to, 'a bit of fun'], so he is,' stammered Katie, speaking even more rapidly; although her enthusiasm had now melted into nervousness. 'I'm just so bored in there, and I…'

'Yes!' I snarled abruptly, interrupting her. 'The operative word in that sentence being *craic,* as in crack-cocaine!'

I was bitterly disappointed. Despite our differences and arguments, I genuinely wanted Katie to get past her addictions. It was then I noticed Katie had arranged the icing sugar from the plate into… lines. *Oh my God. On the plate. White lines. Oh my god! AND* SHE HAD ROLLED HER CHRISTMAS PAPER HAT INTO A SUSPICIOUS-LOOKING, STRAW-LIKE SHAPE.

'KATIE!' I roared furiously, with my eyes almost popping out of my head, 'Look what you've done – you *stupid* crack head! MUM!' I grassed. 'Look at what Katie has done with the icing sugar! And she's moving into a caravan with her new _PIKEY_ boyfriend!'

'… What? Aww bless her… she'll have a grand holiday in a caravan when she's better,' mum said, barely opening her eyes or taking any notice of my outcries. 'Ahh look, she's made some snowy roads on her plate. They're *lovely* pet. She's still such a creative child.'

'I've got her wrapped around me little finger,' Katie mimed behind mum's back, deliberately winding me up now that I had grassed on her. I was overwhelmed by an immense feeling of anger surging through me, catalysed by mum's blind ignorance. Heaving myself off the sofa, I snatched the plate from Katie and marched into the kitchen. In desperation, I started raiding the cupboards, but not a drop of alcohol was to be found. This enraged me even more.

Despite this, I was terrified of ending up like our dad. There was no way any of my children (if I ever managed to have any) would be put in a position where they had to get on their knees begging me to stop drinking.

'If it's good enough for God's disciples to drink wine, then it's good enough for me' was dad's favourite phrase. I used to watch him as a child through the gaps in our hallway. He and Father Brian would drink till they could barely stand. *Then*, we would all be dragged to mass to repent our sins. This, I never understood. Poor mum had to juggle everything with screaming, attention-seeking Katie joined to her hip. Laura would shut her bedroom door and bury her nose in a book, so I always felt it was up to me to help fix the situation and fix my dad.

Dad's once genius mind had turned on itself. His increasingly erratic, madman behaviour escalated to psychotic levels that could no longer be endured. Alcohol-induced schizophrenia took hold. He said he could hear voices that told him he could fly – he nearly threw himself off a multi-story car park.

Later, I had chosen to stay in England with dad, so it had become my responsibility to look after him. As frightened as I was, I couldn't leave him all alone. I convinced mum that I would take care of him. *I'll finish my apprenticeship and by then dad will get better*, I promised.

I still shudder remembering the devastating morning that he left me forever.

I had been out the night before celebrating my seventeenth birthday and sneaked in late after being out with my girlfriends. I'd selfishly gone straight to bed without checking on dad, as I normally did.

The next morning, I found him slumped on the living room floor. Eerily still, he was clutching our old family photograph and the lyrics of the stolen love song he had written for mum so many years ago.

Frantically, I waded through the debris of empty cans and bottles and fell to my knees beside him.

'… Dad?' I called in alarm. 'Talk to me, dad!' I shrieked, beginning to panic as I cupped and pulled at his ice-cold hands. 'You've just had too much to drink - that's all!' Looking at his expressionless face, deep down, I knew that wasn't the truth.

With all my strength, I shook him for some kind of response. 'Come on… sing something! Wake up… please! Breathe. Please. *Please… ' I sobbed.* 'I'm sorry I shouted at you for not taking your tablets. Come on, dad - I'm sorry, please just wake up! Don't leave me…'

I ran to the phone and called an ambulance. Everything was happening in excruciating slow motion.

After what seemed like forever, the operator answered. I begged her to make the ambulance come quickly. She instructed me to stay calm and check dad's breathing. Dropping the phone, I dived down to where he lay. Tilting his head, I placed my ear to his mouth. Nothing. The only sound was my own rapid breathing. I checked his pulse. There wasn't one.

At that moment, my worst fears were confirmed. *I* wasn't going to be able to save my dad.

'It's you and me - we can get through this,' I pleaded. 'Please just wake up!' I cried and cried.

Adrenaline-fuelled hysteria set in, as I attempted to perform CPR. I sealed his lips and tried with panic-stricken breaths to bring him back. 'Please don't go...' I sobbed. 'Don't leave me all alone.'

But he had lost his battle.

His tortured soul had departed this world. I could feel the warmth fading from his crumpled body, disappearing into my arms. I grabbed a blanket, lay on the floor beside him and wrapped us up together.

I held him so tight, with my body shaking and trembling in disbelief, my eyes drowning in tears.

I don't know how long I lay there before the ambulance arrived, but eventually I drifted off to happier times. I saw flashes of dad teaching Laura, Katie and I to play guitar and encouraging us to sing. Laura sounded like an angel. Even Katie showed signs of great talent; with her young, yet undeveloped voice and an ability to pick up and play virtually any instrument. As for me, well, I merely watched on longingly as they shared yet another moment that I wasn't truly a part of.

I wanted to hold dad for as long as possible, but the weight of his body was gradually slipping away beyond my grasp. I knew I had to let him go. But I wasn't ready, not yet. I needed more time with him before the doctors and funeral directors took him away from me, forever.

Supporting dad's head with a cushion, I reached over, grabbed his precious guitar, plucked a few strings and heartbreakingly sang to him for the first and last time.

I shared a final, exquisite, beautiful moment with my dad.

A torrent of pain and regret turned me inside out, as I called mum with the tragic news that dad has passed away.

It all seemed so long ago, but the spirit of our dad still hung strongly about us, even now. Christmas never felt quite right again; even though for so many years the 25th of December only meant an extended day of drinking and arguing for my parents.

Wanting to escape the Christmas family drama and with the bemusement over Siobhan swallowing her SIM card, I decided to give her a call.

'*Merry Christmas!*' I bellowed down the phone.

'Merry Christmas! And greetings from England!' chorused Siobhan.

'So… what on earth was *that* all about? Are you okay?' I questioned, while I made myself comfortable.

'You'll not feckin' believe it when I tell you!' said Siobhan, relishing the opportunity to tell the next crazy installment in her chaotic love life.

'Oh, I *will* believe it… tell me!' I begged.

'Well… you know that ol' tosspot I used to kinda see for a while?'

'Which one? Let's be honest, there have been a few.'

'Danny!' she exclaimed.

'*Danny?*'

'You know, *Danny.*'

'Oh yeah... Danny!' I bluffed (I couldn't really remember this one). 'I just didn't know that you and Danny had split up. When did that happen?'

'Noooo, not Danny #2, I'm still riding that one! I mean Danny #1, the gobshite that was looking to drag me arse up the aisle. You know who I mean, the eejit who got sacked and had to downgrade from a top-end BMW to a clapped-out Skoda.'

'Ah yes, I remember him. The poor guy who lost everything,' I said, sympathetically, as it all came flooding back.

'Poor guy me arse! He knows I'm with the Danny #2 and the stupid fecker's only gone and text me out of the blue. And Danny #2 only went an' feckin' read it! Really, the gobshite should never have been going through me phone, but he did. So, I grabbed it and feckin' *ran* I tell you. So then I locked meself in the bathroom. Danny's on the other side of the door, trying to kick down the door. He hurt his foot, which served him right. But then he starts tryin'a jimmy the lock with a fookin' two pence piece, trying to get me phone back off me! I was like; fook that for a laugh! He would've seen the texts from all the others as well! So I took me phone apart and got out the SIM. The second he comes through the door, he sees me swallowing it to get rid of the evidence.'

'*Shit!* Why didn't you just flush it down the toilet, you nutter?' I asked, baffled.

'He would've feckin' dived in an' got it. He had his feckin' fingers down me throat trying to get it back he's such a feckin' loon. So anyways... I bit the bastard. It's the only way I was gonna get him to stop!'

I burst out laughing, as did Siobhan.

'I was *shittin'* myself, I tell you, Tara.'

After a minute of rolling around, I had to ask, 'Why do you keep dating these destructive men?' shaking my head, still laughing.

'Well... I can't help it really... I seem to just *love* a bastard. He's wild. It really turns me on; even if it does scare the shite out of me. Should probably go and see someone about that really...' she cackled. 'Anyway, I've got to go... I'm meeting Danny #1 for a drink.'

'Err... okay,' I said, now even more baffled. 'I'll call you when I get home from Ireland. Merry Christmas, and see you soon!'

I'm sure she was supposed to say Danny #2...

Heading back into the lounge, I immediately began to regale Siobhan's story. I just had to gossip to *someone* about it, so I broke the ice with Katie as if we'd never had the heated confrontation at all.

'Sounds like she could do with a bit of help if you ask me,' said Laura in her everyone's-dysfunctional-apart-from-me voice.

'I'd love to go and stay with her for a weekend,' added Katie, wide-eyed.

'You're not going *anywhere*, you brazen hussy!' I barked.

'Right... who fancies a game of Trivial Pursuit?' asked Laura, clearly changing the subject to prevent another row.

'Not me,' I protested. 'You're a boffin. You only want to play because you know you would win!'

'Well, you might learn something,' said Laura, all teacher-like and patronising.

'Why don't we all have a nice game of snap?' suggested mum.

Now *that* was a game I could play.

It had been a typical Christmas day (minus the turkey and alcohol, of course). We had eaten, we had bickered and we had laughed. Mum then went to bed whilst Laura, Katie and I stayed up chatting and squabbling until the early hours of the morning.

CHAPTER THREE

My final night in Ireland had arrived. After a few alcohol-free days and nights of staying holed up at mum's to show solidarity for Katie, cabin fever begun to set in. The rehab doctor had given mum strict instructions that Katie was not to go anywhere she may be tempted to look for drugs, and was to be kept in a controlled environment. Long story short: Katie couldn't step a foot outside the house.

Laura and I had more than done our fair share of going without; it was *our* time now. So, Laura and I felt obliged to go out and get rat-arsed.

I couldn't help but feel slightly anxious about Laura's temperament for the evening. Usually she was a wise, intellectual type with patience akin to a Buddhist monk. However, get one-too-many drinks in her and she would revert into a party animal that never wanted to go home. In my opinion, she showed traits of our father's genes in more ways than one. However, needs must, I wasn't going to let anything stop me from going out and having a very good time indeed.

Laura and I made our way to our favourite cocktail bar in Dublin city centre with a *lock up your husbands, we're on a mission* attitude. Upon arriving, Laura approached the doorman confidently, legs first. I stood back awkwardly and wondered what the frig she was doing. I watched her provocatively allowing the side splits of her pencil skirt to flap open as she began wrapping her tanned, toned leg around his waist; using his body like a pole and shimmying up and down him in a very sultry, risqué manner. She was such a show off! *God, I wish I had a quarter of her carefree attitude.*

I looked down at myself, feeling suddenly butt-ugly. *I knew I shouldn't have worn this outfit!* I had agonised what to wear all day. Planning it all thoughtfully, I wanted to look sexy, yet stylish with a carefree edge. But now I felt none of these things. I had stupidly opted for my metallic, silver, skinny jeans and silver, sparkly, off-the-shoulder jumper, with huge, matching silver bangles. Even mum - who never noticed anything important - said I looked like an inflated roll of tin foil (although I think she was trying to be encouraging).

Laura, on the other hand, had just thrown on a tight black pencil skirt, crisp white shirt and pulled it together with a wide, black-buckled leather belt, which gave her the sexiest hourglass figure. Me? Well, there was no strategy whatsoever. I mean for God's sake, I hadn't even put my best assets on show. Jesus, I had paid enough for them. What was I thinking?

I jumped from one foot to the other on the gravel to keep warm - I should definitely have brought my fur coat - it was bloody freezing. I thought Laura was never going to stop flirting with the doorman - I just wanted to get inside - I could hear the band doing a fantastic rendition of 'Valerie' by Amy Winehouse. Becoming impatient, I put my best foot forward and attempted to shimmy sexily to the beat when suddenly a stone flicked back, ricocheting off my ankle. 'Owww...' I was huffing, puffing and hopping around in sheer agony. I thought I was going to pass out.

I reached out for Laura, holding up my ankle, desperate for sympathy, but instead she used my poor, throbbing leg as her handbag holder so she was freed up to finish her seduction of the doorman.

There she was, Ms. Lickarse Laura, perfect at everything, caressing the Incredible Bulk. She was running her hands seductively down his dribbling chops, snapping into some kind of Argentinean tango, with her short, black bob flicking from right to left, left to right. The show finally ended (thank God) with the doorman powerfully cupping the base of Laura's spine and throwing her down into a dramatic, exotic dip.

'Tara!' shouted Laura, her eye's lit up wildly.

'Yep?' I winced, wondering if I needed to get to A&E.

'Bar!' she announced, with an authoritative point.

I couldn't have felt less cool if I had tried, as the doorman made a great show of leading us through the door.

I hopped in, rubbing my swollen ankle, while Laura tangoed through the crowd like she owned the place, oblivious to my practically broken ankle. To our joint pleasure, we found the place was heaving. We noticed straight away the 'pickings' were far from slim. The local rugby team was out on a Christmas jaunt and both Laura and I were very partial to a bit of muscle. We stood at the bar, scanning the crowd. There was plenty of choice.

'We can afford to be picky tonight,' I whispered, nudging Laura.

'That'll make a change for you!' she jibed back, with a mock prim expression. Ignoring her comment, I raked my fingers up through my hair, trying to give it extra height. Pulling the curled length around my shoulders, I applied some more sticky lip-gloss.

Laura confidently ordered our drinks. She was immediately approached by the shortest player of the whole rugby team. He was what she would later dismissively call a 'typical Irish Leprechaun.' However, despite his lack of height, Laura seized the opportunity and flirted unashamedly with him in order to get an introduction to the rest of the team.

He must be the one who ends up on the bottom of the scrum pile, I mused to myself as I watched Laura fluttering her eyelashes and handing me a vodka and coke. This guy definitely had a face only a mother could love.

Laura's flirting did the trick though; before I knew it, we were whisked over and introduced to the rest of the team. *Thank you, God!* Miraculously the pain in my ankle subsided as my focus was instantly turned to the bulking frames of pure muscle in my midst.

I was going to play it super-cool, noticing that one of the rugby players kept staring and smiling at me. He was absolutely *the* best-looking ride I had seen for, like, *ever*. Oh yes, I fantasised about doing some rip-roaring sexual healing with him. I took a deep breath and pretended I hadn't noticed him. No way was I going to make eye contact - which made him stare even more to get my attention. I did my 'I haven't even noticed you' routine and simply exaggerated my body language, oozing femininity to stir him up, while very obviously scanning the rest of the team.

Trying to find confidence from somewhere, I conjured up a little plan. With my heart pounding, I swaggered in front of him towards the toilets. The prime objective of this killer strategy was to give him an opening to whiff my new 'take-me-now' perfume, which perfectly complimented my 'take-me-now-eyes'. As I got within a few feet of him, I opened my mouth as if about to blow a bubble, rounding my lips into the perfect 'O' shape in the hope of the perfect pout. As I drew up beside him, I paused for a few seconds while standing far closer than absolutely necessary and seductively placed my hand on his torso.

'Ex-cu-se me,' I whispered, in the slowest, sexiest voice I could conjure up. Unable to contain myself, I kept moving while sensually trailing my fingertips across his muscular torso. God knows what this was doing to the man, but I could feel adrenaline coursing through my veins. My breathing was short and sharp, as I battled to keep my sexy composure. That's no walk in the park either while wearing four-inch heels, holding in your stomach, sticking out your chest, keeping your shoulders back, pouting your lips and wiggling your backside at the same time. I'd like to see blokes try to pull off that move.

As I slithered across the floor, I could feel his eyes burning into me. A sixth sense told me he was watching my every move. Knowing how visual a man is, I thought I would go one step further and emphasise my womanly sensuality a little more by slightly exaggerating the bum wiggle while sticking my chest out a few inches further for ultimate sex bomb effect. I was nearly at the toilet door, when I felt my (severely battered) ankle give way.

The next few seconds were like a scene from Bambi. My knees banged together while my flailing arms grabbed some poor, unsuspecting woman. God love her, she seemed genuinely concerned as she steadied me. I hardly even managed to thank her because, in trying to re-gain my prowess, I quickly turned around red-faced and saw Laura chatting to my prey.

'Feck... arse... shite!' I scolded myself, as I hobbled through to the toilets. *What if he saw me?* Waving furiously at Laura from behind the door, I beckoned her over.

'Laura. Laura! Come here quick! Oh my God... I'm *so* embarrassed. It could *only* happen to me,' I groaned as I yanked her in.

'What's up?' she asked, ignorant to my nearly fatal mishap.

'Please, tell me you didn't see that?' I begged, as I cupped my hands over my face in shame.

'See what?'

'Did *he* see? Did you see? Did anyone see?' I gabbled uncontrollably.

'What *are* you talking about?' Laura answered, shaking her head, looking genuinely confused.

'Me, falling off my shaggin' heels on the way to the toilets!' I barked.

'No,' laughed Laura. 'I was way too busy checking out the wall-to-wall cock-a-locka.'

'It's karma; I always get punished when I think naughty thoughts,' I sulked.

'C'mon - c'mon,' encouraged Laura as she swung open the door back to the bar. 'We're wasting time in here. I didn't come all this way to spend the night in the bogs - let's go have us some fun!'

'I'll be out in a bit,' I replied, still feeling mortified and not quite ready to show my face.

I really needed to undo my skintight jeans so I would at least make some use of my embarrassing 'trip' to the toilets. Back at mum's, I had eaten the remains of an old box of rejected chocolate liqueurs found at the back of a cupboard (well, all the rum flavour ones anyway). It was a comfort food thing, although perhaps it was through lack of festive alcohol too. Either way, the chocolate liqueurs were now terrorising my insides and giving me windy-pops. Added to this was the small issue with Siobhan's Christmas present (*small* being the key word here). She had bought me a thong which was at least two sizes too small. To be honest, after my chocolate gobbling session, it was maybe three sizes too small. It had felt okay just as I was leaving mums. However, the minute I got into the taxi it felt like my arse was sitting on a cheese wire. The offending garment had developed an unhealthy, intimate appetite for my nether regions. I squeezed my hand down the back of my jeans and tried to release the torment of the string, but within seconds it was back, slicing me in half again.

Realising there was little I could do about the thong issue (perhaps another vodka would act as a pain killer), I fixed my lip-gloss and gently ruffled my hair, making sure my extensions were all in place. I swallowed my pride and nervously came out of the toilets.

I had been single for way too long. It's not like I couldn't find a man or anything. I just had a graveyard full of failed relationships that all suffered the same fate: *him* getting too close and *me* running for dear life. I couldn't help myself. When I found someone I liked, I would even sit down with a notepad and analyse and dissect the relationship to no end. By the time I'd finished over-analsying, I would be so anxious I simply hit the panic button on my emotional ejector seat.

Not this time though. I was only too aware I had wasted so much time in the past, which is why I'm in my bloody thirties with no husband, no babies and a bleak future. Besides which, I didn't need a notebook to know for certain that Mr. gorgeous rugby man outside was absolutely, without a doubt, prime husband and father material.

Taking a little more care this time, I strutted my stuff back into the bar. While trying to see where the object of my attention was, I was stopped by a 'yokel'. A yokel is Laura's code word for local yolk of a farmer who needs a wife, only knows how to speak to the animals and has no female contact in his life except that of his female heifer variety.

'Sure you're a fine looking woman,' said the yokel.

I smiled sweetly, thanked him and tried to get back to the gang of hotties. I was just pulling my arm back when he came right out with it and asked me if I was looking for a husband.

'No!' I replied, trying not to sound rude. *Well, yes actually,* I thought, *but it's not gonna be you in a million years, chum!*

'Can ya milek cows?' he inquired in the strongest Irish accent I had ever heard. It was then I noticed he had a tooth missing - as if there weren't enough nails in his coffin.

By now, I was beginning to really lose patience.

'No!' I said petulantly, putting on a cut-glass English accent. 'Why on earth would I want to fondle a cow's udder, when I could pick up a carton of semi-skimmed from Marks & Spencers?'

Is he mad? Clearly he was. Whilst trying to get away from the eejit, I spotted the ride from earlier staring straight at me… so quickly switched tactics and pretended to enjoy the painstaking conversation with the yokel. I turned back to him and smiled sweetly.

'Actually… on second thoughts, maybe I *would* play with a cow's udder,' I added deviously, slamming on the flirtation switch.

'Sure that's grand news, so it is!' slobbered the revolting yokel, looking delighted. 'Can you cooke? I'm a meat and two veg man meself, so I am.'

'Ah! You're *so* funny!' I laughed, deliberately too loud. 'Me, cook? I can't cook for toffee!' I said, giving him a playful shove; knocking the featherweight slightly off-balance.

'Oh, I'm *so* sorry!' I gasped, grabbing him by the arm. Actually, I wasn't. I took the opportunity to see if the hunk in the corner was still watching. He was.

'Ah, never mind sure, you're me dream woman, so ye are,' said the yokel, steadying himself, shuffling his way closer and closer until I had to take a step back. 'I likes a bit of rough and tumble me self, sure I do.'

He just didn't seem to get it that I really didn't care for his 'meat and two veg'. I wanted the gorgeous ride's meat and two veg - that was far more appetising.

'Can I catch you for a dance later?' leered the indefatigable yokel.

Ah, see mum and dad had very strict views on this. They brought us girls up to know that if ever a man had plucked up the courage to ask us to dance, we were never to say no. They had really drummed it in. So, of course, my answer was 'yes'. However, I drew comfort in my traditional get-out clause – my would-be dance partner would have to try and find me first.

'I'll be back later for that dance,' I grinned, turning to dart away. He picked up my hand and slobbered a kiss on it. Yuck! Smiling through gritted teeth, I worked my way back to the real men.

Shite! I couldn't see him. He had completely disappeared. I didn't want it to appear that I was looking for him - so, disappointed, I sloped over to Laura. She was on her third pint of Carlsberg already. I could never comprehend how she was able to drink beer at the same rate as men and still remain upright at the end of the night. She seemed to be having a ball too and was flirting outrageously with a very handsome six-foot-tall, broad, blonde Adonis. She was in her element. The Adonis pulled her out to dance and I was left alone with the other players, feeling a little vulnerable. Lovely as the rugby boys were, I couldn't help but try and find *my* ride from earlier... Nothing. *That bloody farmer!* My heart sank. Giving up hope, I threw back my vodka and Coke, swallowing it down in one.

Then, suddenly all six-foot plus of *my* hunk emerged from the darkness, striding directly towards me. My heart rate accelerated instantly and my instincts were screaming: *pout, pout, and look cool! Don't look at him, Tara!* I just couldn't help but gawk; he was just so god-damn sexy.

For a few seconds, I felt as though my legs had been cut off beneath me, as I stood paralysed in awe. He was so incredibly, mind-blowingly gorgeous. My stomach flipped over as our eyes locked. I tried to look away but, quite simply, I was mesmerized. I managed to pull myself out of my stupor for long enough to check out his left hand to make sure there was no Mrs. Beautiful - there wasn't. After that I was completely lost again.

'Are you okay?' he asked, in a slow, sexy voice, 'your friend said you fell over.'

'I'm fine, thank you,' I purred (even though I was seething inside with Laura). *The bitch! Why the hell did she have to go tell him that? Sometimes she stoops lower than a centipedes arse!*

'I haven't seen you around here before,' he continued in an English accent. I was completely thrown. I had just presumed he would be Irish. I guess he must have been equally surprised with my own English accent.

'Can I buy you and your friend a drink?' he asked.

'Err, that's no *friend* of mine,' I answered, trying to keep the mood casual, even though I was still raging with her. 'That's my *much* older, big-mouthed sister.' I couldn't help myself adding, with a mischievous grin; 'we call her 'Lickarse Laura'.

'What's the pair of you drinking?' he laughed. *Oh, great, now I'd have to ask for a pint for my boozy sister.* I always felt so embarrassed that she drank pints; it was so unfeminine.

'Err, I'd say she'll have a small glass of Carlsberg and may I have a vodka and cock... Err, I mean *Coke*, please.'

Oh my God... did I really just ask him for some cock? Oh God. I was cringing with embarrassment; I just prayed that he hadn't heard me. He came back a few moments later with a huge tray of drinks and handed me my vodka and Coke, smirking.

'I'll see what I can do about getting you that cock later,' he added with a wink.

Shite! My face was crimson again.

Trying to ignore his comment and steady my breathing, I changed the subject:

'Oh, err, that's a rather big glass for a lady,' I stammered, desperately hoping the flame red of my cheeks would disappear.

'Well, I couldn't help but notice you earlier, and that your sister was drinking out of a pint glass... don't worry,' he continued with a gentle smile after seeing my cringed face, 'it is very acceptable for ladies to drink pints in Ireland.'

I involuntarily laughed as he swept away my anxieties in one foul swoop. Our eyes locked for a moment, unfaltering.

'By the way, my name is Travis.'

'*Travis...* that's a cool name,' I blurted. 'Mine's Tara. Tara Ryan. Nice to meet you. Where are you from?'

'Manchester,' he replied, proudly.

Hmmm, a northern ride, I thought, suddenly developing a thing for northern men. I then explained that I too lived in England and was just over visiting my lunatic family for Christmas.

We quickly became engrossed in deep conversation. I wanted to know every single detail about him and just couldn't get enough of hearing him talk. It turned out he'd had a very successful career playing rugby for England and had toured all over the world. In his mid-thirties, he retired from playing professionally and was then headhunted to become a fitness coach for Dublin for the coming season. He was now living between the two countries, but flew home to see his parents as often as he could. He shared digs with other players in Dublin, but planned eventually to move to Ireland on a permanent basis. *Really?* I thought, slightly disappointed at the latter part of his conversation. I would soon put a stop to that!

By now, the bar was rocking and packed to full capacity. The dance floor was overflowing with the giant-sized rugby team taking up most of the space. I kept hearing rowdy shrieks of laughter coming from them all. Glancing over at Laura, I could see she was in the thick of the dancing crowd, trying to teach them salsa.

Travis and I smiled indulgently at them and then swiftly continued getting to know each other. Despite the noise and wild atmosphere, it really was as though we were in our own personal little bubble. I was oblivious to everything else around us.

I liked him. I liked him a lot and I was certainly getting some high definition flirty signals from him. It took me a little while to ask him the question I really, really, wanted to know the answer to.

'Are you single?' I asked, my heart hammering in my chest.

'I am now,' he replied, very seriously, while looking deep into my eyes.

'Me too,' I added, trying to remain composed while screaming inside with delight. With that, we both leaned forward and our lips touched. He wrapped his arm around my waist forcing me to fall into him. From that moment, something shifted inside me. I felt my emotional floodgates open and the warm embrace of love race through my body. So, this was it. This was the feeling I had heard others talk about. My life had merely been a rehearsal up to this point. This was the man of my dreams, here, in the flesh, with me. I felt like I had been taken to another place, as our tongues gently began to entwine. Everything was happening in slow motion. All the background noise had completely disappeared now. We were in deep embrace, kissing slowly, long and tenderly. My lady-garden's sprinklers were now beginning to activate themselves.

We both pulled back, looking at each other. Everything was in real-time again and all the noise flooded back. Travis, not taking his eyes off me, tenderly raised my hands and kissed them delicately.

'Was it as good for you as it was for me?' he asked with a cheeky smile.

Dumbfounded, I was unable to utter anything. *Phew* was the best I could manage, as I collected myself and licked my lips. *Delicious.*

'Hey Tara, this is Dougie,' Laura panted breathlessly after her energetic salsa moves. 'He's the greatest dancer!'

'Lovely to meet you, Tara. I see you have more than met our Travis,' he said with a sloppy grin.

Laura then dragged Dougie off by his shirt collar to the outside terrace for a smoke. Still high from my love rush and with my head in the clouds, I hadn't noticed that the band had finished and the bar had started emptying. Holding hands, Travis and I followed the crowds outside. I couldn't help but think about my flight home back to England in the morning. I had been in Dublin for the best part of four days and now there was something worth staying for, I had to leave. Typical!

'I would really like to get to know you more Tara. Much more.' Travis stated domineeringly, as he romantically swung me around to face him.

Phwarr. The sheer manliness of him. My lady-garden went into yet another spasm and I couldn't help but wonder what he was like in the bedroom department. I really wouldn't object to him tackling me, at all.

'I would really like that too.' I added, completely away with the fairies. I could hardly help myself – now, I was actually trying to visualize the size of his tackle.

Sensing my momentary distraction, Travis pulled me closer. We kissed again, wrapping our arms around each other.

'Get a load of *them*!' shouted Dougie.

'For the love of God!' jeered one of the team.

'Sweet Jesus...' bellowed Laura, 'get a room!'

We simply couldn't leave each other alone, and I for one, was already aching at the thought of leaving him.

'Come on then, gorgeous,' he slid out his phone from the back pocket of his tight Levi's. 'Let's have your digits. There's no way I'm letting you go back to England without me knowing how to get hold of you.'

Being drunk on adrenaline, nerves and vodka meant I had to repeat my number several times before I got it right.

'Put in the English code!' I added, desperate to get this part of the evening just right. I wasn't going to lose sight of this man now. It was a real pain I didn't have my own phone with me so I could get *his* number. I hadn't even thought of taking it out with me. After all, it was just something else that I had to carry. Lip-gloss and perfume were always my first priority.

Dougie, who continued to rib Travis about being in love, took off his ring and gave it to Travis.

'G'wan n' marry her now!' he slurred, laughing lecherously.

We all laughed in our drunken state as another one of the team members pulled up a flower from the garden, put it in his hair (soil and all) and announced in a gravelly voice that he was to be bridesmaid. Dougie offered to be the priest and Laura, laughing, took a role reversal and was best 'man'. We all roared with laughter and began a pretend wedding ceremony. Travis whispered that he wished it was real and scooped me up in his arms. Then, before I knew what was going on, I was being shoehorned into a taxi. Apparently, the party was to continue back at Dougie's house.

I don't remember much of the journey, as our tongues were doing most of the talking. I was just elated that my night with Travis hadn't ended yet.

We arrived at Dougie's house and all headed for more beer in the kitchen. Six of the players had arrived back at the house too. Travis made it very clear he wanted us to be alone, but there was no way I was going upstairs, as drunk as I was. As much as I wanted to rip his clothes off and feel those muscles, there was no way I was going to fall over with my legs in the air. Well, not yet anyway.

I checked that Laura was okay, but as ever, when drunk she was as happy as a pig in shit; especially when surrounded by gorgeous men and bountiful amounts of booze.

Travis led me into the living room. As I looked around for the best place to get cosy, I noticed he'd begun texting someone. I didn't want to appear nosey, so said nothing.

'I have just sent a text to your phone, so you can read it when you get back to your mum's,' he said, smiling confidently as he sat down on the large sofa and patted the seat beside him.

With a sigh of relief, I sat down beside him. Travis then turned to me with a sexy smile:

'I haven't enjoyed a night like this in a very long time. You're different, Tara. You're very special.'

But, out of nowhere, his mood then seemed to darken. He withdrew slightly, rendering the atmosphere in the room heavy and tense. I felt my heart begin to beat faster as I wondered what had changed.

'I'm afraid to tell you everything about me, in case it puts you off,' he began cautiously, lowering his head, cupping his hands around his beautiful bronzed neck.

I slid off the couch onto my knees and faced this exquisite creature. Meanwhile, that infernal, bastard thong had sliced my arse into two arses - it was so numb, it was such a relief to get up off it. I lifted up Travis' stubbly, chiseled jaw and looked deep into his rich, chocolate brown eyes. It felt as if I could see into his soul. But I could sense something just wasn't right. We both fell strangely silent and I pulled away.

'Look, Travis,' I said, confused and trying to get a grip of myself. 'Are you really single?' how someone this gorgeous could be single was beyond me. He nodded his head, but didn't look up.

'Have you murdered someone?' I asked jokingly.

He shook his head with half a smile.

'My job...' he replied shrugging his huge shoulders and avoiding direct eye contact, 'it's left me with a complicated life.'

Aren't we all complicated? I thought. *Just wait till you meet the rest of my crazy family.*

I know I should have been listening more intently to what he was saying, but his physical presence was just so distracting. God, he was *so* shaggable. While comforting him, I couldn't help myself rubbing the top of his toned thigh. In an instant, I drifted off into thoughts of him in a rugby kit - all dirty, sweaty and powerful.

'I'm so glad I found you, Tara,' he pulled my face gently to his and we kissed again.

'Look,' I said, doing my best to concentrate by slightly pulling away from those incredible thighs. 'I can cope with most things in life, as long as you're single *and* honest with me. The rest we can work through.'

'... Do you believe in love at first sight?' Travis asked with conviction.

Sweet Jesus, I thought, I've hit the jackpot here. Not only is he a gorgeous northern ride, he's also in touch with his feelings. *Stay cool Tara, stay cool.*

'Well... I believe we can feel a deep connection,' I answered, not wanting to give too much away. He interrupted me:

'Tara, I feel like we just fit. It's as though I've known you for years. It's like, tonight, I was meant to meet you. I would really like to see you whenever I can, but as I mentioned earlier, it's complicated and won't be easy for you. I can't be seen out drunk and partying thanks to my job. I'm in a responsible position. Tonight was an exception because we were celebrating a win and it's Christmas. I have to keep a very low profile with my personal life.'

I smiled to myself. *So, this is a role of a WAG* (Wives And Girlfriends). Keep quiet, always look sexy, and always, *always,* have the latest, largest, designer handbag (just in case the paparazzi are out).

I've trained for this job my whole life.

The time was ticking by too fast. It was 4am, my flight back to England was in six hours and I still hadn't packed. My heart and pretty much all of my anatomy wanted to stay, but my head was telling me to leave.

The room next door had gone very quiet. Travis remained seated, but I stood up with the intention of going next door to grab Laura and do the sensible thing, but, before I knew it, Travis pulled me down on top of him. With my legs straddled either side of those firm thighs; he roughly pulled me into him. I could feel his throbbing manhood pushing hard up against me through my jeans. I gripped his huge biceps. He slowly but firmly began thrusting his rock hard cock against my crotch. I gasped in anticipation as he buried his face into my chest and started biting my nipples through my jumper. Oh God, I was so turned on. Running my fingers through his dark brown hair in ecstasy, I pulled him closer, urging him to continue. Was I really about to have a sexual encounter with a man I barely knew?

But then, the unwanted images started. I mentally tried to push them away, but the pictures of my past crawled into my thoughts uninvited, pushing painful, confusing, conflicting memories to the forefront of my mind.

In an instant, I was back to the age of seven; in my usual hiding place, crouched on the bottom of our stairs in between the coats, peering between the banisters through to the lounge. I always took Panda (my teddy) with me. I would cry into Panda and no one could hear me. Sometimes I would put him over my eyes so I couldn't see daddy hurting mummy.

Mummy was sobbing, but it was Friday. Daddy usually got angry or threw his dinners up to the ceiling on Saturdays. He was ranting something about mummy's friend being dishonest to her husband and saying she would go to hell for her sins. I didn't like the word hell. It was a bad, bad place where devils would burn you slowly and then they would eat you alive. I wanted to go in and stop daddy shouting at mummy, but it went quiet, very quiet. I inched forward just so I could see through the crack of the door. I could see mummy and daddy praying. I went upstairs to Laura's bedroom and crept into her bed. She always pretended to be asleep, but I knew she wasn't.

Forcing myself back into the 'here and now' and finding strength from somewhere, I leapt up. It was perfect timing - Laura poked her head around the door at just that moment.

'Err, Travis,' she said very calmly, but unusually wide-eyed for her. 'Some of your players have passed out on the floor while showing me how to do a scrum... and one of them is at the bottom of the pile that appears to have forgotten how to breathe.'

'The lads aren't used to alcohol,' he replied calmly while clearing his throat and trying to hide the huge bulge overwhelming his Levi's. 'Don't worry, they'll be fine.'

Dougie ordered a taxi for us and then proceeded to pull Laura back into the living room for another snog. Travis and I stood waiting in the hallway, holding each other like lovesick teenagers.

'Can I fly over and see you soon?' he asked, tenderly brushing some hair away from my eyes.

'I look forward to it,' I said, dropping my voice a notch or two and fluttering my lashes. YES!! The Big-Man upstairs was on my side for once. We squeezed each other's hands and sadly said our goodbyes. Laura and I then made our way to the taxi.

'I'm sending you another text, gorgeous!' Travis shouted while watching us leave.

I blew him a kiss as Laura and I spilled into the taxi.

CHAPTER FOUR

The journey back home from Dougie's house seemed to take forever. All I could focus on was getting back to my phone and reading the mysterious text from Travis. Not that Laura noticed my excitement. She herself looked like the cat that got the cream.

'I didn't want to tell you earlier, but they're really famous around here!' Laura bragged. Barely pausing for breath, she gabbled on about the antics of Dougie and co. I deliberately zoned out, silently embracing how lucky I had been to meet Travis. In my heart and mind and, well, everywhere else, I already knew he could be *the one*.

I had the passenger door open before the taxi had fully stopped outside mums. I threw the euros I'd been clutching in my hand at Laura and ran to the front door. Laura was oblivious to my torment, chatting away to the driver in what seemed to be slow motion.

'C'mon! C'mon!!!' I hollered impatiently. 'I need the keys to get in!'

Laura staggered out of the taxi still laughing and fumbled in her tiny bag. After drawing out her keys with a triumphant flourish, she dropped them. She reached down unsteadily to retrieve them from the pavement and promptly dropped them again.

'For the love of God, give them to me!' I yelled, the sound reverberating in the gloomy half-light of the suburban street. Snatching the keys from her, I opened the door and dived over to my phone. I flipped it open with a racing heart.

Gulping hard, I shook the phone impatiently. I switched it off and then back on. Nothing.

'BASTARD!' I exclaimed, not caring who I woke up. 'I can't believe it!'

Feeling a mounting sense of desperation, I switched my phone off again. This time, I left it off for about a minute before switching it back on again. *Still nothing. THE LOUSY FECKER!*

By now, Laura and the rest of Dublin could hear me from the lounge.

I felt like I'd been punched in the stomach. Laura, who had by now cottoned on to the fact that I was more than upset, tried to console me by saying; maybe the texts had been delayed for some reason.

'Really?' I asked, feeling a little more hopeful.

'Well, even if he doesn't make contact,' she said, as she staggered up the stairs, 'you've had a great night out, so let it go.'

'*Let it go?*' I convulsed, my momentary good feeling vanishing in an instant. 'You mean, as in, let-it-go, just *forget it?* Are you out of your mind?!'

Silence.

'Laura, come back downstairs!' I demanded, 'What about you and Dougie... haven't *you* two exchanged numbers?'

No answer. *The lickarse*, I huffed to myself. 'To think she has letters after her name,' I cursed, 'and she has the cheek to call herself a psychotherapist!'

To bring some much needed attention to myself, I forced out a few fake whimpering tears at the bottom of the stairs hoping someone, anyone, would come down to me.

Nothing.

I needed to think. '*Come on brain*', I tapped. I stood with my hands placed on my hips trying to focus but the heavily patterned pink and purple flowered wallpaper began to make me feel sick. I perched on the bottom step, held the banister and braced myself before I released a long, whiney whimper. I waited silently… okay, so that didn't work either. I raised the decibels up to as high as I could muster, gathering pace, momentum and volume, letting out a-huge, long, ear-aching shrill.

The house remained silent. Apart from the bloody annoying singing Santa I'd just set off in the lounge.

'Selective hearing gobshites!' I shouted.

I didn't know whose face I wanted to punch the most; the singing Santa's, Travis' or Laura's.

I really didn't fancy sharing the makeshift double bed with Laura in fear of (accidentally-on-purpose) smothering her with something. I stomped up the stairs, loudly flicking on the bedroom light, hoping to annoy Laura as much as she had annoyed me.

I mean, I *needed* her. I wanted to talk through the entire 'if, but and maybe' scenarios. But *no*. I just got ignored by *everyone*.

Laura was by now comatose and didn't even flinch during my continued hissy fit. I deviously ripped out pages from her precious book, doodled some willies in it and switched on the sidelight, aiming the bulb directly in her face for good measure.

Suddenly, I had an attack of conscience and pulled the bulb away in case it burned Laura. It hadn't made me feel any better anyway.

By now I was completely fed-up. I pulled my suitcase down the stairs and flopped on the couch staring at the flashing Christmas tree lights in deep thought. I felt so utterly miserable.

The throbbing pain in my arse from that bloody thong was now being diverted directly to my heart. I threw my skyscraper shoes at the wall, pulled off my skintight jeans and released the offending thong. Then, in a childish fit of petulance, I proceeded to jump up and down on the pathetic pile of clothes like a lunatic. All the while, I recited every obscenity I could think of. Strangely, it didn't make me feel any better at all. For the want of any better way to react to what was clearly the ruin of my *whole* life, I pulled on my inside-out, back-to-front PJs, thought of a few more obscenities and started ranting again.

I threw some things into my case and cursed myself for not taking Travis' number so I could give him a piece of my mind. Who did he think he was? The gobshite!

I decided to try and get some sleep. I lay on the couch and drifted, keeping my phone under the cushion, just in case.

It felt like I'd only been asleep for a minute when it was time to get up. Of course, the first thing I did was to check my phone. Nothing. I felt like such a fool. Thank God I hadn't slept with him!

I felt exhausted and was dreading my miserable journey home. As I threw on some creased, mismatched clothes, I kept having flashbacks from the night before. Retrieving my scattered outfit after last night's episode, I couldn't stop myself thinking these clothes were up against that gorgeous hunk last night. What a wanker!

As I finished throwing the rest of my belongings into the case, I started to feel pretty foolish and embarrassed for getting so carried away.

'Ah sure, are you really going to leave looking like that?' mum asked, as she fussed about, tucking extra stuff into my bag (including what looked like a full packed lunch). She never did trust airlines to feed me properly. She spun around to face me, 'you look like you've been dragged through a hedge arse-ways. Will you not even run a comb 'trew your hair, child? And you've still got your disco makeup on... let me get that for you, pet.'

With that, mum advanced towards me with her thumb, dripping with saliva.

'Oh god... mum... no, don't!' I squealed, backing up in horror. 'I couldn't give two shites how I look right now!'

Mum looked offended, but luckily, before she could reproach me, Laura interrupted:

'Tara, you're going to have to shift that arse of yours if I'm dropping you at the airport,' she shouted over her shoulder as she made determinedly to her car. 'I'll be late for work otherwise.'

I could barely conceal my growing temper as I yelled back. 'Look - I can't find my Jimmy Choo pumps... Mum, have you seen them? ... *KATIE*! Have you *had* them?!'

I wouldn't have put it past that little sister of mine to have them on eBay as quick as a flash to raise cash to feed her nasal hobby.

'Now don't you be blaming the child, Lord knows you'd blame her if it were raining!' interrupted mum whilst wagging her finger at me. Katie, who was leaning on the doorframe looking smug, seemed to be enjoying my discomfort. I didn't want to give her the satisfaction of saying anything, so I became determined to leave immediately, missing Jimmys or no missing Jimmys.

'Right - I have to go!' I bellowed in annoyance, grabbing stuff right and left and shoving it into my case.

'Go on with yourself and hurry over to the car,' said mum, trying to stuff one last Satsuma into my handbag. 'God only knows what the neighbours will think - with you leaving the house looking like that.'

I gave mum a big hug and Katie a halfhearted one, grabbed the first pair of shoes I could find and hobbled to the car with my case in tow. I threw my luggage into the boot and slumped into the passenger seat.

'Are you really going to the airport looking like that, Tara?' enquired Laura, with her well-practiced 'have-you-lost-the-plot?' look. I decided that any answer I gave would be way too foul mouthed, so I didn't answer her at all.

I pulled down the sun-visor to look in the mirror. They were right. I looked rough as a badger's arse. Maybe I should have brushed my hair; or at least wiped away the makeup from underneath my eyes.

I flipped the sun-visor back up and looked down at myself. I really was a mess. My open toed, diamante-encrusted, silver, four-inch heels really didn't look good with socks on underneath. To make matters worse, the socks didn't even match. One was a rainbow inspired stripy sock, the other a novelty Christmas sock with a reindeer's face on it. Adding to my 'bag lady' look was a mismatched, creased, velour tracksuit, which had something sticky on it, more than likely a dribble of rum from those god-awful liqueur chocolates. Finally, completing the tramp-like ensemble was my knee length cream faux fur coat. If James could see me now, he'd have a touch of the vapours and resign on the spot.

No – actually - for the first time in my life, *I really didn't care*. My thoughts had already crept away from my outfit and back to last night. Travis seemed so sincere and above all, so honest. How could I have got it so wrong?

Before I knew it, we were at the airport. Barely a word had been exchanged between Laura and I. I think we were both too hung-over to speak. She did mention her pounding head and not wanting to go to work, but that was about the extent of our conversation.

As I was readying myself to say my goodbyes to Laura, she saw the sadness in my face.

'Tara, today's a new day,' she said gently. 'Embrace it. Now, go and sort yourself out in the toilets. Your hair looks like something that's just been emptied out of a vacuum cleaner.'

'I don't care,' I replied with a half smile before half-throwing my arm around her in a belated attempt to be sisterly.

'Sorry, Tara, I have to run. I have to return a book that I borrowed from my boss before I start work. I'll call you later.'

Oh… FUCK. The book! I had flashbacks of a drunk, immature me doodling random penises all over it the night before. *Shite.* Right then, right there I didn't have the courage to own up to what I had done to her boss's book. I decided I would text her instead *after* I had put my case through, that way I'd be out of punching distance (plus there would be lots of security around).

I limped over to the departure lounge with my flapping, short ankle-bashers revealing my interesting choice of socks and four-inch stripper stilettos.

Checking-in at the airport was the last thing I wanted to do. I kept fantasising that Travis would make it to the airport in time to stop me from leaving, but I hadn't even told him what time my flight was. I dragged my weary, hung-over head (closely followed by my body) across the packed Departures hall to the check-in point.

'Good morning, Madame,' said the check-in assistant with a forced smile.

I didn't give her any sort of acknowledgement; I just threw my passport on the counter with a big sigh.

'Thank you,' she said with just a hint of sarcasm in her crisp, perfect little voice that matched her crispy large bun. 'Could anyone have tampered with your belongings, Madame?'

I really wasn't in the least bit interested in this boring procedure. My thoughts had once again returned to Travis. That devious, silver-tongued bastard!

'Yes yes, everybody tampers with my things,' I mumbled irritably while wondering where the hell my expensive Jimmy Choo pumps had gone.

'*Madame,* are you saying that someone has tampered with your luggage?' questioned the check-in girl, her eyes widening.

'Err, no… sorry,' I stammered, snapping back to the here-and-now, becoming aware I'd said something stupid. '*I wish Travis had tampered with my things though…*'

The snotty check-in girl gave me an alarming look.

'Oh God, did I… did I just say that out loud?'

'Yes, Madame, you did,' she announced in a matter-of-fact tone. She seemed to take delight at my expense. 'Madame, are you saying someone has tampered with your bags?'

My stupid loose tongue seemed to be taking over before my foggy, hungover brain could filter its content.

'No - no, not at all,' I said nervously, in response to her ridiculous reaction. *What is her problem? Seriously?* I could tell she was on the verge of summoning some sort of assistance. I attempt once more to calm the situation.

'I mean,' (drawing myself up straight) 'I have nothing to clare… err no - I mean *deeee*clare.'

I saw her eyes narrow as she leaned in closer to look get a good look at me, sniffing me as though I was some kind of animal.

'That's not what I asked you, Madame,' she yapped, articulating every syllable with cut-glass clarity as though she was speaking to an imbecile. 'I believe you could be highly intoxicated and therefore *unfit* to fly. I'm going to have to call security.'

'Sweet mother of God,' I said, as the enormity of the situation began to hit home. *Was this idiot really going to kick me off the flight?* 'What have I *ever* done to you?!'

'There's no need to be abusive, Madame,' she returned, primly. 'We have strict guidelines that we must follow. Passenger safety is paramount.'

Alarmed, I watched her perfectly manicured hand pick up the phone.

'Can you get security over to check-in four?' she rapidly ranted into the receiver, while never taking her eyes off me. 'We have a code yellow situation. I can smell alcohol and the passenger is being particularly abusive... Yes... Yes, I also think she might be on drugs.'

'Wait... what? *Me?*' I exclaimed, looking around in disbelief. The woman behind me was avoiding all eye contact with me, and the teenagers behind her were snorting with laughter.

'What the actual fuck is wrong with you!? I'm just trying to catch a flight... I want to be left alone!' I snarled over the desk.

'Make that a code orange – please hurry.'

IS THIS REALLY HAPPENING TO ME?

My heart was pounding; I could see the situation was now beyond saving. To top it all off, my hangover from the night before was now in full swing, as I broke out into a cold sweat and started shaking.

By now, a large and very unhappy queue started to form behind me. I could feel the stares burning into my back and could hear the huffs, puffs and loud clicking of tongues. I tried to make light of the situation.

'Not to worry,' I announced, bravely turning to address the people behind me. 'There's a slight problem with my booking, they're just phoning to get confirmation.' But, if anything, this only made the situation worse.

'Jaysus, she's not to be messed with - she'll be from the travelling community,' whispered one elderly lady to her companion in a voice loud enough for everyone to hear. 'Thank the Lord for airport security.'

By now, I didn't know what to do. I just pulled on my oversized Bvlgari sunglasses in an effort to hide my identity as best as possible. I figured it didn't help much. And I certainly felt no better. All I wanted was for the ground to open up and swallow me whole. I could see heads poking out from the back of the queue, like a Mexican wave trying to nosey what was going on up ahead.

'It's simply a misunderstanding,' I added, addressing the crowd again; this time raising my arm in a theatrical gesture designed to show my innocence. Looking at the stony-faced reception I was getting from my audience, I decided my salvation laid in one more last-ditch attempt to appease Ms. Polyfiller-face, the check-in assistant.

'Do I look like I attend AA meetings?' I asked, trying to sound reasonable. Okay, I knew I hadn't exactly covered myself in glory this morning and I did look pretty rough, but this lot were really taking this to the extreme.

Clearly trying to reason with this size 12 woman (who was obviously in denial and had convinced herself she could squeeze in to a size 8) was a mistake.

'Look… Miss,' I implored, trying to be even more respectful this time. 'I just want to get home. I went out last night and it was a complete disaster. I met a well-known man and, yes, I did perhaps have one too many, but… '

'Madame,' she sharply interrupted, 'are you trying to bribe me? With celebrity name dropping?'

'No, I am not!' I retorted in disgust, genuinely shocked and now even more pissed off. *How dare she?* I was wasting my breath. Everything I said fell on deaf ears. She quite obviously had it in for me from the beginning.

'Please move over to one side Madame - there are *sober* passengers waiting for their flight,' she said pointedly, pouting her lips with a dismissive hand gesture.

Cheeky bitch, I thought, as I scrambled in my handbag for chewing gum to disguise the smell of alcohol.

Today is really not the right day to pick on me… the obstinate twat. Despite my feigned defiance, my face was still smarting with embarrassment. I quickly pulled out my phone to call Laura to come and vouch for me and help me get out of this dreadful mess. But, before I could, security had arrived. Two guards linked both of my arms and hustled me into a room, while a third walked behind, dragging my case. I tried to distract myself from the embarrassing walk of shame by imagining how I'd tell this story to my friends. It would have to be something like; 'who would have thought it, three burley men ushering little old me'. But I wasn't ready to laugh. Not by a long shot. It was so mind-feckingly awful. The floodgates opened and I began to cry like a baby.

In the end, they questioned me for over an hour while I polished off ten cups of coffee on the trot. I was more than relieved that they didn't decide to body search me, my arse was sore enough thank you very much. In fact, they decided not to take the matter any further after all. Maybe they subconsciously realised there was no further indignity that could be heaped upon me. I was now a broken woman.

Even so, while all of this was going on, there was still a part of me listening out for my so-called 'delayed texts' from Travis. I really, really had it bad.

Despite feeling completely demoralised, after they released me, I still managed to catch the original flight after rushing through security. I was still in complete shock when I boarded the plane and while trying to find a seat, the whispers began again. It was all those feckers from the queue.

'Seeeee,' I announced in a booming, devil-may-care tone, gesturing at my own presence. 'Innocent… till proven guilty.'

To complete my act of nonchalance I kissed my teeth and shook my head in pure defiance. 'That will shut them up!' But, for once, I did as I was told and switched my phone off during the flight and just sat in tearful, mopey silence.

As soon as we touched down, I switched my phone back on. I had a new message – please let it be Travis…

[Text from Laura]

Omg are you ok? Mrs. Flanagan saw you getting arrested at the airport. Tried to call you but can't get through, phone me ASAP x

[Text to Laura]

Tell Mrs. Flannel face I WAS NOT ARRESTED!! There was merely a misunderstanding. Will call you when I'm home. Still haven't heard from Travis by the way :-(x

Shite. Now the whole of Dublin will know what's happened at the airport, great. My life is on the floor, I despaired.

I sat pondering on the parked plane, still bewildered and shaking my head in disbelief at the last 12 hours of events. Unbelievable. *So, here I am, back in England, exhausted, confused, un-refreshed, it's pouring with rain and now I'm meant to put on a brave face?* I just couldn't.

I text Jackie turning down her kind offer of picking me up from the airport, pulled on my coat, collected my luggage and grabbed a taxi home. I felt exhausted and frankly, quite depressed. I returned to London with a hangover from hell, a case full of dirty washing and a thong-induced, red-raw arse (that wasn't even the result of having amazing sexy-times). I was already sick of the festive season.

I just wanted to sleep the whole sorry nightmare away. I switched my phone to silent, dumped my case in the hallway and got into bed fully- clothed, pulling the comfort of the duvet around me.

I woke up four hours later to find I had several missed calls and three text messages.

[Text from (Unrecognised)]

Hi Tara, hope you don't mind, but when I didn't hear from you, I wasn't sure if I had the no. down correctly... So I tracked down your sis this morning and she gave it to me. I miss you already. How're you feeling today? Travis xx

I screamed with excitement and jumped up and down on the bed. I was like a frantic child, I was so deliriously happy. I couldn't help but read the text over-and-over again. Deep down I always knew he wasn't a gobshite! I can't believe I thought he was a wanker. Oh bless him!

I went back and read the first of other text messages from Laura saying Travis had tracked her down at her workplace, because she had told Dougie the hospital where she worked in the hope of a 'visit' one day. The missed calls were from Laura too, she'd been trying to get hold of me. All of a sudden my trip to Dublin was the best trip ever. A whoosh of love fell over my quickly recovering body. I returned a text immediately:

[Text to Travis]

Hi Travis, so good to hear from you! I'm glad you went out of your way to get my no., really enjoyed your company. I hope to see you again very soon xxx

Life was *so* worth living again.

I immediately dialled Laura and shrieked down the phone to her on a euphoric high while demanding every little detail of how Travis got my number.

'So, what did he say?' I asked, ecstatically.

'The same as what I just told you five times,' she said with a sigh.

'Okay… sorry. So what did he wear?' I begged.

'The same outfit that I described just a minute ago.'

'Was he still gorgeous?' I wheedled. Stupid question really, *of course* he was still gorgeous. 'D'you think he really likes me?'

'I'm sure…' began Laura.

'Did I tell you what he has text me?' I asked, interrupting her in my excitement.

'Yes,' said Laura evenly.

I somehow sensed she was bored with me, so ended our conversation and read my newly received text.

[Text from Siobhan]

Boo hoo... I have a sore tummy. I think me sim card is on its way :'(x

I woke early on the morning of New Year's Eve with a smile. I checked my phone to find out if I had received a text from Travis. I had. It was a whole wonderful page full of kisses. Just as I was about to reply, I received another one...

[Text from Travis]

Hi babe, hope your well. Have decided 2 go 2 Manchester for new yr. Really want to see my parents x

My heart leapt with excitement. I rang Laura immediately.

'Laura! Laura! Guess what?' I yelled, the second she picked up the phone.

'What?' mumbled Laura, in a grumpy, *I've-just-woken-up* voice.

'Guess!'

'Whaaaaaat?'

'Guess! Guess!' I implored, wanting her to play the game a little and be happy for me.

'You've won the Lotto?' she sighed.

'No,' I tutted, 'it's even better than that!'

Laura continued grumbling and was obviously not in the mood for guessing games.

'Oh you'll never guess!' I added impatiently. 'Travis has just text me. He's flying to Manchester. For New Year. Do you think he is coming over as an excuse to see me?'

'It's 7:30am,' she butted in. 'All I can say is; if he's sending you text messages at this hour of the morning, then that must be the case. But, has he even bothered to call you yet?'

'Well, no, not exactly,' I admitted, 'he has been *texting* me though… I don't want to call him yet because I have to play it a little cool, don't I?'

'Well that's up to you, but you could perhaps ask him if he would like to come and see you while he's in the country, that would be nice,' she counselled.

'Nice? *Nice?* I can think of a *much* better word than "nice"! Sorry… I didn't mean to wake you. It's just that he's the first and the last thing I think about. This feels so, well, different. It's like he's switched a light on inside me that's never been on before and I'm kind of afraid of how I feel. I can't really explain it. I think I have found something I thought I would never find. I feel sick, but not unwell. I can't eat, yet I'm hungry. Oh… I don't know,' I sighed. 'I just feel totally lost in him. Every time I hear a song it reminds me of him and it's like he's singing it to me. Every time I see a man on the TV I compare them to Travis.'

'It's plain and simple,' groaned Laura. 'It's just infatuation. Enjoy the ride and chill.'

'So, I'm not going mad then?'

'Not at all, get a grip of yourself! Just send a text back and get on with it.'

'Okay, I'll text him. Speak to you later - and thanks, Laura.'

[Text to Travis]

How lovely for you. I'm sure they will be very happy to see you. If you fancy coming up to me afterwards let me know, as it would be more than lovely to see you! xxxx

I knew I wouldn't be able to concentrate on anything until I'd heard back from him, but I did have to at least go through the motions of going to work. Apart from anything else, I needed a blow-dry ahead of the fancy dress party Siobhan was holding at her house for the New Year. It was bound to be a mad one, her parties always were. I also needed to pick up my costume from James.

I checked my phone before I walked into the Salon; no new texts. It had been two hours now and still no reply from Travis. I tried to keep myself calm by reasoning that, maybe, he was already on a flight over and had switched his phone off.

'Morning everyone!' I beamed as I arrived at the Salon, brilliantly masking my lovelorn anxiety.

'Hi Tara, I've picked up your outfit… and it's just *fabulous*,' pouted James. 'I'm so jealous. I've always wanted to wear a Miss Santa tutu in public. It's hanging up in the staffroom, darling. Ooh and by the way, can I detect a bit of a glint in your eye? What have *you* been up to in the old Emerald Isle?'

'I'll tell you another time,' I smirked, grinning from ear to ear.

'Oh no! You are *not* doing this to me,' said James, practically breaking into a run to cut me off before I could get to the staffroom. 'I have to know. Pweeeaaase! Is it juicy? As in, *really* juicy? Have you finally had some action?'

'Well, no, James, not - yet, but watch this space and get saving for a hat!' I purred coquettishly.

'So, no sex then?' said James, suddenly looking very deflated.

I shook my head.

'Oh, right,' said James, now confused at how this might possibly have worked. 'So not even a little lick of his lollipop?'

'Erm, no,' I said with a shrug as I battled out of my coat.

'Hmm. Well, anyway,' said James, losing interest fast and miming an extravagant yawn. 'I have to finish my nails for tonight. See you later.'

'James, before you go, is Jackie okay after that text from Pete?' I asked, suddenly remembering the offending message (even though it felt a million years ago, pre-Travis).

'Oh yeah, everything's fine now,' James said dismissively, 'someone was playing with Pete's phone or something. She's in the beauty room at the moment but she'll be out in a while if you want to see her.'

'No, it's okay,' I said, feeling relieved. 'I don't want to bother her. I'll catch up with her at the party.'

I opened the staffroom cupboard to inspect my outfit. It was just what I wanted. Miss Sexy Claus would be wearing a short, frilly tutu and a cape edged with white, fluffy fur. I'll match it with a low cut top, some stockings and bright red heels.

'Jayde!' I could hear James yelling from the Salon floor. 'Stop stuffing pork pies down your hole and come and do Tara's hair!'

I watched her through the corner of my eye walking past James with her middle finger raised, finishing her pork pie, she was trying to say swivel, but it came out as 'thwivel', along with some pork pie.

'Come on then, Tara, let's get you lookin' even more gorgeous,' said Jayde, popping her head around the staffroom door and wiping the crumbs away from her mouth and uniform.

'Jayde - I saw that, and if *I* can see those gestures, half the Salon can too with the amount of mirrors in here,' I admonished. 'If you're going to raise your finger at James, try not to get caught, eh?'

Jayde looked sheepish. 'Sorry, you know what he's like.'

'Yes,' I interrupted, before I could be drawn into a long discussion, 'I do... but stop taking the bait, Jayde.'

To be honest, I felt so loved-up I just didn't want the discussion at all, so I let it go. I checked my phone again. Nothing.

'Right, Jayde, I want sexy, half-up, half-down, with tousled curls cascading down my shoulders please.'

It didn't take Jayde long and she did a great job. I didn't look too bad at all, even if I do say so myself. I didn't want to hang around the Salon too long though. I had too much on my mind. With my hair done, I got up to go home.

'Right, see you two tonight - and James, can you let Jackie know I was here?' I said, as I swept out.

I drove home with my phone in between my legs just in case I heard from Travis. But still, nothing! He had *still* not responded. Once home, I read back the text that I had sent over-and-over again. *Yes,* it was clear enough. I guess he must just be busy. Or, maybe I hadn't made it clear enough that I was inviting him down? Either way, I was starting to feel pretty desperate all over again.

CHAPTER FIVE

After a two-minute walk, I arrived at Siobhan's house. I could hear the music blasting and saw hordes of people dancing through the kitchen window. Ringing the doorbell, I was greeted by James.

'Oh my God, James!' I shrieked, taking a step back in shock. 'What *are* you wearing?'

'I know there's not much to the outfit,' said James, as he gave me a suggestive twirl, 'but I love it. Don't you just love it, Spencer?' asked James, turning the full spotlight of his attention to a young man who had appeared from nowhere, and was also waiting to be admitted to the party. Poor Spencer looked mortified. It was *very* clear he didn't bat for the same team as James, nor did he intend to.

'Do the angel wings do it for you?' continued the irrepressible James, turning around and pouting back at Spencer over his shoulder. In James' view, any heterosexual man could be turned.

'Hmmm? What about these skimpy, silky shorts then? They don't leave much to the imagination do they, Spencer? I've got a spare pair if you'd like to try them. Or maybe you'd like to get into my shorts, sweetie? Anyway, come in, come in.' said James, standing back with a flourish. He looked a bit disappointed as Spencer put his head down and darted through the doorway without giving him a second glance. *Gay is the way* sweetheart. You'll find that out sooner or later,' James called out to the rapidly retreating figure. 'Call me when you're ready!'

Recovering his composure, James turned to me; 'Oh well, plenty more fish in the sea, as they say. Everyone's well on their way, getting leathered.'

Poor James. His posturing was lost even on me. While he'd been tormenting Spencer, I'd been busy sending Travis yet another text. This one was a guaranteed showstopper though, because it had a selfie of me in my Miss Sexy Claus outfit attached to a very suggestive few words.

'Where's the lady of the house, James?' I asked, as I clicked *'send,'* hoping against hope this text would stir Travis into action.

'Well, the last time I spotted her she was trying to hump the Christmas tree,' replied James, brightening now I'd finally looked up and taken notice of him.

'Oh, okay, sounds about right,' I giggled, despite my desperate mood. 'Thanks, James. Nice wand by the way,' I added, nodding at his nether-regions as I stepped through the door.

'Thanks, honey. I get that a lot,' he grinned. 'If only the right bloody people noticed it!'

I elbowed my way through the crowd of people, checking my phone as I went. Even in my distracted state, I could see there were some great costumes - everyone had gone to a great deal of effort. Outfits ranged from cute animal onesies to the very outlandish, human-sized whoopee cushions. Some outfits were, I might even go so far as to say, shocking. I mean, a green glitter mankini? Really? Yuck. Yet, strangely, it was impossible not to gawp.

I could hear Siobhan's bellowing voice long before I spotted her. She was making an attempt to sing along to Wham's 'Last Christmas'. Entering the lounge, I spotted

Siobhan just in time to witness her humping session with the Christmas tree go horribly wrong. In some sort of grotesque finale, she took a tumble backwards, pulling the tree down on top of herself with a huge crash. Baubles and bits of tinsel flew into the air and the tree itself was plunged into darkness as the fairy lights gave up against the relentless assault from Siobhan.

For a few moments the room was plunged into silence. Everyone stopped what they were doing and looked over, unsure of how to react. Everyone, *except* James, that is. He'd clearly abandoned his door duty and was now up on a chair wiggling his toosh and his magic wand (the plastic one) about in the air. I'm not sure he'd even registered our friend's predicament.

I hurried over to see if Siobhan was okay. From what I could see, she was comatose, as she lay trapped under the tree with her legs wrapped around it. One of her hands was sticking out from between the branches, still grasping an empty wine bottle.

'Siobhan!' I yelped, pushing the tinsel aside and plunging my hand into the foliage so I could force open one of her eyelids. 'It's only 9:30! Have you been on the sauce all day?'

'Feck… what? I wuv you, Tara… I wuv *everyone,*' she slurred.

'James, get down from your stage and get me some water for Siobhan will you?' I yelled across the room. Most people had already decided the show was over and had drifted off as someone had cranked Lady Gaga up to full blast.

'But 'Poker Face' is *my song!*' whined James. 'Can I get the water in a minute? Actually, where's that lard-arse of a donkey, Jayde? She can get it.'

'James, I don't care who gets it, just please hurry up,' I said in my best I'm-in-no-mood-for-messing-about voice.

'Ugh! Fine!'

Still wiggling his toosh, James minced off to the kitchen and shortly returned with a glass of water. It was hopeless though, I couldn't get near Siobhan's mouth. We needed another strategy. I began barking instructions.

'James, go and find me some strong men to help get this Christmas tree up and then get Madame onto the couch.'

Gawd, I am so wasted on this lot, I thought. *I'd make a bloody brilliant parent. Look at how effortlessly I take charge in a crisis. None of this lot are lifting a finger. If it weren't for me, Siobhan would be trapped until morning!*

Then suddenly I had an awful thought. *What if something dreadful had happened to Travis? What if he had been in a car accident somewhere and veered off the road and no one had noticed? Or worse, what if he had been kidnapped and held up for ransom? OMG, maybe I should call the police or something? Mind you - and say what? 'Err, my boyfriend - possibly my potential husband (who I've actually only known a few days), seems to have disappeared and is not responding to my text messages and his phone is constantly going to voicemail?'*

'There aren't any decent men - believe-me - I've already checked,' shouted James, above the din of the opening lines of a Spice Girls track, forcing me to tear my thoughts back to the here-and-now.

'I'll go and pull Jayde's head out the fridge,' James sniggered. 'She's the closest thing we have to a strong bloke. She's built like a brick shit house.'

However, James couldn't find Jayde anywhere. She'd completely disappeared - which she seemed to do a lot of lately. Luckily, while James was looking for her, he managed to gather a group of willing bodies, and together we managed to heave the Christmas tree off Siobhan. I moved swiftly to get the baubles out from her bra but I needn't have bothered. She looked a terrible state. Her St. Trinian's outfit was now a complete mess, her stockings full of ladders and her skirt was tucked into her knickers.

Hauling Siobhan onto the nearest couch, I called to James; 'Okay, James - give Siobhan that glass of water.'

'Open wide, Siobhan,' he said, yanking her head up by one of her pigtails and pouring a huge glug of water down her throat. 'There's a good girl.'

'This water tastes as good as feckin' vodka!' Siobhan sputtered, as her tongue lapped up the remaining liquid around her face.

'Oops, my mistake,' said James sheepishly after whiffing the few drops left in the glass. 'I could have sworn it was water.'

'James!' I shouted in horror. 'She's had far too much already! She's gonna be as sick as a flippin' pig!'

As if to prove my point, Siobhan immediately pulled *that* face. Oh feck, it was the *oh-my-god-I'm-going-to-puke-on-you* face.

'Shite, are you going to be sick?' I asked, preparing for a dive out of the way.

'EVERYBODY OUT - *NOW!!* SHE'S GUNNA BLOW!'

With that, I heard my phone go off. I'd left it on the side table in all the excitement (but I reckon I'd have heard a message drop if it was two miles away). Ecstatic, I promptly dropped Siobhan's head that I had been cradling. It landed with a sickening thud.

'Oh shite, sorry!' I shouted back to Siobhan as I dived over to my handbag to retrieve my phone. 'Hang on Siobhan - don't be sick yet. Travis has text me!'

Flipping open my phone I saw I had more than one message. Beaming with excitement, I scrolled through them. Arse, feck, shite. Not one of them were from him. The bastard. The only one that was vaguely interesting was one from Jackie saying she wasn't coming to the party 'for personal reasons'. The rest were all "before the sun sets... happy clappy New Years wishes" and all that nonsense. Honestly? I couldn't give a flying feck about the sun setting.

I turned back around to my patient, only to discover she had clambered her way off the couch, and was now standing, green-faced, with the unsteadiness of a one-year-old learning to walk. That wasn't the real problem though. Looking on, I could see Siobhan's face contorting as she began to wretch, her eyes widening. I grabbed the nearest thing to me - which turned out to be a Christmas stocking - and held it out for her. Of course, she missed the stocking completely. Sadly, I couldn't say the same for my outfit, which bore the full brunt of Siobhan's projected stomach contents.

'I feel feckin' great now!' spluttered Siobhan, who had somehow miraculously and instantly recovered. 'Where's the feckin' party gone? I need a drink!'

However, after taking one wobbly step forward, her eyes rolled to the back of her head and she collapsed face first on the floor. I stood there with my mouth open, dropped the stocking and held my arms out in disbelief.

'Great, just bloody great!' covered in vomit, I tiptoed out to the kitchen with my face looking like a slapped arse. I poked my head around the door to find James had moved stage and was now on the kitchen table doing the YMCA.

'James, I'm having a nightmare,' I said, trying not to breathe in as I talked - the stench of Siobhan's sick was making me feel nauseous. 'Can you watch Siobhan? And DO NOT give her any more alcohol. I need to go and get changed.'

Pissed off, I stomped up the stairs into the bathroom, peeled off my *not so sexy* hired outfit, showered and thudded into Siobhan's bedroom. I flung open the wardrobe, flicked morosely through its contents and eventually I opted to put on one of her Juicy Couture tracksuits. Checking my hair and makeup in the mirror, I couldn't help but think about Travis once again. I couldn't believe he still hadn't text me. The tosspot. He's probably down the gym working out those fantastic abs - just when those abs should be working out on me.

The party was still in full swing downstairs. I could hear all the commotion as I descended into the madness once again. Feeling more miserable than ever, I headed to my bag and got out my phone. It was now 10:15pm. No new messages. In a huff and utterly fed up with watching everyone else having a good time snogging under the mistletoe, I burst into the kitchen in search of disinfectant and rubber gloves. As I was rummaging around the cupboards, I heard what sounded like Siobhan shouting: 'Jam it up her arse!'

I looked round to find Jayde (who had finally appeared after her mysterious absence) doing her best at running in her homemade donkey outfit. The costume was just a grey t-shirt (three sizes too small), accompanied by leggings that (bless her), gave her an awful camel-toe that she was completely oblivious about. It was completed with a set of wonky ears on a headband. Yet, that wasn't the most ludicrous part of the picture. Jayde was being chased around the room by James *and* Siobhan...! *SIOBHAN!? She had puked all over me not even half an hour ago and now she's running around with another glass of wine in her hand!*

'Come on, everybody,' shouted James encouragingly. 'Pin the tail on the wobbling donkey! There's enough arse for everyone to have a go, you can't miss.'

'Don't worry, you all just carry on - and I'll clean up the mess!' I moodily shouted at them in a bid to get some attention. Nobody paid me a blind bit of notice though. I moodily checked my phone again.

Not being able to contain myself, I called Travis' phone after carefully making sure I'd withheld my number.

It was still switched off. But why?

In a daze, I threw back a vodka and Coke and finished cleaning. I did my best to join in and mingle with some of the other guests, but my heart really wasn't in it. I couldn't help wondering; *where is Travis? What is he doing?* I knew that in my miserable, discontented mood, I was half-heartedly joining in conversations just to kill time; but I wasn't kidding anyone, least of all myself.

By 11:55pm we all congregated into the lounge to see the New Year in. I rang Travis again. His phone was still switched off.

'*I'm* doing the countdown everyone, so shut up!' announced James. 'Everyone make sure you have some Champers - and Jayde you get your cake ready. I've got a surprise for everyone at midnight. Spencer, darling! I *so* caught you looking at me just then. My eyes are up *here*, sunshine!'

'James, I'm getting in there first with Spencer, you jammie fecker!' slurred Siobhan, who seemed well on her way once more. 'You can have sloppy seconds. Isn't that right, Spencer?'

Poor Spencer. He looked like he was at the wrong party.

'Ten, nine, eight, seven, six, five, four, three, two, one... HAPPY NEW YEAR, bitches!' James cheered, throwing glittering fairy dust everywhere.

Feeling incredibly sorry for myself, I faked the smiles, the kisses and the hugs. Just a simple text from him would have made me enjoy the celebrations so much more. Am I really that forgettable? Clearly I was, because I was standing alone on New Year's Eve.

At 2am I slowly swept my tired eyes across the smoke-filled room and sadly brushed away the 'happy' glitter. I noticed that everyone had paired up in some form for the evening. That is, everyone but me and - oddly for once - Siobhan. Emboldened by too much drink, she had told both Danny's to 'feck off' because she 'couldn't give a shite' about either them. Now she was curled-up on the couch surrounded by her empty bottles, sleeping like a baby. The only other singleton was Jayde who had claimed the buffet and had brought a chair up to it to give it her full, undivided attention.

James was making best friends with Siobhan's much-loved inflatable man, Barry, who she usually carried around in her handbag. Unaware he was being watched, James could be seen chatting Barry up in the corner and cupping his gentleman's area. *I must buy James the 'Inflatable Ben',* I thought, as I overheard him ask Barry if he would like his fingernails painted.

Everyone else in the room was with their real-life partners, or who-ever they'd copped off with for one night. And then there was me, all alone, holding my silent phone.

The following day I felt even more flat. I certainly didn't feel like I was starting the New Year off in good spirits. All my resolutions to find a husband and get pregnant now felt completely foolish. I couldn't even keep a man for more than a night. And, worse still, I hadn't *even* slept with him and he'd still done a runner!

No! I shouted at myself, clicking my tongue. My New Year's resolution is to bag that man! He's *the one*. I just know he is.

It was back to work soon, which I wasn't in the mood for at all. My thoughts were only of Travis - and work completely interfered with that.

As I looked at my phone, my thoughts turned once again to Travis. *Maybe he's just turned his phone off over the holidays,* I wondered. What if he never got those texts? I checked my sent messages for the twentieth time. *I'm being ridiculous,* I thought. *I'll just send him another text, what have I got to lose? But what should I say? I just need to think of something he has to respond to.*

Feeling a little braver, I began to compose a text:

[Draft message to Travis]

Did you have a nice eve?

[Delete]

[Draft message to Travis]

Hi gorgeous, where are you?

[Delete]

[Draft message to Travis]

You WANKER! Why don't you reply?

[Delete]

[Text to Travis]

How's the family? Wish them all a Happy New Year! Look forward to meeting them all one day! Xxxx

Fuck it. [Send]

I spent most of New Year's Day waiting to hear back from Travis (the same as every other day for the last week, then). I hate waiting!

Get a grip. I thought. *It's New Year's Day, he's probably in bed with a hangover. Oh, I wish I was with him.* I pictured him laying in bed, imagining his body. I could see him naked, with a white sheet only just covering his manly-hood, with me laying next to him. Running my hands down his ripped six-pack and carrying on down to his... *Ahh for feck's sake. I need to pull myself together. Big time!*

But then my thoughts started to change. *The fecker better be alone. What if he met someone last night while he was out? What if he is in bed with her right now? Oh my God. The WHORE, sleeping with him on the first night. I bet she's blonde and skinny, with huge boobs. Oh my god, he's cheated on me already. BASTARD!... I hate him!* My stomach sank as my thoughts spiralled out of control. *I'm going to text him a piece of my mind!*

[Draft message to Travis]

Have you forgotten about me already!!? Met a whore then have you? Let me guess her name... CHLAMYDIA???!!!!!

[Delete]

[Draft message to Travis]

I miss you so much. Where have you gone?

[Delete]

Eventually I thought better of it and decided not to text him. *Oh god,* I huffed as I slumped on to the couch, *I wish he would just contact me so I could know one way or the other!* I decided to call Siobhan for some advice.

'I have text him loads of times and I haven't heard from him since yesterday morning,' I moaned, trying with my voice to get over just how wretched I felt. I wanted to reach out to someone so they could understand how badly my heart ached. 'He went to visit his parents in Manchester and I text him saying he should come down and see me, but I never heard anything back.'

'Ah c'mon now, if he doesn't get to see his parents very often, then it's probably a case of catching up,' she counselled. Siobhan could really be quite sensible when she was sober.

'Really? Do you really think it's that?' I wheedled, praying she was right.

'Yes, I'm sure he'll be in touch,' she said, reassuringly. Then she ruined the effect by adding: 'And if not, I'll get on the next flight and deck the bastard!'

'So how's your head, Siobhan?' I giggled, despite myself. She always did make me laugh.

'Well, I'm in top form - but you'll not feckin' believe this, right,' she gabbled on, talking at her usual break-neck speed. 'I wakes up this morning with two guys in me bed, all three of us stark-bollock-naked, not a clue who they are. Then, I went downstairs to find some eejit has knocked over me feckin' Christmas tree - and James was still fast asleep on top of me blow-up Barry!'

'Oh Siobhan, don't you remember anything at all?' I sighed heavily.

'Well, I know I had a great feckin' time, that's all that matters right?' she laughed back. 'I'm just in the middle of dragging one of those guys out of me bed to get the Christmas-tree spines out of me fanjita!'

'Okay, well I'm glad someone's still having a good time,' I sighed, feeling a cloud of despair descending on me again as I was reminded how rubbish my night had been. 'I'll let you go then.'

I had to end the call quickly. I felt like I was going to cry. Maybe my sister could be of some comfort? I rang Laura and gave her the same story.

'Has he *still* not rang you?' asked Laura, with her usual infuriating air of snotty concern.

'Well, no, but Siobhan thinks that he needs to spend time with his parents,' I stammered, instantly regretting making this call.

'Hmm…' pondered Laura doubtfully.

'What do you mean, 'hmm'?' I huffed and rolled my eyes. 'I rang you to make me feel *better* not *worse.*'

'It just doesn't sound right to me,' said Laura, moderating her tone. Gawd, I hated it when she talked to me like I was one of her mental patients. 'Perhaps you should give him a call and put yourself out of your misery.'

'*Me?* Call *him?* Again? No way! I'm not running after him. I want to be different. I bet all the girls that come into his life do the chasing thing with him. And I'm not going to be like *that.*' I pronounced defiantly.

'Well, fine then, don't call him; *stay* miserable,' said Laura, who clearly couldn't think of anything else to say. Bloody hell, I thought she was supposed to be trained to deal with these situations. She was rubbish. What were all those years in university for?

'It's simple, you either do, or you don't,' she concluded.

No shit, Sherlock! I thought.

'Shall I *text* him?' I asked, partly because I was feeling rather unsure as to how to behave, and also because I was still desperate to try to find some comfort from our conversation.

'Yes,' sighed Laura, 'if that's what you want to do, then do that.'

'But I don't want to appear like a bunny boiler!' I wailed.

'Then don't text him!'

'You're right. Okay. I won't!'

The following day I returned to work with a heavy heart. It was days now since Travis last contacted me. By now, I had completely given up all hope of hearing from him.

To stop me from making even more of a fool out of myself, I painfully deleted his number from my phone. Then, after enjoying the brief moment of control, I swiftly deleted every in and out text message. I felt momentarily liberated, but then immediately regretted it.

So, here I was, 2nd January. I had gone back to work and life had gone back to normal. Except it hadn't. Not quite. I felt a hole. A great big gaping hole - which no amount of shopping or wine could fill. It was as though Travis had never existed. I felt as though I had been on a rollercoaster that had only one peak. I simply couldn't understand. Whilst I had only met him once, he had made a huge impact, making me feel something I had never felt before. It was as though I had unfolded for the first time in my life.

I found it really hard to concentrate at work - and even the usual madcap banter didn't distract me from my thoughts. I kept flashing back to that magical night. But each hour, his face was becoming less clear. It was like I had dreamt the whole thing. *Why did I erase his number?* I felt like I had lost the only connection with him that I ever had. But then, what's the use of keeping the number when you get no reply?

'Tara… earth calling Tara…' called James, as I moped around the Salon. 'You have two broken nails. Let me fix them for you.'

'Not today. Tomorrow, maybe. Just not today.'

'Tara, you're not yourself,' he said, looking concerned. 'Has that rugby guy got to you that badly? I hate to see you so sad. Have you noticed that Jayde and I aren't bickering? We're trying to make you happy. Both you and Jackie don't seem right. Come on, let me take you out for a boozy lunch and we can do a bit of shopping. That's always fun. I always think the first day back after a break is too depressing, so it should only be a half-day. I don't know why schools don't do it - the half day, that is, without the boozy lunch of course.'

'James, I don't think I'm up to it,' I cut in. Blimey, I must have looked bad if I've driven the irrepressible James into a nervous babbler. 'It's just hard to explain. Even though I only met him the once, it felt like… like he was… well, the one. I've just never felt those types of feelings before, *ever*. Why did he come into my life, turn me upside down and give me a taste of hot passion, just to bugger off? I mean, James, you're a man - well err, kind of, no offense - why do they do that? They give you all the bullshit, practically get in your knickers and then, nothing! I don't understand why he left my life so quickly. It's just really hurting right now.'

'Right,' James said, grabbing my hand and marching me to the office. 'Pull up a chair. Come on.'

'What are you doing, James?' I asked feeling alarmed.

'I've got it all worked out. We're going to Google him of course, so you have a picture and maybe you can email him?'

'But I don't even know his full name.' I interrupted, overcome with a feeling of hopelessness. 'What's the point? He certainly isn't bothered about contacting me.'

'Tara, listen sweetie, I'm an expert in tracking down the male species, trust me,' pronounced James, swatting away my objections. 'Are you really going to give up that easily? Now, do you want a picture? Or not?'

'Well… yeah, I do, but…'

'Right then!' interrupted James, suddenly all business-like, tapping away on the computer. 'So, it's Travis. A rugby coach for Dublin, right?'

'Yes.' I sighed heavily, slumping down on the chair beside him with my jaw resting heavily in my hands.

'Travis… Travis Coleman - is *this* the one?' James asked, jabbing the screen and turning it to face me. I let out a shriek and shook.

I trembled as I turned to face the computer. There he was. I felt like my heart was about to burst through my chest. I could feel a build up of familiar emotions of loss come rushing forward. My eyes, which were wide open, then filled with tears. More than anything, I wanted to jump into the screen and grab him - just to ask why he had done this to me.

'Stunning, Tara,' sympathised James, getting out of his chair, so he could step back and take a good look. Standing with one hand on my shoulder and the other perched on his slim hip, he nodded in approval.

'Really stunning,' he whispered, before he turned on his heel with a sigh and left me alone.

I was lost in my memories. Everything came flooding back. There were those beautiful brown eyes that once stared into mine and his mega-watt smile that melted me from the first moment I saw him. As I stared at the picture, willing it to come alive and step out of the screen to make everything right, I realised this was becoming even more destructive to my already fragile mood. I was feeling frustrated and confused, wishing I had never seen a picture of him. In fact, I wished I had never met him at all.

I ran to the toilets to fix my makeup and sort myself out. *That's it!* I thought, *I just want to go home.* Overflowing with angry emotions, I readied myself to run to my car and drive home. I just wanted to be alone.

'Tara,' shouted Jayde from the staffroom, 'your phone's buzzin' big time.'

'Tell them I'll call them back.' I answered bitterly, as I stomped around gathering up my stuff.

'Ello,' I could hear Jayde answer my phone, 'oh, alright mate?'

'Give me that!' I heard James growl, as he snatched the phone from her. *'Good afternoon*, thank you for calling Glamma-Puss, this is James speaking. How may I help today...? I'm afraid Tara isn't available at the moment, can I take a message...? Okay... okay, and who shall I say is calling?' he asked.

The next thing I knew, James was running across the Salon towards me with a dropped jaw, pointing frantically at the phone, mouthing, *'T-R-A-V-I-S'*.

'Stop mucking about, this really isn't the time!' I snarled, furious that they could possibly think this was a funny prank. This wasn't something for Salon banter. This was my bloody life.

Shrugging his shoulders and giving me a 'you're-going-to-be-sorry' face, James continued on the phone. 'Travis, thank you for calling,' he purred. 'We have your details and I will pass the message on to Tara personally. Thank you for your call and enjoy the rest of your day.' He then hung up.

'Tara, darling,' he said as he handed me the phone with a 'told-you-so' smile. 'Look... it's an Irish number. It *was* him.'

Shaking with shock, I finally realised James was telling the truth. I excitedly grabbed my phone and ran to the toilets to call him back.

'Travis?' I mumbled nervously, shaking from head to toe. 'It's me, it's Tara, Tara from England.'

'Hey gorgeous, yes, I know it's you,' Travis laughed softly. 'I was just lying on the bed reading *all* your text messages. Miss Naughty Santa outfit, eh? Very, very nice indeed. And those stockings… wow, how am I supposed to concentrate on work now?'

I practically fainted with desire just listening to his devastatingly sexy voice.

A short while later, I proudly strutted back out of the toilets. Jackie had now joined Jayde and James and all three were waiting patiently for me to say something.

'He had only gone and accidentally left his phone in Dublin,' I said, feeling ecstatic and a little sheepish at the same time. 'He returned from Manchester this morning and has only just received all of my forty-something text messages. Or maybe he said fifty? Ahh well - who's counting? I feel *so* stupid. But guess what? He's flying over to see me next week. I'm so excited… I feel sick!

'James,' I added with a beaming smile. 'Do you fancy fixing my nails now?'

CHAPTER SIX

I had been planning what to wear for the best part of three days. I had tried on practically *everything* in my wardrobe in various combinations. Nothing seemed right. There was nothing else for it. I had to call in my local fashionista: James.

The next day, we headed to the West End of London, armed and dangerous with my credit card. For two hours we went from shop to shop, hunting down the perfect outfit. I liked almost everything, but James insisted I needed to make a huge impact of looking sexy and 'fierce'. We both agreed on one thing though: there was no room for error. Nothing other than *complete* perfection was acceptable.

James had been pitching 'fur coat no knickers' from pretty much the moment we'd first met at the train station. I resisted for a long time, but eventually, fuelled by Dutch courage (thanks to a liquid lunch), I agreed to meet him half way. I would get a new *faux* fur coat, but there would *have* to be underwear underneath, very *sexy* underwear. So, after we left the noisy Italian restaurant, which was tucked away in the corner of Shepherds Market, we set off with renewed vigor. The next stop was Agent Provocateur for some saucy pieces.

'It's got to be all black,' ordered James as we wove our way down Brewer Street. Then, after pausing to wink at a couple of pretty young men who caught his eye, he added;

'Apart from the diamond earrings and the soles on your Christian Louboutins, of course.'

The shop in Broadwick Street was buzzing with pretty young things. James and I did our best to look like we shopped there all the time and picked out some lace hold-ups, with a forties-style black line running up the back. Then, we added a pair of hipster French knickers and a matching bra that would give you the type of cleavage you could park a bike in.

'Right! Next stop: Harvey Nicks!' declared James, while the assistant wrapped my precious lingerie. 'Let's grab a cab.'

'James, I'm not a bank.' I protested weakly.

'Oh come on! This is *Travis*, the man you thought you'd lost only a few days ago. We've already agreed every detail *has* to be none other than perfect.'

He's right, I thought to myself. *And Travis is my Mr. Right. I have to invest in my future and the future of my (hopefully-soon-to-be conceived) children.* Mentally I prepared myself to give my plastic another bashing and followed James out of the door and into the back of a taxi. James confidently told the driver where we wanted to go and proceeded to flirt with the poor man all the way to Knightsbridge.

As soon as we got to Harvey Nichols, James instantly forgot about the driver and headed purposefully towards the store. Once inside he went straight for the furs.

'You know I don't do real fur!' I said, looking around me desperately in case an animal lib fanatic spotted me.

'But it's already dead!' James exclaimed, with a puzzled face as he smoothed down a coat. 'It's not going to mind. Besides, someone has gone to the trouble of skinning all these fluffy animals. We can't let them go to waste.'

Shamefully, despite my reluctance, one coat did catch my eye. It was a long, black, luxurious D&G mink. Carefully avoiding looking at the price tag, I gingerly put it on. With a theatrical gasp, James collapsed into the chair behind him.

'Tara, it's got your name written all over it! It was made for you,' he said, fanning his face as though to prevent a full swoon. 'That's definitely the one. You *have* to get it!'

'Come and look at the price tag for me, I daren't,' I said, feeling a pang of guilt as I stroked the gorgeous mink. It felt so dreamily soft to the touch, falling in smooth sleek lines as I ran my fingers through it as if I was stroking a Persian cat.

'Fate has stepped in - it's in the sale!' he whooped. 'It's only £3,000. What a bargain! That's a sign for sure!'

Gulping hard, I began a fierce mental argument with myself. *Can I justify this? Of course I bloody can't! But it fits so perfectly,* I thought, as I swirled around, hugging the fur and standing on my tiptoes for added effect. I imagined Travis looking at me in my black, raunchy, luxurious fur. I savoured the mental image of that beautiful mouth curling into an appreciative grin. Game over. I peered over my shoulder to take one last glance at myself in the mirror. I *had* to have it.

I winced at James as I handed over my credit card to the smiling shop assistant.

'Isn't it just *fan-fucking-tastic*?' James cooed, clapping his hands in glee.

'I love it,' I breathed, 'can't you tell?'

'Well, not really, you've paralysed your face in that, sort of, vacant look,' said James, with his usual teasing pout. 'Perhaps you should've waited for those first two vials of Botox to kick in before having the other three vials injected?'

'Oi, you!' I replied, giving James a friendly shove. 'Well, I'm pleased to hear it's worked. Not that you are a discerning enough judge to tell.' I added, as we both fell about laughing.

'Right – shoes,' instructed James with a snap of his fingers, oblivious to the looks the sales assistant was giving us as he rapidly wrapped the fur. 'Let's stop buggering about - pun - *definitely* intended - and get on with what we're here for.'

'James, that's enough,' I said, still chuckling as I accepted the enormous Harvey Nichols bag from the stony-faced assistant. 'I have a beautiful pair of Louboutins at home. No more spending. I will be living on beans on toast for a year.'

'Come with me,' said James, who was clearly not going to take 'no' for an answer today. 'You only have the five-inch heel. We are going to get you the full six-inches because, as we both know from experience, anything less than six inches *really* doesn't register, sweetheart. And anyway, there's nothing quite like the unspoiled sole of a Louboutin.'

'But, oh my God, I could have bought a car with the money I just spent on that coat,' I groaned, beginning to panic.

'Shoes, Tara. Come along. This way. First floor…'

James linked his arm tightly around mine and marched me over to the escalator. Just as we reached them, I heard a text come through and eagerly fumbled for my phone in my bag.

[Text from Travis]

Just booked us a room @ The Sanderson. Only the best for you, can't wait to see you Xxxxx

'James, look at this!' I screamed, ecstatically jumping up and down like a crazed schoolgirl, waving the phone in his face.

'Bring on the Louboutins!' I shouted in a frenzy.

'And there they are, Tara… your *new* shoes,' announced James; pointing theatrically the second we reached the shoe section. *Jesus, that guy can spot a pair of decent shoes from 10 miles away,* I thought.

'Oh my God,' I gasped, once I'd clocked them. 'They're not shoes - they're stilts! There's no way I could stand in those - let alone walk in them. I'll break my neck.'

'What on earth are you talking about?' James said, looking utterly bemused. 'Of course you can! Let me show you how it's done.'

I sat down and watched on with embarrassed fascination as James did his Cinderella act, squeezing his perfectly pedicured (but wide) foot into this slender, four-sizes-too-small stiletto. I looked on in disbelief, as he then proceeded to strut provocatively around the shoe display with ease and grace.

You had to hand it to him. If a man can walk like that in a six-inch pair of heels, then so could I (even if I did have to be lifted and lowered into them). They were beautiful stilettos too, clad in black silk, complete with matching bow cascading from the top of the heel almost to the floor. They were extremely raunchy, yet classically elegant. Sure, they were practically identical to the ones I already had at home, but still… in for a penny, in for a pound. While the cashier delicately wrapped the shoes up, ready for purchase, I tapped out a reply text to Travis. After showing it to James, we both grinned as I pressed the send button.

[Text to Travis]

How does fur coat, 6 inch heels & lacy knickers grab you? Xxx

I have never recalled feeling such a rush as I did when I sent that text and then keyed in my PIN code. It was albeit short-lived, once I began totting up all the spending in my head. By the time I picked up my perfectly-gift-wrapped shoes from the counter, I had more than a twang of inevitable guilt. Bang goes the new sun-bed I was saving up for in the Salon.

In an attempt not to spend any more money, I made a desperate plea to drag James out of Harvey Nichols. But as we headed for the door, I spotted my last, potentially fatal purchase.

'*Don't* think I didn't see you looking at that handbag!' said James, raising his eyebrows in glee.

'No… I shouldn't. I *really* shouldn't,' I protested, more weakly than ever. 'I probably *couldn't* anyhow. I think the credit card is already maxed.'

'Well, let's go and find out,' said James, propelling me closer to the handbag section.

I picked up the black fur Versace handbag that I'd spotted in passing and, right on cue, another text from Travis came through.

[Text from Travis]

The thought of you in fur coat & lacy knickers has made me rock hard! Xxxxxx

'Okay - he obviously likes fur,' I said, showing James the text. 'Let's do it. I'm going to try and buy this handbag - and if I can't pay on my credit card, it's clearly not meant to be.'

I held my breath as I handed my card over. Amazingly, the purchase went through. I wasn't sure if that was a good thing or not, but by now it was too late. With my bank account nearly £5,000 lighter, we left Harvey Nichols with just two shopping bags.

'I'm glad we went with fur coat and naughty knickers, as there's no way I would have been able to afford a dress as well,' I giggled, as we dived down into the tube station to begin the journey home.

After a sleepless night, I raced to my Salon where I decided to have the works done. To begin with, I pleaded and pleaded with Jackie to give me yet another Hollywood to remove what little fluff there was (although I had to stoically block my ears to her sternly delivered advice against it).

'I don't care if it looks like a plucked chicken, as long as it's smooth,' I said, stubbornly. 'Vajazel it after to cover the sins.'

Next, Jayde did my hair, while James fixed diamantes to my long, glossy, black acrylic nails and matching pedicured feet. This was followed by a session with Jackie *and* James jointly applying my makeup. Everyone agreed that smoky eyes suited me the best, I had silk false lashes fixed on to finish off that sultry look I desired.

Frankly, I'd have gone through anything to look my best. Travis and I were only to be together for such a short space of time and I really wanted to make that huge impact James was so insistent on. I already knew that with my outfit (or lack of) I was well on my way to doing so. Therefore, I had to make sure the rest of me was up to scratch. I wanted him to walk out of the arrival gates of the airport and think proudly: 'She is mine.' To achieve that sort of 'wow' factor, I needed every millimeter of my body to exude sex appeal.

After a couple of hours being poked, prodded and tweaked into shape, I left the Salon. Draped in all my brand new finery, I began my journey to the airport to pick up Travis. Internally I was squealing with frenzied wild thoughts, but knew I must stay calm, because calm equals sexy. That's not easy when you feel like there are a million gymnasts somersaulting in your tummy all at once. *The next time I get back in this car, OMG... I will have probably had the best sex in my entire life, with – OMG - the best looking ride, ever.* I had to pinch myself.

… And Breathe.

I must not talk incessantly.

And breathe…

I must not try too hard.

And breathe…

I wonder how big his cock is?

And breathe…

His flight was due to land at Heathrow at 8pm. Sadly, we wouldn't have long. He had to fly back at 8am. the next morning for an important game.

Not long after I set off, with my music blaring on the car radio to give me a bit of a gee-up, my mobile rang. I ignored it. I could tell from the ring tone it was Laura. She then rang again. With a sigh, I turned down the radio, switched my phone onto speaker mode and answered it, 'Tara have you left yet?' asked Laura.

'Yes,' I said, still a bit peed off that she had interrupted my singing along to Michael Bublé. 'I'm on my way now.'

'Have you seen or heard the news at all?' Laura enquired.

'No. Why? What's wrong?' I gasped.

'Most flights in and out of Ireland have been cancelled,' she said flatly.

The news hit me like a bullet.

'WHAT? No! Why?' I stammered.

'There's thick, thick fog everywhere and a plane had to do an emergency landing at Dublin,' she said. 'You know what it's like, the news is pretty sketchy right now.'

'I don't feckin' believe it.' I said quietly after a long pause.

'I suggest you ring Travis and find out whether his flight is going ahead or not.' Laura suggested gently.

'Shit. Okay… well thanks for letting me know. I'll keep you updated.'

I pulled in at the next service station and nervously rang Travis.

'Well Dublin airport seems normal babe,' he calmly stated, in his slow, sexy, gravelly voice. 'Hold the line gorgeous, I'll just go over to the information desk.'

I could just make out what he was saying in his delicious accent;

'I've got the love of my life on her way to Heathrow - I need to know if my flight is going ahead.'

I couldn't quite focus on the reply he was given because, quite frankly, I was dazed by what he had just said about me being the love of his life. I was overcome with a warm, fuzzy feeling.

'Okay babe,' he said, coming back to me, 'there could possibly be some delays, but the flight *is* going ahead.'

'Thank God for that!' I answered, relieved, completely forgetting to even attempt to play it cool. 'I can't believe that in just a few hours we will be together.'

'I just want to hold you so tight,' he replied. 'See you very soon, babe.'

All mashed up with love, I started the car and continued my journey to Heathrow airport. Once I navigated around the heinous one-way system, I parked up in the short stay zone. I really didn't want to have to walk very far in these stilts. Flipping down the mirror, I checked my makeup, but I couldn't even focus on that. I just wanted to look out into the dark, cold, starry sky and wonder what our night would bring. Nervous anticipation about making love with Travis filled my mind. I giggled to myself as I got butterflies in my stomach. I had tingling sensations all over me. It would be strange yet, so exciting. Just the thought of touching him, stroking him, smelling him, taking him all in made my lady-garden moist. Very moist indeed. I would have to try and resist launching myself at him. All I wanted to do was rip his clothes off. I had never experienced a lusty feeling like this ever, ever, ever.

My raunchy thoughts were brought to a grinding halt when I received another text from Travis.

[Text from Travis]

Babe, I haven't boarded yet, there has been another delay, but should be boarding in 5 mins xx

I knew it wasn't his fault, but I felt really peed off. I returned a text with a simple:

Okay x

The flight would only take around an hour so, having some time to kill, I stayed in the car. I applied more lip-gloss, put some music on and chain-smoked a few cigarettes. Soon though, I started to feel cold, very cold. Nice one Tara. Only I could come out in January with just a fur coat and skimpy knickers on.

[Text from Travis]

Babe the flight has been delayed again! This time by 2 hours!! What do you want me to do? Xxxx

A poxy phone call would be nice, I thought, completely pissed off by now. I punched the direct dial number in my phone to call him. This time I was not quite so happy.

'I do wish that you would *call* me instead of texting all the time,' I began, trying to control my tone the best I could. I was just so desperate about the way things were going.

'Sorry babe, it's just so noisy here with announcements and so on,' Travis said, sounding as damn calm and lovely as ever. 'Do you think someone is trying to tell us something?'

'Maybe,' I answered, still a little sulky.

'Babe, I hate the thought of you waiting around all this time. Are you okay? Why don't you get yourself to the hotel and I'll get a taxi over to you when I land.'

And that was it, his voice and concern melted me. I was *so* ready for this, to be part of a couple, to have a man. My Mr. Right, worrying about me for a change, making sure that I'm safe was like music to my ears.

'I'll go into the airport for a coffee and wait for you, as I'd rather we arrive at the hotel together,' I said, once again bright and happy.

'Okay, gorgeous, if you're sure. I will let you know the minute I board.'

'Well, with such little time left, we won't be getting much sleep,' I added with a suggestive giggle.

We both laughed and that ended the conversation. *Go to the hotel?* There was no way. I had been dreaming about this perfect meeting of Travis and I for days and days. I'd mapped out every second in my head again and again. I had even watched 'Love Actually' several times so I could make sure our airport meeting went just like it did in the film.

Travis and I were two souls destined to be together and a delayed flight was NOT going to ruin that for me. With a face full of determination, I climbed out of the car, locked it and strode purposefully towards the main terminal building.

The second I walked into the Arrivals hall, my resolve vanished. Standing in my beautiful fur coat and stripper heels, I stood out a mile in the crowd of backpackers and tourists. I immediately felt so over-dressed as I awkwardly maneuvered myself deeper into the arrivals lounge. It didn't help that there were bodies lolling around everywhere. There were even people sleeping on the floor. It was surreal, like something out of a disaster movie. I had descended into absolute chaos. The fog delays must be a lot worse than we thought.

Precariously I made my way over to Starbucks, stepping gingerly around the prone figures. I couldn't believe what I was witnessing. It was as if the airport was hosting the whole of England. Doing my best balancing act in my shoes, I eventually carved a path through the crowds to find there was no coffee, no seats… no anything.

The only thing I did find was a lot of *complete* perverts. I don't think I've ever been gawped at by so many dribbling old men. They all seemed to enjoying their drinking Stella-Artois as they followed me around the terminal with their eyes.

I started to feel like a circus act. I had over-the-top hair and over-the-top shoes. I was dressed like nobody else in the airport - and the amount of makeup I had on would rival that of any clown.

My head started to spin with the embarrassment of it all. I hated the light in places like this. Those fluorescent bulbs were always so cruel. *And why are the floors so damn slippery? Surely not everyone has to wear hiking boots for a flight? It must have been a man that chose this stupid floor. I would love to get him to try and walk on it in heels while carrying a ton in a suitcase.* The fact that I didn't have a case was irrelevant. I had my brand new handbag with me, which was, in my opinion, the same weight as the average weekend case, if not heavier. I had everything with me too; hair irons, hairbrushes, perfume, phone, tissues, 'protection' (and lots of it), keys, nail varnish, nail varnish remover, purse, chewing gum, baby wipes, baby oil, spare knickers and two pairs of sunglasses; one Versace and one Bvlgari. Oh yes, and a bit more makeup.

For what seemed like ages, I traipsed round desperately trying to find somewhere to sit and try ever so subtly to kick off the killer heels, which were crippling me, but to no avail. The airport was now giving out sleeping bags to delayed passengers. What on earth was going on? It felt like the world was coming to an end.

It didn't take a genius to work out it was going to be a long night, so I headed for the ladies. I just wanted to sit down on a toilet for a few minutes to rest my weary, throbbing feet. I was also now desperate to scratch my lady-garden. *(Why, oh why didn't I listen to Jackie? I should never have had another*

123

Hollywood). When I got to the ladies I found there was a massive queue, with dozens of poor mums trying to calm their bored and screaming babies. *Honestly, could this get any worse?*

As I walked back into the concourse to seek out another loo, a group of drunken gobshites caught my eye and beckoned me over. I lowered my head trying to make out that I hadn't seen them.

'Oi sexy,' they called, 'yeah - you in the black fur coat! C'mon over and share our sleeping bag. There's plenty of room for one more!'

The cheeky feckers, I thought, as I ignored them and carried on walking around in circles, hoping to find a seat. Suddenly, I spotted a family ready to leave their table. The trouble was, so had everyone else. There were many of us predators dotted around, poised and ready to pounce on the almost-free table. Everyone's eyes - mine included - were darting around, assessing the competition for the great race to the table. As soon as the last family member raised their arse off their seat – that was it – the flag was down and we were off! The whole world and his screaming child made a dive for the seat, but, as I started to run, I felt my left hold-up coming loose and sliding down my leg.

'SHITE!' I yelped desperately, as I clapped a hand over the trailing end of the hold-up. *A chair?... Or dignity? Feck dignity - I want to park my arse!* A chair was just within my reach, but I would have to let go of my hold-up if I was to make a proper grab for it. So I reached out, releasing my hold-up. The chair was almost mine. I was so close. At the last moment I saw someone out of the corner of my eye. Without looking up, I gave them a shove and told them to 'feck off.' Then, looking up, I realised what I had just done. The 'someone' I had just assaulted (after winning the chair of course) was a… priest. *Shite*.

Hardly surprisingly, he looked none-too happy with me.

'Oh… Father - I'm *so* sorry,' I said, mortified. 'Please, take the seat.'

I stood back up, unable to look him in the eye, my face red with shame.

'Ah bless you my child, sure it's like a game of musical chairs, is it not?' The portly priest said, nodding approvingly at my quick volte-face.

As I watched him sit down, on *my* hard earned chair, I felt my hold-up hit my ankle. The priest didn't say a word as he slowly looked down at the offending object, but I can tell you now… the look on his face was of utter bemusement. The sight will stay with me for life.

I didn't want a man of the cloth to see me trying to recover my hold-up from around my ankle. Surely I had suffered enough? I swiftly swung my big fur handbag off my shoulder and draped it nonchalantly in front of my leg, as I shamefully backed away with an uncomfortable smile.

'No problem, Father, no problem.'

'Hey, Nora Batty!' shouted some clever dick behind me. 'Do you need help pulling your tights up?'

The cheeky gobshite. 'Tights indeed. They're hold-ups! So *there*, you thick-arse!' In a huff, I shuffled backwards; red-faced and trying to retrieve my hold-up that was still dangling around my ankle. 'You wouldn't know your arse from your elbow!' I cursed back, ready to punch something.

[Text from Travis]

Just been an announcement over the tannoy: Would the man meeting Tara Ryan please make himself known, we want to tell him he's one lucky bastard!
Xxxxxxxxxxxxxxxxx

In an instant, a warm feeling flooded through me. I decided Travis was definitely worth the wait (and the embarrassment). To compound the good feeling, as I began to type a reply, I spied a nearby café opening its shutters. They had coffee! *Thank God (sorry, Father).*

[Text to Travis]

God, you have so said the right thing. You have made me smile. I will wait all night for you if I have to Xxxxx

The two-hour delay became a three-hour delay, but we were still told the flight would definitely be going ahead. At this point, Travis and I decided we had both waited so long that we might as well just sit it out for as long as it takes.

While I waited, I discreetly put my fingers into my coffee to add moisture to the top seam of my hold-ups. The last thing I needed was another hold-up collapse. My bum was so numb, but I didn't dare move off my chair in the recently-opened coffee shop. No, they were like gold dust. Indeed, I had just witnessed a guy asking someone to mind his chair. As soon as his back was turned, the chair-thief ran off with it. I wasn't going to be fooled. Numb bum suits me fine. I just switched the pressure on my bum cheeks every ten minutes or so.

After an hour, I managed to shimmy the chair (albeit rather noisily) to the other side of the café to flick through an abandoned magazine. *Ugh! They can look up with daggers all they like, the chairs mine, you losers.* I even stood up at one point to tease them and just to show pure defiance, lifted the lightweight chair up with me. Then, after stretching out as though to leave, I pulled up the collars of my beautiful coat and flopped back down again. Well, what the hell else was I supposed to do to pass the time?

After what seemed like an eternity of mindless people-watching, my phone started to ring. It was Travis. They must be boarding at last.

'Babe, I'm really sorry... The flight has just been cancelled.'

'... Please tell me you're joking?' I begged, although I already knew he wasn't.

'Babe, I'm so sorry; I'm not joking.'

'Oh... (long sigh)' I replied, trying desperately to stop myself crying like a baby whilst still on the phone. My hissy fit could wait until later. 'I see.'

'Babe, I know you're upset; I am too,' he said. I held my breath as his soothing tones washed over me. 'You get yourself home and text me when you're back safe and sound.'

'(Sigh)... okay,' I grumbled, swallowing a large lump in my throat.

Staring into oblivion, I shut my phone. I felt numb and in shock. My feet felt glued to the ground. I couldn't move. It was like I was having an out-of-body experience. The Big-Man upstairs had thrown me a double-whammy. *First my hold-ups - and now this? All that pruning, all this bloody itching.* That was it. *I'm not itching myself through the pocket lining of my fur coat any more.* I wrenched my fur coat back in temper and gave my lady-garden a much-needed scratch. I was almost orgasmic with relief. Everything was throbbing: my head, my feet, my arse cheeks; everything was pulsating and for all the wrong shagging reasons!

Forcing myself to come back to the here-and-now, I began rummaging around in my bag. Eventually I found my car parking ticket under the pile of beauty products and headed to the kiosk to pay.

'That'll be eighty five pounds please, Madame,' said the bored-looking man behind the Perspex.

'Hang on... what do you mean, EIGHTY FIVE POUNDS?!' I screamed incredulously. 'I've just blown nearly five grand on a date that I didn't even get to have because...' I paused to draw breath, doing my utmost not to start bawling then and there,

'Miss, there's nothing I...'

'DON'T interrupt me!' I snapped, as I continued on my rant. 'First, the fecking flight was cancelled and now you're suggesting I pay £85 for the pleasure of waiting around for four hours to find that shit out?'

'As I was just trying to say... there's nothing I can do,' he began, with the practiced patience of one who is used to being yelled at by furious customers. 'You should have parked in the long stay car park, Miss; the Short Stay is just that... short stay. If you want to dispute it, I'll give you the address where you can write to complain. But, if you wish to leave the premises with your vehicle today, you will have to pay first.'

With my feet now throbbing thanks to James and his bright ideas, I took off my shoes and threw them on the ground in protest. I felt so helpless; there was nothing I could do.

'For feck's sake.' I shouted, reluctantly handing over my credit card and watching in mounting fury as he punched in the details.

'…Your card has been declined, Miss. Do you wish to try again?' said the car park man, showing me the card reader as evidence.

'Oh, feck!' I spat, through gritted teeth under my breath. 'Right, just give it back. I will just give you all the cash I have in the whole damn world, shall I?'

'Thank you, Madame,' he said, his face completely impassive as he took the wad of notes I handed over.

I stropped off to the car park in my stockinged feet with the killer heels dangling from my fingers. And sure enough, the next crisis hit. *Where is my car? I'm sure I parked on the third floor, didn't I? Can you not be on my side? Just for once? Please?* I mouthed up to the sky.

Maybe he heard me this time because, after walking a bit further on, I eventually spotted it tucked behind a big van. Both relieved and infuriated, I dashed over to the car and swung open the door. *Ewww.* I had stepped in a puddle. But by now, I really didn't give a shit. I just jumped in the car and gunned the engine. After a long sigh, I put the heater on full blast to warm my frozen wet feet and headed for the car park exit.

Driving away from the airport, I noticed an overwhelming smell… *Is that…* I sniffed and sniffed until I discovered the source.

'Oh… my… fecking God!' I burst out loud, banging the steering wheel in protest. 'I've fecking stepped in fecking PISS! Some *grotty little wanker* has pissed next to my car. MY CAR!'

At boiling point, I started to have a serious evaluation of my pathetic life. *Shite. I've spent nearly five thousand pounds on a date and I've come away without a man, significantly poorer and with sore feet that smell of piss. Feckin' great!*

CHAPTER SEVEN

The following day I was like the Antichrist. I rang Laura and explained the nightmare episode, even though I knew there was nothing she could say that could make me feel any better. Sure enough, her *I-told-you-so* attitude instantly got on my nerves, so I ended the call quickly.

I hated Sundays, they were always so lonely, boring and way too long. The fact that I hadn't heard from Travis since I had text him to say I was home safely, made me feel even worse. There *was* plenty to do, of course, apart from chain-smoking and shaking my phone, but I didn't feel like doing the washing, ironing or any of that crap. I wanted *Travis*. God, I was so hungry for him. I felt miserable and unsettled. Why couldn't he just text me? *All that effort I went to, all that debt I'm now in and yet, nothing. The cheek of him. Who does he think he is? He's Travis... that's who he bloody is. A fecking gorgeous gobshite. Way-too-busy-Travis; clearly too important to pull his poxy finger out and text me!*

Utterly dejected, I sat with my hands in a box of Rice Krispies, mechanically shoveling them into my mouth.

I shovelled another handful of Rice Krispies in my mouth and sighed so hard that most of them came flying back out, but I didn't care. I had every right to be feeling this way. I wanted to feel sorry for myself - and that was that.

Then, I heard a familiar beep of a text coming through and instantly snapped out of my misery-fest. Spitting and choking out the remains of the cereal, I fumbled to pull my phone out of my dressing gown pocket.

[Text from Siobhan]

I have had the worst night of my life. R u home yet from your shag fest? x

...

[Text to Siobhan]

His flight was cancelled, I feel really down, what happened to you? X

...

[Text from Siobhan]

I don't believe u!! I'll b round in 5 mins 4 a cuppa xx

'Are you okay, Siobhan? You look a little... disheveled,' I said in a flat tone while I filled the kettle.

'Am I feck! I spent the night in the cop shop!'

'Jesus! What? Why?'

'Well, I was minding me own business, driving to Luke's and I needed some petrol,' she began, speaking even more rapidly than usual in her distress. 'So, there I was with a lit fag, when me mobile started ringing. Thing is, it was in my jeans pocket. I un-did me seat belt and answered me phone. I'll be honest with you now, I did use me elbow just a little to steer me car as I pulled into the petrol station. So, there I was in deep conversation with me mammy and filling the tank - you know, it is hard to smoke, hold a phone *and* fill up at the same time. I coulda done with three hands so I could. Anyway, I kept the fag in me mouth, so I could hold the phone and fill up me car...'

'Oh-my-god, you didn't?!' I gasped, my eyes widening in horror. I was so shocked by the story I momentarily forgot about my own life trauma.

'I know, right,' shrugged Siobhan, ignoring my reaction and ploughing on. 'I was feckin' proud of me multi-tasking, so I was. The next thing I knew, the gobshite fuzz was beside me. Well, he thought he was the fuzz when he tried to feckin' arrest me. So I told him to feck off with himself, and told him, "you're no policeman, you're one of dowse community support officers". Then he only went and rang the real fuzz!'

I winced. I knew there would be more.

'So I got feckin' fed up of this *arse* telling me he could arrest me, so I says to me mam, "I'll have to let you go, but I will get back to you in a bit". Then I put me phone in me pocket and threw me fag on the floor, cus I mean business now right.'

'Siobhan…' I gulped, cupping my face in horror.

'Tell me about it. Some eejit pretending to be the police, someone had to sort him out. I decided I would do one of those citizens arrest thingies for impersonating the law. So there's me, right, trying to shove this loser into the back of me car, when three feckin' gorgeous policemen turn up. And what do they do? They feckin' cuff me and put me in the van, that's what they do. They only released me an hour ago! The feckers are taking me to court! I don't even know what for. I don't see their feckin' problem,' concluded Siobhan, shaking her head in genuine bewilderment.

'I… I don't really know what to say… apart from cigarettes and mobiles don't go with petrol stations,' I lectured.

'I hope I don't go to prison, but if I do, I hope by then I can go to one that's mixed,' she said. Then she grinned: 'Imagine the wall-to-wall cock!'

'*Jesus*... that's not funny,' I said, struggling to keep a straight face. But her crazy antics got the better of me once again and as usual, I started laughing.

'So, what happened with you last night then?' Siobhan asked, turning the tone.

'Oh... I don't want to go through it again,' I said, waving away the question. 'Let's just say, the only part of me that got wet was my bloody foot.'

'So... the drought continues for you,' Siobhan remarked, shaking her head in wonder as she got up to leave. 'Well, I'll have to skip the tea because I've got to go and see a man about a dog. I'll call you later to make sure you haven't hung yourself from the curtain rail. Look on the bright side, at least you now have a fur coat I can borrow.'

After she'd gone, I realised my mood *had* lifted a little. It always did when I saw Siobhan. *Actually* I thought, God love him, *Travis must just be so busy. He does have to organise a whole rugby team. Maybe I'm being a little too hard on him.* I decided to send him another text.

[Text to Travis]

Hello gorgeous, I hope you're ok? What will happen to your flight ticket? Surely they will refund you? Xx

After a few hours of not hearing from him, my thoughts started to shift again. My light mood darkened and I began to feel like I was about to lose the plot again.

[Text to James]

I'm sure you know about last night from Siobhan, but I haven't heard from him since!! Do you think he's had enough already? Xx

…

[Text from James]

Darling, I heard it all from Jayde this morning. Sweetie do u really think he would sit in an airport 4 hrs if he wasn't mad about you? Xxx

…

[Text to James]

How does Jayde know? Xx

Hmm, I guess James was right - news certainly travels fast. I glanced at my watch. The day was nearly over and the house was a right mess. I was crunching my way through the sea of dropped Rice Krispies in an effort to start clearing up, when I heard another text come through.

[Text from Travis]

Hiya babe, sorry for the delay. Don't worry about the ticket. I really want to see you ASAP Xxxxx

Oh the relief! Thank you, thank you! I jumped up and down in joy and quickly returned a text.

[Text to Travis]

Hi gorgeous, want to see you ASAP too! Don't worry, I know you're busy - I'm just so pleased to hear from you Xxx

...

[Text from Travis]

Okay gorgeous, well my work schedule is hectic. I have some free time, but not enough to go out the country. Any chance you could come over to Ireland? Please? Xxxxx

I was ecstatic, but I had a one big problem: money. I was so stupid to have spent all that money for the meeting at the airport that never happened. If this date was ever going to happen, I really did have no choice but to figure out a way of persuading Travis to pay for my visit. Yet, my pride would never allow me to admit to him that I now had a severe cash flow problem.

[Draft message to Travis]

Are you going to be a gentleman and pay for me?

[Delete.]

[Draft message to Travis]

Spent all my money on a fur coat and knickers

[Delete.]

[Draft message to Travis]

I would love to, but the Salon has hit a quiet spot

[Delete.]

My phone vibrated suddenly.

[Text from Travis]

Let me know if you're ok to go ahead, I'll book it for you babe xxx

YES! The relief. I ran to get my diary. *He must be keen,* I thought, sending two messages that quickly!

[Text to Travis]

Tomorrow's good for me Xxxx

...

[Text from Travis]

Haha, you're funny, babe! I like a sense of humor in a woman. How about 10th of Feb? I do have to go to a meeting though early the next morning though Xxx

'10th of February?' I shouted out, after reading the text. *How am I supposed to wait for that length of time?*

That was a whole feckin' two weeks away. *Stay calm Tara, stay calm.*

[Text to Travis]

Can't wait! Book away, sexy Xxxxxx

The next couple of weeks building up to my trip were grueling. I had to work non-stop in an effort to claw in some money to make up for my stupidity. My mood made for a very uneasy atmosphere in the Salon.

It probably didn't help that I had my phone practically fused to my hip at all times on constant text alert. I mean how long does it take to book poxy flights? I had given him my details days ago!

I couldn't help but get totally frustrated with his snail-like responses - I stomped moodily around the Salon with my head swiveling between hot and cold with anxiety.

'It's easy!' I spat in temper to the staff and customers, my eyes almost popping out of my head as they looked back at me nonplussed. 'You just press some buttons on a computer, tick a couple of boxes and *voila* it's done. Flight booked.'

Of course, my meltdown dispersed with immediate effect the moment the textual healing landed on my phone with the flight details. I was euphoric. The staff breathed a huge sigh of relief too, as did my clients.

'Sorry,' I giggled. 'I haven't been that bad, have I?'

My question was greeted by silence. Clearly I had. Oh well, I was happy now anyway.

The day finally arrived, I woke very early in the morning like a five-year old at Christmas. In fact the only thing to dampen that overwhelming feeling of excitement was the vile smell of the fake-tan wafting up my nose. I couldn't wait to shower it off. I wished they would come up with a perfumed fake-tan, one that didn't leave all the evidence on the bed sheets. I dived into the shower and gently washed myself while trying my best not to rub it all off as I watched the water run orange around my feet.

Whilst packing for the trip I received a text:

[Text from Travis]

I have a permanent grin on my face, so excited. Can't wait to see you xxx

I grinned and carried on getting ready, as I was a little behind with my packing. Within a few minutes I received another text.

[Text from Travis]

Are you okay??? Xx

Huh! He makes me wait hours, or even days, for a response and because I haven't responded immediately, he's panicking. Good, I thought, it shows he too has a vulnerable side. I will respond when I'm ready, he can just wait.

God, I feel unusually powerful today. Perhaps it was because I knew he was waiting around for me (for a change). It gave me the chance to have the upper hand.

I set myself a target: *I'm going to make him wait at least an hour before I respond. Maybe even two hours. In fact I may not even text him till I land.* I managed about fifteen seconds before I responded just incase he got put off waiting... I was never very good at meeting targets anyway.

[Text to Travis]

Hello gorgeous. Will set off to airport in 10 mins. Can't wait to be with you Xxxxxxxx

This time around, I was going to go less extreme in my choice of outfit. I opted to wear a very simple, figure-hugging, nude, woollen dress that sexually draped off one shoulder. Hoping the Big-Man upstairs wouldn't notice, I had decided not to wear any underwear. I accessorised with a leopard print belt that pulled me in at the waist, a matching bag, along with brown boots complete with leopard print heels. All of which were courtesy of the fabulous Mr. Jimmy Choo. Even though these were from last year's collection, they were timeless classics. I completed the effect by applying soft gold tones of makeup and lashings of lip-gloss. Stepping back, I pulled a few poses in the mirror and then excitedly left for the airport.

I arrived in plenty of time, making a note of where I parked the car this time. I also made sure to listen very carefully to the attendant who checked me in. (I wasn't going to risk anything, given my recent experience).

It was unusually warm for the time of year, yet the heating seemed to be on full blast in the airport. I began to regret wearing a woollen dress. I could feel beads of sweat appearing on my forehead and squelching under my armpits. Nonetheless,

I teetered my way through to the departure lounge and waited to be called. *So far, so good.*

With time to spare, I decided to take my obligatory walk around the Duty Free section. As I idly wandered around, a flamboyant male makeup artist caught my eye. What intrigued me was the fact I could hear him bitching quite distinctly in a repulsed tone to what appeared to be his assistant;

'… he was like a Monet, incredible from a distance, but *revolting* up close,' he was saying in a heavy French accent.

Fascinated by his mystique and conversation, I lingered. Glancing through the corner of his eye at me, in an exaggerated 'I'm busy' fashion, he sighed and turned back to his assistant to carry on with his conversation. Not one to be easily put off, I approached the counter with slight apprehension.

'Excuse me,' I said, hesitantly. Without even acknowledging my presence, the man immediately raised his voice and along with his hand, right up to my face. It was a deliberate attempt to completely cut me off, the cheeky froggy fecker! Then, once he had decided he had finished his conversation, he lowered his hand, swiveled on his heels and with a snooty expression, sighed heavily at me.

'How can I help, Monsieur?' he said, turning his eyes away from me to inspect his manicure.

'Pardon?' I said in horror, as I looked around for this 'man' he was addressing. Nope, the froggy fecker was most definitely addressing me!

'Err, pardon… Madame?' he said, his face utterly deadpan.

'I'm… I'm looking for some perfume.' I stuttered as I tried to come to terms with his insult. Did he think I was a Lady boy?

'Okay,' he snarled with wide nostrils. He couldn't have looked more disinterested if he tried. 'Daytime? Evening? Floral? Musky? Woody? Light? Spicy? Sexy…?'

With my confidence feeling severely knocked, I ploughed on, ignoring the slight lump in my throat;

'Well… a sexy one. I'm meeting someone very, very special and I'm looking for something a little… provocative? What would you recommend?'

He offered no reply, tutting as he proceeded to make his way over to me from behind the counter.

'Right, Madame, I am presuming you are referring to a fragrance?'

'Yes,' I replied gingerly, as I took a step back in confusion and weighed up in my mind whether this guy was on something. What the feck else would I be referring to?

With an increasingly disgusted look on his face, his eyes darted over to his assistant.

'Sacre bleu…' he muttered. Then glaring back at me he gave it to me with both barrels while shaking his head vigorously. 'Non-non-non. Madame, surely we need to sort *this* [waving his hand around my face] before we can deal with your [whiffing through his flared nostrils]… odour. But it's okay, I understand *that* time in a woman's life - those hot-flushes - it must be… difficult – *non?*'

Is this man Satan's very own PR? I took a deep breath and tried to square my shoulders and verbally attack him back, but the words just wouldn't come out. Instead, I found myself reaching round for the shoulder strap of my handbag and with a tight grasp, uncomfortably pulling it closer to me. The makeup on my face had obviously melted with the heat.

'Please don't leave me like this' I blurted, suddenly desperate and convinced I must look like a complete horror. *How could I possibly let Travis down like this?*

'Can you fix me, like NOW?' I begged, panic stricken.

Silent once more, his eyes zoomed in at my boots from last season.

'Well, I cannot work miracles my dear. But I am *ze* best, so I will do what I can.'

Empowered by his own self-righteousness, I watched him flick his perfect mane to one side as he turned to walk off. His exaggerated steps and thrusting of the hips made for a magnificent stride that any catwalk model would have been proud of.

'Chantelle. Candice. Come,' he demanded, summoning his assistants with a fierce snap of his fingers.

'Yes Franc,' [pronounced 'Fronk'] chorused two young women who came hurrying across.

'You!' he ferociously commanded to one of the girls. 'Pallet. Now. And get me *ze* latest collection, we will surely need it. I am going to prepare,' he announced with a sharp clap of his hands before propelling me into a chair.

As he and the assistants busied about me removing my existing (albeit melted) makeup, I took some time to analyse my ridiculer. Despite the fact that he was a *complete* bitch, I was ever more curious about him.

He was incredibly beautiful, with amazingly high cheekbones and a raven black, Vogue-esque haircut that complimented his perfectly chiseled features. He was tall and super-slim. There was no doubt about it, he had the ultimate size-zero waist; from which he draped a shimmering, studded black leather belt, complete with a pouch, overflowing with makeup brushes. His all-black outfit left nothing to the imagination; it consisted of skinny leather jeans (through which I couldn't help noticing that his manly-hood was parked to the left) and a very tight fitting, deep V-neck t-shirt. Of course, Franc was more than aware of his superiority. We were mere mortals compared with this god-like, captivating creature of beauty. His sheer glamorous presence was intimidating to say the least.

While I was acutely aware I severely disliked him, I also knew I wanted to be just like him. He was everything I was not. I was the woman, yet he was infinitely more feminine and sexy. He was effortlessly glamorous too - with such grace, beauty and confidence. Strangely, I wanted - no, in fact, I needed - to be liked by him.

Why is life so cruel and unfair? How is it fair that I should have work so hard trying to look good, and yet still hate what I see so much?

I swallowed hard because I knew these thoughts were eating away at what little self-confidence I had. I did what I always did and raised my emotional shield, burying my painful thoughts deep down where nobody could get to them - not even me.

I've always known I was different to everyone else. I will never forget the light bulb moment when I decided to do something about my looks and change my life forever...

I was a schoolgirl at the time. I used to spend most of the day at school in sheer terror, or sobbing. The minute the bell rang, I'd be up like a shot from my chair to make a run for it. But the bullies were fast - faster than me, anyway. I never asked why they did what they did.

'You're the runt of the litter,' they insisted. Then, using various terms of abuse, they'd explain just how totally un-cool I was; with my carrot-coloured, unruly and frizzy hair; my pale white skin, unfashionable clothes and, of course, the crazy, alcoholic dad.

I used to lie in bed holding my fluffy covered hot water bottle over the latest bruises and cuts and wonder: *why don't they taunt Laura?* We both had the same dad after all. Turns out, the answer was simple: Laura was beautiful and I was not.

Then, one night, I had an epiphany. I made a decision to physically change everything about me that was humanly possible. I would recreate myself to fit into society. I've spent the last twenty or so years doing just that, even though - as my current experience indicates - I have never really managed to rid myself of that gawky teenager underneath my recreated self.

Willing myself to appear confident, I cleared my throat.

'I need to look as good as possible,' I said.

Without acknowledgement, Franc began pulling my face into different lights (which was now bare of any makeup).

'These lights Madame... they do you no favours,' he announced, after taking a step back.

I tried to fight back the tears. My worst fear... confirmed by an expert.

'You should invest in some of the Botox,' Franc pronounced, as though this was the most obvious thing in the world.

'I've just had some,' I replied, utterly deflated. In fact, I'd had the maximum I was allowed. 'But maybe it's not all kicked in yet, it does take a...'

'Hmmm, I would ask for a refund,' he interrupted. 'It 'as obviously not worked.'

I bit my lip and dug my nails into my hands. I deeply regretted ever having come to the counter. I just wanted to get up and leave.

'However Madame, I can make you look *magnifique* with this new collection,' he added in a slightly more humane tone. 'It has just arrived from Paris.'

'Maybe this isn't a good idea, I only have about twenty minutes before I board,' I lied. I had nearly an hour, but I wanted to get away from this froggy fecker and his abuse as soon as possible. In fact, I wanted to report him. He was *so* rude. Better still, I wanted to deck him round the head with a breezeblock or two. *Then,* I would report him and get him fired.

'Madame, you are in *ze* best hands,' said Franc, tutting away my concerns. 'I will create a work of art from you. You will look and feel *fantastique,* do not worry.' With that, he pinched his fingers together and kissed them with a load of '*mwahs*'. I didn't think people actually did that - maybe Franc wasn't so cool after all.

Still, Franc's insults had clearly hit their target. I still felt in quite clear need of his help. I decided the best thing to do was let him work his magic. Maybe I wouldn't report him. Not yet at least.

Strangely, as I indicated I would let him get on with the job, Franc became a little nicer. As I started to muse over how much commission he gets, my beautifully blow-dried hair was pulled back to within an inch of its life as the transformation began.

The makeover seemed to go on and on as he blended in *this* and rubbed in *that*. After half an hour, I nervously looked at my watch, knowing that it was nearly time for boarding.

It gradually began to dawn upon me that every passer-by was staring at me, as they hurried to their flights. I even caught the sound of the occasional 'wow'. My stomach butterflied and flipped with excitement. *God he must be doing a great job,* I thought. I wished I could see myself, but he'd positioned me well out of sight of any mirrors.

Finally, Franc stepped back and, together with his assistants they *ooh'd,* and *ahhh'd* his 'masterpiece'.

'Can I have a sneaky look?' I asked.

'Non!' he snapped. Recovering himself, he smiled, 'wait till I have completed my artwork. Just a few final touches...'

'I'm so excited. I can't wait to see what you've done.'

'Candice! Get ze mirror for ze gorgeous mademoiselle,' said the evidently satisfied Franc, clicking his fingers impatiently.

'I am a *God* - and now you are a *Goddess,'* he gloated with absolutely no trace of irony. Then, he flipped open his Prada wallet and flicked a business card at me. Candice, stony faced, handed me the mirror.

'HOLY-MARY-MOTHER-OF-GOD... what have you done?' I shrieked, as I surveyed this stranger's face in the small hand mirror. I moved it to arms length and then close to my face to check it was really me.

'I look... like a corpse bride!' I wailed, flinging the mirror down. By now I was having difficulty breathing. 'Oh my God... you said... oh my God... you would... oh my God. I've

got a date… AND I LOOK LIKE I'VE HEADBUTTED A
MAKEUP COUNTER!'

Franc, the froggy fecker, had given me a white, ghost-like
face, with dark, black, sunken, scary eyes; nearly black lipstick
and a charcoal blusher.

I covered my mouth to stop the screams and tried to look up
to tackle him eyeball-to-eyeball. But thanks to the super-heavy,
peacock, feathered, false lashes welded to my eyes, I could
hardly open them at all.

Franc raised his pencilled brows, dropped his jaw and
glared at me with wide mascara eyes. He was clearly
flabbergasted by my reaction and the few traces of niceness
had well and truly vanished. He probably knew there was no
way he was getting a sale, let alone a tip.

'Well, my dear,' he scowled with a razor sharp tongue, 'you
cannot polish a *turd*.' Giving me one last death stare with his
devil-like eyes, he pursed his lips and snatched his card out of
my hand. He then swiftly turned on his Gucci loafers and
minced off muttering what I imagined to be French obscenities
under his breath.

I started sobbing uncontrollably. 'I'm being taught a
lesson!' I wailed as I dramatically flung myself into Candice's
enormous silicone valley.

Poor Candice looked alarmed as it all flooded out of me;
'I'm being punished for being a floozy. You see… I'm on my
way to have sex with a man and I'm… I'm not wearing a…
braaaaaaaaa, or kniccccccckeeeeeeeeers,' I sobbed.

By now I was howling and Candice was desperately trying
to prise my fingers off her shoulders. I carried on, oblivious to
her discomfort, or the shocked faces of the other Duty Free
shoppers. 'It is, isn't it…? - ISN'T IT? The Big-Man upstairs

always knows, you know. Do you wear a bra, Candice?' I sniffled.

As I picked up the mirror and took another look at Franc's so called 'artwork' I didn't take any notice of Candice's' response. I did, however, hear the call to board my flight to Dublin.

'This is the final call for flight number WWFR12Z to Dublin. Would all remaining passengers please make their way to gate number 12.' Boomed the tannoy.

'Oh shit!' I screamed, as I shot up out of the chair. 'That's my flight!'

Almost hysterical, I scooped up my handbag and ran out of the shop. Once outside, I span around six times looking for a sign for the toilets.

'Where's the feckin' toilets? Huh?' Not directing the question at anyone in particular. I was directing it at the whole feckin' airport.

Finally, spotting the 'stick lady' toilet sign, I put the door firmly in my sights and, covering my face as best I could, I went on a one-woman stampede for the entrance. Sweating profusely, I flung the door open, wide-eyed. I must have looked like an unhinged mental patient. I scrambled over to the mirror and winced as I saw my reflection. *Arghhhh!*

Even though my flight was boarding, there was no way I was getting on that plane looking like this. I whimpered as I ripped off the peacock lashes. I then held my hair back with one hand, squirted soap into the other and flicked the tap on. Yet, the more I tried to wash the nightmare away, the more the dark colours and lashings of eyeliner just smudged around my eyes.

I began grieving at the thought of my glorious array of makeup tucked away inside my bag, which was in turn buried deep somewhere in the airport baggage system, completely unreachable.

'Would a Miss. Tara Ryan make her way to gate number 12 immediately,' announced the tannoy. **'This is your final call for flight WWFR12Z to Dublin.'**

'Oh God… feck… arse… shit… bastard… bollocks!' I spat, my heart racing. *I can do this, I can do this.*

Using both hands and much more soap, I started to scrub again. After a frantic minute, with my face feeling raw and my eyes stinging from the soap, I took one final look in the mirror. My face was bare once again and my once sparkly blue eyes were now red and squinty. I looked like a heroin addict, but feck it, I really want to see Travis - even looking like this.

I grabbed my bag, a wad of toilet roll to dry my face and began my sprint to the gate. I gasped for air as I reached it and, with the shakes, handed over my passport and boarding pass. I was fully aware of the pieces of toilet roll stuck to my face and the small trail attached to my heel, but was almost beyond caring now.

'Sorry… sorry… sorry… ' I apologised to the stewardess who looked less than amused. *Yes, yes,* I thought. *You don't need to rub it in. I already know how much everyone hates the last person to board.*

She waved me through the gate and I ran down the ramp to board *just* as they were closing the doors. As I made my way towards the back of the plane, I became aware that I was getting some strange looks. I really couldn't understand why. I had removed most of the makeup and most of the toilet paper and anyway, I was here now. I hadn't made us late. Well, maybe a little bit late. So what on earth were they staring at?

They could all feck off with themselves. I pulled out my little mirror and checked my face, yes, it was red and blotchy, but it didn't warrant the gawping stares. I closed my stinging eyes to shut them all out, took some deep breaths and continued to tell myself that I would be able to sort myself out at the other side.

As the plane descended into Dublin, I readied myself to run. I know I was the last person to get on the plane, but I was going to make sure I was the first one off it. I legged it through passport control and shimmied between the crowds at the baggage reclaim, managing to get myself a prime position in front of the carousel. I was like a woman possessed. Right now, I needed my makeup like I needed air.

[Text from Travis]

Hi babe, have landed. Just in baggage reclaim xxx

'FOR FECK'S SAKE!'

What the hell is he doing in baggage reclaim? I didn't know he was flying into Dublin! I thought he was already here! I immediately dropped to the floor, left my bag on the carousel and made a dash for the toilets on all-fours. My bum was sticking up in the air as if on an assault course. My eyes darted around. *Any one of those pairs of legs could be his*, I thought to myself.

Relieved to be in the safety of the ladies toilets, I took a few moments to compose myself. Exhausted, I walked warily over to the mirror to survey the damage. My trendy symmetrical fringe was now in kiss-curls after it got wet, whilst I was trying to remove Franc's so called *magnifique artwork.* Deciding not to linger too long on the face, I let my eyes travel down my body. It was then I spotted some strange markings across my chest.

No… No!! Sweet Mother of God. So that's why everyone was staring at me on the plane. There, for all to see, were two *perfect* circles, one on each breast. I stepped closer and closer to the mirror for a better look. All the sweating and perspiring had made my fake tan seep through the wool of my dress, leaving me with two perfect sweaty brown circles on my enhanced boobs, complete with sweaty brown dots in the middle.

Shit-shit-shit! I had no jacket to cover up my sins, no makeup to fix my face and no straighteners for my fringe. Meanwhile, the man of my dreams was somewhere just the other side of the toilet wall.

I couldn't have looked more like a poxy pig if I had tried. I had little piggy eyes, all red and swollen and great big piggy teats ready for a feeding. It couldn't get any worse. I turned on my heels and slid down the wall by the washbasins. As I slumped down, I lifted my knees and bowed my head. I felt sick. I just wanted to go home.

Startled, I felt something hard hit my arm and then clank to the floor… Looking over, I could see it was a euro. The well-dressed woman who was rapidly leaving the loos had mistaken me for a down-and-out.

This had to be one of the lowest points of my life.

Then, my phone rang. It was Travis. Typical. He never phones me and the one and only time I don't want to speak to him, he calls. I let it ring off. If I was having a nervous breakdown, I wanted to do it in private.

'Why does everything have to be so difficult?' I shouted to the heavens above, as I threw my hands up into the air. 'Why me?'

[Text from Travis]

Hi babe, got my bag. Will head over to the bar in airport. I hope u r okay? xx

I let out a huge sigh of relief. Now it was possible to run out, get my bag, fix my face, fix my hair and get my jacket to cover my boobs. *Or, I should just get the next flight home?*

I peeked my head around the toilet door and out into the terminal, just to check Travis wasn't there. I could see my bag going round and round the carousel all on its own and decided I would just make a run for it.

I charged over, grabbed my bag and ran back. *Okay,* I thought, in front of the mirror. *If I can fix this mess that was staring at me, I'll go ahead. If not... I'm going home.*

As I opened my bag, I discovered even more horror to follow, as I pulled out my one and only other outfit. My crisp-white shirt and bright-red skinny jeans were now in the colour of "Warm Beige" after my foundation had exploded inside my bag.

After ten minutes of wailing like a banshee and kicking over three sanitary bins, I calmed down. But only slightly.

This isn't how a WAG acts, I scolded myself, clouting myself around the head a couple of times.

I grabbed a toilet roll and began rinsing and wiping each item that could be salvaged.

I smeared my face with my white shirt collecting as much foundation as possible from it and blended in some concealer, then some more concealer, then, more concealer on top of that.

In the end, I decided it wouldn't take as much of an overhaul as I feared to sort myself out. Pretty soon, my face started to resemble that of a human being once more. My breathing thankfully returning normal...

[Text to Travis]

Just waiting for my bag. Be with you in 10 mins xxx

I expertly applied soft, smoky browns and golds again while simultaneously rehearsing a pout and a sexy smile to help me get back into the moment. I knew deep down I was kidding no one, especially myself, but... well... I did look a little better, even if a little piggy-like all the same.

With no power socket for my straighteners, I had no choice but to pin my fringe back with a diamante clip. As much as I didn't like to have my hair off my face, needs must. After agonising for a few moments, I sadly tossed my now unsalvageable "Warm Beige" shirt and jeans into the bin.

I elected to put my dress on back-to-front. There was one disadvantage to this strategy. The dress was woollen, so the fabric was not what you'd call 'forgiving'. In fact, there was an arse-shaped bulge stretched in the material, now flapping in front of my lady-garden. Still, it was better than before. I put on my jacket, gathered my things and headed out of the toilets.

Utterly exhausted, I dragged myself towards Customs. *Please... please God,* I prayed, *please don't let them pull me over.* A female security guard suddenly darted towards me and asked me to stay where I was. *For the love of God... Not again,*

I thought as I prepared myself to break down in tears. I was so on the edge, so close to touching Travis now, I thought I might actually kill *anyone* who stood in my way. Luckily, the security guard walked straight past me and began questioning a shifty-looking man that seemed to be hiding behind me.

Feeling dishevelled and disoriented, I hurried through security and headed straight for the bar.

'Pull yourself together,' I whispered to myself under my breath. 'Think about your entrance.'

Trying to emulate Franc's perfect catwalk strut, I held my head high and began a hip-swirling, lip-pouting walk to the Arrivals bar.

'Oi you, gorgeous!' shouted a strange voice from across the terminal. 'The party's this way!'

'Oi - she's with me mate - back off,' I heard another voice say. I knew immediately it was Travis. My heart was beating so hard in my chest I thought it might burst straight through. I turned slowly to face him.

'The cheeky sod,' said Travis playfully, giving me a smile that made me want to faint. 'You're all *mine*.'

With that, he picked me up and hugged me so hard that it hurt. I blushed and smiled as he held me back at arms length and searched me from head to toe.

'God, I want you,' Travis said in a low voice as he gritted his teeth and drew in air. 'But first, lets get us a glass of Champers.'

He gave me a wicked dirty smile, grabbed my hand and my bag and eased me towards the bar. For once, I was speechless. I just couldn't believe we were together at last. Despite the

endless struggles to get here, nothing could possibly ruin this
moment…

CHAPTER EIGHT

'How was your flight, gorgeous?' asked Travis, cool as a cucumber, adjusting his Ray-Bans and striding purposefully with me through the crowds towards the bar.

'Perfect,' I lied, smiling sweetly as I checked out his gorgeous arse whilst holding on to him for dear life. I tried desperately to retain my cool, but I was overwhelmed and slightly star-struck. It was a surreal feeling. Here I was, after all this time; able to see him, touch him and smell him. I wanted to pinch myself. *I am finally with Travis at long last.*

He looked smoking-hot as ever, wearing a dark blue Ralph Lauren top with the collar popped, sexy Levi's and tan builder boots. He really was every inch the perfect man. Why on earth had I ever fantasised about marrying a pot-throwing, temperamental chef when I could have a high-flying, rugged rugby coach? This was much better in every way.

'You're even more beautiful than I remember,' he commented, suddenly swinging around to face me.

'Oh... thanks,' I replied nervously, feeling even more light-headed. I hoped I just didn't spoil the moment by tripping over someone's suitcase and falling flat on my face. I was just so unbelievably mesmerised by his presence.

'Sorry about the rush,' said Travis, as he picked up the pace - we were by now almost sprinting, 'I just want to have you alone with me. We'll have a quick drink in here, and then...' Travis looked at me grinning and biting the side of his lip, 'then... I'm going to eat you alive.'

Say something... say something! I screamed to myself. But nothing came out of my mouth. I was utterly spellbound. Thankfully, he leaned into me and delicately kissed me on the lips.

'I... I... like your top,' I began to stammer, nervously pulling away from him. 'It's... err... a very nice colour.'

Oh my god! I have the most exquisite creature that I have ever set eyes on right in front of me and I tell him his top is a nice colour? Get a grip, Tara. Stop letting your nerves get the better of you. Luckily, Travis didn't seem in the least bit phased.

He smiled his delicious 'come-to-me' smile, then turned and signalled to the barman with a nod.

'Two glasses of your finest Champagne, please,' he said firmly. I couldn't help but get turned on by his authority.

Reaching across, Travis tenderly caressed my cheek. The second he made contact it was as though a thousand volts passed through me. Then, guiding my jaw to him with his finger, he pulled me closer. By now we were so close I could feel his warm breath on my face. Teasing me, he pulled back and looked at me, cocking his head to one side while coolly removing his Ray-Bans. We were silent. Despite the fact we were standing in a packed, noisy bar, it was as if nothing else existed. The atmosphere between us was inexplicitly charged, as his penetrating stare bore deep into my soul. His pupils, large and dilated, danced into mine. The air around us was almost sparking. I would have dropped my knickers right there, right then (if I were wearing any).

I felt an endless swirling pleasure as Travis slid his hands down to my waist. I had to bite my lip to stop myself crying out as his hands travelled further down the small of my back. And then, with a deft movement, he pulled our nether regions tightly together. The whole time he was doing this, he kept his eyes locked firmly on mine. As I stared back into those deep brown eyes, I felt hot with intense desire as he sensually squeezed my bum cheek, sending shivers down my spine.

Was I really about to make love for the first time in my whole life? And with this beautiful man? Hell yes! I mean, I know it's not like I was a virgin or anything, but I'd never actually *made* love, because I'd never really *been* in love. Not up until then, any way. This was completely different. I actually ached for him. It was an exquisitely beautiful pain.

'You've... got no knickers on,' whispered Travis, widening his eyes excitedly.

His hand continued to circle my cheek as he leaned in even closer, with his face touching mine so he could whisper into my ear. I could feel his warm breath.

'This *delectable* derriere is all mine,' he said, as he squeezed a handful of butt cheek, his voice husky with pleasure.

I giggled and blushed simultaneously. I couldn't help it. I felt like a teenager all over again. Eagerly responding, I moved my head back and kissed him gently down the side of his neck. Taking in the smell of his spicy, sexy aftershave at such close quarters nearly made me convulse on the spot.

'*Jesus*, Tara, you're making me tingle. Like *everywhere*,' his voice purred darkly. We were still locked together, but to emphasise his point, he pushed his groin even harder into me. He was rock hard, a fact I couldn't help but greet with moan of tantalising pleasure.

The intensity of the moment was interrupted by the barman placing two Champagne flutes on the bar in front of us. Travis stepped back and deftly flipped open his wallet, handed the man a few notes and indicated with a wave that he should keep the change.

Drinks in hand, we headed for a table in a quiet corner.

'God, I've missed you,' said Travis shaking his head, as we slipped onto the red, velvet bench, getting as close as it was possible to get without me actually sitting on his lap. 'I keep forgetting just how beautiful you are.'

Travis rubbed my leg seductively, gently easing my dress up by a few inches. I smiled, with what I hoped was a naughty, *'that's-for-later'* expression and emphasised my point by smoothing my dress back down.

'Patience. Anticipation is the strongest aphrodisiac,' I commanded, with a girlie giggle.

'And you're just so *natural*,' he breathed, drawing me even closer. 'I love natural beauty.'

Hearing that, I had to use every ounce of strength I had not to choke, splutter or laugh. There really was very little left of my face or body that had not been tampered with in one way or another. I recovered well though and even managed a polite - and dare I say it, demure - thank you. Well, who was I to burst his bubble? Sheila had done the most fabulous job of ironing my face out.

We kissed again, but this time a little harder. I felt so alive the second his full lips touched mine, my fingers gently trailing the outline of his tapered jaw line. He wrapped his hands in and around my hair, pulling me ever closer. Suddenly, remembering about my extensions, I panicked. *What if he feels my glued-in bonds?* But he clearly wasn't thinking about such minor details, or maybe he didn't notice. Either way, he never said a word.

'G'wan der my son!' shouted an old git from the bar, it was obvious that the remark was aimed at us. We pulled away from each other with a little laugh and I became aware that a number of people were staring at us.

'Shall we go?' we both said simultaneously.

Travis pulled his Ray-Bans on, so I fumbled into my bag producing my huge Victoria Beckham pair. *He must want to avoid being seen by the paparazzi,* I thought excitedly. *That's something I would have to get used to.* (Note to self: carry a wig, or possibly a large hat at all times, might come in handy. However, this may depend on size of handbag being used at the time).

'Ready?' he enquired, with an amused grin.

'Ready,' I answered, downing the rest of my Champagne, straightening my sunglasses and picking up my bag. Taking my hand, Travis determinedly led us through and out of the crowed Arrivals hall. *This is how a WAG must feel,* I thought as I proudly kept a very tight grip of my man.

Once outside, Travis hailed down a taxi and gave the address of the hotel. Off we went, snogging each other's faces off the whole journey. We were utterly oblivious to the nosey glances of the taxi driver who seemed to be doing his utmost not to get caught looking at us.

After a short while, I became vaguely aware of the luxurious sounds of crispy, deep, gravel crunching under the wheels as the cab slowed down, eventually coming to a grinding halt. The driver turned off the radio and, clearing his throat, indicated we had reached our destination. Prizing myself away from Travis' mouth and removing his wandering hands from up inside my dress, I tried to survey the unfamiliar surroundings through the steamed-up windows. I suddenly felt very nervous and off balance about what lay ahead.

I ruffled my hair back into place as best I could and smoothed my dress back down.

I glanced over at Travis who was, as usual, oozing confidence as he gathered our belongings. He really was impossibly handsome. So calm, so collected and *so utterly perfect.*

'My Princess, your castle awaits,' he gestured proudly with his arm, while simultaneously bowing his head like a manservant. Then, he took my hand while shoving a wad of notes in the direction of the cabbies.

I was completely speechless at the overwhelmingly spectacular sight in front of us.

'It's a castle!' I gasped, steadying myself. 'It's just like the Magic Kingdom castle at Disneyland. It's even got flags on poles and everything!' I cupped my face in childish astonishment, utterly overwhelmed. I had always wanted to come here. I didn't even have to look for the hotel name. I had eagerly read reviews of the boutique hotel Castle Clontarf after Siobhan attended her posh cousin's wedding here. *Oh my God, wait till I tell her!*

'You're my Princess,' Travis whispered passionately. 'I want to look after you, always.'

I swung round to face him, my eyes brimming with tears. I was finding it hard to speak. 'Sorry, sorry…' I eventually stammered, my voice constricted with emotion. 'It's just all so beautiful. And what you just said, well, it's kind of blown me away. Where have you been all my life?' By now the tears were streaming down my cheeks.

'You can stop crying now. You're safe. I've got you, Tara,' his voice now rich and protective.

'Even the stars in the sky look like shimmering diamonds,' I babbled, trying desperately to pull myself together. But, once I had started sobbing, I couldn't stop. *Jesus. Come on, Tara, he's got the message. Yes, I love it. I love it all.*

I knew I really did need to stop crying. Blowing my snotty nose and sniffing like a two year old really was *most* unattractive and very un-WAG-like indeed. *I mean for God's sake, what if the paparazzi got a picture of me like this? Now that really would be something to cry about!*

I really couldn't help it. I stood, spellbound, facing the picturesque castle, squeezing Travis' hand tightly. It was like I was in a fairytale. I freeze-framed the moment in my mind, absorbing the idyllic surroundings and savouring every detail.

A bedazzling array of spotlights in whites, vivid blues and pinks bounced romantically off the trailing ivy leaves covering the soaring castle walls and turrets. The picture was topped off by a pair of giant, weathered, moss-laden stone lions sitting at the entrance, powerfully guarding their fortress. It looked like a Hollywood film set.

'It's *the* most romantic setting I have ever seen!' I wailed, almost breaking into another sob.

'I knew you would love it here. It's the best hotel in town,' chorused Travis, effortlessly picking up our bags with one hand. 'Come on, gorgeous, let's get you inside - you'll freeze out here.'

Walking into the vast, richly decorated lobby, I suddenly began to feel weak. It was probably a combination of over-excitement, lack of food and the glass of bubbly at the airport. I took an opportunity to sit on one of the entrance hall thrones, which were covered in plush scarlet velvet. The one I chose was in front of a large, ornate stone fireplace. I took great pleasure from the intense heat radiating from the roaring open fire. As Travis checked us in, my eyes traced the lavishly carpeted stairs and the exquisitely engraved granite stairway. I instinctively knew these were the stairs that would take me to heaven.

In the distance, I could hear the rich tinkling of a piano playing soft jazz, together with soft murmuring voices. It all served to give off an intimate, relaxed vibe. I closed my eyes, savouring this precious moment. I had never felt this special… ever.

I shivered at the thought of what lay ahead. I turned my attention back to the grand reception desk where, I realised with a start, Travis had been watching me the whole time. Mentally, I was already undressing him, my mind spinning with possibilities. I fluttered my lashes back at him, my gaze slowly roaming over his luscious body; taking in his solid legs, narrow waist, strapping chest and those magnificent strong arms. Of course, that's not to forget his perfect 'come-to-bed' smile. I had to be the luckiest girl in the whole wide world.

All those days and nights of texting, the wanting, the waiting, all those text-sex conversations about what we were going to do to each other; finally, it was all moments away from happening.

Having now checked-in, Travis nodded over to me.

'Come on, princess. Let's go,' Travis beckoned, as he strode over, eyes fixated on me. 'We're on the top floor, so we'll take the lift.'

Leaving the beautiful, soft sounds of the piano behind us, I remained silent and swallowed nervously. The tension between us was mounting by the second. We entered the lift, gazing into each other's eyes as the doors fell shut.

The moment we were away from watchful eyes, Travis exercised full, hot-blooded assertiveness. He whipped me up into his solid arms and separated my legs as to straddle him. I felt a rush of adrenaline as he slammed me into the wall, violently juddering the lift on its suspensions. He bit my neck ferociously, sending orgasmic, shooting pulsations straight through me. His hips were grinding up against me, sending me into overdrive. I started trembling in synch with the rumble of the elevator, panting and ready for more. But our lusty encounter was over too soon, as the brass doors subsided, letting in some much-needed oxygen.

'... And that's just the warm up,' he smirked, gently easing me down and leading me into the corridor.

I was already fully stimulated and we hadn't even got in the room yet.

Struggling to steady myself, I felt the thick, plush red carpet beneath me; as we glided down the long, empty, softly lit corridor.

Arriving at our room, Travis eased open the large wooden door, revealing a suite fit for royalty. My eyes zoomed straight towards the magnificent, heavily carved, mahogany four-poster bed; then all around the majestically decorated room. I was overwhelmed. It all felt so surreal. I was speechless.

'So... do you approve?' Travis asked with a smoldering gaze, looking like an advert for designer aftershave.

I frantically nodded, still taking in all the finery and soft furnishings. I knew *this* was the lifestyle I had always craved.

'Perfect. The Champagne is still chilling,' said Travis, rattling the ice around the bucket. 'I've been saving *this* for a very special occasion. I had it sent here earlier today.' He picked the bottle of Dom Perignon 2003 out of the ice bucket and showed it to me.

I didn't know much about vintage plonk, but what I *did* know was that some more Dutch courage was very much needed. Travis quickly found some glasses and tore the metal wrapper off the top of the bottle. I felt yet another rush of adrenalin as he popped the cork with masterful ease.

'I know I could've gotten a bottle from Room Service, but it wouldn't have been as good as *this*,' he smiled, dashingly.

'To... us,' I toasted, my heart racing. We chinked our glasses and sat down on the bed. 'Oh... look at the spring on this mattress,' I commented, bouncing around with childlike exuberance, thus causing me to spill some of the extortionate champers down my already-stained dress.

Travis smiled, ignoring my clumsiness.

'Sorry, gorgeous... I've just remembered,' he announced, sounding sincere. 'I have to make a quick call... I don't want anyone to interrupt us later. I'll take it in the corridor.'

'Okay, no problem,' I conceded, trying to disguise the feeling of annoyance in the pit of my stomach while frantically wiping down my dress.

Travis headed towards the door, dialing a number as he walked.

'Take your time. It's really not a problem,' I said, sweetly lying through my porcelain veneers. 'I've got urgent calls I need to make myself.'

The tosspot!

I've waited all this time to see him and he fecks off to make a call... in private! Who could possibly be more important than me at this precise moment? Whoever they are, they're a wanker, and so is he. Don't they understand how little time we have and how precious it is? I may not even have sex with him if he's not careful. No... that's a lie, I will. But, still.

It's a shame Travis wasn't <u>this</u> reliable with calls to me. Well, two can (and will!) play that game. In the future that is, not now. I'm gagging for it way too much to be playing games at this precise moment.

As soon as he'd left the room and the door was shut, I shot up off the bed and darted over to the huge, exquisitely-carved gold mirror. I needed to see how my piggy eyes were doing and douse myself in perfume (not forgetting a quick spray of the lady-garden of course). *Well, I may as well take advantage of this interlude and spend the time usefully.*

Despite having drank yet another glass of Champagne, I had become increasingly self-conscious as I waited in the huge room all alone. I decided to soften the unforgiving lighting and so dashed around the bedroom drawing the heavy red curtains, switching off the main light and turning on the table lamps instead. Once I was happy with the ambience, I hurriedly took my 'relaxed' position on the bed once more and waited. And then I waited.

And waited.

'Sorry, Princess,' Travis apologised unconvincingly, as he strode into the room a whole fifteen feckin' minutes later. He didn't look the least bit sheepish, *the wanker.* 'Now, where were we?' he asked, easing himself down beside me on the bed.

Although I was still trying to retain my cool allure, I would have loved to have given him a swipe for leaving me for so long. Instead, I raised my Champagne flute to my lips seductively, forgetting completely that I had already emptied the glass while he was out of the room. *Maybe I ought to lay off the Dutch courage for now.*

'Let me top you up there, babe,' Travis smiled, jumping up to retrieve the bottle. Turning back to face me he gave me another one of his killer smiles. 'I still can't believe we are *finally* together.'

My stomach whirled with anticipation. I was powerless to his presence and forgave his inappropriate absence as I silently held my glass out for him to fill. I was trying so hard to be seductive but was sure I was failing miserably. As for Travis, he just looked like a sex-siren. It seemed so bloody effortless for him.

There was an uncomfortable silence, as he looked deep in to my eyes. I drew my breath as though in preparation to start gabbling my usual stream of nervous nonsense.

'Shhh,' whispered Travis, as he put his finger to my lips. 'Come here to me, baby. I'm going to kiss and lick every inch of you. I want you to watch me, guide me and lead me around your perfect body.'

I gently placed my glass on the bedside table and turned back to face Travis, who was climbing onto the bed. I let out a moan, as he gently lay beside me. I kept my body as rigid as possible, to avoid the gathering of any stretched skin that had not been fixed by surgery, or the occasional few minutes in the gym.

'I want to undress you, but can I leave your boots on please?' Travis asked, gently unbuttoning my dress. *What is it with men and long high-heeled boots?* Well, it certainly broke the ice.

'You dirty perv,' I laughed nervously.

'I know,' he replied with a resigned shrug of his beautiful, square shoulders. 'It's how you make me feel. I can't help myself around you.'

'I will leave them on, if that's what you desire,' I said in a slow, sexy voice and bit my lip purely for the girly effect. I'd have covered my feckin' boots in Marmite and eaten them if it meant he would make love to me.

In a single, strong move, Travis straddled me and whipped his top off. His herculean, polished, buff torso was staring me in the face. It was hard to concentrate on the top half though, because I could see his manhood growing, barely contained in his jeans. Travis ran his hands through his hair and gritted his teeth.

'You're a keeper - you really are,' he stated with darkening eyes.

My heart flooded with joy.

Releasing the built-up tension within me, I pawed and squeezed at his muscle-bound flesh and frantically undid the buttons on his jeans. I wrenched them down and his massive, now-throbbing manhood burst over the top of them. Panting with lust, I went to yank down his boxers to release him fully, but he grabbed my wrists and pinned them to the bed.

'Fuck... I want you!' he demanded. 'Don't move. That dress is coming off.' He lunged forward and purposely undid the rest of the fastenings, expertly undid my belt and in one swift movement threw my dress up and over my head.

Easing himself further towards the end of the bed, he slowly bent down over my lower regions. Inch-by-inch he kissed my thighs, working his way slowly, inexorably towards my lady-garden. I arched my back in ecstasy, closing my eyes, as he gently bit and licked and firmly guided my legs apart with his hands. God I wanted, no, I *needed* something in my mouth. I reached down and felt his pulsating, wet tip. I don't know what came over me, but I pushed him off me and aggressively climbed on top of him, sitting astride his knees. Pushing him down by the shoulders, I took his rock-hard, dripping cock in my mouth and sucked and licked it like a woman possessed. Travis groaned like a wild animal, tearing his fingers in and out of my hair, repeating my name.

I never wanted this moment to end.

'Stop, Tara, stop, you're going to make me cum... it's too soon,' he panted. To emphasise the point, he yanked my hair back, forcing himself out of my mouth. I crouched down, smiling up at him and slowly licked my lips.

Travis looked back at me.

'You dirrrrty bitch...' he growled in a strong, gritty voice.

With that, he grabbed my hair dragging me back up level with his face. Then, to my complete and utter shock, he spat on my face.

Horrified, I pushed him away. This was not what I had expected at all! I was in complete shock. I put my hand up to wipe my face and instinctively, I spat back. Staring hard at him, I slapped him across the face with all my strength.

'Turn around,' he commanded forcefully, absorbing and ignoring my slap. I didn't have a chance to protest as he swung me around, lifted me up onto my knees and slammed me up against the cold, hard headboard. He used one hand to firmly pin both of mine together behind my back. With his other hand free, he gathered up my long hair in a vice-like grip.

I felt him pull back and then push forward hard, capturing and penetrating me in one masterful movement.

He writhed hard against my backside, moving powerfully back and forward; crashing in and out of me with wicked skill. *So I guess this is what they call 'doggie style'.*

'Tara – you are on the pill, aren't you?' he panted, presumptuously.

'Err… no, I'm not,' I managed to squeak, my hands fisting the bed sheets. 'Do you not have anything with you?'

'Okay, no worries,' he rasped. 'I'll be careful. I'll pull out. I'm not stopping now, not for *anything.'*

I could barely move, but I did my best to follow the rhythm and the pace that he had set. I ached to turn around and kiss him passionately. I was desperate to see his face, but I was totally imprisoned in his grip. I felt dizzy with the pleasure he was giving.

Then, suddenly, as I was reaching a crescendo of pleasure, he pulled away. I struggled to release myself from his entrapment, but he hadn't finished with me yet.

'No, wait,' he ordered, easing me further down the bed so I was now virtually on all fours with my curved backside offered to him. He still had my hands gripped firmly behind my back in his one hand, but took the other from my hair, placing it firmly around my stomach. He leaned in closely, teasing my inner thigh with his tongue, lapping up the moist liquid that was dribbling from me. He groaned as he deeply inhaled my feminine scent.

I was quivering in ecstasy, with my breathing becoming increasingly erratic as he licked and teased me, gently alternating pushing his finger and his tongue inside me. I wanted to faint with pleasure as he tickled my sex button, sending me into orbit.

'That's it, baby,' he whispered as I groaned and moaned. 'Cum for me baby, cum for your man.'

His nimble fingers continued to push hard and fast inside me. The feeling was unexplainably exquisite.

'You're soaking wet. Fuck, I'm in heaven,' he groaned as he rubbed and manipulated my button in every conceivable direction. I knew I couldn't hold on much longer - and I wasn't sure I wanted to. I was overwhelmed by a tsunami of emotions and sex liquid, gathering at a phenomenal pace. It was a force so strong I wasn't sure if I was dying. Then, in a fantastic release, out it poured onto the bed, dripping down my legs and on to my boots.

'Holy Mary Mother of God!'... Had I just fecking pissed myself...? O-M-G... like a baby? My eyes practically popped out of their sockets in horror.

Travis - had released my hands and was on his haunches looking at me with unbridled gratification. Mortified, I used my newly-free hand to quickly cup my lady-garden in embarrassment, confusion and panic. I didn't want anymore to come out.

'I love a squirter,' said Travis, with evident satisfaction. 'I want you to cum again, just like that.'

'You do?!' I asked, still feeling the humiliation. I was scared to look at him properly. 'I've never... ever... ever cum like that before.' My eyes fixed to the floor in shame.

'Don't go shy on me now, baby... We have unfinished business,' he grinned, stealing a glance at his still rock hard cock. My face flamed a brilliant shade of red, whilst he moved closer to me, looking masterful. Throwing me down hard, he scooped my legs up high across his broad shoulders and entered me. His eyes never left mine as he began to thrust in and out.

'I fucking love you, Tara,' he groaned as he gathered his pace. I had to close my eyes because I was on the point of reaching another orgasm.

'I love you too, Travis,' I managed to whisper. I whole-heartedly surrendered myself - mind body and soul. I was vaguely aware of tears of joy snaking down my cheeks as I climaxed again. I just couldn't get over feeling the wonder of him, all of him. I opened my eyes to drink in the sight of him enjoying my body and my well-watered lady-garden.

By now, he too had been forced to close his eyes. His slightly open mouth and blank expression told me he was now on another planet. Nothing else mattered. Nothing else existed. He powerfully shot himself into me and promptly collapsed.

It was the most sexually erotic experience of my life.

CHAPTER NINE

I had mixed feelings when Travis began to unwind himself from our sweaty, post-coital embrace early the next morning.

I knew he had to go to a meeting here in the hotel in one of the conference suites. That was, in part, why we were at this incredible hotel. But I'd have given anything for him to say: *Sod it! I am with the most amazing woman in the world, let them get on with it without me for once.*

Even though part of me wanted a breather for a few minutes to mentally relive every detail of our night of passion, I would have said 'yes, yes, yes!' in a nanosecond to a repeat performance.

Instead, I felt Travis tenderly brushing the hair to the side of my face and kissing me gently on the lips.

'I'm sorry, baby,' he breathed, looking intently into my eyes. 'Leaving you here... looking like *this*... after what we've just experienced... is the hardest thing I've ever had to do in my whole life. You are the sexiest woman I have ever seen.'

As he stood up, he let his hands slowly trail down the whole length of my body. I felt the familiar tingle of anticipation and did my best to arrange myself in a coquettish pose to tempt him back.

'Stop it,' he grinned. 'You know what that does to me.'

Without a word he dived back on top of me and kissed me long and hard, his tongue searching deep into my mouth. His hand roughly grabbed my breast as he began to work his way down my body, licking every inch of me.

I was in ecstasy. I could barely wait until he reached my lady-garden and stretched out my legs in eager anticipation.

Then, I heard the familiar painful ring of Travis' phone.

'Leave it,' I begged, not knowing if I could physically cope if he stopped right now.

It was too late though. With one movement and a hint of a growl he was off the bed, tending to his phone.

'Hi, yeah, sorry, I got a little held up,' he said, in a completely matter-of-fact tone which showed no hint of what he'd just been doing not ten seconds earlier. In fact, if he wasn't standing there with a massive, glorious erection, I'd never have believed he was the same man. *He was clearly a very accomplished actor,* I thought, with a glow of pride at his endless talents.

'Yeah. No problem,' he continued, as he began to busy himself around the room, picking up his scattered clothes and putting them on as he spoke, his mobile cupped under his chin. 'Yeah, well, if you have the contract ready, we won't have any trouble. Okay. See you down stairs in a few minutes.'

Snapping shut his phone, he looked over at me as he dressed. He looked genuinely distraught to be leaving me. Standing there with his fists clenched, he let out a groan.

'Sometimes work *really* sucks,' he said. 'Will you wait for me? Order yourself some Champagne and something to eat. I will be back as soon as I can - sooner if possible.'

Then, leaning over, he put his mouth close to my ear.

'Don't bother to get dressed, you'll only have to take it all off again,' he whispered. 'I've got plans for you, Tara Ryan.'

Before I could respond properly, he'd walked out the door.

Lying back in the crumpled bed, I revelled in what had just happened. *We've just had unprotected, baby-making sexy times - that's what just happened!* And, best of all, he didn't even seem the least bit phased, in fact he had almost implied that he wanted me – yes, me - to be the mother of his babies!

I shivered with excitement, pushed my tummy out and then gently rubbed it. I didn't want to disturb his super-charged sperm after they had just left their testicular boot camp. I shoved a pillow under the small of my back to keep my oven at the correct tilt and lay still. *Swim my little ones, swim,* I thought, encouraging them on their long journey to my 'petit poi'. I visualised the sporty ones in Nike tracksuits with cool Ray-Bans and others in Speedo trunks wearing swimming goggles. Some will get lost and just give up, some will be confused and idly shoot-the-breeze with each other; probably go cross-eyed from swimming around in circles, pissed after our Champagne-fuelled binge.

On the other hand, there will be those who will be swimming down a NO ENTRY ZONE. They'd be swimming past the tonsils and wondering where the feckin' hell they were going. By now, my imagination was in overdrive, as I envisaged the sperm race.

'Overtaking the lot of them with super charged stamina, comes the super-dupa sperm whale,' I mentally commentated, like an over-excited sports presenter.

'His Olympic medals are shining brightly - this dude is so relaxed, he's even wolf-whistling and winking at the very receptive petit poi. Oh no, she's barricaded the doors and appears to be throwing handbags and lipsticks. Ah no, it's a poor defense. Old super-duper has simply flashed his medals and she's opened the door to let him in. What a performance, ladies and gentleman!'

I don't know how long I'd laid there going over it all in my head, but I was brought back to reality by the arrival of a text. Bursting with excitement, I dashed across to the side table to retrieve it and was rewarded with a message from the Love God himself.

[Text from Travis]

That was outstanding sex!! Never felt anything like it. Can't concentrate on meeting Xxx

I know Travis had told me not to leave the bed, but I was up now as I really needed to pee. Walking through the heavy door, I couldn't suppress another smile. It really was *the* most incredibly posh hotel. There were mirrors everywhere in this hotel room. You could see yourself from every angle in the most intimate detail. That was not, as I quickly discovered though, such a good thing.

Peering into the largest of these mirrors I could see there were no two ways about it: I had a severe case of FFG (Freshly Fecked Glow). My face looked and felt like it had had a chemical peel. It was red-raw and patchy. Meanwhile, my lips were so swollen they wouldn't need filling for at least another six months. But worse was to follow, as I looked closer at myself in the beautifully lit bathroom mirror.

Oh my God. I had a great, big, pus-filled pimple staring right back at me - right on the end of my nose. *Shit. Is that why he was looking at me so intently? That's so disgusting.* Horror took over me as I grabbed some tissue in preparation for the operation that was so urgently needed to get rid of the offending mass. I didn't want to leave any marks on my face, as he would be back at any moment, but on the other hand, it couldn't stay. Taking a deep breath, I positioned a finger either side of the offending spot and pushed them together - hard… *'Feck, that really hurt!'* What made it worse was it wasn't that long ago I'd had a proper peel, so my poor face was super-sensitive. Still - no time to be squeamish. I was on full shag alert.

As soon as I was done and had carefully wiped my face clean, I remembered I was desperate for a pee. Following the events of earlier, I gave myself a treat and actually sat on the toilet instead of performing the usual muscle-spasm-inducing hover, which I normally adopted over a strange loo, (even one as clean as this one). Alas, I had to sit on the perch, as my thighs were so sore I just couldn't squat anymore.

Seated at my throne, I could hear my mobile receiving text messages. I was reluctant to leave the bathroom though in case Travis decided to do a quick detour back to the room. I needed to check my face wasn't bleeding where I had drained the life out of my pimple before I re-entered the fray. Eventually though, curiosity got the better of me and after a quick glance in the mirror, I stuck a piece of tissue on the end of my nose and made a dash to the bedroom to grab my phone before dashing back and locking myself into the bathroom. A sigh of relief washed over me because at least I could make myself look half decent before he returned.

[Text from Travis]

Hoping to break for lunch at 12 x

[Text from Laura]

Well??? Come on!!! How did it go???? X

I went straight into reply to Laura;

[Text to Travis]

I faked a couple of orgasms. But the real ones were brilliant!! Google 'wet-the-bed orgasms'!! Woke up with a great big fecker of a pimple, but burst it. Talking of heads, get saving for a hat - I'm in love!! Call you later xxx

I giggled smugly as I watched the envelope on my phone whisk away to Travis... *Shit!! That was meant to be for Laura!!*

Shit! Shit! Shit!

OH FUCK! OH MY GOD... NOOOOOO!

I could feel my face burning. What a stupid, stupid, stupid cow! I felt so completely helpless. I can't believe I just sent that to Travis. I just wanted to put my hand into my phone and pull that awful message back. There was nothing I could do. It had flown off into the airwaves, around the swanky corridors of this five-star hotel and straight into the mobile phone of the gorgeous, cool and sophisticated man I adored.

Frantically, I read the text back. Then I read the text back again, and again a third time. It got worse each time I read it.

I started to sweat and feel dizzy. Dropping the phone onto the sink unit, I ran away from it and stared at myself in the mirror in agony. Then, I ran back to the phone, picked it up and read that awful feckin' message again. I switched the phone off and then back on again. I don't know why I did this I knew it was working fine. Somehow I thought it might just un-send the text, but I already knew in reality there was no going back. I was doomed. There was nothing I could do apart from jump out of the window; but that would hurt - we were on the top floor, after all. Whilst I did want to knock myself out, I didn't want to die.

'Pull yourself together, Tara,' I screamed silently to myself. *You can't fall apart now. You have to think - and think quickly.* Quite frankly that's not always something I was good at. With shaky hands, I began to compose a text.

[Draft message to Travis]

Hi gorgeous, sent you a text by accident. Really sorry...

[Delete.]

Shit! That's crap. I cursed at myself, sinking down to sit on the edge of the loo as my legs turned to jelly.

[Text to Travis]

A text has been forwarded to me from a friend. I meant to send it to Laura. But sent it to you, by mistake! lol xxx

I clicked send, accompanying my message with a silent prayer: *'Please God, don't let him think I was referring to him.'*

I put the phone down on the toilet, feeling utterly helpless. Obviously I'd need to leave the hotel right away. That was a given. There was no way I'd ever be able to see him again (that is, if he ever *wanted* to see me again).

Disconsolately, I turned the heavy lever that worked the shower to one side and watched as the generous spray of water cascaded into the tray below. Jumping into the warm water, I tilted my lady-garden forward and frantically began washing the sperm away… there's no way I was going to be a single parent from day dot!

I began to plan how I would escape the building without running into Travis. I couldn't face him. Not now. Not ever. But I already knew in my heart of hearts; I couldn't bear not to see him.

Maybe I should send another text, I thought, as I practically poured the entire bottle of Molton Brown Black Peppercorn body wash onto my hand and began to soap myself. How could I undo this mess? Every time I thought about the text, I cringed. I can't believe he will have read that bit about faking orgasms. For lack of any other options, I let out a huge, dramatic sob. Since it felt a little soothing, I did a few more for good measure. I did, however, frequently pause to peer across at my phone to see if a message had arrived. It lay deadly silent.

Maybe he hasn't been able to read the testosterone-destroying text yet, I thought, brightening. *After all, he is stuck down stairs in that meeting, so at this moment, in his eyes - I could still be the woman he wants to be with. Oh, that would be so perfect.* I smiled faintly, feeling calm for the first time since I'd sent that stupid message.

But, it won't stay that way, will it Tara? Feckin' texting. Whoever came up with that stupid idea needs a breezeblock around their face. I wish I could turn the clock back. Bloody Laura and her need to know everything. Nosey cow. It's all her fault. I'd called him a Sex God only a few hours ago, now he wouldn't believe me. I've completely insulted Travis and made out he was a crap lay. To make matters worse, he was actually really good in that department. Most men need a feckin' sat nav to find their way around our lady-gardens, but this one knew exactly where he was going. He didn't think that my nipples were for tuning a 1970's-style radio either.

Oh God, well... that's it, he will never forgive me. I will probably never hear from him again.

As I stepped out of the shower and reached for one of the over-sized, white, fluffy towels, I heard a text come through on my phone. Wrapping the towel around me in trepidation, I picked it up. Looking down at the screen, I gasped as I read: '**New message Travis**.' My whole body trembled as I sat down on the edge of the loo once again. With my eyes half closed and holding the phone as far away as my arm could stretch, I pressed 'read'.

[Text from Travis]

Lol. She needs to find herself a real man if she needs to fake. Meeting's running over babe, not sure when I can get back. Miss you Xxx

'There is a God. There is a God. Thank you, thank you!' I screamed out loud and kissed my phone. I read the message again and took some deep breaths.

As I stood up to dry myself properly, I realized all was going to be okay. He wasn't angry and he'd completely believed my little white lie. Then I cursed, thinking about all the little super-duper-charged sperm swimming through the hotel pipes that I had scrubbed away. Well, hopefully one may have swam to the finish line in time.

After all that stress and excitement, I was dying for a ciggy (or ten). Completely ignoring the 'NO SMOKING - MAXIMUM PENALTY €120' signs, which seemed to be everywhere, I hung out of the window and counted my blessings as I puffed on my cigarette. *Perhaps I am a quick thinker after all.*

After chain-smoking a few cigarettes, I began to feel a little light-headed and restless. Now I knew I was in the clear, I really hoped that Travis' meeting wasn't going to run on for too much longer. I was desperate to spend as much time with him as possible before I went home. My flight was at 4pm, so we were already cutting it fine.

Waving as much cigarette smoke out of the window as best I could, I slammed it shut, fastening the catch irritably. *What the feck was I going to do now?* I wondered, as I ambled aimlessly around the room, listlessly opening drawers and cupboards and peering inside. For the want of anything better to do, I took out my phone and began recording a video diary of the plush hotel room. I'd been begged by James and Siobhan to record the dirty details. I decided to begin where it all began, so I laid my now crumpled dress flat on the bed and started with a shot of the back of those awful fake-tan stains. After verbally pointing out the two brown titty circles, for good measure, I began the tour. I started in the bathroom, filming the huge, Victorian, freestanding bath; the 'his and hers' sinks and the sparkling shower unit.

'Plenty of fluff, very high quality white towels - right up your street James,' I commented while filming myself in one of the large mirrors. 'Oh wow, look at the beautiful dressing robes.'

I pushed my phone deep into the white pile showing off the embroidered castle logo.

'Moving swiftly on, this is the lounge area.' I stated, proudly trailing my hands over the dark red, soft leather

Chesterfields strewn with raw silk scatter cushions laid out in perfect formation.

I stopped filming for a minute while I fiddled around with the TV remote. I was trying to locate the music channel on the huge plasma screen. I had to scroll through hundreds of channels before I got to it, but when I did, I was rewarded with my favorite song in the whole wide world ever; 'Je T'aime'. *OMG - Je T'aime!* Serge Gainsbourg and Jane Birkin bought the world to their knees when they released it in 1969.

I vaguely remember mum years later boasting to all our neighbours excitedly that dad being in the music industry had managed to get her an illegal seven-inch vinyl. She was red-faced and sweating profusely clutching a 'Learn French' manual.

'It was banned in England and Ireland years ago and now it's been re-released,' she whispered in a smug tone to a slightly nonplussed Mrs. Murphy.

'Those French men,' added Mrs. Murphy, folding her arms under her large breasts and raising her eyes skywards in mock disgust. 'Dirty little feckers, so they are, sticking their tongues in your mouth when they kiss. Disgusting really when you think of those slimy snails and frogs they eat. Couldn't be very hygienic now, could it?'

'But that's the French for you,' added mum, 'so bloody sexy - only they could get away with that.'

I turned the volume right up as my thoughts plunged back to the past. I remembered when I first clapped eyes on the most beautiful, most perfect woman I had ever seen, Brigitte Bardot. I can vividly recall dad actually salivating watching a TV documentary about her and Je T'aime was the backing track. She was the epitome of sexiness and beauty. She had it all. I wanted to be her. It wasn't that I fancied her (well actually, if I ever was to become a lezzer, she'd be my type). I was just in awe of her stunning beauty *and* she just seemed to be idolised by all.

Seeing Brigitte Bardot on the TV as when I was a schoolgirl meant that I decided not to throw myself in front of the no.10 bus after all. Instead, I decided to change everything about myself. I would start with my carrot hair. I had been dragged to enough Salons to witness mum having her tightly-wound perm and mile-high bangs to know anything was possible. I would turn *myself* into a blonde bombshell.

I waited till the house was empty and I gathered my tools carefully. My attempt to create a homemade hi-lighting cap involved; one Woolworth's carrier bag placed over my head, one strip of thick Sellotape (to tape the bag to my forehead) and one sharp, rust-free screwdriver (to prize areas of hair through that I wanted to be baby-blonde). Oh, and not to forget, one extra-large bottle of Co-op economy toilet bleach.

Sadly, instead of Bardo-esque blonde curls (perhaps predictably) I ended up with a head of hair that represented all the colours of the Irish flag: orange, green and white. When I saw what I'd done, I was hysterical.

'What in God's name has the child done to her hair?' Dad asked, horrified, as I passed out and tumbled down the stairs in mortification.

'Lord have mercy,' gasped mum, slapping one hand across her mouth and using the other one to cover over Laura's eyes to shield her from the horror. 'Am I hallucinating?'

No matter, I thought, breaking my heart in the Salon chair as they clipped my mass of smoking burnt hair away. I had to shove mums knitted tea-cosy over my head. *It will grow back and there's always a no.10 bus tomorrow.*

As the song faded away, I snapped back to the present. Pressing the video icon on my phone, I resumed my diary.

'And this is the friggin' empty bed,' I yelled, pulling back the heavily embossed gold throw and the crisp white sheets in sheer temper and frustration. 'We should be Fifty Shading in this four-poster right now!'

With that, I flung myself backwards, flopping onto the large bed and moodily threw my phone at the chair.

After a while, I decided I couldn't very well stay naked all day, whatever Travis had requested. I wasn't used to spending this much time in the buff and was feeling a little self-conscious. Apart from anything else, it wasn't doing my self-esteem any good, because every time I caught sight of myself in the enormous number of mirrors dotted around the place I felt compelled to look more closely at all my flaws and defects.

Eventually, I decided there was nothing for it. Tutting, I popped a hand towel around me. Travis wouldn't mind. I was only dressed scantily.

Desperate to keep myself occupied, I started to pack my things away. At least that way, when he did return, we could use the time usefully.

Thinking about it, I realised that was part of the reason I was so on-edge (apart from the fact my lover had shagged me and gone off to a meeting) was that I knew I was on the precipice of something big with him. I didn't want things to go back to the way it had been; where I spent my life simply waiting for text messages and barely speaking to Travis. Everything was different now. We had exchanged bodily fluids. *I mean, we could be pregnant.* We were in love. Travis even passionately shouted it to me mid-orgasm.

'Is that the sound of wedding bells?' I giggled to myself, as I mentally relived the moment for the hundredth time. 'Actually, imagine being *Mrs.* Travis Coleman.'

Just thinking about it gave me a warm, loved-up feeling. Then, my imagination racing, I hared off through my wedding day in my mind's eye. I saw exactly how my wedding gown would look. It would be a white, fairytale puffball that gathered underneath the bust line, ruched and with a full skirt, shaped beautifully by layer upon layer of organza, and a bustle on the back. *Yippee! It sounds totally like Cinderella already.* It wouldn't be backbreaking with millions of Swarovski crystals, just a thousand or two, because I'd need to glide around effortlessly. I did have to remember that there was a strong possibility that I could be at least five months pregnant by then, so my huge dress would need to cover that fact while still making me look, dare I say it, *virginal.* Very clever of me really, thinking ahead like that.

Oh, and I want a towering tiara with a bling bouquet and three-inch bejewelled acrylic nails. The wedding cake would be, err... a castle! It could be covered in mini candles and have glittery mechanical butterflies and feathers sprouting everywhere. All tastefully done, of course. There'll be nothing tacky allowed at my wedding, no sir-ee. God, I wonder if it would be possible to... I've got it... to have our wedding at Castle Clonarf! Jeez, I really think I'm in the wrong profession. I should be a wedding planner.

In my fabulous daydream I saw myself standing next to him at the altar; Travis wearing an all-white, long-tailed tux and looking like my knight in shiny Armani. My mind wondered further and further. There would be white horses and carriages...

I wonder how he would propose? Would I give Hello magazine the contract or OK?

[Text from Travis]

Babe, wont be back till 2. They have laid on a lunch. I'm so sorry, I will call you asap Xx

In an instant, my fluffy world fell apart. *The feckin' bastard gobshite!*

I had pictured Travis and I going to the airport together, hand-in-hand, us both sobbing uncontrollably and having to be prized apart. Surely he'd remembered I had to leave to get my flight by 1:30 at the latest? He'd booked the feckin' thing after all. I despondently put back on my tit-stained woollen dress, suddenly feeling quite low.

[Draft message to Travis]

Travis?? Where for art thou, Travis? Xx

[Delete.]

[Draft message to Travis]

I want to puke, maybe morning sickness? Xxx

[Delete.]

[Text to Travis]

Oh no. I won't see you before I go. I have to get a taxi by 1:30 latest. Can you come to say goodbye. Properly? :-(X

I held my breath, waiting for the return text. But, nothing. I watched the hands of the large antique clock tick on, but my phone was silent. I couldn't leave it like this. It just didn't seem right.

[Text to Travis]

Please call me. I would just love to hear your sexy voice before I leave xx

Glancing at my watch, I held my breath as I waited for the return text. It was now 1:15pm and I knew I should be phoning reception to order a taxi, not staring at a blank screen. I felt like my oxygen supply had been cut off. I couldn't believe that one minute I'm practically babysitting our potential child, haggling vast amounts for our wedding pictures and dreaming about mechanical butterflies and in the next minute it turns out that I have… zilch, diddley-squat, niente. *Nothing.*

Bastard! I felt suddenly very hot and faint and couldn't stop the tears tumbling down my face. I rubbed my tummy and whispered to it in a huff: 'Don't tell me you *and* your father are both going to be bastards?'

By 1:25pm I still hadn't heard from him. Holding back the tears, I dialed zero and asked the very annoyingly cheerful receptionist to order me a taxi to the airport straight away. I picked up my bag and after one last glance around our love nest, I picked up his Castle Contarf dressing robe, inhaled his sexy scent from it, shoved it in my bag and walked out the door. Part of me still hoped that I'd see Travis running down the corridor in a last desperate bid to see me before I left. But no, the corridor was eerily quiet. I could hear some other guests chatting in the far distance and the low sound of the lift rumbling, but that was it.

Walking back into the vast lobby I realised I was a completely different person from the one who had been sitting in that chair, only a few hours before, bristling with anticipation. Yes, I had experienced everything I had expected and more, but at the same time, it hadn't turned out anything like I had expected it to. Here I was, slinking out of the hotel alone, like some guilty hooker.

The smartly dressed doorman opened the door for me and gave me a kindly smile as he showed me to the waiting cab. It was all I could do to hold back the tears, which were building up in my eyes.

'Airport, please,' I said to the driver, keeping my head down and staring at the blank screen of my phone on my lap.

Come on, Tara, I said to myself, in a vain bid to gee myself up. *You hate goodbyes anyway.*

I'd just have to console myself with the flashbacks that continued to send my stomach flipping with fuzzy wuzzy sensations in my lady-garden. That, and the fact that Travis would definitely have to pay for the wedding now - to make up for letting me down on our first proper date.

[Text to Travis]

I'm so sad that we didn't get to see each other before I left for the airport. About to board, hope your meeting is going well. Call when you can xxx

Right up until the moment I boarded the plane, I honestly believed he would call. But he didn't. I tried switching my phone on and off, but there was still nothing wrong with it. He

190

just wasn't calling. I kept it turned on right up until the moment when the trolley-dolly hissed to me that the seatbelt sign was on and we were preparing for takeoff - so all electronic devices had to be switched off. I needn't have worried though. The phone would have stayed resolutely silent. When I flicked it back on after we landed, there were still no new messages or missed calls.

Amazingly, by the time I arrived back home I'd managed to get myself into a better place emotionally. Yes, I was exhausted and every part of my body ached, but it was worth it - Travis was worth it. After a few stretches to straighten my back out, I had managed to convince myself that poor Travis would have been suffering as much as I was. There I was, cursing him while he was stuck in a boring meeting, desperate to see me and hating himself for letting me down like this. What was it he said? Yes, 'leaving me was the hardest thing he had ever had to do in his whole life'. Why had I been so hard on him?

I just wished he would call, though, I thought as I placed my phone beside my bath and eased myself into the hot, bubbly water for a well-deserved, long soak. I looked down at my body where he had laid his, just a few blissful hours ago and closed my eyes. I smiled and drew in a deep breath. I wanted him in my life, now more than ever.

After my long bath, I wrapped my Castle Clontarf dressing gown around me and lay on the sofa, ignoring all calls from friends and family. Eventually, I drifted off.

[Text from Travis]

Hi babe sorry it's so late, had a mad busy day. I hope you got home safely Xxx

Checking the time on the phone, I saw it was midnight. He had certainly taken his time getting back to me. *The cheek of him,* I thought. *I've a good mind to tell him to feck-off with himself.* But to be honest though, I just felt so happy to have heard from him at last.

[Text to Travis]

Thanks so much for such a lovely time. I'm home safe and sound. Can't wait to see you again xxxx I'm still awake if you want to call?

CHAPTER TEN

I'd been back at work for three days and still had no contact from Travis whatsoever, which left me more than confused.

The last time I'd spoken to him he'd been climbing out of bed with me, after the most incredible night of sex. However, I didn't dare tell anyone he'd not spoken to me since (except for a brief text complaining that the hotel had tried to charge him for a bathrobe he hadn't bought). *How do you tell a man that you stole his bathrobe so you could retain his scent?* There was no way I could admit that I had taken it, but I did phone the hotel and pay for it on my (already dented) credit card. I begged the receptionist to tell Travis there had been some sort of admin mix up and they had made a mistake. She must have thought I was *nuts.*

My phone never left my side. In a desperate bid to be strong, I did resist texting him, but it was nearly killing me.

'Tara, darling,' said James, clearly about to begin yet another tactic to cheer me up after I'd spent another day moping about the Salon. 'You know that New Year's resolution we all made last month? About going to the gym? Well, I've found the perfect class for us all. It's street dancing. Jackie, Jayde, you and I are all going, so go and fetch your gym kit and we'll meet you there at 6:30?'

'Ummm… not sure if I'm in the mood James,' I said, feeling rather flat.

'Of course you are, Tara, you want to be in shape for Travis, don't you?' James said, waving away my objections. 'He will be constantly surrounded by rugby groupies looking to sample what he has on offer. You've got to keep in shape, okay? Fabulous. See you there.'

Just as I was about to tell James to bugger off, my phone received a text message. It was all I could do to stop myself shrieking.

[Text from Travis]

Hi babe, I miss you & love you. Sky Sports tomorrow. Live match. Watch it. I'll scratch my nose to say hi xx

...

[Text to Travis]

Omg, so pleased to hear from you. I love & miss you too!!!!! XXX Can't wait to watch you and the match. Xxxxxxx

...

[Text from Travis]

How about me popping by after, gorgeous? It's not that far from you and we've got some unfinished business... ;-)) xx

...

[Text to Travis]

What??? Yes, yes, yes!! When? Where? Are you serious? Xxxxx

...

[Text from Travis]

Yep, I'm serious, we fly over to London tonight ready for match tomorrow xxx

...

[Text to Travis]

OMG!!! What time do you think you will be here? Shall we go for dinner? What type of food do you like? Soooo excited! xxxxxx

...

[Text to Travis]

Did you get my text? Xxxxx

...

[Text to Travis]

Tried to call you 100 times, can't get through! Can you please let me know ASAP, OR I WON'T BE THERE, ALL DRESSED UP SEXILY, WAITING FOR YOU! XXX

...

[Text from Travis]

Hi gorgeous, sorry, it's mad busy, I will call you when I'm on the way to you. What sexy clothes are you going to wear? xx

Huh! I will let him know when I know myself. It's funny that when I mentioned not being there he magically responded. I clearly needed to get better at the whole *treat 'em mean, keep 'em keen* tactic.

Feeling like a completely different person (now that I had heard from my love), I turned around to face my colleagues with a beaming smile.

'Right everybody!' I announced with a big smile on my face. 'Who wants to see rugby players getting all hot and sweaty?' For once, I immediately had James' attention and the girls weren't far behind.

'We're all going to watch my husband-to-be on Sky Sports,' I grinned. 'We can watch it here in the Salon, but afterwards you've all got to feck off, because he is coming here to whisk me off as a romantic gesture and then have rampant sex with me.'

With that, I grabbed my stuff and marched out of the Salon, leaving everyone speechless at my transformation. I didn't care. I had less than 24-hours to get into shape. Sod the dance class though. I didn't have weeks to hone my body. I needed to fast track my glamour. Heading towards the shopping mall, I quickly called Travis to ask his preference of food so I could book a restaurant but, just as per usual, his phone was going straight to voicemail.

[Text to Travis]

Good luck tomorrow, darling. I can't wait to see you on TV. (And in the flesh) :-) Xx

Arriving at the mall, I headed straight for Ann Summers. I wasn't messing about. Walking purposefully around, I surveyed the lingerie on the rails with deep intent. As I headed through the shop, I couldn't help but notice the merchandise seemed to grow more intriguing the further back I went. A black leather whip caught my eye. *Hmm,* I mused, my imagination boggling for a moment. Alongside the whip was a PVC catsuit, also in black. Strategically placed beside it was a matching pair of leather handcuffs. A whoosh of domineering thoughts overcame me.

I should whip and tease that gorgeous fecker into place. I could dominate him for a change. My mind flashed to images of Travis tied to a bed, unable to move. This was somewhat appealing on more levels than one.

That's what you get for being a gorgeous, inconsistent pig, I giggled to myself. *On second thoughts, he would probably love that.* Okay, well so far, that's the favorite scenario for tomorrow night. I made a mental note of this scene, but couldn't stop myself wondering what the Big-Man upstairs would think of me.

As my eyes then traced over to the next section, my softer, more feminine side came out. My eyes dreamily gazed upon a row of soft, feathery boas in a spectrum of beautiful pale pinks and whites, laid out beside matching frilly bras and lacy knickers. Walking down the row, I slowly caressed and ran my hand gently across the array of fluffy fabrics, imagining what they may feel like on.

What to choose? I was awful at making decisions lately. Far too loved-up for my own good. Completely baffled, I stood back, feeling dizzy with the choices in front of me. I really needed some advice. *Do I go hardcore (with a few Hail Mary's for my sins)? Or girly? Gosh, where would he take me this time?* I had to be prepared for anything.

I sighed deeply as I tried to organise my muddled thoughts. Then, just as I decided the only thing for it was to try everything on that Travis might like, I was distracted by a noisy customer.

'Well,' continued the tall, tanned, blonde, tattooed, mid-thirties hunk, 'she's kind of *this* big.' Without a trace of embarrassment he was cupping his hands on his own chest in an effort to show his girlfriend/wife's breast size, which was apparently considerable.

'What do you mean, her *back* size?' he asked, confused; clearly in answer to the questions of the bored-looking assistant. 'I don't have a clue, does it really matter? She's... well, err... *her* size, over there.'

He pointed frantically at a girl the size of a toothpick.

'Is the underwear for your wife?' asked a nosey woman standing in the queue. 'Because if it is... you *really* don't want to get that wrong,' she smirked.

Men really don't have a clue, I thought, shaking my head as I wandered back to the front of the shop and started my search all over again. *But bless him* (I turned back around for another sneaky look), *at least he's trying.*

Right, time to focus. Time is of the essence. Let's see. To give myself some momentum, I grabbed a couple of items and tried out the colour next to my skin. Black balconnette bra, or a red? Side-tied, bowed, or crotch-less undies? Commando was so much easier, but never, ever, would I be doing that again.

Then, barely thinking about what I was doing, I marched over and picked up the black, PVC catsuit. I'd barely laid hands on it before an assistant popped out, as if from nowhere, making me jump.

'Madame, would you like to try the catsuit on?' she asked, with a sweet smile. Then, before I could answer, she prattled on. 'Because of the rubbery texture of this item, we do recommend a small sprinkling of talc on the inside. They can be quite tricky. Would you like me to fetch some talc for you?'

'Erm... not to worry,' I insisted, feeling a little embarrassed. It felt like I was advertising to the world I was about to have a steamy session of S&M sex. 'I don't have that much time. I'm not actually going to try it on.'

'Would you like me to put the catsuit to one side for you then?' she asked, completely unfazed.

'I'm just going to hold it up against myself, if that's okay?' I said, clutching the suit closer to me in case she tried to walk off with it. 'I'll just try on the other bits I've got here real quick.'

Apart from the fact I really didn't want to admit to liking such an outrageously raunchy outfit, I was afraid the shopkeeper's white talc would have an adverse effect on my newly applied spray tan. I only had a few hours to get body-perfect. I couldn't afford any fuck-ups.

I disappeared into the tiny changing room and wrestled my way out of my clothes. I'd hung the catsuit on the hook behind the door and did my best to ignore it, as I tried on the other, safer garments. After trying on endless sexy pieces, the devil knocked at my door. I turned to look at the slinky PVC suit and swore quietly to myself. *Lord, I will seek forgiveness after I've worn it,* I thought, biting my lip hard and blessing myself.

I'd better just quickly slip it on though. I can't afford to waste any money. I took the catsuit off its hanger. It felt surprisingly cold and slippery. I slipped a foot in each leg hole and I heaved and pulled. *She certainly wasn't kidding about the talc,* I thought, as I yanked the catsuit up just past my hips. I paused briefly to see what it looked like so far. *Hmmm... not bad. Not bad at all,* I thought as I swiveled around to take a look at the back view in the mirror. Still, I did have to see the *whole* thing on to be sure.

The further I pulled the catsuit up my body the more complicated it seemed to be. I simply couldn't figure it out. There were definitely no zips or buttons. Meanwhile, there was a large opening around the chest, yet a small neck collar. Completely thrown, I lifted up one component after the other of the outfit that flopped around my waist.

Determined not to be beaten, I challenged the seemingly indestructible material. I pulled it back down to waist level and put my arms through the only two holes I could find - which then automatically pulled the back of the outfit up. I winced as the crotch piece nearly fractured my lady-garden. Straightening up and surveying myself in the mirror, I could see the neckpiece was still flapping. *What the...?*

Scratching my head, I wondered how the hell I would ever get the rest of it on. I pulled it back down to waist level and started again. Okay, this time I would put my arms and head in at the same time. *It's about co-ordination,* I told myself. With another supreme effort, I tugged the suit so hard that for a moment I thought I dislocated my arm. It really hurt. The collar was now stuck around my nose, I was seriously losing my temper.

'There must be a fault on this one,' I cursed, sweating profusely.

But then, with one final yank, the bastard was on. *Ahh, no one messes with Tara; the Sex Goddess.*

Feeling not unlike a lump of jelly in a vice grip, I stood back and squinted into the mirror. I forced myself to visualise the 'sexy' me, with bright red, glossy lipstick and come-to-me eyes. To complete the effect, I stood on my tippy toes and ruffled my hair. I roared like a tigress under my breath and pouted at my reflection.

Hmmm. After all that, I really wasn't sure. In fact, if I was honest, I looked like a she-devil gone wrong. This outfit probably looks better on a twenty-year old. Feeling turned off, it slowly dawned on me that the catsuit was probably even more difficult to get off than it was to get on. Good job I didn't need the loo. Sod's law though, the moment the thought entered my head, I realised I was actually busting for a pee.

Oh my God. How on earth am I going to get out of it? It was that hard to get into, I would probably have to be cut out. Oh the shame of it. My bladder was now feckin' bursting. Crossing my legs, I grabbed hold of my lady-garden, mumbling frantically at my poor, constricted bladder to *hold on, hold on.*

Pulling desperately at any loose fabric I could find, I started to jump up and down, frantically wriggling this way and that. But every time I pulled it back over my head, the body of the catsuit shortened and pulled itself even tighter. *Oh God,* I was going to pee myself for the first time in thirty years. (My orgasm with Travis doesn't count, I Googled it. And I was asleep when I did that other one last year, so it doesn't count either). No matter how much I pulled my butt cheeks and pelvis in, it was a no-go. By now I was in a serious flap.

'Pull yourself together, Tara, for feck's sake!' I admonished, realising with a start I'd actually said it out loud. Hoping no one heard, I began a frantic conversation in my head. *Think! Think! Come on, brain - please start working.* After a moment's deliberation, I decided to try and catch the catsuit off guard. To surprise it, I closed my eyes and meditated briefly while I planned a sneak attack on the costume. This was war! However, as I quickly found, fighting a battle in the dark with my eyes closed against the rubbery predator was probably the worst idea I'd ever had. My assault was immediately repelled and I was thrown back against the changing room door.

Defeated, I slid down the length of the door in to a panting mess. I'd lost.

But what now? I was too ashamed to ask the assistant for help, they had warned me about the talc. Hysteria began to kick in. I needed to make an SOS call.

Then a thought hit me. Maybe I could rip it off? Damn it, that should've been Travis' job, but it was too late now. I began to hunt for a good place to start picking at a seam with my tweezers.

Then, like a godsend, a voice from heaven filled my ears. It was James. I knew that voice *anywhere*.

'James?' I hissed over the top of the changing room door. 'Is that you?'

Easing the door open, just enough to pop my head out, I could see the back of his highlighted hair.

'James!' I snarled. 'Come here!'

Looking confused, James leaned back away from a shelf full of sex toys and pouted his heavily glossed lips. His eyes and head darted in every direction before he finally spotted my torso-less head, peeking around the changing room door.

'Come in here,' I demanded through gritted teeth. 'I'm stuck.'

I watched his eyes light up and his mouth open wide. God, he can be a bitch at times.

'Oh my god. So this is where you dashed off to in such a rush tonight. We all decided to abandon the dance class because you wouldn't come with us. Never mind, we can all go next week. At least you can now meet my new boyfriend - I'll bring him over...'

'No! Listen to me,' I said, unable to disguise how desperate I felt as I opened the changing room door fully. 'I can't get out of *this*, I'm stuck.'

As I revealed the full extent of my humiliation, I dropped my arms to my side in exhaustion. I already couldn't stand what was inevitably coming next.

'But, you look fabulous, Tara,' James announced theatrically, gasping through his fingers which he's raised to his mouth in mock admiration. 'Christian, sweetie, come quick! Come see what my boss is wearing. We have just *got* to get us one of these!'

'*Please...* I've been like this for half an hour. Just come in and help me out of it,' I wheedled, my feeling of horror and shame growing each second.

I saw Christian hurrying over, noting he was James' usual type; about 19-years old, athletic and achingly good-looking.

'Christian, be a love and hold this butt plug, Tara needs me,' James declared melodramatically as he swept into the changing room, slamming the door behind him. 'Wow,' he gasped, this time in apparent genuine admiration. 'It looks like it has been sprayed on. It's fabulously raunchy. I hope you're going to buy it? If you're not, *I* certainly will. Does it feel good on? Do you think it would fit me?'

'Shut up!' I brutally interrupted, puffing with the exertion of trying to get out of the feckin' catsuit. 'Just get me out of it!'

'Oh Tara, look at me - I look like boiled shit,' said James swiveling around, distracted by the wall-to-wall mirrors. 'All this wind is doing no favours for my hair... and, oh my God, my arse is so massive in this mirror!'

'Hey, Christian… Christian!' he began yelling over the top of the door. 'Does my arse look big today? Looks like I'll need an extra large butt plug after all,' he laughed.

'James, please stop poncing around,' I begged, desperately.

'Sorry,' said James. Then, tilting his head to one side, he said, 'It just doesn't leave much to the imagination, does it? I can see all the weeds in your lady-garden.'

'I'm going to bloody wet myself in a second and I will hold you fully responsible!' I spat, giving James the evil eye. 'Now please just hold the collar and stretch it apart as far you can.'

I spun around to give him better access and waited for him to do what he needed to do to help release me from the clutches of this evil black suit. I tried to ignore the feeling of his fingertips vibrating as he held back deep shudders of laughter.

'Christian,' cried James, again, snorting heavily with the effort of it all. 'We need all hands on deck here. There is a big black rubber to deal with. Come on in and help.'

Then, looking conspiratorially, he whispered to me, 'It's okay. He's seen far worse.'

It didn't matter. I didn't care anymore. I'd gone past that point. Christian hurried in and then, after the briefest of introductions, the gay brigade set to, pulling and pushing me this way and that. It seemed to take forever. Meanwhile, my eyes were rolling into the back of my head with the pain of it all - I had to constantly bite my lip to prevent myself from pissing everywhere.

'Tara… have you tried undoing the Velcro on the back of the collar?' James asked, still trying not to laugh.

'What?' I spat in horror, swinging around to look at him.

'You mean you got that on with the VELCRO done up?' he said in amazement. 'Wow, get *you*. I bet you're a *right* minx in the bedroom!'

By now, both he and Christian could no longer hold back the hysterics and both were howling with laughter; tears rolling down their faces.

'James, I implore you – *DO NOT* mention this to *anyone*,' I instructed, as he finally released me from my bonds. It was such a relief as I rolled the hot PVC prison off each leg. 'I'll give you a bonus at the end of the week. And Christian - you can come and have a couple of sun beds - but both of you please just keep shtoom!'

'I swear on my *huge* bonus and Christian's twenty free tanning sessions; we won't tell a soul,' chanted James, placing his right on his chest (around about where his heart would be, if he had one).

I flopped down into the chair and both James and Christian held the catsuit by the ankles and pulled and heaved. To help ease things along I peeled the rest away from my now chaffed, sweaty skin. Then, *voila,* it was off! The feeling of freedom was immense.

I shoved both my saviours out of the dressing room, got dressed at lightning speed and raced towards an assistant whilst cupping my lady-garden, jumping desperately from one foot to the other.

'Please,' I winced, 'where are the loos in here, please?'

'They're staff only toilets,' she replied snootily, returning her gaze to her notebook.

That was it. I had had enough. I told her in no uncertain terms that unless she let me use the loo, she was going to have a fine mess to clear up. For good measure, I added that I had eaten a mean curry for dinner last night. The assistant's face said it all. She hastily asked me to follow her.

My pride and reputation emptied down that toilet. After the most gratifying wee of my life, I composed myself and left the shop without looking at anyone, not even James. I just wanted to go home.

Still, at least I had tomorrow to look forward to. Hearing a ping from my phone, I dug it out of my handbag excitedly. *It'll be Travis, making last minute arrangements, I'm sure.*

[Text from Jayde]

Just fort I wud let u no, James has sent every1 a picture of u trapt in a gimp outfit, in a sex shop. Is it tru or is it photo shopped?

The following day, I decided to close the Salon slightly earlier than I should've but, hey, it's not every day you get to see your man live on TV, or that you have the second hottest date of your life. I instructed Siobhan to come over with enough alcoholic provisions to last her the night. No doubt she would end up crashed out somewhere completely arse-faced, but the deal was that we'd all watch the match together on the Salon TV and that when the match was over, she'd be in charge of getting everyone out of the Salon so I would be alone when Travis came. In a brief text exchange that morning, Travis had said he expected to be away from the stadium by 6pm and would meet me at the Salon as soon as he could. I'd bombarded him with questions about where we'd go once he got to the Salon, but as always, his text messages abruptly dried up. I didn't care. This was already shaping up to be one of the best days of my life.

James walked - or should I say limped - in, around 30 minutes before kick-off, making his usual dramatic entrance.

'Fuck me sideways and call me Samantha, I've only gone and pulled my groin!' he grimaced as he tenderly walked through the door with a frozen bag of peas over his manly-hood. 'I've spent my whole day off in Accident and Emergency! Five hours I was sitting there. But worse than that, the only Vogue magazine they had was three years out of date. All they did in the end was tell me to go home and take some paracetamol. Well, I said to them, 'only if you can give me a suppository'. I don't think the doctor had any idea how much danger my moneymaker was in. Mind you, I did get him to have a cup of the plums before I left - just to make sure I hadn't pulled them as well.'

'Oh *poor* James,' I replied, sarcastically eyeballing him. 'Could that have been Karma… as a result of his gossiping? Or perhaps from sending crude pictures of *a* helpless victim trapped in a catsuit?'

'Don't ya be worryin' about screamin' queenie over there,' interrupted Jayde. 'He just wants even more attention than normal. Oh and by the way, Jackie text me on me way over and she ain't feeling great. So she's gonna stay home tonight.'

'Oh that's a shame,' I replied, feeling rather disappointed. This was my big night after all. 'I wonder what's up with her lately. She never seems to want to come out anymore. Anyway you two, help yourselves to drink and nibbles over there.'

Just as I turned to follow James into the staffroom to give him an ear bashing, I heard a crashing thud against the front door. It was then flung open by Siobhan accompanied by her usual manic grin.

'Sorry, Tara. It's this feckin' trolley. Got a mind of its own, especially now it's only got three wheels. By the way, if the neighbouring shop says anything about their car being dented; it wasn't me, right? It's just a coincidence. Me fourth trolley wheel is stuck underneath his car, along with me right shoe. That dent was feck-all to do with me,' Siobhan stammered in a continuous stream of speech. She then hobbled through the door, dragging a wobbly Tesco trolley that was filled to the brim with wine boxes. 'So you alright then?'

'Yeah, I'm really happy about seeing my man on the TV,' I replied, laughing at her scatty behaviour. 'I can't say I'm surprised Siobhan, but I have to ask… what's with the trolley?'

'Well, I was going through Tesco looking for a little something for tonight, right? I see these boxes of wine on offer. *That'll do nicely,* I thought. So I pile them into me trolley and you know how it is, you try a little tipple on your way to the till. Who doesn't? But I took a little detour and didn't realise I'd been through nearly a whole box. Anyways, I get outside and I can't remember where I parked the feckin' car. So here I am, trolley and all. I've paid a feckin' pound for it anyway. That reminds me, Tara, I'll be needing that pound back. Have you a fork or something so I can jimmy it out?'

'Oh, Siobhan,' I replied with mock reproach at yet another dose of her crazy antics. 'Help yourself, but leave the trolley outside please. Now come on - the match is about to start.'

We all crowded into the staffroom, finding space as best we could around the tiny TV. As I took a seat, I began to gloat to myself; *not only am I going to watch my future husband at work, I'm going to tape it so I can show everyone (including our future children).* I was so very excited that I could finally see Travis in his kit. As an added bonus, I would be surrounded by my girlfriends and gay best friend. I felt so proud that at last they could get to see what I had been going on about since I returned from Ireland.

The game finally got off to a cracking start. For what felt like ages, I was glued to the TV but I still had not caught a glimpse of Travis. The camera was on *everyone but* him. I kept scanning the team and mistakenly shouting 'there he is, there he is' before correcting myself and beginning my search afresh. Luckily, after a few minutes of this, Jayde gently told me I was looking at the wrong team entirely.

After a quarter of an hour of pointlessly scanning the TV, the game broke for a few minutes while some man in a tracksuit ran on to rub an injured players leg. In the distance, I could see another man running on to the pitch with water bottles. *Was it him? Please God. Please God, let the camera do a close up.* With that, my prayers were answered.

There he was. *Oh my god.* I turned to my friends, my hands clasped to my face in joy.

'Is he not the most beautiful creature you have ever seen?' I said, turning quickly back to stare at the man of my dreams. My face felt like it was on fire from the minute I saw him. I was glowing with pride, torn between serenely watching his every move and screaming and jumping up and down like a child. Then, he reached up with one of those wonderful hands and scratched his nose, just as he had promised. That was it for me. Game over.

I was hysterical. All hopes of playing the calm Goddess of Love were gone. There was my man, standing on a pitch, wearing the sexiest pair of shorts and trainers I had ever seen. And he was sending a signal to me!

God, he was so manly. I was beside myself. I couldn't help it, so I ran over and kissed the TV. *I, Tara Ryan, had made love with that man.*

By now, play had resumed and it had started to rain heavily on the pitch. I *so* wished I was there. The mud, the sweat, the ear pulling (they really shouldn't do that), the diving, the skidding and scrumming – the whole thing left us all *ooh'ing* and *ahh'ing*. Everyone in the staffroom was caught up in the excitement of it all and we were all chanting and singing so much we completely drowned out the commentary. Sometime in the second half, I caught another glimpse of Travis; soaking wet and running his hands through his hair. I squealed like a teenager and everyone else in the Salon joined in too. We laughed and embraced each other as though we'd witnessed our own team win the league.

By the time the match was over and Travis' team had won, we were all completely hysterical; laughing, crying and screeching at the top of our lungs while swigging Siobhan's supermarket wine. I watched with pride as the manager, Travis and the subs poured onto the pitch embracing and congratulating each other.

'Tara, darling,' sighed James, 'does one know if the gorgeous Mr. Coleman is into spandex at all? That's what the good Lord invented it for, sexuo-erotic Gods like him. He's just so… so… *so*… dick-matising! Pwweeeese can we stay to meet him, just for a nanosecond?'

'James!' shot back Siobhan, 'I've made a promise to Tara that we would vacate the Salon without a fuss.'

'What? Huh? Sorry James, hang on, I'm just texting Travis,' I said, utterly oblivious to his comments.

[Text to Travis]

Well done!! I'm so proud of you! You looked so utterly gorgeous in your kit Xx

'But I want to meet him,' pouted James, tugging at my shirt. 'Can't we just stay here for an insy-winsy bit, just so I can checkout his cute-t-cles? He might want a manicure or something. I'd be perfectly happy to give him a quick soak and a hand job.'

[Text from Travis]

Thanks babe. See you in 30 mins or so. I'm rock hard just thinking about you xxx

'James!' hissed Siobhan placing her hands firm on his shoulders and dragging him over to the corner of the Salon. 'Shhhh. Don't say another word.'

'But...' stropped James sounding not unlike a two-year-old.

'Come here to me, James,' ordered Siobhan cutting him short. He looked very sullen before she began to whisper urgently into his ear. Then, in an instant he started to grin like a schoolboy and even did a little excited jump.

I didn't give a second thought to their mischievous antics. I had far too much on my mind, such as my tingling lady-garden after Travis' last text, for one. Turning, I raised my hand to calm everyone.

'Sorry, James, what was it that you wanted to say earlier?'

'Nothing that can't wait,' James stated, his eyes darting quickly over to Siobhan's.

'Okay, well sorry to be a party pooper guys, but I'm throwing you out,' I said, trying to stop the grin that was spreading across my face. 'I'm about to do some intense scrumming of my own - and guys, sorry but this isn't a team game…'

Jayde already had her coat on and was rushing out the door. And surprisingly, James and Siobhan were also very compliant, heading purposefully to the door without a murmur of complaint or even a ribald comment. *They really are great friends,* I thought. Very understanding and supportive indeed.

CHAPTER ELEVEN

I squealed out loud like a child, excitedly sprinting around the Salon checking and everything was perfectly in its place. *Finally,* here was my opportunity to show off my Salon, Glamma-Puss, to Travis. It was, after all, the one thing that I had got right in my life. It was nothing but a shell when I had first viewed it but with blood, sweat, tears and sheer determination, I had achieved my dream of creating a successful, top-class Hair and Beauty Salon with a reputation to match.

Dashing over to the staffroom, I put on my all-time favorite CD from the 'Bam-Buddah Grove' collection. I've always loved its spiritual blend of tones that were relaxing, yet rhythmic; with hedonistic and erotic pulses. Just hearing the first few bars of its smooth sounds sent shivers down my spine. It sent me wild with thoughts of Travis and I getting up to mischief. *I really must remember to take the disc home with me tonight. Oh-my-god!* Just the thought of what was about to happen suddenly stopped me in my tracks. I could just imagine making love to him with those head tripping sounds in the background. That really is the ultimate setting for an all-night, steamy sex session.

I walked back into the Salon and switched off the main overhead lighting; preferring the soft, seductive glow from the two huge Bourgie gold table lamps that were placed either side of the chaise longue. The Salon looked perfect; towels stacked and rolled, colour coordinated in minks and creams, large ornate mirrors gleaming and workstations neat and tidy. I was desperate to impress Travis. I would show him around the Salon, show off my entrepreneurial flair and then we would get a taxi to the fancy, romantic restaurant I had booked. After that, I'd whisk him back to mine. After all, he had set the standard so high on our last date, it was the least I could do for the man I wanted to spend the rest of my life with.

I prayed the outfit I had chosen to wear was worthy of his presence. Pacing nervously over to the Salon mirror, I did a quick check of my efforts to pull off the perfect WAG-like look. Hair; ruffled and humungous, *check.* Acrylic, nude nails; still attached, *check.* Lashes glued securely, *check. Oh, that one looks a little loose. Bugger. Well, I'm not risking fiddling around with glue now, it will have to do.* Lips lined and dripping with nude lip-gloss, *check.* Black sheer shirt, daringly transparent; *check.* Lacey black bra; still visual *check. Oh feck it.* Pouting at my reflection, I popped open another button. Cleavage on display; very visual, *check.*

Suddenly startled, I swung around to face the Salon door. 'Travis… is that you?' I totted over and peered through the blinds. I couldn't see a soul. I could've sworn I heard someone.

Right, back to the preparations. After witnessing countless men dropping their jaws over Laura's Christmas outfit, I had decided to copy it for my big date. Of course, my version *had* to be more expensive. This wasn't deliberate one-upmanship; it was simply that the sales were over now, which forced me to spend considerably more than I had wanted. But hey, Travis was worth it. I smoothed down my horrendously uncomfortable tight black leather skirt and heaved the thick, black, waist-emphasizing belt-buckle in by one more notch. I had teamed it with a very elegant Yves Saint Laurent sheer black shirt with diamante fastenings and statement satin cuffs. *Beat that, Laura.*

I quickly shoved on my skyscraper Louboutins and straightened my stockings. No more hold-ups for me - I'd certainly learnt my lesson. This time I was wearing an extortionately priced silk and lace black suspender belt. I hoped they wouldn't *just* be more reliable, but more comfortable too. So far, that was not the case. When I attached my stockings to the clips of the belt I'm almost sure I damaged my spine. How the feck are you meant to clip the damn things on behind you and keep your stockings straight? Thankfully Siobhan had lined them up for me earlier on.

By now I was starting to feel very nervous. Travis could walk through that door at any moment, flashing me one of those oh-so-sexy smiles. I glanced up at the Salon clock. It was nearly 7pm.

Where should I be waiting? I wondered, as I paced around the Salon taking up various nonchalant poses. I wanted to appear very busy and sexy as he arrives. Eventually, I decided the best first impression would be if I were on the Salon phone taking a pretend booking. Yes, that was it.

Just as I picked up the phone in readiness for my charade, I spotted him trying the door handle. My heart leapt.

'Push the door harder Travis,' I mouthed, busying myself with my fake conversation. To be honest though, I lost the thread of it the minute I saw him walk in. My gaze was completely riveted by his presence.

'Hey you,' he smiled.

I blew him a kiss and pointed theatrically at the phone, swinging myself around in the opposite direction.

'Come on, come on,' he whispered loudly, tapping at his watch impatiently. His eyes were wild with excitement.

I smiled nervously, indicating with an elaborate mime that I wouldn't be long. To raise the stakes in my game, I provocatively eased myself around the front of the reception desk. Now he was standing just inches away.

I had never seen Travis in his kit before, well not in real life. I had to pinch myself that this was really happening to me. One minute he's on the TV in front of thousands of fans and groupies, and the next, he's *here,* with *me,* in the flesh. The fact that he had mud all over that flesh just added to my aching longing to touch him.

Forgetting completely that I was supposed to be in an intense client conversation (albeit a pretend one), I exhaled in a rush. I became acutely aware that my breathing was now quite audible. In fact, I may even have been panting. Heated anticipation ran through me as I watched him casually stride back to the Salon door. He nonchalantly leaned back against it, propping his muddy boot up against the once spotless sill. Without looking at me, he whipped out his phone and diverted all attention to seemingly more pressing matters than me.

'Sorry,' I mouthed, 'I won't be long.' He didn't seem to notice.

A lump appeared in my throat. I began to kick myself that I hadn't jumped the bones off him the second he arrived, but not me, oh no, I have to plan a stupid staged greeting and he's bored shitless with me already.

'I'm gonna fuck you hard when you get off that phone,' he stated without even looking up as he continued to tap into his phone.

'Not in your dirty rugby kit, surely?' I whispered back, pressing the button to end my call.

'Oh yes I am,' he added, without a trace of humour. He took one last, quick glimpse at his phone before tossing it over to the chaise longue. His eyes finally met mine as he peeled off his hoodie in one swift movement, pausing only to wipe his brow with it.

'Tara, you look so fucking hot in that outfit. I want you - and I want you *right now.*'

'This old outfit?' I gestured down at myself nonchalantly, tutting and fluttering my lashes. 'I haven't even had time to get changed from work yet, what must you think of me?'

'Right here, right now I want to rip it all off you and fuck your brains out,' he said in a low voice, stepping closer.

For a few seconds, I was completely taken back. This didn't seem like my Travis at all. He didn't seem to have any of his usual charm. He seemed utterly focused on one thing. It wasn't that I was complaining because, to be fair, I was thinking the same thing. I just expected… well, I don't know what I expected. Perhaps a yielding soft mattress would have been a good start. It must be the adrenaline still pumping around him from the match. *I must be understanding. It's very important that I support him at a time like this.* I'd been reading all about this in my research on all the do's and don'ts of a WAG.

'Err, would you like me to show you around the Salon first? I simpered. 'Or, we could go straight back to mine, freshen up and then dinner?'

'Babe, I've already eaten,' he said. 'I grabbed a quick bite after the match and had a protein shake. I just haven't had dessert… yet.'

There was no mistaking it. His voice was laced with unfamiliar tones of urgency. I swallowed hard and picked up my glass of wine from earlier and gulped some down.

'Okay, well perhaps you might eat later,' I smiled, doing my utmost to appear calm and accommodating.

'By the way, where are your bags? I asked suddenly, noticing he had nothing with him, 'because if you have left

them in your car, I'm happy to come with you to get them?'
Move over all you WAGs. I'm on top of this, big time.

Travis didn't respond. Without uttering a word he lunged over to me, shoving both his hands through my hair, causing me to lose my balance and fall backwards onto the desk. His lips pushed hard against mine and I could taste the saltiness of his sweat. He pinned me down with one strong arm while using the other to clear the reception desk in one foul swoop, sending everything in its path smashing to the ground. I released an involuntary moan, almost dissolving on the spot.

'Fuck, I need this Tara,' he groaned, keeping me firmly and masterfully fixed down to the desk as he buried his stubbled jaw into my shirt, tearing at the remaining fastenings with his teeth to gain further access. He breathed me in; inhaling my sweet perfume and nuzzled his stubble roughly over my décolletage; skillfully teasing, nuzzling and descending lower with his tongue. I felt wild with passion; encouraging him, pulling him into me, weaving my fingers in and around his sweaty, sexy hair. I could feel him sucking, poking and prodding. His tongue was in desperate search of my erect nipples; finding them through the lace of my bra and teasing them with groaning sounds until he had one breast bursting over the cup. My breasts were heavy with aching for more stimulation. Every move he made sent shivers of lusty longing surging through me.

He abruptly stopped, tearing his black rugby shorts and boxers down over his trainers before kicking them away. He then began frantically hitching up my skirt, steering me effortlessly into position. I watched his eyes widen as he caught sight of my sheer stockings and suspenders. The sight seemed to encourage even more crazed, wild behaviour. He worked his way down my body, plunging his tongue through the lace of my scanty knickers tracing my lady-line folds, inhaling me and panting like an animal.

'Travis, not here... we can't! I moaned. 'Anyone could walk in. The doors are not locked and the blinds are still open.'

'I don't mind, if you don't mind,' he growled, ripping his t-shirt over his head and flinging it into the air.

'*I* mind,' I said, weakly. I was both slightly disgusted and yet completely and utterly turned on by his suggestion. 'Travis, stop!' I whispered, slapping his hands playfully as he started again.

'I can't stop,' he groaned, 'I don't want to.'

'Please, not like this... Slow down,' I teased determinedly, slapping his hands away again, pushing him off and pulling myself up and away from the desk. I clutched his beautiful hard-set jaw at arms length and stared deeply into his chocolate brown eyes before kissing him tenderly.

'I need to lock the door and close the blinds, okay? There's no rush, we've got all night.'

I let out a huge, bewildered sigh and swallowed hard while I set about covering up my modesty. I popped my boobs back into their lacy cups, shimmied my skirt back down into place and headed over to lock the door.

As I adjusted the blinds, I turned back round to him, Travis was beautifully butt-naked apart from his trainers. Christ, he was a sight for sore eyes. He looked like Action Man, with perfectly formed, rippling muscles and his hard glory-crown glistening, dripping and ready.

I hardly had a second to dwell on the vision as he stepped forward impatiently, dragging me over to one of the mirrored workstations.

Pulling me in front of him, I stumbled slightly in my skyscraper heels, grabbing the styling chair to balance myself as his powerful body enveloped me from behind. In spite of my panic about how quickly things were progressing, my body responded as he began rocking and swaying behind me.

'How fuckin' sexy does this look?' he whispered closely to my ear, sending shivers straight through me as we watched each other in the mirror.

'We make the perfect hot couple,' I purred back at him, sticking my bum out further to greet his hardness while trying to absorb the madness of it all.

'No,' he responded forcibly, shaking his head. His voice was deadly serious. *'This* is hot.'

With that, he pushed himself hard into the back of me, tugging my hair back roughly. 'Do you feel that, baby? My cock is gonna take you from behind. You're gonna watch me fuck you… in this mirror.'

I gasped in a loud moan, trembling all over.

'I have a panoramic view,' he gloated, throwing his head back in pleasure. He began peeling my shirt back off my shoulders. I shuddered in delight as we watched it float, then pool onto the floor.

'You're gonna get this hard cock inside you,' he stated, shoving me out of the way to view himself fully in the mirror. Instantly I seized an opportunity to turn around and face him, but without ceremony he turned me back around to face the mirror ahead of us.

Shocked, I placed my hands tenderly on top of his; desperately trying to follow his erratic lead as his hands travelled fast and furious all over me.

I was finding it hard to keep up with him in any sense. I swung between being paralysed and confused by his playboy mood and then being completely turned on by it. He urgently ripped down both straps of my bra, whipping my arms free.

'Look at me squeezing your tits, Tara,' Travis gloated towering behind me.

I watched his hand swaying and swooning at a crazy pace. Then, with his other hand he began pulling my hair backwards and forwards, rocking me wildly.

Desperate to get this new turn of events right, I kneaded his tightly toned butt, my fingernail's digging deep and passionately into his soft supple skin. I did my best to follow his crazy rhythm as his hands descended with lightning speed, aggressively hitching up my skirt to waist level.

I felt so dizzy, alarmed *and* turned-on I nearly fainted with desire on the spot.

'Those fucking stockings and suspenders are driving me wild,' he teased, completely immersed in the moment. He weaved his nimble fingers in and around the lace knowledgeably, pinging one of my stockings free from its clip.

I smiled faintly and nervously and ran my hands down his hot, naked flesh, still reeling in confused pleasure. Just as I felt I was getting to grips with the moment, he had me by the back of my neck and was forcing me to bend over.

I gripped the Salon chair to hold myself steady as he yanked and stretched my knickers aggressively to one side, mounting me like a bull from behind. Not quite ready to accommodate him, I yelped out loud in pleasurable pain.

'Feel that, baby,' he moaned, as he writhed harder into me, kicking the chair away and out of my reach. My heart pounded hard in my chest as I fell forward, my hands catching the floor just in time. I was totally encased by Travis and his muscle-bounding strength. The sounds of his body slapping hard behind mine, enjoying me, made me feel suddenly powerful and almost brazen.

'You're a great fuck, Tara,' he grunted.

With just a view of the Salon floor and his trainers (due to me being folded over), I cocked my head round to the side. I could see the rear of him in another mirror. His perfectly formed butt muscles were working at a phenomenal pace, fucking me hard.

His strong, muscular back was flexing and dripping in sweat, while his huge arms held my waist in place as he continued thrashing in and out of me.

'Look, look in all the mirrors around us. It's like I'm fucking ten women. Fuck. I'm in heaven.'

I was just about to grab a pair of thinning scissors and stab him in the ankle when he quickly added; 'I meant ten of *you.*' His hard pounding and last comment left me feeling stung. In my struggle between feeling confused and turned on, the anxiety about his erratic behaviour definitely had the upper hand after that. I tried to raise myself back up to move into a more loving position, but Travis was having none of it.

Looking into the mirror to the side of me, I caught a glimpse of his stormy expression, as he pulled me around like a rag doll.

'I can see every angle of us both, we look so hot, so horny,' he panted, apparently oblivious to my change of mood. He just continued banging harder and harder against my female form, which looked so small in comparison. His breathing became ever more frantic as he pushed and stretched me to my limits.

'I'm fucking your pussy, Tara; your sweet, tight little Catholic pussy,' his voice now wicked with enthusiasm.

I was just about to take a bite-sized chunk out of his calf in protest when I felt awash with *the* most erotic leg trembling sensation. Zillions of powerful volts flooded through me and a kaleidoscope of colour misted over my vision.

'T-R-A-V-I-S! OH-MY-GOD!' I pitched at a soprano level. 'Whatever you're doing… oh my God! I… can't… I… can't-catch-my-breath… don't stop. I beg you, don't stop.' I wailed whilst simultaneously turning to jelly.

'I knew you'd love a fingering up the bum… I just knew it!' he said with undisguised relish.

'WHAT THE FUCK!' I gasped, horrified, punching his hands away from behind me. 'Get out of my allotment!'

I would do anything for him, but not that! Nobody goes up my back garden! 'That is sacred, Holy ground!' I began wailing and balling like a brat. Suddenly distracted, I heard sounds in the distance again.

'Did you hear that, Travis… did you hear that noise? I'm sure I can hear voices.' I slapped the back of his leg to still him. He grunted loudly, still pounding away at me and ignored me completely. I cocked my neck around to get his attention, puffing my sweat-soaked hair from my face.

'Travis… Travis! Please stop, or just cum, I can't take anymore,' I began to plead, trying to raise myself up.

But he didn't show any sign that he'd heard me. He just held me tightly in place, plunging harder and faster, gathering in momentum and pace. He kept one of his hands strategically placed around my waist to still me and the other over my forehead to keep me steady. His fingers grossly dropping over my eyelids, then into my mouth. I heaved at the thought that one of those *polluted* fingers had been fiddling where it was forbidden to be. I held my breath as my eyes crossed together in total disgust.

Finally, giving an almighty yell that sounded like Tarzan, Travis powerfully shot himself into me. He buried his sweat-soaked face into my back, the jerky movements indicating his load had nearly emptied, as his body juddered behind me.

Not a moment too soon he folded over me. We stood, bent over, both panting breathlessly in the otherwise silent Salon.

In less than two seconds, he retracted himself out of me and staggered over to the chaise longue to retrieve his phone, collecting his strewn clothes along the way.

'Damn it. I've got to go, there's a crisis with one of the players,' he said, shrugging his shoulders and rattling through his texts.

'Oh no,' I said, feeling utterly wretched. 'What's happened? Do you want me to come with you?' Realising I was standing in just my stockings, suspenders and shoes, I grabbed a cutting apron to cover my modesty.

'No, I really don't have time to wait,' he said dismissively. With that, he paced eagerly over to one of the washbasins and splashed soapy water over his manly-hood before grabbing a clean Salon towel to wipe him-self dry. As soon as he was done, he tossed it carelessly onto the floor.

'Will you come back to my place... tonight?'

'I doubt it,' he said, without even looking up from his phone.

The blood drained from my face at his snap decision. I stood, paralysed, leaning my hip against the washbasin and folding my arms tightly around myself. My gaze narrowed as I watched him pulling his clothes on and striding towards the Salon door to leave.

'I can be ready to come with you in seconds,' I pleaded, suddenly running over to him.

'Gotta go. Sorry,' he said, barely turning around and unlocking the Salon door to leave.

'Please don't go,' I begged, as my eyes filled with tears - my hands involuntary pulling at his hoodie.

'Please try to be more understanding Tara, its part of my job,' shrugged Travis, completely devoid of emotion. *'Don't* make me feel any worse than I already do.'

'Sorry,' I whimpered, hanging my head in shame for even asking. I raised my hands gently to his face to brush away one of my lash strips that had attached itself to the side of his neck. Before I could get it, he grabbed both my wrists together and pushed them away.

'I'll call you soon,' he said abruptly. With that, I watched him scamper off into the darkness.

I stood, shivering in shock and pressed my head despondently against the door. My quivering hands clasped around the keys for support as I locked it. The blood drained from my face and my legs gave way. I slid into a trembling, crumpled heap on the floor.

Eventually, trying to pull myself together, I attempted to piece together what had just happened. Time seemed to have stood still. I glanced at the clock. *Could it really be only 7:30pm? Had the love of my life actually just come and gone in less than half an hour?* I had been in the shower, getting ready for him longer than that!

I double-checked the time on my phone to see if either the clock on the wall or my watch had stopped. Nope - he'd been here for a matter of minutes. The reality of what just happened began to dawn on me, like a drawn-out punch in the face.

Shivering, I shoved my arms through the cutting apron and helplessly crawled over to the reception area on my hands and knees, dragging my body through the chaotic paraphernalia of clothes, towels, gowns and desk debris strewn around me.

Something glimmering in the low light caught my eye. It was my cherished pen mum passed down to me after dad died. It was shattered into bits and scattered across the tiled floor. Dad had written his last love song with it. I picked up the broken pieces and held them tightly against my heart as a flurry of emotions overcame me; guilt, anger, shame, longing and loneliness. Without knowing which emotion was most dominant, a torrent of tears swiftly and uncontrollably followed.

A muffled noise sounding close by suddenly interrupted my misery. Was that voices I could hear again? I'd been hearing them on and off all evening. Were my dad's schizophrenic tendencies now also affecting me? I mean, I always thought Laura had it - definitely Katie - but *me* too?

The voices were getting louder and moving closer too. With my vision totally blurred by tears, I quickly shot up from the cold hard floor, praying Travis had come back.

'Travis?' I cried.

I rubbed my burning eyes and makeup-smeared face to find James and Siobhan striding towards me from the *back* of the Salon.

My jaw dropped; 'What the fu...?'

'No need to say anything, we saw the whole thing,' James said gently, taking me in his arms and holding me tight. 'The total-toss-potting-feckin'-arse-wipe-of-a-bastard.'

'Oh, James,' I howled, blubbering and trembling into his tight grip. 'He's gone, he's left already... It's only been half an hour and he's left.'

'Right!' spat Siobhan furiously down the phone. 'He's wearing a grey hoodie and black shorts. Shoot the fecker on sight! - But don't kill him... Cos me fag mate wants to ram a rusty nail file up his jacksy, that's why...'

'... *And then*, I'm gonna cut off his oversized dong and feed it to Jayde,' interrupted James, finishing Siobhan's order.

'Siobhan, James, stop it - please don't make it worse by getting him done over,' I pleaded breathlessly.

By this point, Siobhan's face was bright purple as she frantically paced around the Salon, shouting profanities down the phone. 'In fact,' she finally turned to me, covering the phone as to not be heard, 'we should start by ruining his reputation with a vicious rumour or two. I'll get on the blower to the paparazzi now.'

'Say his dong is bent,' James added, looking straight at me for approval, his eyebrows raised in hope.

'Siobhan, please give me the phone... just leave it alone,' I begged. 'I've been through enough this evening. If you do that, there's no going back. Not that I ever would, but still, please.'

Especially if I'm pregnant, I thought. I didn't want our baby being bullied in the playground having to deal with a family name tarnished by a rumour. *Oh my god, what am I thinking?* I surely didn't still expect to walk off into the sunset with that brute.

As my mind spun, something else began to trouble me. It suddenly occurred to me that the response time from my life-saving emergency team was suspiciously short. They also seemed to be very knowledgeable about my ordeal. *What was that all about?*

'Excuse me, you two,' I broke in, as the pair argued urgently about a strategy to destroy Travis. 'How *did* you two even get in here, and so quickly after this all happened?'

'Ah yes, well, err... you see - we were, err... doing a stock count upstairs,' fumbled James, looking over at Siobhan for support. 'Weren't we *Siobhan?'*

Even though Siobhan nodded enthusiastically, it was easy to see this was a blatant fabrication.

'There's nothing up there but cobwebs and sawdust, you fibbing, spying toe-rags!' I shrieked.

'Oh, okay, don't go on about it, woman,' said Siobhan, waving away my protest. 'We just wanted to make sure that you were okay, isn't that right, James? Which reminds me, it's all on your CCTV if you still wanted to go to the press with a sex tape. We could blur your face out and everything. You would make a fortune.'

James turned to me with a curious pout on his face. Oblivious to my baleful look, he leaned in conspiratorially; 'Would now be the wrong time to say, *I told you so* about your back garden? *Any hole is a goal,* you know. I saw your face change to a very peculiar shade… It did that to me the first time, but I never looked back since.'

I cupped my face in shame, 'Oh God… you saw that as well? Is *nothing* sacred?'

'Hmm… no,' they both shrugged in turn. 'Not now we have CCTV and the internet. It could even go viral with that kinda footage,' they both agreed, nodding.

'Carry on,' egged Siobhan, turning excitedly to James. 'Tell us more about *your* first time James.'

Not one to turn down a request for a life story, James sighed and gave a huge grin, 'Well, if you insist. See… I knew that I wasn't a diner for vagina after my first and *only* hetro encounter. The smelly bitch tasted like a nine-volt battery. I actually had to gargle white spirit to get rid of the taste.'

'I've never so much as even had a suppository up there,' I spluttered, but the words fell on deaf ears. James' story was clearly far more entertaining. 'He committed one of the worst sins possible under the eyes of the heavenly father and worst of all,' I whispered, sobbing, 'I didn't exactly *hate* it either.'

'Fook off,' gasped Siobhan, still ignoring me completely. 'We taste like batteries?'

'He's a complete gobshite, doing that to me and taking my bum-ginity without my permission...' I carried on, largely to myself, 'an outrageous invasion of the worst kind.'

The phrase 'bum-ginity' seemed to finally catch their attention and they both swung round to face me.

'Here,' said James, 'knock this back.'

He passed me the glass of warm, flat wine that I had left earlier. 'It will calm you down. Siobhan and I will clean this up. Stay calm – we've got everything under control.'

I felt so dirty and so used; everything was spinning around my head in a twisted mess. I was overcome with the discrepancy of my strong commitment versus Travis' complete lack of any loyalty whatsoever.

'He's a complete shambles of a very well-endowed beast,' ranted James, picking up the overturned chair.

'Stamina like that would give you an early heart attack,' added Siobhan thoughtfully, as she bent over to pick up the appointment book.

I broke out, sobbing and wailing like a banshee again. 'But I really love him,' I cried, 'I will never meet anyone as gorgeous as that... *ever again.*'

'Course you will - listen to me,' said Siobhan. 'Sex is like bungee jumping; you know you're gonna enjoy it but - if he's really butt ugly, just don't look down.'

'But I don't want babies with just *anyone*. He was my last hope.'

'Oh, darling,' hushed James. 'Whilst he's undeniably delicious looking – and, in fact, I would go so far as to say built like a human tripod, with two legs and a third *huge* stump in the middle – he's a total shit. I mean to say; shagging you senseless and just abandoning you in split seconds like that. What a dastardly man-whore!'

'I hate to say it,' agreed Siobhan, 'but I think he planned it that way.'

'So do I,' whispered James, rubbing my arm tenderly. 'Never see that poor excuse for a man *ever* again. Tomorrow, I shall wear a black sequin armband in his memory, out of respect for you of course,' he added with a pout, clicking his tongue.

'Shall we have a group hug?' asked Siobhan. The thought of which, made me sob uncontrollably again.

CHAPTER TWELVE

I'm not sure how I made it through the next couple of weeks. I was in a complete daze. I certainly didn't hear from Travis and for a short while I was happy about that. But then, once the shock wore off, I started to see things differently. Maybe he was just over-excited and on a high from winning the match and hadn't realised how much he'd hurt my feelings. I mean, if it makes him happy, maybe a little rough sex is okay every now and then. Or worse – his silence could be his way of punishing me for that 'faked orgasm' text I accidently sent him at the hotel?

I had resumed texting him about a week after our Salon encounter, but he'd not answered even one of my increasingly desperate messages. I just couldn't understand what I had done so wrong. I hadn't even complained about, well… what he'd *done.*

So here I was, yet again, hiding away from the world in the Glamma-Puss staffroom. I'd been doing it for so long now, no one even bothered to pop in anymore with some inane bid to cheer me up. Even the indefatigable Siobhan seemed all out of crazy ideas. James too was strangely distant. A constant pain in the pit of my stomach didn't help my mood. It was a physical pain too, not just one of those I-have-a-broken-heart pains. Plus, the misery of it all left me feeling so horribly tired all the time.

For a few fleeting moments, I'd considered it may be the telltale signs of early pregnancy. There might be a happy ending to that first fairy-tale night after all. *Perhaps a baby might be all I needed to tame Travis. Maybe at this stage in both our lives it would be the perfect solution to bring us together as a proper family at last.*

Logically though, it couldn't be baby pains. Bloody hell, it was only a few poxy weeks ago. It didn't stop me hoping though - or making an appointment to see a doctor. I didn't want one of those blue line pregnancy tests from Boots to tell me my big moment. I wanted a white-coated hunk of a doctor to look deeply into my eyes and say: 'Miss Ryan, I have the most incredible news. You're pregnant.'

I closed my eyes tight shut and muttered yet another silent prayer.

Dear God, if Travis phones now and everything is okay, I will be so good - you'll never believe it. I'll go to church every Sunday and will help poor people and everything.

I waited with baited breath, my eyes still tight shut. Then, my prayer was answered. My phone rang. It was surely a miracle. My eyes flew open and my heart started hammering in my chest.

Then I saw the name on the little screen. 'Laura'. Shit.

'Hi Tara, do you have time for a little chat?' asked Laura, in her usual, patronising manner.

'Hi… what about?' I asked, deliberately sounding as unfriendly as I could. I really was not in the mood for one of her lectures.

'I'm rather concerned about you… you seem so unhappy - and I hear that you're spending less and less time at work,' she continued, blithely ignoring my reaction to her call. 'Is he worth all this heartache?'

'I'm fine,' I insisted, switching my tone to sound as nonchalant as possible. Maybe this was the best way to get her to butt out of my life. 'I'm entitled to some time off Laura. Anyway, I'm sure I'll hear from him soon, then I'll be okay.'

'So you're only okay when you hear from him?' she brutally continued to interrogate.

'That's not what I meant!' I protested. This wasn't going well. I didn't have the strength or energy to see off her clever, *psychobabble* questioning.

'He loves me, Laura, I know he does,' I lied, hoping this would see her off at the pass. Oh well, in for a penny, in for a pound. I'd better make this sound convincing.

'In fact, he text me last night and told me again how much I mean to him,' I said airily *(oh I wish)*. 'In fact, we had text sex till 3am!'

In actual fact, the incident in question had been weeks ago. Not long after the night in the hotel, we'd gone through an orgasm-inducing series of messages when he'd text me out of the blue at 2am one night. But, the minute his manly-hood had cum, he was gone, leaving me to play with my lady-garden while staring at a non-responsive phone. The gobshite had disappeared off the face of the earth. All the time I was texting, 'I'm nearly there, I'm nearly there,' (well if I'm honest, by the time I had written the text, I wasn't there at all). For all I knew, he had probably switched his phone off and gone to bed.

'But Tara,' sighed Laura, 'that's not real. Did he call you? And *actually* speak with you?'

She had a point. In fact, in our entire relationship, I could count the number of times he had text me on two hands. As for real-life calls, well that was probably only one hand's worth. Bloody hell, I had only seen him three times in my entire life and on two of those times he had shagged me and then buggered off!

I shook my head to get rid of the unwelcome thoughts. I knew he loved me. He'd said so, hadn't he? It was just... well... complicated.

'I don't mind, because I know how much pressure he's under,' I began to stammer, drying up almost immediately because I couldn't think of how else to defend him.

I could feel the tension as my sister fell silent. She always did this. It was something they taught her at 'Shrink School' I guess. I hated it when she did this. My mind reeled as I desperately sought ways to excuse Travis' behaviour.

'Laura, he texts me as often as he can. Why would he waste his time contacting me at all if he didn't love me?'

'Love,' said Laura, primly, 'is an *action* word. If he really loved you, he would show you.'

Lickarse! Only *she* would know something like that. I never did get that grammar stuff at school. All those 'action' words, 'doing' words and God knows what else. Please don't even get me started on the 'pro-nouns', what the feck were they? Heck, nerdy lickarse even knew how to do 'logarithms' - I had always thought they were some kind of street dance.

'*So what* if he puts his actions in a text and doesn't see me very often. Don't you think he cares about me at all?' I spat, recovering my poise somewhat valiantly, I thought.

'But your so-called relationship is *purely* virtual,' she said, beginning to sound exasperated. 'At best, it's a fantasy pantomime played out over a plastic handset.'

I sniffed hard and had to bite my tongue to refrain from telling her to feck off.

'I'm sure he does care about you, but he does seem wildly sporadic and inconsistent,' she added, poking at my insecurities like they were on display.

'Please stop confusing me with your big words, you sound like you have eaten a dictionary!' I blurted out, trying my utmost to steady my quivering voice.

'Okay, sorry. It just makes me feel sad when I hear you so down,' she said, switching to her 'soothing' shrink routine. 'It just seems that Travis is nearly *always* the cause.'

She was right, but there was no way I would admit it. I wanted *everyone* to love him. I hated the thought of my family not approving of Travis. I would have to be careful what I told them in future.

'Okay… but I do really feel I have met *the one* and, you know Laura, they do say *the course of true love never runs smooth,* don't they? We have *so* much in common. He's a Virgo and I'm a Taurus, so we are *both* earth signs. Also both of our names begin with the letter *T.*'

Warming to my theme, I prattled on excitedly. 'If you think about it, what were the chances of us ever meeting, with him working in Ireland and me living over here? Yet, we both just happened to be out on the same night. I think the universe pulled us together. It was like fate and destiny all wrapped up in one!'

As I paused for breath, I could hear Laura sighing down the phone. She wasn't buying it. But I needed her approval, I always did. Nicknames notwithstanding, I admired Laura so much. Nothing ever seemed to phase her. She always came up smelling of roses. After her husband walked out on her, she didn't fall apart for a moment. She simply dusted herself down, went to university and studied Psychology. Now she had an amazing, high-flying career. If I could have just a drop of her drive and confidence, I'm sure I wouldn't be in the situation I am today; hurtling towards forty, childless and in a (now clinically diagnosed) dysfunctional on - but mainly off - relationship with the world's most elusive man.

'It may appear that you have a lot in common,' she continued, 'but these commonalities are just circumstantial - they don't really mean anything. You're not looking at the relationship itself.'

Each sentence was a like gunshot wound and yet she just wouldn't stop.

'It's not really a relationship when you think about it. Those few conversations you have had are just hollow words typed on a mini keypad that get sent through the airwaves. Your two 'dates' have been extended, meaningless shagathons. You know each other more orally then emotionally. I bet you've had more conversations with his balls than his face. How can you base a loving relationship on *that* alone? Where is the effort there? Have you two even been out for a meal?'

I was devastated. My head started to throb and I felt like it was about to explode. I felt sick and dizzy and the pain in my stomach now felt like someone was stabbing me with a knitting needle. I had to end the conversation quickly.

'Laura, I have to go now, I have an appointment at the hospital and I'm running late.'

It was true. In precisely one hour, 'Dr. White Coat' could step into my life and make all my dreams come true. I was vaguely aware Laura was beginning to launch into her next attack as I dug about in my handbag for my diary to double-check the time on my hospital appointment. My hand fell upon the Perspex of the small plastic vial the surgery receptionist had given me with the curt instruction to bring a urine sample. I headed for the loo and put Laura on loudspeaker, placing her on top of the cistern and flushed it (not the short flush, the long flush), drowning out her lecture, literally.

Did people really pay for this kind of demoralising bullshit?

I sighed heavily, yanking my tights and knickers down and placing the narrow vial underneath myself. Even though I could feel it was in the correct place, I just had to tuck my head down in between my legs making sure that enough urine was being collected.

It wasn't. Instead, my wee shot out in every conceivable direction and dribbled down my hand.

For the love of God! I stopped mid flow and adjusted my stance.

My lady-garden used to pee out in the most beautiful, reliable, straight and gentle stream. Now it resembled that of an old, broken showerhead; leaking and pissing all over the place. I peered through my legs, concentrated and tried again. Managing to catch the some of the spraying splutters that were shooting to the left, I screwed the lid on and popped the sample beside Laura. I inhaled deeply, shook my head, pulled up my underwear and washed my hands, only to find that she was *still* talking…

'Okay, look, I'm sorry if it appears that I've been a bit hard on you; it's just… I don't want to see you get hurt,' Laura summarised. 'How about you do a little work on yourself?'

'What do you mean?' I queried, snapping out of my reverie about my peeing ability. I didn't understand… I had already had more Botox than I was allowed.

'Well, how about trying some emotional-personal development? Try and fill your life with things that don't involve *him*, some structure of your own that fulfills and nourishes you.'

'Structure? Actually Laura, that's not such a bad idea. Sheila was going on about a new nourishing filler that can plump your cheeks out, I might give that a go…'

'Not *that* type of nourishing structure,' sighed Laura impatiently, 'I meant in the *emotional* sense.'

Are you serious, I thought? I'm not exactly the happy-clappy personal therapy type. I realised quickly that if I didn't get off the phone fast, I'd probably never get away.

There was nothing else for it. I'd have to humour her.

'Yes, yes, that's a great idea,' I said, trying to sound enthusiastic, 'well done you. You really are so clever, Laura. Thanks so much. I do have to go now, but I swear I will do some personal stuff. Call you later.' I stabbed the hang-up button on the phone so hard, I chipped a nail.

(Sigh)… Personal feckin' development! What the feck's she on about now? She has no clue of how I'm feeling. In fact, I really don't like her attitude today, I thought, as I stuck my two fingers up at the phone.

Stealing myself for my appointment and needing to feel better after Laura's lecture, I decided to read back some of the (admittedly few) filthy, dirty text messages Travis had sent me. My insides started racing and dancing with desire again. He was just so exciting and unpredictable. But *yes,* I sighed to myself, *maybe Laura did have a very minor point about his inconsistencies.*

Sitting in the hospital waiting room, I slid my phone out from my handbag and stared at the blank screen. *No new messages.* The aching for him to contact me was never-ending. My heart descended ever deeper into the achy land of limbo. Reluctantly, I looked at the clock. I had been in this poxy hospital for two hours now. I was far from meeting the hunky 'Dr. White Coat' - so far I had just met a bored-looking, grumpy nurse who ordered me to go upstairs for blood tests.

'It's on a first-come, first-served basis,' she said, as she handed me a form, barely looking at me. 'You might have a bit of a wait. When you've done that, come back down here and the nurse will go through the rest with you.'

I sighed heavily. I really couldn't be bothered to hang around anymore. But I had to go; I had been feeling too poorly for too long.

It had been 13 days, 3 hours and 23 minutes since I had last received a text from Travis, but even that was only to confirm he was meeting me at the Salon for our 'date'. Having said that, this was the longest he had ever gone without contacting me. It was nearly two whole weeks of crippling uncertainty. It had been nearly 14 long, wine-indulging, nail-biting, comfort-eating, uncontrollably sobbing *'bastard-I-hate-him - fuck-it-I-love-him'* days of hell.

Clutching my phone close to my heart, I decided it was time to have another go at bargaining with the Big-Man upstairs.

'Please, let him contact me today and I promise - in fact - I swear on everything I own, I'll say a decade of the Rosary and I'll go to your house and light a candle for St. Jude, the patron Saint of lost causes,' I muttered. *This has surely got to work, hasn't it?* Mum always said that if we did this, we would have our request granted.

'Now, I know it seems that I only talk to you when I want something,' I continued, oblivious to the looks I was getting from the elderly man sitting beside me. *Feckin' hell, I was only whispering, why doesn't he mind his own business?* 'I know that you're busy, with at least a million other requests from all your real fans who actually attend mass every week, but to hear from him now would really be good for me. A call, or even a lousy text with just an 'x' is all I ask for'.

I drew a slow, quivering breath. Moments passed, but there were no immediate results. Maybe I wouldn't see the results right away, or my request was waiting in line and would come through shortly. Mind you, the Big-Man hadn't even got to my prayer from this morning. Strikes me, he might need a few angels to sort out his admin for him. I counted to three, then to ten, then to thirty very slowly. Nothing. I stared at my phone willing it to stir into life. Giving it a shake, I performed my now obsessive switch-off/ switch-on routine. This was now becoming a fully-fledged compulsive disorder. *Okay then, your Holiness, when you're ready then... but can it please be today?*

Travis' silence was eating me up from the inside out. Come to think of it, my phone had been very quiet in general. Maybe there was something wrong with my network. Craving some form of acknowledgment, I decided to give it a test.

[Text to Siobhan]

I'm testing my phone - I think its broken, did you get this? And if you did, can you text me back ASAP? Thanks Xx

[Text from Siobhan]

Testin testin! I like 2 b wined dined & 69nd. I take it u haven't heard from him then? Did u get this?? xxxx

Disgusted, I threw my phone into my handbag and headed towards the ladies. I'd been dying for a pee for ages and couldn't hold on any longer. If my appointment with the nurse came up, they'd just have to wait.

'Jesus!' A flash look in the grubby hospital mirror made me jump. My peroxide blonde hair, recently extended by ten inches, had settled itself into a shape that could only be described as resembling that of a cat's arse perched on top of my head. It had a mind of its own. What was happening to me? I also had started to notice that the growth of my leg hair had slowed down in recent days too. *Excellent,* you may think - Wrong! It seemed all my leg hair had actually decided to migrate to my upper lip. Adding to that, my newly acquired 'retained water' look left me with a permanently jutting tummy. It was safe to say - I was not looking my best. It was no wonder Travis wasn't returning my calls.

Forgetting all about my pee, I stepped up close to the mirror and began my routine facial inspection; pulling the skin by my hairline tightly upwards, momentarily taking away ten years worth of the effects of gravity. Of course, this only ever lasts about a nanosecond. As I let go, ten years came flopping back.

'I don't remember *that* line in my face,' I gasped. This was becoming a regular catchphrase of mine. *It certainly wasn't there yesterday.* Frantically I tried smoothing it away with the tips of my fingers, hoping it might be a crease mark from frowning so much. No such luck, it was most definitely a new wrinkle that had crept up on me.

You, little bastard, are going to get filled tomorrow, I said to myself, wagging my finger at the offending wrinkle. I pulled my face this way and that, lifted my brows up with my fingers and tilted my head at different angles. God I looked rough. I need a face-lift. I'll have to put that on my *want-it - need-it - must-have-it* list. *Oh, I wish my Botox would hurry up and kick in,* I thought, as I continued scanning the rest of my ageing body. I hated this cruel mirror. I was almost certain that it was faulty. *Hang on a minute.* I staggered back from the mirror in horror.

No. It can't be. It's not possible. WHEN DID THIS HAPPEN? I could actually see my own arse without even turning round. Bloody fantastic. *I am definitely going to demand a refund on my poxy gym membership.* Could things get any worse?

Miserably, I walked over to the loo and had my long awaited pee; hovering as far away from the porcelain as was physically possible without peeing on my shoes (which wasn't easy now I could apparently no longer pee straight). Thankfully, I managed to wash my hands and exit the room without catching another glance of myself in the *Mirror of Horrible Truth.*

As I headed towards an empty seat, I heard an exasperated voice shouting my name.

'Tara Ryan? *Tara* Ryan?'

'That's me,' I shouted, rather too loudly.

I'm sure I saw her tut and shake her head as she motioned me to follow her into the brightly lit consulting room. Everything about her demeanor screamed that she didn't want any small talk. *That's fine by me. I'll save my sweet talk for Dr. White Coat. I don't need to impress her.* The wrinkly old camel. *She needs a good old rodgering,* I thought. *I bet she hasn't had sex in years. Mind you, who would want to, with a face like that?*

Anyway, back to the point in hand, I mused. *How would I go about giving Travis our wonderful news?*

I would wear a white, virginal diaphanous flowing gown and cook a candlelit dinner for two (okay, actually I can't cook, but I can certainly order food in that will look like I've cooked it).

Then I would make my announcement:

'We are with child.'

No.

'We are pregnant.'

No.

'You've scored.'

Hmm… maybe I might need to work on that line. I'm so not going to let myself go while I am pregnant either. No way.

MENTAL NOTE TO PREGNANT SELF:

1. No puking – it's very unflattering. Morning sickness, if applicable, must wait till Travis has left the house.

2. No leggings, no anoraks and absolutely no lesbian haircuts.

3. No stretch marks. I will bathe in Bio-Oil for at least two hours every day.

4. Buy a sexy Agent Provocateur Babydoll nightie to give birth in; with fully-matching mules piped in their classic colours with the initials 'TC' (Tara Coleman) on them.

5. No screaming or howling during labour. I will breath like a Buddha; controlled and in a peaceful manner.

6. Must schedule tightening of lady-garden immediately after birth of our perfect baby.

7. Breast is best. Hmm... not sure I want to have my silicones removed. I will definitely have to think about that one. I will miss my chin-hitting friends.

8. Caressing of breast area will only resume once re-inflated with new 'sticky up bosoms'.

9. *Book a tummy tuck. And throw in a sneaky facelift for good measure (they might do buy one, get one free!)*
10. *Must ask Travis to give me a list of his celebrity buddies, need to choose suitable Godparents.*

Satisfied with my to-do list, I began to picture what I would wear whilst pregnant. I would definitely need to wear sexy skintight dresses to show off my long-awaited event. I would wear my beautiful Louboutin heels and look every part the radiant mummy to be.

Meanwhile, we would keep up a strict regime of mind-blowing sex daily, maybe even three times a day, or for as long as is possible.

Lost in my dreams, I stuck out my arm and let Nurse Ratchet tap on my veins till she announced she had found a juicy one.

'Nearly done,' she said grabbing another vial to fill. 'Right, that's it. We'll call you soon with the results.'

And that was that.

I drove home in a trance. *I can't believe I had to spend three hours in hospital for nothing. No big announcement. No 'congratulations, Miss Ryan'. Nothing. I should have gone feckin' private. Then, I wouldn't have to wait to hear what was plainly obvious to all. I am pregnant. I must be, mustn't I?*

This should be the happiest time of my life, but it just stubbornly wouldn't fall into place. Nothing was going to plan. Why was everything so complicated? And why did I have to fall in love with someone who is in the public eye? And why couldn't he be seen out with me and have a normal life?

Most importantly, *why can't he simply get in touch with me?*

I just had to send him one more text. *Now, I know all the self-help books tell you not to chase a man.* (I had cleared the shelves at Waterstones in the past two weeks in a bid to understand Travis better). *And I get that you are supposed to leave them alone once they've gone into their cave.* (Thank you, *Men are from Mars and Women are from Venus). But come on, he's been in his 'cave' way too long now. And surely, even if a man is padding about in a cold, dark cave, he'll at least bring along some boys toys in with him? Like his phone for example?*

Maybe one more text won't hurt, will it?

After an unsure moment, I made up my mind. I'd take the risk. I'll just give him a gentle reminder, whilst not directly addressing his lack of contact (okay, I didn't say that I had read those self-help books to the end).

Scrolling through my contact list, I looked for a name that would make my text to Travis appear like an innocent mistake. It has to be someone with a name beginning with a 'T' I thought, deviously. I felt delighted with myself for having thought of such an ingenious way of provoking a text from him.

[Text to Travis]

Hi Teresa, here's your requested reminder of your appointment at 4:30pm today. Please confirm back with Glamma-Puss Salon. Tara.

My heart pounded as I pressed the send button. *Clever Tara. Now Travis will have to respond and let me know that I have sent him a text that was obviously meant for someone else.* Knowing I would surely get some kind of response before the appointment momentarily made me feel devilishly empowered. I now even felt like I might be able to muster the energy to go to the gym (to refund my membership, of course). But I didn't.

I settled down to wait.

The witching hour of 4:30pm came and went at a snail's pace. Nothing. Not a peep. I could barely believe it. I sat on my sofa, rooted to the spot, staring into space. *What the feck will it take to make him react?*

I don't know how long I sat there, hours maybe, but suddenly I was overcome by a hidden rage. I was now a woman on the edge. I couldn't take anymore. I was consumed by a mentalist idea that only a woman in desperate need would consider. Acting like an automaton, I withheld my number and called the bastard's phone.

I wasn't even sure what I was going to say, but I had to do something.

To my complete astonishment, the line at the other end clicked. My heart banged as he answered. I instantly hung up.

I was utterly traumatised. The fecker was clearly alive and had not lost his phone. After all my wild allegations and imagined disasters, nothing was wrong at all. He was, in fact, completely ignoring me.

I flopped back onto the sofa and started retching. I could barely breathe. My heart was in pieces. I honestly thought I might pass out with the sheer agony of how I felt. My phone suddenly pinged a text in my shaking hand - I could see it was from him.

[Text from Travis]

Tara, it's over. Never contact me again.

'OH - MY- GOD… He's finished with me!' I screamed in disbelief.

I read and re-read the devastating message. My insides collapsed with such a force that another boiling hot wave of nausea pricked and prodded my entire body. Without warning, I threw up all over the sofa and myself.

Those ensuing minutes I experienced were, what I can only explain as a complete mental and physical breakdown.

It felt like my eyes were popping out as I desperately tried to catch my breath. My face contorted into the ugliest expression imaginable, while I pointlessly waved my arms in the air. I was left panting and sobbing; trying desperately to find a position on the vomit-riddled sofa where my heart didn't feel like it was about to explode from my body.

I don't remember much about the next few hours. Piecing it together later, I think I began to hysterically phone anyone who would listen. They didn't listen for long though, because I was blubbering an incomprehensible language that nobody could understand. 'They said *not* to go into his cave but I *did*,' I screamed, like a woman possessed. 'The dragon has burnt me.'

Call after call, I wailed and repeated the verbal diarrhea like a mantra. I bemoaned my absolute failure in life, love, and everything in-between before clicking the red button and phoning the next number. Siobhan was call number four.

Actually, she'd been call number one, but I hadn't given her a moment to respond.

'Calm down and breathe,' Siobhan interrupted, the second I got through. 'Who has burnt you? A dragon? Tara, are you hallucinating? You haven't had a party without inviting me... have you?!'

I didn't reply. I just wiped the dribbling snotty mess from my face to my sleeve and forcibly lobbed my phone at the wall.

Watching the object of my addiction explode mid-air made me change my mind. Frantically, I began searching on my hands and knees for the scattered remains of my phone.

'What if he thinks he has made a terrible mistake?' I wailed, as I struggled to piece the various pieces of my phone back together. My world was tipping and crashing on its side at a rate that I couldn't control. I felt like my life support had been cut off. My emotional stability was hanging by a thread, as I rocked myself back and forth curled up in a ball on the floor, cradling my burning, tear-stained face. *What the hell had I done so wrong that he could do this... and by text?*

I dug my nails deep into my head, howling and raging like a wounded animal. My heart hammered and thumped so loud I thought I was dying - I was now vaguely aware that I was on the verge of self-destructive melt down.

Forcing myself to stand up, I wiped my face with grim determination. 'I'm worth more than this!' I screamed at the top of my lungs. 'Feck the world... Feck everyone... Feck what's right and what's wrong!'

Engulfed with toxic rage, accompanied by waves of intense despair, I raced upstairs to the bathroom mirror and searched my tangled, twisted face.

Come on, Tara. You are better than this. You are not going to lie down and take this one. I was going to win that bastard back if it killed me. I knew he still loved me. I just needed to remind him of that fact.

'I have to fight for him,' I told my distorted, tear-stained reflection. 'I have to fight for *us*.' I have no idea how I made it to the bottom of the stairs, or really how I planned to 'win' him back. The last thing I remember was booking the first available flight to Dublin.

CHAPTER THIRTEEN

The first thing the following morning, I launched myself into the shower like a woman possessed. I was on a mission and there was a hell of a lot of work to do.

Once I had towelled myself down, I looked at my swollen and blotchy face with grim determination. *Feck.* I was gonna need a lot of work. A face-lift at the very least. But, there was no time.

My initial attempts at vajazzling myself were thwarted by my trembling hands. That, and the fact I kept pausing to sob my heart out and wail loudly. I plastered on layers of makeup and smeared on some slutty red lipstick. Then, after looking at my reflection, I promptly burst into tears. Big black stains of mascara streamed down my face. *Feck. Feck. Feck.* I reached into the cupboard for the Clarins makeup remover, wiped it all off and started all over again. *Just don't feckin' cry, Tara,* I warned myself. *I'm not sure I have enough mascara left to do all this again.*

Flipping my hair 360 degrees, I pushed through diamanté earrings stabbing myself in the neck in the process. The shock nearly made me start blubbing again, so I dug my fingernails into the back of my hand to distract myself. *There. Floodgates closed.*

I walked purposefully from the bathroom and into my bedroom. Swinging open my wardrobe door, my eyes fell upon my prize. My beautiful black fur coat. As yet, Travis had still never seen it on me. I fanned myself frantically, my head zipping back to the euphoric high that had spurred me on to max out my credit card and purchase it.

I thudded my head hard against the wardrobe door remembering the highly suggestive and erotic texts that sizzled back and forth between Travis and I that afternoon. One particular text he sent was burnt into my mind:

"The thought of you in fur coat and no knickers has made me rock hard."

Laying the bag carefully down on the bed, I slowly unzipped the fur coat out of its pristine holder and paused. This coat was to define my mission, to ensnare his heart and win him back. I stood back and stared at it. It was a lot to expect from a coat.

'Travis Coleman - I'm coming to get you - in a fur coat and no knickers!'

My eyes suddenly caught sight of the clock beside the bed. *Shit! Look at the time.* If I didn't leave there and then, I wouldn't be able to get another flight till tomorrow. Without a moment's hesitation, I took the fur coat out of the bag and slung it on. Then, I floundered for my passport in the cabinet drawer, wrestled on my tatty slippers, shoved my Louboutins underarm and ran out of the house.

As I raced along the motorway to Heathrow, I tried to reflect on what I was doing and why. *This is lunacy, isn't it?* Travis had told me *never* to contact him again. I had screwed things up good and proper and managed to alienate the man of my dreams. Maybe I deserved to feel like this.

I felt heavy with failure, shifting around uncomfortably in my car. My thoughts were flashing back to the rip-roaring (albeit very agitated and somewhat unusual) sex we'd had that night in the Salon.

I shook my head, thumping the steering wheel in temper. 'Damn it!' I exclaimed in despair.

It was all *my* fault. I hadn't responded in the most grown up manner to his mischievous wandering finger. I mean, there he was taking our sex life to a whole new level - and what did I do? Bless myself and begin reciting a Hail Mary! Then I accused him of taking my bum-ginity! No wonder he buggered off and never wanted to see me again.

Suddenly my bum twitched and began to sweat at the thought. 'No bloody point in sweating now!' I yelled down at my quivering arse.

I cringed as I reflected on my appalling behaviour. I had almost cried like a baby in front of him when he left. I must have made him feel terrible. I had totally embarrassed myself, and worst still… I had embarrassed him so much, he felt compelled to end us, forever.

Gulping back the sob that was growing in my throat, I desperately tried to see the bright side of my situation. I *had* to or I would be howling and smudging my feckin' makeup all over again. Now… what was it James used to say? Oh yes. If someone turns their back on him, he sees it as more of an opportunity.

By the time I had arrived at the airport, my stomach was clenched with anxiety. As I sat in the queue outside the Short Stay car park, I checked my makeup in the vanity mirror. God, I looked a mess. No wonder he didn't want me. I shook my head. *Come on, Tara, be positive.* What would lickarse Laura say right now? Probably some psychobabble stuff about positive thinking and making things come right; I was gonna need a barrel-load of that babble, that was for sure.

After I had nosed my car into one of the few parking slots, I yanked off my warm cosy slippers and slipped on my cold skyscraper Louboutins. The second I opened the door to get out, I felt a whoosh of cold air cut through me.

Clutching my bag, I ignored my mobile that was buzzing ten-to-the-dozen with calls from family and friends. I walked purposefully towards the main terminal; except, I couldn't seem to get my feet in rhythm with each other. Something was seriously wrong. I was totally off-balance and wobbly. I looked down at my feet and immediately saw the problem. I cursed James and his bright ideas. Thanks to him, I was wearing two shoes from different sets: one a five-inch Louboutin, the other a six-inch. *Argh! JAMES!*

I couldn't stop now. I had no choice. Setting my course firmly in the direction of the main terminal, I forced myself to continue hobbling in my odd shoes. I had a driving force of passion and love and nothing was going to stop me; not even you – *yes, you* – Big-Man upstairs. *I don't care if it's a sign, or if you think I'm doing the wrong thing. I'm going to ignore you, the way you have ignored me.*

Once I had struggled through the interminable queue at security, I threw what little possessions I was traveling with onto the conveyer belt.

'Remove your coat please, Miss,' said the tall security guard, barely acknowledging me as he continued to stack up the trays. 'And your shoes.'

'I-I-I… can't,' I stuttered, frozen in horror, my face now flaming red.

'Remove your coat please miss, or you're not coming through,' pronounced the guard who had abruptly stopped stacking his boxes. His brows were now knitted together with annoyance, as he stared straight at me. I stepped to the side, closer to the guard who visibly tensed in apprehension of what I might be about to do. His hand twitched to his side, where there was a large truncheon fixed to his belt.

'Listen, I really can't take off this coat,' I whispered, looking pleadingly into his eyes.

And now the humiliating confession. 'I'm… not wearing anything underneath,' I said, my eyes dropping to the floor in shame.

'Really?' he questioned in disbelief.

May God forgive me… I threw my head up and sideward, inhaled a deep, nostril-widening breath and opened my fur coat for a nanosecond, revealing my entire naked body (well practically entirely naked, if you don't include my vajazzle). I saw his eyes widen in shock and then he broke out into a full-grown smirk.

'Ah hem… okay… please remove your shoes, Miss,' he said, still aghast, grinning and shaking his head. He then called over a female security guard to search my coat.

'Boyfriend problems,' I said, trying to keep my voice as casual as possible to justify the obscenity. The two security guards exchanged glances, with raised eyebrows. 'Trying to win him back,' I continued, as I looked up at the ceiling with my arms stretched whilst being patted down.

I couldn't wait to get away once through security, I dashed towards my gate with my face still flushed red. I deployed all my usual tricks to keep my mind off what was hurting me so much, but nothing seemed to be working. I just couldn't tear myself away from my paranoid state by thinking ahead to what I was actually going to do, or say, on the other side. It didn't help that my eyes were irritated from a combination of tiredness, excessive crying and sloppily applied mascara. But I was on a mission. *Okay, Tara, visualise how you think this will play out.*

Of course, the first thing I would have to do is actually find Travis. I hadn't actually thought properly about how I would do that yet.

I decided he could be in one of three possible places. I would grab a taxi to the training ground first, and then swing past the local coffee haunt. Failing that, it's then going to have to be Dougie's house. If Travis wasn't there, I would just have to wait it out till he was.

Once on the plane, I struggled past the cramped flight deck and down the aisle while desperately trying to prevent my fur coat from accidentally flying open to reveal all. That really would be a humiliation too far. Eventually, I spotted an empty seat near the back and squeezed my way into it. As soon as I had fastened my seatbelt, I immediately closed my watery eyes to avoid talking to anyone. For good measure, I sent my best, cold 'do-not-even-try-to-talk-to-me' signals to the young girl sitting next to me.

I needed a stiff drink. My nerves were absolutely shot to bits. I really hadn't thought of what I would even say to Travis when (or if) I eventually found him. Maybe I wouldn't say anything at all. Maybe I would simply drop my fur coat to the floor in front of him and that would say it all for me?

I visualised the scene of his stern face breaking into a smile as my coat floated to the floor. He'd step forward and take me in his arms and it would be just like it was in that fairytale hotel where he had confessed his love to me.

The vibrations of takeoff shuddered me back into the real world. I opened my eyes because I knew I could never sleep. I just didn't know what to do with myself. As soon as the seatbelt sign flicked off, I pressed the call button for a hostess to come to my aid. I didn't really know what I wanted, but I needed something to bring me up and out of this stupor. I was in a complete mess and unable to stop myself analysing *this* and dissecting *that*. I just couldn't get my head around what had happened.

I needed a drink and I needed one *now.*

As my mind raced, I became aware of the young girl sitting next to me retching. *How gross.* I really didn't need this. I fumbled around in the seat pocket for a sick bag for her (or, more accurately, for me). *Please don't get any vomit on my fur coat,* I thought, eyes rolling. I turned my whole body away from her, my mouth now filling up with warm, foul-tasting saliva at the sounds of her gagging.

These kids obviously can't hold their drink, I thought, condescendingly.

'One too many?' I enquired, perhaps a little heartlessly. Post-drink recriminations are always better for the morning after. I wasn't exactly sure if what I had said was a question or a statement, but never mind. As far as I was concerned, I really was going above and beyond. She shook her head as I handed her another sick bag while I was simultaneously pushing the help button frantically above me. I really did need a hostess to come and help. Right *now.*

'I'm so, so sorry,' she spluttered between retches and then pointed at her tummy as she continued to gag. Now I looked at her properly, I was overcome with a wave of empathy. She was clearly pregnant.

'Oh, you poor thing,' I said, my voice now full of maternal sympathy. I immediately felt awful about my snap judgment of her.

'Five months gone, still being sick,' she confessed with a tiny embarrassed smile.

She looked way too young to be having a baby. Her face was small and pale with neat little features. Despite my sympathy to her plight, I couldn't help thinking her boring brown hair blended in seamlessly with her boring brown poloneck. Pushing the thought away, the mother in me took over and I pulled tissues out of my bag to pass to her. *She really doesn't want to let herself go like that,* I thought to myself, turning away from her to avoid the wafting stench.

That's dangerous territory, letting yourself go like that. And it's certainly not an excuse to wear those colours. You wouldn't catch me throwing up in public with morning sickness like that. I mean, she could have at least waited until she was off the airplane and worn something a little more fetching.

I discreetly slipped my hand inside my fur coat and smugly patted my tummy, proud that my unborn baby knew how to behave. Good genes you see, they make all the difference.

Lost in my dreams, I didn't even notice the girl had left her seat. She'd obviously gone off to finish her puking in the loos. Good… ahh yes… my double vodka and coke had arrived. I had a momentary internal tussle as to whether I should be drinking spirits in my condition, but decided one couldn't do much harm. My baby was probably only the size of a jellybean anyway and I was sure it wouldn't count. Besides, these were exceptional circumstances. I made my mind up and swigged it back. I instantly felt a lot better. That was a good thing, because we were just about to land in Dublin.

I don't know what they put in that stuff, but within a few minutes I was experiencing a fully blown, out-of-body experience as I left the aircraft. Adrenaline was rushing around my body. I honestly felt like I was on drugs. I had the sensation that I was watching myself from above, like it was happening to someone else. But the intense longing to confront and seduce Travis was more powerful than anything I'd ever felt. The internal conflict waved backwards and forwards constantly. The feeling would cycle from my head all the way down to my stomach, endlessly pumping through my veins. I couldn't resist the feeling of hope that I could somehow win him back.

Then the doubts came flooding out. *Was I really going to walk into his life and demand an explanation, with no warning?* A little voice in my head knocked at my heart. *What if he rejects you? What if he laughs in your face? No, no, I can't let myself think like that,* I said, trying to bury the little voice. I was entitled to get some answers and I wasn't leaving without any. Travis owed me that much.

I paced numbly towards the exit, swept along by the crowd of people leaving the plane. My body shook and trembled with every step. Most of my confidence and bravado had disappeared. My legs were on autopilot, yet I felt like I was free falling out of control. Once through passport control I had to try and pull myself together quickly, so I diverted my path to the toilets. As I walked through the large swing door, a familiar retching sound crept its way back to my ears.

'Pregnant girl from the plane, is that you?' I called over the cubicle where the noise was coming from. No answer. 'Are you okay?'

'Yep... fine...' the splattering she was making in the toilet bowl suggested otherwise.

Why did I have to develop a conscience now?

'Umm…' I rested my head on the outside of the cubicle door, unsure of what to do next. 'Is anyone coming to get you?'

[Louder splatters and splashes.]

'Eww… I'm fine! Don't worry about me, I'm being picked up…' she gulped.

'Okay - well, good luck. Bye!' I said with relief as I detached myself from the situation. I was really glad I wasn't in her shoes. I'm sure Travis would never tolerate such weakness. I am so glad my pregnancy is trouble-free.

I took one long, lingering look at myself before I swung the door open to leave the ladies. My footsteps echoed eerily in the now-empty terminal building as I proceeded towards the Arrivals for Dublin, my eyes immediately spotted a gorgeous hunk of man.

'Travis?' my scalp pricked as I did a double take.

There he was. Right in front of me, casually leaning against a pillar, waiting. I saw him glance up in surprise, his body now rigid as he spotted me.

The surprise and colour drained from Travis' face and was replaced with an expression full of wide-eyed horror.

I stopped in my tracks: happy, shocked and confused.

All my plans and elaborate scenarios disappeared from my mind. The only sound I was aware of was the loud thump of my heart which seemed to be trying to break through my chest.

Then, two things happened very quickly. I heard footsteps close behind me and saw Travis' expression change. It softened, but still looked full of panic. He was looking at the source of the footsteps behind me.

I turned my head just as the person behind drew up beside me. It was the young, sick, pregnant girl. She wasn't looking at me though. She was staring straight ahead at Travis with a huge, sloppy smile.

'Thank you,' she whispered to me gently as she walked past. Then, as she picked up speed walking straight towards Travis, she called out to him. 'This kind lady has been like a mum, looking after me and your baby on the flight.'

Each word was like a knife stabbing me in the heart. I was frozen to the spot, my head spinning, unable to take it all in. Looking at Travis I could see his pleading eyes burning into mine, begging me not to say anything as she enveloped herself into him.

And I didn't. I *couldn't*. I was utterly paralysed. I wanted to scream at the top of my voice, 'but I'm wearing my fur coat and no knickers…!' surely he couldn't pick that dowdy, pregnant, sick girl over *me?*

Pregnant sick girl turns to give me one last cheery wave, grinning all over her little pretty face as she buries herself under the protective cloak of Travis' arm. Tearing his eyes away from me, he bent down and kissed her tenderly on top of her head. Then, for one more kick while I was down, he leaned over and rubbed her tummy and whispered something into her ear. I caught sight of her giggling. Without a second glance back at me, the pair of them turned and walked away. As I watched them go off hand in hand, I felt compelled to scream out and say something, but no words would leave my open mouth.

Then, as they reached the sliding doors of the terminal, I saw Travis briefly turn his head to look over his shoulder. Our eyes met, for what I knew would be the last time ever. The expression within them was so unlike anything I had ever seen before. Travis, my own love God - the man who had made me feel like no one had ever done before - looked at me with complete, chilly disdain. With that, he turned back and he and his pregnant girlfriend disappeared into the crowd outside the airport.

I don't know how long I stood there, unable to move or speak. I felt sick and numb as I became vaguely aware that tears were falling down my cheeks. Then I heard my mobile begin to ring. I hadn't even realised that I had it on during the flight.

Fumbling around in my bag, I finally managed to locate it and answered it without looking at who was calling.

'Miss Tara Ryan?' said the caller. The voice didn't sound familiar.

'… Ye, uh… yes?' I answered, feeling nailed to the spot.

'It's the practice nurse here, calling from the doctors surgery,' went on the brisk, professional sounding voice. 'We have your blood test results through and there is a note here that you wanted to be called as soon as the results came in. This is just to let you know there is nothing serious to worry about. It looks like you are simply entering into the menopause.'

At that moment, I felt my legs crumple beneath me and my whole body crashed to the floor.

CHAPTER FOURTEEN

[Text from mum]

I think that Botox has made u go a bit funny. Get the doc to check it hasn't leaked into your head. Love u xx

...

[Text to mum]

No mum, it can't leak into your head!! I'm just tired and can't sleep X

...

[Text from mum]

Ur such a beautiful looking girl, u really don't need all that stuff. Please leave ur self alone Xxx

I pulled up to the surgery in a daze, not quite remembering the drive. My breathing was short, shallow and I couldn't stop my hands from shaking. I placed one hand on top of the other to try and control the anxiety. Just getting out of the car felt like an impossible task.

After enduring two weeks of this hell, I was so tired of my thoughts, so tired of the pain, so tired of not being able to sleep. All I wanted was for my head to shut up, but it just kept on chattering - I was utterly exhausted from it. My mind had become my enemy.

Each waking moment was an overwhelming emotional battle that I could no longer endure. *He* wasn't mine to love. *He* never was mine in the first place, but that didn't stop the waves of grief or the stomach-churning misery that continued to peak as I thought about Travis and her together.

I wrenched my weary mind back and began to gather myself to face the fact that… I actually couldn't face the facts. Mustering up all my strength, I counted to three, held my breath and made a run for the doctor's surgery. I prayed no one would see me. It wasn't just that I was still wearing my pajamas, covered with a hastily donned overcoat. I just wanted to hide myself away from the world. I just wanted to go back to the familiar sanctity of my bed, away from everyone.

Luckily, it didn't take long for me to be seen by the doctor. But, the minute the doctor made eye contact and asked me how I was, that was it. My chin started to tremble and my face contorted as I fought the tears back. I gulped hard in an effort to pull myself together. I wanted to scream and shout about what I was feeling, but I knew it was pointless. I knew I could never be fixed. I just hung my head and sniffed hard.

'I think I may be a little down,' I finally blurted out, along with a torrent of tears. 'I can't cope.'

The doctor handed me a box of tissues.

'I can't sleep. I can't eat. Please can you give me something to make this pain go away?'

'What pain are you feeling, Tara?' he asked gently, looking at me over his glasses. I sat in silence and shrugged my shoulders. 'Are you having suicidal thoughts?'

'What?!' I asked abruptly. 'Of course I'm not. I would never commit such a sin!'

I couldn't bring myself to admit that in fact, I had been praying every night to the Big-Man upstairs, wanting him to take me away in my sleep. After all, he decides when your time's up. But as of yet, my prayers had gone un-answered.

'What do you think is making you feel this way, Tara?'

'Where do I start?' I began, my head spinning with what I should say. 'Anything that *could* go wrong in my life *has*. Everything is just such a mess. Work has really slowed down and I just feel under *so much* pressure *all the time.*'

'Okay,' he nodded encouragingly, 'do you get much exercise? It can really raise your serotonin levels.'

The silly fecker, I thought. *I'm sure I had some of that injected into my face recently.*

'Well I used to, but now I can't seem to muster up the energy,' I said, my voice faltering. This wasn't going as I expected. I would just have to be very specific.

'Doctor, *please* can you give me something so I can calm myself down? Maybe some sleeping tablets? And some triple strength Prozac? Can I have the strongest ones you have please? I just want to stop feeling like this.'

'I don't think that would be the right solution for you,' he said in a patronising tone.

'Pardon?' I said sharply, the tears stopping instantly.

'Well, Tara, all the pills will do is simply mask the problem... what we need is to *resolve* whatever it is that is making you feel this way, not cover it up.'

'So what are you saying?' I asked uncomfortably, twitching in my chair. I knew that no amount of time, money or comforting conversation could undo the past. Or change the fact that Travis - the man who had practically asked me to

265

marry him - was having a baby with his *young* girlfriend. 'Surely you're not saying I can't have any happy pills? Can I just have double strength Prozac then?'

Maybe I was being a little greedy asking for triple strength.

'Well, it sounds like you have a lot of emotional issues to work through. I think it would do some good if you talked to a professional. I'm suggesting we get you to see our counsellor.'

'I don't need to see a counsellor!' I barked sharply, unable to hide my annoyance. 'I want to be numb so I can't feel anything. Is that really too much to ask for?'

'You need to feel something, Tara. I'll get that referral for you.'

'But that could take weeks and I can't spend another hour feeling like this,' I said, starting to *really* panic now. 'Will they give me some numbing tablets?'

'They can be highly addictive, they only add to the problem.' He said, sounding very matter of fact.

I couldn't take in what he was saying. My nerve endings were screaming: *please God; not another day, hour or minute like this.*

'Look, I know that you're a really busy man and you probably have a queue of *real* lunatics who need to see a counsellor... and it's really kind of you to offer... but if you can just give me a prescription I can get out of your way,' I pleaded, 'and I won't tell another soul - I promise.'

'I'm just booking the referral now,' he said, tapping on his computer.

A boiling temper began raging inside me.

'I am *not* happy. I am not happy *at all*. I am not leaving till you give me something. It's not fair! All my friends are on numbing tablets (*well, all the fecked up ones anyway*). In fact, all the celebrities are on them… you know, life is hard enough.'

By now, I was up on my feet and pacing the floor. 'It's one big battle out there. I'm tired of fighting - so don't you battle with me too. You're supposed to be *helping* me. You're supposed to be on *my side*. Just give me the God damn pills!'

With that, the Doctor's face showed that he had given in, as he silently printed me off a prescription. Immensely satisfied with my performance, I calmed down.

'I will give you a four-week supply, by which time your referral to the counsellor will be through,' he said handing over the precious prescription. 'But please remember, Tara, this is only for the short term.'

'Are they nice and strong?' I asked shakily, snatching the prescription from him and shoving it in my pocket in case he changed his mind.

'They will help you sleep. Make an appointment to come and see me next week.'

Will I feck come and see you next week, I thought, as I dashed out of the door. *I'll be La-La Land.*

I raced to the chemist to pick up my prescription.

Come on, come on, I thought, as I stood in the long queue full of dawdling old biddies on a day out (probably picking up their incontinence pads). Actually, I wasn't sure who smelled worse - them or me. *I will shower tomorrow, maybe.*

I finally got my hands on my precious numbing pills and promptly shoved two in my mouth. I know the packet said take one just before bed, but I figured they would take a while to kick in.

[Text from Siobhan]

Me and James came round to see u but no one's in.
Hope ur feelin better, we are worried about u xxx

[Text from Laura]

Mum, Katie and I are very concerned about you, can
you please stop ignoring our calls and pick up your
phone!

Lying on the sofa, reading the other texts from friends was
the last thing I remembered until the following morning. I
woke up freezing, still fully clothed and holding my phone. But
at last, I had something that knocked me out and removed the
pain (for a while, anyway). I had just had 12 hours of
nothingness where I wasn't obsessing about Travis.

Light-headed, I stumbled into the kitchen for a drink and
collapsed in a chair beside the kitchen table. Feeling relief, I sat
and stared into space for a while. Soon though, the pain and the
pictures in my head started creeping back. They started as a
dull ache, but increased with vivid intensity.

I couldn't face work, so I called in sick… again.
Swallowing another two pills, I went to bed and buried myself
away from the world under the duvet. I lay there, waiting for
them to take effect, desperately trying to push the images away.
I felt so drained. All I wanted was to go back to nothingness,
where I wouldn't feel the pain of real life. But, much to my
despair, an hour later I was still awake.

Convinced that the pills weren't working, I took another
one, but I was just drifting in and out of sleep. I wanted a
proper sleep; a deep, undisturbed sleep. I wanted to be

anywhere but here. I wanted to be anyone but me. I hated the 'now'. Maybe I didn't want to wake at all.

So I swallowed another two for good measure.

I repeated this pattern over the next week, but by Friday, sheer terror took over. In one week, I had taken a whole month's supply of pills. I needed more, but what would I say to the doctor? How could I tell him that I had only one tablet left? I would have to make up some wild story.

Taking a deep breath, I called the surgery and left a message. The doctor called me back within minutes.

'How are you, Tara?' he asked with a cheery voice.

'Much better, thank you... but I do have a very small problem,' I added cautiously. 'I went to stay with my sister for a few days in Dublin, you know, to get some fresh air, exercise and have some company. She has these two mischievous dogs and, well, one of them actually ate my whole box of numbing pills, straight out of my bag! The whole packet, even the foil… *everything*. He had to have his little doggy stomach pumped. Such a naughty pup! He slept for three days and was very sick.'

I paused, listening hard to hear if there was any reaction.

'My sister is very angry with me,' I continued, throwing in a few sobs for good measure. I had to do something. I could feel I was losing. 'But, doctor I'm feeling so much better – all thanks to you and your brilliance,' I added very quickly. 'If I could just sleep a few more hours a night, I'm sure I would cope better. And I have decided to really embrace the counselling thing. In fact, I can't wait to start. You are an amazing doctor and…'

'I'll leave a prescription at reception and we will have that appointment with the counsellor for you soon,' he interrupted abruptly, 'and Tara... please be more careful this time.'

Breathing a huge sigh of relief at my potentially Oscar-winning performance, I clicked the receiver.

A week later, a letter arrived from the surgery with the date of my counselling appointment. I really didn't want to go. If they weren't going to give me any numbing pills, what was the point? I cancelled it, saying I felt too unwell to attend; promising I would re-book, as soon as I felt better.

My pills were depleting fast though. I felt sheer terror at the thought of having to ask for more, but I had gone through all my pills again in just over two weeks. Even though I was feeling more unwell as time went on, I had at least achieved what I had wanted; to feel numb; to feel nothing.

I mentally prepared myself, thinking up different stories, different excuses, something - anything to get more pills. I then nervously rang the surgery to make the dreaded appointment.

'I'm afraid your usual doctor is away on holiday, Miss. Ryan,' chorused the receptionist, 'will you see Dr. Arahna instead?'

'Of course, no problem.' I answered, instantly relieved.

When the time came, I easily pulled the wool over Dr. Arahna's eyes by rambling through one of my old stories.

I'm getting good at this; I thought. *I should have taken a career on stage.*

Dr. Arahna barely lifted his head to acknowledge me, but that suited me fine. He didn't care and neither did I as he handed me my prescription.

Now I was popping the pills like sweets, it was only a matter of time before I would be in the same situation once more. But, for now, I could breath again. Or sleep more in my case - that was all that mattered.

Meanwhile, I continued to fob-off friends and family with tales of flu or a stomach bug, whatever I could get away with. I became a good, convincing liar.

All too quickly though, the time arrived where I needed another prescription and I made an appointment heavyhearted. I couldn't recall when I had last washed. I looked bad, smelt bad and felt bad. In an effort to look a bit more *together* for the doctor, I dragged myself under the shower. The water hurt as it pounded my fragile body. I felt so weak. I convinced myself I may really have been coming down with flu. I had no clean clothes so picked the least-creased ones off the floor, pulled them on and set off nervously for the surgery like a zombie.

As I was called to go through, I kept telling myself to keep my composure, stay calm and in just a few short minutes, I would have what I needed.

'Hello Tara, how are you?' my usual doctor said cheerily.

'Really well, thank you. I just need to get a repeat prescription please,' I said gulping hard.

'But you should have enough to last you at least another two weeks,' he replied after consulting his computer. 'And I notice here that you have not yet been to see the counsellor?'

'Err... no, not yet,' I answered, blushing. 'I was a little poorly and I forgot to re-book. As soon as I get home I'll make the appointment.'

He clearly wasn't impressed with the bullshit I was spewing. I knew he could see right through me. He knew - that I knew - that he knew I was bullshitting. He sat, looked at my bullshitting face, turned back to look on his screen and then looked back at me.

'Tara, I can't give you any more.'

I was instantly filled with rage.

'WHY NOT?!' I exploded. 'But I need them. They take the pain away. They stop me from thinking!'

'With the amount you've been taking, they'll stop you living altogether. Please, remove your coat so I can take your blood pressure.'

'I haven't taken *all* those tablets you know,' I protested. 'One of my friends had a couple, my sisters cat - err... I mean dog - had nearly a whole packet. And, and...'

'These pills are highly addictive. By the looks of things, you've been taking enough to knock out a horse.'

'I hope you're not implying that I'm addicted,' I said, doing my best to sound indignant, '... or the size of a horse? And you call yourself a *doctor*. It's not cocaine or alcohol, it's a little white tablet that helps me sleep; nothing more, nothing less.'

'... On the scales please,' he continued, completely ignoring my pleas of justification.

Petulantly, I removed my coat, with a few huffs and puffs thrown in for effect. I stomped onto the scales, hands-on-hips.

'Hmm... just as I had suspected. You have lost nine kilos since I saw you last.'

'So?' I snarled, secretly wishing he'd told me what it was in stones and pounds (I could never work it out in kilos).

'*Nine* kilos in just over a *month*? I am very concerned.'

'What's a few pounds?' I snapped, getting more irritated by the second.

'Nearly a stone and a half in such a short space of time is *not* healthy.'

'A stone and a half?' I stammered, quite stunned. What a shame that I didn't take these tablets when it would have mattered.

The doctor continued his checks. My blood pressure was through the roof, I was becoming underweight, *blah, blah, blah.* The gist of it all: I was a train wreck.

'I am *not* addicted,' I defied desperately. 'Surely I can't just *stop* taking them? Don't I need to come off them slowly?'

It's not good when you have to tell a doctor how these things are done, I thought to myself.

'I cannot give you any more, Tara. Besides, if you're telling me that you're not addicted… then you won't miss them, will you?'

'But that's not fair.' *The smart arse.*

'So, are you willing to admit you have probably become addicted?'

'No, because I most certainly am not!'

The cheeky gobshite. That's Katie's department. She's the druggie of the family - not me. Why did I have to end up with a doctor who does everything by the book?

'You're going to have to go cold turkey. By the end of the week your sleep pattern should go back to normal.'

'Fine!' I snarled. 'That's fine. You're the *so-called* expert.' I added in a sarcastic tone; 'My life is in your hands!'

He ignored me as he picked up his phone to make a call.

'Ah, she's still here,' he said into the receiver. 'Can she see a patient now? Yes… I would consider it an emergency, thank you, I'll send her through now.'

'Right then,' he said turning back to me, 'let's get you back to a good state of mental health. The counsellor is here and she will see you now.'

'But… I don't need to see anyone. I'm not mental!' I protested. 'I don't want to talk to anyone, I just want to sleep…'

Unable to even finish my sentence, I broke down. I was then gently escorted into another room, where there was a very large, rounded lady waiting for me.

'Hello Tara, come and sit down,' she smiled soothingly. 'My name is Dawn. How are you feeling right now?'

'I'm fine,' I sniffed, feeling completely drained, almost falling into the chair. I was just petrified, now that I had no more numbing pills.

Apart from my sniffling, the room fell silent. Sadly, my head wasn't silent. The same thoughts pounded my brain. It hurt to think, really hurt. To add to it all, there was the certainty of going home empty-handed. I felt like my life support had been switched off - I couldn't breathe.

'If the doctor could just give me a few more numbing pills I would feel better, please can you go and ask him for me?' I implored, running my hands through my greasy, matted hair. 'Please, I'm begging you.'

'That's a very interesting name you have called your medication,' Dawn said, completely ignoring my plea. 'Tell me how you are feeling right now? Try and use a *feeling* word if you can.'

'… Broken,' I said, sobbing into a tissue, '… broken.'

'Broken,' she repeated softly, nodding her head in sympathy, 'tell me about *broken*.'

'(Snivelling)… I hate myself… I hate what I have become and *this*,' I said bitterly, pointing at my heart, 'this has had enough. No more. No more. I'm done.'

'So, what I am hearing is… you hate yourself and you hate what you've become?'

'We love and we lose love… and it hurts,' I gulped, 'it hurts real bad… *real bad*… What's the point of anything? It's all pointless. We live and then we die and… Look, I don't want to waste your time any more. The short of it is - I'm just ready to die and get out of everyone's way…'

'… Okay, Tara… it's okay to cry...'

She let me cry for a full ten minutes without saying another word.

Eventually I was able to piece some words together. 'I feel so alone. Just so, so lonely. I'm in darkness. There isn't a way out. When you need people the most… they're gone.'

'So you're in darkness and you're feeling alone?'

'… But you know, you get fooled because they are there in *body,* but not there in *mind…*' I babbled.

'Someone is there with you, in body, but not in the mind?' Dawn questioned.

Who is that somebody? I asked myself. *Sweet Jesus, I really do sound like a mental patient.* Was it my dad? Was it Travis? Stumbling over my own thoughts, I remained silent for a moment.

'… And you end up trying everything – anything – to get that person back,' I began welling up again.

'It's okay, Tara. It's okay. Stay with those feelings.'

'… But it's all too little, too late!' I barked back in anger. 'He took what he wanted out of life to cope and now the person they once were has gone… it fucking hurts. We consume things and then… they consume us.' The grief and pain became so overwhelming I began to retch.

'Please… please help me. The pain… I can't bear the pain. I miss him. I miss him so much. I failed. *I* failed. He didn't want to be with me.'

A tidal wave of emotions crashed into my whole being. I felt faint and unsteady. I felt sick.

'Dad… Travis,' I mumbled in confusion. I shook my head… 'I don't know.'

'It was your dad or Travis?' repeated Dawn, in a calming voice.

'I don't know… My dad went and died on me. He never even said goodbye. I looked after him as best I could - but he still left me after everything I did for him.

'You think it was your fault your dad died while you were looking after him?'

'I couldn't stop him from drinking. I should have been there 24/7, but I was working so hard to keep a roof over our heads.'

'So, you couldn't stop him drinking? So, it's the child's job to look after the adult is it? How does that make you feel?'

'Guilty,' I whispered. 'Really, really guilty.'

I buried my hands in my face as the feeling of guilt engulfed my mind.

'You feel guilty for putting a roof over your dad's head and for doing your best as a daughter?' Dawn pressed.

'I feel guilty about everything... I tried my best. He was an alcoholic. Then he got diagnosed with schizophrenia and didn't take his medication. I didn't know that he wasn't taking it. So yes, I feel guilty. It *was* all my fault.'

'Your father *chose* not to take his medication and he *chose* to continue drinking - and this makes you feel guilty?'

I nodded as the tears fell down my face and on to my lap, soaking into my clothing.

'How does that make you feel?'

'Like a failure... very lonely.' I answered quietly.

'Tara, we've made some great progress today,' said Dawn, sitting up in her chair and glancing at her watch, 'our time has come to an end.'

'But... I haven't even started on the other fecker who abandoned me!' I stammered. 'And he's gone for a child as a lover! ... *And* I'm in the *menopause. Me*... in the menopause! I'm only in my feckin' thirties!'

'This is good, Tara, would...' began Dawn.

'What the feck is so *good* about that?' I interrupted sharply, feeling my anger rising. 'All you've done is just repeat everything I've said... Feck it! Just get me my numbing pills. I've kept my end of the bargain. It is time for *you* to keep *yours.*'

I stubbornly folded my arms, feeling angry that I'd done what was asked and they didn't even given me what I wanted.

'Another appointment would be far more beneficial for you Tara,' she said smiling and shaking her head at me.

I made another stupid appointment, to shut them up. But I already knew I would cancel it.

I arrived home distraught, empty-handed and pissed off. The slightest noise drove me insane. I ripped the phone, TV and radio out of their sockets and pulled down the blinds in every room of the house. I needed to get some more pills. Reluctantly, I switched my mobile back on, deciding to ask Siobhan for help,

'Hello?' Siobhan answered, sounding surprised.

'Siobhan, it's Tara. I need a favour.'

'Well, feck me! We all thought you had been abducted by aliens!'

'Very funny.' I really wasn't in the mood for Siobhan's humour.

'How've you been? *Where* have you been? Are you alright?' she said, sounding genuinely serious for once.

'Siobhan, I need you to go to the Doctor's for me.'

'Oh... okay...'

'I'm still not feeling well and I can't sleep. Can you make an emergency appointment for this afternoon and get some sleeping tablets for me? Please?'

'Okay... *anything* to make you feel better. We're all missing you so much.'

'Thanks... All you need to do is tell the doctor you can't sleep. Come round for a cuppa when you've picked them up.'

'No problem, I'll be there as soon as I can. Call me if you need anything else.'

I paced the floor for an hour before Siobhan turned up. She flung open the back door, grinning from ear to ear.

'Well?' I said, wide-eyed with my hands out ready to snatch the booty from her.

'You're not gonna feckin' believe this right.'

'Did you get my pills?' I asked impatiently.

'Well, I goes in right and your doctor's feckin' gorgeous. I thought, right, I'm not missing out on this. I says to him, me fanjita's feeling a bit funny like, can you gimmie a once-over? Y'know, get right in there and make sure everything's hunky-dory. So he goes, "that's fine, lie on the couch and I'll get a nurse". I wasn't sure about that at first, but then I thought, the more the merrier, you know. Anyway, nurse walks through the door and her face is like a bag of boiled shite and she's built like a brick shit house. I thought *there's no way she's fiddling with me flaps!*'

'Siobhan! Did you get my tablets?!' I snarled through gritted teeth.

'Wait, wait, wait,' says Siobhan, doubled up in hysterics. 'I threw me thong to the floor and spread me legs, guiding him in like. It was fookin' great. I was lying there, with me legs practically wrapped round his neck, pretending it was me first time and that I was frightened. Meanwhile, while his head was in me crotch, I was waving me middle finger at the sour old bitch in the corner. It was fookin' great. Oh yeah, I forgot to ask for your tablets. Sorry… but, if you want cheerin' up, go and have your fanjita inspected. It's far better than *any* pills, I'll tell you that for nothing.'

'FOR FUCK'S SAKE!' I raged at her. 'What the hell am I going to do now? All I asked was for you to do one simple thing for me, Siobhan. Just go and ask for some bloody pills. That was it. But you can't even do that!'

'Oh right, well sorry for having a laugh,' Siobhan said, looking genuinely hurt by my outburst. 'Well I can pop down to the offie for you and pick up some brandy. Few of those will knock you right out.'

'No,' I signed, completely exasperated, 'I don't want a drink. It keeps me awake. You *really* don't understand. I needed those tablets like you would not believe.' God, I felt like punching her. My whole being was shaking in temper.

'You're not addicted to these pills are you?' Siobhan asked looking more concerned than ever.

'Don't be stupid!' I hissed, squeezing my eyes tight and gritting my teeth in pure frustration. 'I just need to get a good night's sleep, that's all.'

'Are you sure now? Because you don't look *or* sound so good.'

'Please, stop asking silly questions. It's purely the lack of sleep… I'm fine.'

With that, I abruptly shoved her out the door and locked it. If my doctor and my friends can't help me, then surely the internet could.

After a few days spent glued to my bed in my own private hell, my supply of internet-sourced numbness arrived. *Hallelujah.*

After catching up on my dosage, I drifted in and out of dizzy spells and restless, foggy thoughts.

Everything became grossly distorted. My brain was spiralling at an incredible rate. I was helpless to put the brakes on. It felt like I was suffocating. No, it was much worse… like I was being squeezed to death.

On-and-on I plunged, ever further down within myself towards the bottom of the deepest, darkest ocean, all the while being tossed brutally around by cruel forces and relentless currents. Every time I opened my eyes, it seemed as though everything was closing in on me. The ceiling, floor and walls were haunting as they swayed backwards and forwards.

I tried to get up out of bed, to go downstairs and get more sleeping tablets - my legs gave way completely. As I tumbled to the floor, I reached out to grab something – anything – and as I did, I came crashing down, along with the curtain rail.

I lay in the foetal position for what felt like hours, gripping myself tight and gasping for air. Somehow, eventually I crawled out, pushing my way through a mass of crap in my path to the top of the stairway. I placed my hands over my ears and begged the ringing sounds to stop. Blood was seeping from my head.

Unable to catch my breath, or hold myself steady, I began to bum-shuffle down the stairs. My mind was in fast-forward, playing pictures of the past, present and future, all flashing like sirens around and around. My dad drinking, mum sobbing as she goes to mass, priests and images of the cross, bullies and cruel school teachers, Katie screaming, Laura laughing, Travis grinning with his newborn baby. I begged my head to stop the incessant thoughts and began retching with each step down.

Reaching the bottom of the stairs, I crawled over to lean against the kitchen door. I pulled up my knees and cradled myself tight. *Please, please God, help me. Make this stop.*

Every inch of me was juddering. I tried clutching my hands over various body parts to make it stop - no use. I could hear the inside of my mind screaming. I couldn't control anything. I was spiraling, deeper and deeper down. My jaw started to chatter and my eyes began twitching. I couldn't anchor myself. I didn't have the power. I didn't have the will. The depths of my very being ached. My soul was tortured and tormented. I was consumed by dark black thoughts of pointlessness. I was going down.

Then, suddenly, a blanket of complete calmness washed over me. I realised with utter certainty that death was the only way I could escape this pain.

I didn't want to be here anymore. I grabbed a pen and began scribbling desperate last instructions on the wall and emptied the remaining supply of the internet-sourced pills down my throat. *Reasons to live: ... none.*

Then everything went dark.

CHAPTER FIFTEEN

I am alone, shivering in the dark. My neck and shoulders are throbbing but I lay still. I am paralysed with fear.

Scared of what might happen if I open them, I clamp my eyes shut as flashes of terrifying feelings flood through me. I begin to wonder if I have been buried alive. Even so, I dare not move. I fear feeling the coffin around me.

My whole being was dominated by the deafening drum of my heart, banging so violently it could burst through my chest. It's agony. My ears are ringing with the sound of the blood rushing and gurgling around my body. Everything is pulsating.

I try to clear my constricted throat and I hear a small whimper in the distance. I realise with a start… it's *me* whimpering. An involuntary sob escapes my throat.

'Hello, you,' said a kind voice. I recognize it immediately - Laura.

I become aware of a soft light turned on beside me. Even though it generates barely a glow, it hurts my eyes. I quickly raise my hand over my eyes to protect them.

'Back with us, then?' she presses with a gentle tone that throws me slightly.

I don't answer. I'm swamped with an overwhelmingly intense confusion. I can't find any words.

'Okay, so do you really want to die from terminal disappointment?' her voice, now back to the Laura that I know.

I gulp hard as the tears stream uncontrollably from me. Turning onto one side, I pull my knees up to my chest and scream so loud I even shock myself.

'Good girl, let it all out,' Laura said encouragingly and pulled me into her with force.

'Please don't let go of me,' I begged in a hoarse whisper. 'Please, don't let go…'

'I'm not going *anywhere*. I'm here. We're all here for you. We've sat with you all night. Mum's been here with Katie. We all flew in yesterday after receiving a distraught call from Siobhan.'

'I'm sorry… I'm so sorry.'

Laura hushed me gently and continued cradling me.

'What's happened to me?' I sobbed, completely exhausted. 'Have I gone mad?'

'You took an overdose. Siobhan and I have had a chat and we think you've had a breakdown. But you will get better, I promise. There's a limit to us all and there's a limit to how much you can cope with too. You have just reached your limit. You're not going mad. You're just at the end of your tether.'

I released myself from Laura's tight hold but continued gripping her shoulders.

'Can I be fixed?' I ask, opening my eyes fully for the first time. In shock, I realised I was in hospital. Seeing Laura's concerned face, I promptly broke into floods of tears again.

'Listen… my reputation's at stake here. We can work through this; slowly and together. If I can't help my own sister, then I'm not much of a psychotherapist, am I?'

I closed my eyes and shook my head, already feeling defeated.

'I'm just so tired.'

'Yes, well, I am not surprised,' interrupted Laura as she opened the curtains, filling the room with blinding light, 'your stomach has been pumped within an inch of its life.'

The horrific pictures in my head flashed back. My stomach churned.

'Do you even remember going to the hospital in the ambulance?' Laura asked, poker-faced as she settled back down beside my bed.

I shrugged feeling slightly ashamed.

'It's all a bit of a blank.'

'Hmm… poor Siobhan found you at the bottom of the stairs.'

'I…'

'She thought you were dead, Tara.' Laura interrupted sharply. 'She said she only came back because she felt so damn guilty for not getting you the sleeping pills that you begged her for. She'd had no end of trouble persuading the doctor to prescribe her some. She said something about being forced to change surgery because her doctor refused to be left alone in a room with her any more. Does any of this ring any bells?

Anyway - if she hadn't have come back with those bloody pills and broken in when she didn't get an answer, God knows where we'd be now.'

'Oh God… I'm sorry to have been such a trouble to everyone. What have I done? Will they ever forgive me?'

'Your friends know you're okay. They're a resilient lot. Meanwhile, you've also had quite a few packages arrive that you bought off the internet. You could open a feckin' pharmacy with the amount of pills you were buying. What on earth were you thinking of?'

I shrugged, keeping my hands over my burning face. I just really wanted Laura to bloody go away.

'Sleeping tablets via the net?' Laura eyed me sternly. 'Deadly concoctions, the lot of them, but I guess you knew that.'

I hung my head in shame, my mouth completely dry.

'Doctors had to fight for your life... do you understand?!'

I nodded.

'Your doctor and I had a meeting. After reading your medical notes, he's more than a little concerned, as am I. The surgery said you've cancelled countless therapist appointments. Why?'

'They couldn't fix me,' I shrugged helplessly.

'Your relationship with Travis seems to have brought on totally obsessive irrational thoughts and behaviour. You became completely fixated on something that could only really be described as a virtual relationship. You *are* fixable, but only if you *want* to be,' she dictated. 'This isn't normally recommended, but I've convinced your doctor to allow me to counsel you,' she said, suddenly becoming very animated. 'He did express some concerns that, as I'm your sister, I won't know when to pull back and when to push.'

I sighed hard, wishing I had never woken up.

Laura ignored my reaction and carried on; 'I have given him my word that I will look after you, but you have to promise me you won't take *anything* without me knowing what it is. In fact, all medication has been removed from your whereabouts.'

I wrenched my head back and let out a moan to the skies (or, more likely, asbestos hospital ceiling), coming to terms with the fact that I couldn't get my hands on more drugs even if I tried. They might as well lock me up and throw away the key.

'Tara, they were about to admit you into a psychiatric unit... Do you understand what that means?'

'Yes... I do, okay?' I tutted, eyeing her coldly, 'you've made your point - lecture over. Lower your voice, Laura. I just need a little painkiller for my head.'

'NO! For God's sake, Tara. You're unbelievable.'

Then Laura checked herself and reverted back to her calmer voice. 'You can't have *anything*. Your body still has toxins in it. I'm waiting for the doctor to pop by to chat with you and hopefully sign you off. He's writing you a prescription for some antidepressants that *I* will be administering to you. Then, we will get you back home.'

I didn't argue. I couldn't be bothered. Part of me wanted to launch into a full 'mind-your-own-fucking-business' verbal attack, but whatever I was feeling stayed trapped inside. I had nothing left to give. I felt tangled and twisted. Every vein in my body was leaking pain and confusion. Dark feelings and raw emotions still rolled over every inch of me. *Surely it's was easier to be dead than alive*, I thought, as I slowly turned to face the wall.

God, I am such a screw-up. I was and always will be a failure on so many levels. I couldn't even manage a simple task of suicide.

I came home the following day. I was ushered straight to bed and left alone while my mum and sisters presumably tried to tackle the devastation I had left downstairs. It looked like I had been burgled.

'Today is the first day of the rest of your life,' Laura chanted when she burst into my bedroom, presumably on the next stage of Operation Muck-Out. She continued to chat away happily whilst picking up the debris from my bedroom floor.

'Lay down till we get some food inside you,' insisted Laura, as I attempted to get out of bed. 'Mum and Katie will be up in a minute. They've gone to get some provisions in. Now you've had some rest, there are things we need to talk through. Things that have happened, that I'm almost sure you're unaware of.'

I cupped my throbbing throat, vaguely remembering that awful rubber tube going down into my stomach. The thought made me shudder. I couldn't imagine anything happening in the recent past that was any worse than that.

'Did you know your Salon has closed till further notice?' Asked Laura, settling gingerly on the edge of the rubbish-strewn bed, her face filled with concern.

'Really?' I countered, pretending to give a shit (when I really couldn't have cared less).

With a barely discernible tut, Laura got up to leave my bedroom,

'I'm putting the kettle on,' she called back over her shoulder. I slouched back down into the bed, wearily pulling the duvet around me. I wasn't quite sure how I was feeling, but the words 'unbearable' and 'miserable' came to mind.

Hearing the kettle boiling downstairs felt strangely comforting. It was nice to know someone was here with me, even if it was Laura. To be fair, I knew deep down she was the best person to have by my side. Well, that's if I did really want to live. The trouble was, one minute I did - the next I didn't.

My eyes searched around my bedroom. Everything felt so strange. My recent memories were all jumbled together - it was impossible to make sense of them all. I knew bad things and bad feelings had taken place in this room. I had spent so much time in here, counting cobwebs, looking at cracks in the ceiling and studying anything around me to take away the pain and grief.

I caught my breath as my eyes settled on the fur coat laying redundant, half-on and half-off my chair. The half trailing on the floor was grubby with dust and grime. I hated that coat. I despised the very sight of it. I closed my eyes to shut out the offending sight and turned away.

My attention was caught by the sound of Laura chatting on the phone downstairs, I needed the toilet badly. As weak as I was, I'd have to try to get up. As I pushed the duvet off me, the stale smell of my bedding hit me. I also became aware for the first time there was an array of crap littered all over my bed. Clothes, notebooks, makeup boxes and a selection of self-help books were strewn about everywhere. I shook my head in disbelief. Then, I gasped as I spied the snapped heels of my precious Louboutins. Four of them. Snatching them up, I tucked them quickly under my once pure white pillow with utter shame. *All four pairs?* I had no idea where the remains of the shoes were.

I didn't want Laura to see this, or anyone else for that matter. I eased my legs around to the side of bed, suddenly desperate to find the rest of the shoes. I couldn't see them anywhere though.

I was interrupted in my search by the sound of Laura coming up the stairs. I leapt quickly to my feet, but light-headedness instantly engulfed me. Dizzily, I tottered to the chest of draws and clung to it for support. Slowly, I began to make my way to the bathroom; using the walls as support, my eyes searching the floors as I went. I finally reached my goal and flopped down onto the toilet, trembling. I hung my head down in my hands, unable to find the strength to keep it upright.

'Here's your tea, Tara,' called Laura from the bedroom. 'Your bread is growing the next best antibiotic known to man.'

I sobbed quietly to myself, unable to move.

'Go away, just for a minute. Please, I beg you.'

Before I knew it, Laura was in the bathroom with me crouched down and holding me once again.

'Tara… come on… back to bed, you need food and fluid…'

I sighed heavily as I looked up and caught sight of Laura's watering eyes. I don't think I'd *ever* seen Laura cry before. I was completely and utterly thrown by her sadness. *Maybe she is human after all,* I thought.

'My bed smells awful, I can't get back in there,' I said, raising a slight smile as she walked me back to my bedroom. My breathing was now slowly coming back to a bearable pace.

'Hmm, *that* I agree with,' Laura said, wrinkling her nose as she eased me down onto my bedroom chair, having deftly dropped the fur coat to the floor unceremoniously.

'There should be some clean covers in the airing cupboard,' I said, still stunned by her tears. I watched Laura begin to efficiently strip my dirty, fake-tan-covered bedding. Before I knew it, Laura had thrown that bastard fur coat over me. I pushed it away as though it was poison.

'I see you've been giving that fur coat a haircut,' Laura pointed out as she struggled with the duvet. 'The arm of it is downstairs.'

'Oh God,' I sighed, rolling my eyes, cringing at the thought.

I watched wordlessly as Laura tossed the heels out from under my pillow. She said nothing though; she just turned and stared at me for a few moments. *I wish she wouldn't do that.* Within a few seconds she was back, perfecting her hospital corners.

'In!' commanded Laura, escorting me back to bed.

'Laura, he's, he's… having a baby,' I sobbed. Just saying the words hit me like a ton of bricks. 'And she's… only a baby herself. And I've gone into the menopause too. Me… *me* - in the menopause!'

'Tara… I went into the menopause *years* ago.'

'What? …Really?' I asked, completely stunned. I patted the bed, indicating for her to sit with me.

'Yes, *really*. It's just part of life now. It happens to every woman in the world. It's fine. Just think: no more heavy periods. It's great. I'd just embrace it if I were you. It is what it is. Get a bit of HRT in you and you'll be a new woman.'

'So you don't feel old and useless?' I asked, fumbling with the corner of the duvet and wiping my tears with it.

'Children *aren't* everything,' insisted Laura.

'But I've always wanted a baby. I know I won't ever feel complete without one. My baby would have never left me. It would've always needed me.'

'Children are merely borrowed,' said Laura rubbing my shoulder gently. 'They too, will eventually leave the nest and make their own way in life. Nothing stands still forever. If something's not growing and evolving, it's dying.'

'But I wanted to dress a baby up in beautiful designer clothes, take it to the park and baby groups… I've got so much love to give, and nowhere to put it. It hurts so much.'

I pulled the covers over my face, hiding my tears.

'When you're ready and feeling stronger, get a pooch. You can stick it in one of your designer handbags.'

'It's not the same and you know it!' I muffled through the sheets.

'No, granted, it's not the same. It's cheaper. No tantrums, no arguments and they're *always* pleased to see you. Frankly, it's bliss if you ask me. And by the way…' said Laura easing the sheets away from my face, 'my friend Kath just recently rescued a Bichon Frise; it's the cutest thing I've *ever* seen. A whole ball of white fluff - she's even put a diamante collar round her neck. I've got pictures of her on my phone if you want…'

'I don't want a bloody dog!' I snapped, interrupting Laura and pushing her phone away from me. 'I want a baby and I want Travis. You get another bloody dog if you want one!'

'Kath called her Gucci,' Laura continued, ignoring my outburst, 'she hadn't been treated very well, the poor little thing.'

'If I had a little white fluffy doggie,' I sniffed eventually, 'I would've called her Miss Dior.'

'That name is *so* you,' jibed Laura, smiling. 'As for me, well, I am taking time to enjoy my life now. I enjoyed the children and still do, but they've grown up now so it's allowed to be all about *me*. And, as for that Easter egg you were supposedly 'dating' Tara… Well what can I say? Gorgeous on the outside, but very disappointing on the inside, when you took the foil and ribbons off. He was - and is – empty, Tara. He was never, *ever*, going to be good father material.'

'I miss him,' I shrugged helplessly, 'I know it's wrong, but I *do*.'

'You've got to stop chasing every shiny thing you see. He was like a virus with shoes on.'

I hung my head again.

'Is she awake?' bellowed Katie, bounding up the stairs.

I wanted to hide under the duvet. I felt ashamed that Katie and mum were seeing me like this. But I was too weak to move a muscle. I just had to brace myself.

'Hey Tara! Jeez - you look… interesting,' said Katie, brightly. 'Jesus, I forgot how good-looking the fellas were in England. Even mammy was chatted up by the shop assistant. At her age too… can you believe that?'

'Katie, I'm sorry you have to see me this way,' I said with a wry smile.

'No worries at all,' she grinned, planting a kiss on my forehead. 'Laura will get you sorted good and proper, won't you sis… if not, can I have first dibs on your clothes?' asked Katie grabbing my hand and winking at me.

I cracked a faint smile.

'I have to ask you something though, mammy told me that when you were younger, you borrowed her metal nail-file and filed down your big rabbit teeth, is that right?' asked Katie with a baffled expression.

'Hey pet,' interrupted mum, out of breath from climbing the stairs. She threw her arms around me and gave Katie a stern look. 'Don't be telling fibs, Katie, I never said no such thing about her teeth.'

'You did so, mammy. You said that she had enormous rabbit teeth.'

'Tara, I merely said that your head took a little while to catch up with the size of your teeth, that's all,' said mum interrupting, 'Will I run you a nice bubble bath pet? Don't you take any notice of your sister.'

'I think mammy's trying to be polite… You *do* smell bad, real bad. But I got you some nice body spray if you wanna use it after your bath?' asked Katie, her usual insensitive self.

'Katie that's so thoughtful, thank you… I might just do that later.' I nodded.

'No bother… can I go through your wardrobe?'

I smiled, despite myself. Even a near suicide didn't deter my little sis.

'Boiled bacon and cabbage for lunch,' said mum, theatrically licking her lips in my direction as though I was still three years old.

'Katie! Are they my Jimmy Choo pumps you're wearing?' I barked, sitting up.

'Not at all. They're mine! Sweet Jesus, you really are a complete loon. You gave them to me.'

I tutted in annoyance, she was lucky I didn't have it in me to argue it out with her.

'Mum… I'm sorry to put you through this – especially… well, you know – after what Katie did,' I said, eyeing Katie, who was now deep in my wardrobe.

'It's okay. Just promise me one thing, pet,' said mum, pointedly ignoring my reference to Katie's errant past, 'please stop putting that poison in yourself. I know that's what made your head go, well, strange. I had the fright of my life earlier when I found a sleeve of a fur coat downstairs. I thought you had killed a cat or something. That's that Botox you have sending you loopy. You're just so beautiful as you are pet.'

I looked straight at mum. I have to confess, I was beginning to quite enjoy the attention.

'I just want my girls to be happy. Saints preserve us. That's not too much to ask for is it?'

It was now Laura's turn to pipe up; 'Botox wouldn't do that to you mum. Leak, I mean, into your brain. Although, studies have shown that people who have aesthetic work or plastic surgery carried out do often suffer with low self-esteem.'

Hmm... I vaguely remembered Sheila refusing me more Botox and fillers, questioning my mental state; I had thought she was just being awkward. Quite the reverse, now I think about it. Even she knew, back then, that I was going too far.

'What a gobshite that Jackie's husband was, eh?' Katie pronounced as she popped out from the wardrobe, beaming. 'And that Jayde! Who would have thought? The dirty bitch.' Katie lobbed my heel-less Louboutins out of the wardrobe with a grimace.

'Katie, not now,' Laura snapped in a low voice, 'I haven't discussed that with Tara yet.'

'What?' I said, suddenly alert. 'What's happened to Jackie's husband and Jayde? Oh my God. Don't tell me they're together?'

'Yep - he's a perv,' said Katie with glee, still knee deep in my clothes. 'And he's at least thirty years older than her!'

'Katie… get out of my wardrobe please,' I said, feeling confused again. God only knows what else I've stashed in there.

'Tara, it's all on your phone. There are tons of voicemails, text messages and missed calls from Jackie,' said Laura shaking her head, 'I didn't think you were ready to hear that just yet.'

'I can't believe it. Poor Jackie. How could Jayde, sweet little Jayde, do that?'

'Well, that doesn't matter right now. Without sounding heartless, this means you now have no staff left at Glamma-Puss. James tried to manage the Salon in your absence. Even Siobhan tried to pass herself off as a beautician in the evenings, after she'd finished her work - God help us. Don't worry though, it's nothing that can't be fixed. Granted, it may require a lawyer or two.'

'She was trying to do backs, sacks and cracks,' Katie interrupted, cutting Laura off, 'Siobhan couldn't get any models to practise on and James wouldn't allow her near his crown jewels. So in the end she practised on Barry [her beloved blow-up doll] and melted his bollocks!'

I cringed and sank further down my bed. Clearly, my Salon's reputation was now in shreds.

'She tried to patch Barry up, but he looked like a melted burns victim,' said Katie, feigning deep shock. 'His memorial service was last week. I wanted to come over but mammy wouldn't let me.'

'I lit a candle at mass for him, poor old Barry,' said mum, solemnly shaking her head and blessing herself.

'Mum, it was a blow up doll. He's not real!' I wished I'd never purchased that bloody Barry in the first place!'

'Siobhan threw caution to the wind,' giggled Katie, oblivious to the fact I wasn't finding this at all funny. 'She booked in some furry blokes and went for it. Siobhan rocks. She burned the idiots' arses, so she did.'

'And now she could be facing a lawsuit and that's not funny at all.' Laura broke in. She didn't sound happy and was glaring fixedly at the wardrobe door, clearly trying to get Katie's attention.

'Jeez, I mean, I like a man to be a *man*,' Katie mumbled as she paired the heel-less Louboutins. 'I mean, what's the point of your man acting like a pussy? I have a perfect pussy of my own, I don't need another one.'

'Language, young lady! Lord bless us and save us,' said mum, blessing herself all over again.

'So what's going to happen now?' I asked. While I was completely horrified with the news from the Salon, I was also distracted by Katie holding up my Louboutins. I was just waiting for her to question the state they were in. *Oh God. The next thing I know, this will be all over Facebook.*

'It's all a bit of a mess. And it's all been happening right under your nose,' said Laura compassionately. 'But now is *certainly* not the right day to talk about it.'

I burst into floods of tears.

'It's all a mess. A great big mess; my life, my Salon, everything.'

'Ah c'mon now pet,' mum said, stepping forward and trying to comfort me. There was nothing she could do though. I was distraught.

'Tara, can I borrow this?' Katie came out the wardrobe holding up my silk Yves Saint Laurent shirt.

'Yes… err, no. You can't. Katie - please, not now!' I screamed in a ferocious temper, reliving my last fateful evening with Travis at the Salon where I was wearing just that shirt. 'I can't breathe… I can't breathe.'

'Everybody out!' ordered Laura. 'Katie, get out of Tara's wardrobe now. Go downstairs. Mum and Katie, OUT. NOW. Mum… MUM, your bacon's burning. Breathe… Tara, take deep breaths… It's okay. It's okay.'

'But, I've no bacon on yet pet…' stammered mum, looking confused.

'Then go and put some on!' Laura snapped brutally.

'Right so,' said mum, turning back and looking at me with tears in her eyes.

I inhaled deeply, closing my eyes, revelling in the silence now it was just the two of us. 'Will this ever end, Laura?' I asked.

Laura tripped over the over-flowing ashtray on the floor as she came to perch on the side of the bed. 'Do you want a cigarette?' she asked with a smile, pushing it with her toe.

I smiled weakly as she passed me my tea, 'Love one.'

'When was the last time you laughed, or smiled?' Laura asked, getting up to close the bedroom door and open the windows.

'I don't know,' I shrugged, sipping my tea.

'Mum's reading Fifty Shades of Grey,' Laura grinned and scrunched her face up in disgust.

We both threw back our heads and began to laugh. And it felt good, it really did.

We talked for a while about nothing in particular. I know it was 'what Laura did' but I had to admit, she was feckin' good at it. I really did feel much calmer. It was as though a thick mist was beginning to clear from my head.

After a few more cups of tea and a pause for a bacon butty, Laura decided I was strong enough to start the next stage of my recovery. That is what I assumed anyway, because otherwise she would never have broached her next question.

'Okay Tara, a breakdown doesn't just happen overnight,' she began, looking searchingly at me. 'There will have been a buildup. Can you recall a trigger?'

I took a deep breath. Was I ready for this, I wondered?

'Travis,' I said at last, with a sigh and a shrug of my shoulders, 'I ran into that baby girlfriend of his when I was on my way to win him back, wearing…' I paused, hardly able to say the words, 'that feckin' fur coat. I sat holding a sick-bag for her on the plane. She's barely out of school and she's pregnant. All ripe and glowing with his sodding baby inside her! I thought I was pregnant too. Then, I found out at the same time that I'm *not* pregnant – but I'm in the shitting menopause! It's all made me feel so… useless… old and redundant.'

'But… do you *really* want a baby?' asked Laura.

'Well… that's not the point!' I added bitterly. 'Actually yes. I do want a baby. It means everything to me. It would make me feel whole – complete – I suppose.'

'Really?' said Laura, cocking her head to one side, obviously trying to make me think about what I had just said.

'Owh it's too hard to explain, I don't want to talk about it,' I said, beginning to feel the mists falling again.

'Okay,' said Laura.

'Everyone leaves me in the end, Laura,' I blurted out, shocking myself at my own admission.

Laura remained silent. She just tilted her head to one side again. 'Who is everyone?' she asked quietly after some time.

I remained silent.

'Do you miss dad?' she asked a few seconds later.

I always got a stabbing pain in the pit of my stomach whenever I thought of dad.

'Terribly,' I finally answered, closing my eyes and picturing his face.

'Why… why didn't you help me with him?' I said, turning suddenly to face her. I felt such a rage erupt within me - I wanted to slap her.

'You, mum and Katie left me to deal with dad on my own and I couldn't manage him with his illness and everything else. You,' I added bitterly, 'just had your nose stuck in books, ignoring the fact that our dad was sick.'

'He was an alcoholic, Tara.'

'But why… oh why, didn't *you* do something?' I pleaded bitterly, almost spitting the question out.

'Did you ever notice what books I had my nose 'stuck in' Tara?'

'No, I wasn't interested. I was too busy looking out for dad!' I glared at Laura angrily. 'While you were reading shit, our dad was losing his mind.'

Laura looked horrified.

'I was… I was reading up on alcoholism and researching schizophrenia,' her voice shook slightly. 'I was convinced if I kept reading, I would find a cure for him. Don't forget, I was hurting too…'

For a moment, there was pure, undiluted silence between us.

'I didn't know.' I said, shaking my head, letting out a pain-filled sigh. 'How could I have got that *so* wrong?'

'It was my nerdy way of coping I guess,' Laura added, pulling tissues out of her pocket.

We both sniffed hard as she handed me a crumpled tissue. 'I read every book that I could - most of which I didn't understand – but I just kept reading and reading in the hope of finding a cure for dad. I wanted to wake up one morning and be able to wave a magic wand and make our family… well, okay again. It wasn't easy for any of us. I could never bring any of my friends back to the house like they could. I never knew what mood dad would be in from one day to the next.'

'I had no idea.' I said shaking my head.

'We were very young - we weren't expected to know what to do.'

I nodded. She was right.

Staring outside the window, I felt something shift inside of me. I had carried that resentment towards Laura for years.

'*We* were the children, *he* was the parent,' Laura continued, her mind also now drifting back to those dark days. 'You know, poor mum became so frightened of dad. She feared for her safety as he became more and more unpredictable. Can you imagine; the man you've been in love with all your life, suddenly starting to hear voices? Voices telling him that *he* was the chosen one? And he had an evil wife?'

I just gulped hard and grabbed Laura's hand tightly.

'Poor mum… she had to deal with Katie, who was a young baby back then,' Laura added empathically.

'Hmm… she was a nightmare of a baby though,' I recalled, 'she was always attached to mum's hip, howling.'

'Why do you think that was?' Laura asked, grabbing my other hand, searching my face for some sign I understood.

'She was spoilt?'

Laura shook her head and smiled pitifully at me.

'Okay, let me put this another way. Katie was always crying, right? Do you think she was scared because her mammy and daddy were always fighting? We were at school when the worst was going on Tara. Katie had full view of the damage every day.'

'I've never thought about it like that before... Oh God, poor Katie.'

I felt suddenly ashamed and wanted to hold Katie to make her feel safe.

'Mum was crying constantly, begging dad to get help,' Laura continued, barely hearing my replies. Her eyes filled with tears.

'Dad just carried on getting worse and accused mum of having affairs, making out he had detectives following her - sometimes worse than that. He even maintained that Katie wasn't his child. Can you imagine?'

I was speechless. The pain in my chest gripped me further.

'Mum had to leave, Tara. You didn't want to come, even though we all begged you. It broke mum's heart leaving you behind. Don't you remember the night we all left? I clearly remember saying that you should keep an eye on dad and I would keep an eye on mum and Katie. It wasn't fair, I know, but the family was divided. It was divided by a terrible situation, not because we didn't love each other.'

Laura and I sobbed together for the first time. Our whole family had been caught in the crossfire of living a life with an alcoholic.

'I know you didn't really understand this at the time and neither did I, but I understand it now and it's so important that you understand it too. Mum really loved dad, Tara, but he wasn't well. Alcoholism is an illness. None of us got away without being damaged. My marriage failed, you're an emotional wreck and Katie became an addict herself. None of us could help someone who didn't want to be helped.' continued Laura knowingly.

'Travis played a very large part in this recent episode, but I don't think he was the *sole* trigger for where you ended up. If you want to fully recover, we need to dig a little deeper for a greater understanding. You don't need mind-numbing pills, or a brood of perfect children, or some phony love-God to make you complete. You are already *the* most incredible woman. It is time you started to realise that and learn to love your crazy, funny self.'

CHAPTER SIXTEEN

Over the following few months, Laura slowly pieced me back together. She was the epitome of patience, as I spent days and nights sobbing, screaming, shouting and working through many painful issues; from our dad, Travis and not being a mum; to being a boss, a friend, a sister and issues regarding my low self-esteem.

In Laura's professional opinion, the key to my cure was to change how I perceived myself. I tried to tell her it was because I was wired up all wrong, but she wasn't having any of it. Laura forced me (and I mean physically forced me) to go out for walks with her to build up my strength and get me out of the house. I was terrified at first, I often wondered if I would I ever be the same again. Would I ever feel normal? I'd forgotten what that felt like.

But the world looked different now. I didn't know why. It just did.

Laura was my lifeline as we slowly rebuilt what I had smashed apart. We spoke of our father on extremely deep levels, leaving out none of the pain, sadness or guilt. Together, as sisters, we bonded tightly for the first time. It was so painful for us both, yet we helped each other as Laura too found herself revealing issues that had lain unresolved.

We drank tea until it was oozing out of our pores, as we chatted, laughed and cried.

One of Laura's biggest bugbears turned out to be my fixation on my looks. Apparently it was an indication of how negatively I felt about myself.

'Let's start with the fact that you have beautiful, piercing blue eyes and yet you wear coloured contact lenses. Why?' She asked.

I shrugged.

'Okay, think about that one for a moment. Why do you cover your beautiful milky skin in orange muck that quite frankly makes you look silly?'

Sometimes Laura was so annoying.

'Laura, you're meant to be helping me. Not making me feel even worse!'

'I'm peeling back the layers. I'm trying to get to *you,* the real you. The real *you* is hidden, covered up. You are beautiful, but I know you can't see it. You never have.'

And, so the process went on.

After she'd decided we'd made sufficient progress, Laura allowed Siobhan and James to come back into my life (and not a moment too soon). The pair of them had been bugging Laura almost daily to spend time with me and I think she finally relented as much for herself as for me.

I felt a glimmer of excitement as I heard them both bounding up the stairs together, like a couple of children on Christmas morning.

'Hey, you guys,' shouted Laura after them both, 'Try and keep it as calm and as light as possible, eh? She's still quite fragile. I'll be downstairs if you need anything.'

'No problem!' they chorused, flinging the bedroom door open and bombing on top of my bed like a pair of naughty kids.

'Hi,' I said tearfully, hugging them both and doing my best to ignore their matching, fluffy fuchsia onesies, 'it's so damn good to see you!'

'(Mmmwha, mmmwha, mmmwha) We're just so glad you're back with us!' they said, smothering me in hugs and slobbering kisses.

Then suddenly, in unison, they turned their backs on me. The backs of their onesies were both emblazoned with the words 'Team Tara' in day-glow yellow.

'Team Tara!' they both yelled.

'We've had these printed in your honour,' announced, James proudly.

'We've got you one too!' exclaimed Siobhan excitedly, jumping up and down shaking a huge plastic-bag in my direction.

'And black sequined UGG slippers,' interrupted James, jumping off the bed to do a few ballerina-style pirouettes to demonstrate. 'Look how sparkly they are.'

Then, with a wince he flung his slippered foot up and over his head.

'You still look gorgeous,' pouted James, as he returned to the bed, adjusting his crown jewels with watering eyes. 'Being sexy never takes a day off.'

Then, before I knew what was happening, the pair of them dragged me up and out of my bed, stripping me out of my old PJs and shimmying me into my 'Team Tara' fuchsia onesie along with the sequined slippers.

'But Tara just got a whole lot sexier,' Siobhan bellowed energetically.

I couldn't help myself. I felt instantly lifted.

After they had both finished bouncing all over me, and the three of us did a quick ring-a-ring-a-rosey, I put my arms around the pair of them and sighed heavily before flopping breathlessly back down to the bed.

'I'm sorry guys,' I began tearfully, pulling them both down and closer to me. Our three heads now rested into each other's.

'For what?' asked Siobhan.

'For everything,' I shrugged.

'Nonsense,' retorted James with a dismissive hand gesture, 'anyway, you're back now from, err... wherever you've been in your little head, and now you're getting better. That's all that matters.'

'We love you,' James said pouting, 'we miss you. Glamma-Puss misses you too!'

He kicked off his sequined slippers and snuggled down closer beside me.

'We come baring more gifts,' added Siobhan, bolting out of the bed.

'Ta-dah! Wine. We bring wine!'

'Shhh... don't let Laura hear you,' I whispered urgently, while inadvertently licking my lips.

Good old Siobhan, she even managed to produce three wine glasses from her bag.

'Okay,' mouthed Siobhan removing the cap, 'it needs to breathe for a while, so I'll just leave it for a bit.'

She placed the wine and glasses on the table and tiptoed back into bed for another cuddle.

'So, come on you guys, what's been happening out there in your crazy worlds?' I asked.

'Well, I've been head-hunted,' gloated Siobhan, flicking her ponytail at us both, 'by a sexy wexy, crazy s-c-i-e-n-tist!'

'I'm always getting head-hunted,' snorted James, 'it's no big deal.'

'Not that sort of head-hunted, ya big gobshite.'

'Hush James,' I giggled shaking my head at the pair of them, 'let Siobhan speak. Carry on.'

'But-I-wanna-tell-you-*my*-story,' winged James in a whiney baby voice.

'Soon, I may be packing me rucksack and setting off for the Arctic,' she said whilst raising her hand up, indicating faraway shores. 'I've adopted a baby polar bear and may go and see it.'

'Oh!' squealed James, 'I've always wanted to adopt a chimpanzee. We would have matching diamante sunglasses and a vest top saying 'we like monkey business'... I just never got around to it,' mused James thoughtfully.

'Err... okay,' I said, sensing where this conversation was heading. Bless them both. I don't think I would ever be allowed to adopt a baby now with my medical history and notes. The thoughts of not ever having a baby broke the surface of my conscience a dozen times a day.

'Well,' sighed James clutching at his heart dramatically, 'Christian finally got the job of his dreams. The *'tea, coffee or me' job.'*

'I'm lost, what does that mean?' I asked, confused.

'He's a trolley dolly!' spat James furiously, 'I wanted to be a trolley dolly... but I didn't get the job... and he did. It's not fair.' He pouted and clicked his tongue.

'But James, you're my nail technician. You can't leave Glamma-Puss.'

'Well hurry up and open it back up then!' James insisted.

'I will, I promise… soon.' I said, suddenly feeling a strong inner-resolve.

'James,' snapped Siobhan, 'what the feck are you doing?'

'Checking the wine is breathing darling. It's not, so I'm giving it mouth to mouth resuscitation.'

'Feck off with you, James.'

'It's delightful and plummy,' commented James in laughter, hiding the bottle in-between his legs.

I was laughing. Actually, really belly-laughing. It was something I never thought I would ever do again. It felt wonderful.

'Tara,' said Siobhan suddenly serious and trying to catch her breath, 'I've got a letter for you. It's from Katie; she came to see me before she went back to Dublin with your mammy.'

'Okay,' I said, puzzled. Taking the letter from her, I opened it and read it out loud;

To my sister Tara (AKA head nut case) ☺

By now I hope you are well on the way to feeling better. If you wanna do drugs in the future, come to me and I'll get them sorted for you, but you have to share them. (Only joking).

Mammy and Laura have told me that your baby oven has blown its fuse and over-heated itself and can't be repaired.

I'd just like to let you know... my oven is your oven. I have already discussed this situation with James. He's offered to have a party in his designer pants. So between James and I, we can make you a sprog.

Siobhan wants to be the birthing partner.

Think about it. I love you.

Katie x

For a while I said nothing, I let the thoughts of what I had just read run through my head like cool water on a migraine.

'You okay?' they both asked in soft, comforting voices.

My voice was constricted with joy. I grabbed both their hands in gratitude, injecting love into them.

'To absent friends,' sniffed Siobhan handing brimming glasses of wine to James and me and raising her own glass.

'To Katie,' I sobbed, shocked by her thoughtfulness and surprise offer of becoming a surrogate mother for me.

'And Barry,' toasted Siobhan, 'may God forgive me for singeing his bollocks. May he be resting in plastic heaven.'

'To Katie and Barry,' we all cheered tearfully.

Though Siobhan and James were exhausting, it was so good to see them both again. To be honest, I felt more energised by their visit than the endless hours I spent talking with Laura. Maybe I am being unfair here. I know Laura had done an awful lot to help my recovery. Feck, without her I'd still be gibbering in my bed, or worse.

My reunion with Siobhan and James forced me to face up to what I was going to do about the Salon. As we talked about the various options, I realised how strongly I felt about the place. I was proud of it. I didn't want to give it up.

As if Laura hadn't taken enough on her plate, she decided to take charge of a plan to get the Salon back up and running. That also meant taking charge of Siobhan and James who were both eager to get involved, but taking charge of those two wasn't for the faint-hearted. Laura was pretty good at it though. She held court with the two of them, pointing out random facts, figures and preaching about 'synergising'. Neither Siobhan nor James questioned or dared to refuse Laura's suggestions.

My sister declared that our first mission was to get money coming in again, as I had not even managed to pay my mortgage, let alone the rent on the Salon or staff wages.

It didn't help that financially I was an absolute mess. I needed to raise cash (and fast).

'Open a high-class brothel,' James suggested, 'you can be the Madame - actually, on second thoughts... Captain Laura can be the Madame. No one would dare mess with her. She could whip anyone into place with that tongue of hers. I can so see her as a dominatrix, tying up a man-slave to a bed and whipping his poor ass. Scary thought,' shivered James.

'I've got it!' piped up Siobhan, slapping her thigh with excitement. 'You can still sell your story, it's not too late! Do a 'kiss and tell' on that gobshite Travis. Call it... Death at the Blarney Stone.'

'I can't do that,' I said, speaking with conviction. 'I wouldn't lower myself. Plus, I would have to re-live the whole poxy ordeal all over again. No, that's definitely not the answer.'

'Don't be a wuss, he deserves it,' Siobhan assured me fluttering her hands excitedly. 'The world needs to know what he did to you.'

'Siobhan, I really don't want the world to know that he broke my heart and got a girl half my age pregnant.'

'I don't mean that bit. I mean the bit where he slithered his slippery finger in your tea-towel holder.'

'NO WAY! Jesus,' I huffed, hysteria beginning to bubble below the surface, 'I would never be able to look anyone in the eye ever again!'

In the end, I turned down most of their wackier ideas. I did, however, relent to selling some of my stuff, even that poisonous fur coat. Mum had done a fantastic invisible mend on the sleeve before she and Katie had gone back to Dublin. I let Siobhan open me up a new eBay account and do the listings for me:

Seller: Gay-bay69

For sale

<u>*Dolce and Gabbana Mink Fur Coat*</u>

As new, apart from left arm that has been sewn back into place, (easily unpicked though, if you wish to cut other arm off using this fine fur as a long, trendy gilet instead). Could also be used as a rug for shagging on in front of a cosy fire.

*Has been **nearly** touched by high profile celeb, who will remain anonymous for **now**.*

All offers will be considered.

After that, Siobhan and James rummaged through my wardrobe, sourcing bits to sell. In no time at all they had amassed an impressive pile of my beautiful, once prized-handbags, designer clothes and even my jewellery. Everything was slapped on eBay and I really didn't care one bit.

Laura placed an advert on line asking for experienced staff to replace Jayde and Jackie. When I thought about the pair of them, it made me feel so sad. I missed Jackie and I missed the Jayde that I once knew. I still found it so shocking that Jayde would even consider having an affair with Jackie's husband.

Poor Jackie. Poor, poor Jackie. We'd both gone through similar situations in the recent past. Both our men had gone off with younger women. The thought sent shivers down my spine. Jackie had been with her husband since they were teenagers. *How was she coping? I wished she would make contact.*

My mind wandered once more to Travis and his young, pregnant girlfriend. She would be due soon. My mouth filled with acidic vomit at the thought. *Stop thinking like that, Tara,* I chided myself. *It's over! You are better off without him. You've got lots of good things to look forward to.*

When the dreaded day of the interviews came, I have to confess I didn't feel positive at all. I had to bring myself to face the busy outside world for the first time in months. The interviews were to be held at the Salon, because I couldn't very well invite candidates to my sickbed. There were two positions to be filled; one to run and manage the hairdressing, the other to look after the beauty side.

As I tried to work out what I should wear, I noticed the days where I obsessed about what I looked like, were long gone. I managed to get myself dressed in something other than a tracksuit to appease Laura, throwing on some skinny jeans, a dark blue sweater and some comfy old brown boots. I scraped what was left of my now-very-thin hair into a ponytail and applied a little mascara.

Arriving at the Salon like greeting an old ghost. Memories flashed through my mind as I stood hesitating outside the front door. Eventually, after waiting respectfully for a few moments,

Laura impatiently grabbed the keys and opened the door. She held the door wide and motioned that I should go in. After taking a deep breath, I entered Glamma-Puss once again

As the familiar sights and smells filled my head, my eyes flooded with tears. I trembled from head to toe as Laura held out her hand to encourage me further inside.

'Tara, it's okay. What you're experiencing is just association,' she said reassuringly. 'It's normal and it's okay.'

Slowly letting go of her hand, I walked around the Salon; taking in the old smells, remembering flashes of laughter, scenes of sadness and the place where I once stood allowing Travis to take advantage of me.

My eyes travelled over to the staffroom where I once sat for hours having text-sex with Travis. Of course, I also spent more hours in there on edge and staring at the walls waiting for texts from him too. It all felt like a lifetime ago. The Salon was cold, lifeless even. There was dust and grime everywhere. It was as though someone had died in there. My heart and my head pounded with the memories.

'Greetings, ladies!' James chorused as he came bounding into the Salon. 'How are you, Lady Laura?' he enquired with a curtsey. 'You okay, Tara, darling? Looks like you've seen a ghost. Shall I pop the kettle on?'

The very fact James was here made everything feel better. Within moments, the music was playing, the kettle was boiling and it felt quite… dare I say, 'normal' (whatever that was).

The roar of a motorbike outside interrupted my thoughts. James almost knocked me over as he dashed to the window to take a peek.

'Oh my,' James drooled, shaking his head from side to side whilst peeking through the Salon window, 'utterly, slutterly gorgeous.'

'Is she?' I asked very nervously, hoping she wasn't *that* beautiful.

'Not *her*. *Him.* I love, love, *love* a man in black skintight leathers. And look how he's parked to the left. I wouldn't mind getting my hands on his helmet.'

'James, please come away from the window, you're making me jumpy,' I begged.

James completely ignored me as he raced to get to the door first.

'Well… hello gorgeous man, come in, come in,' he simpered. 'Oh sorry - *and* you dear - I didn't see you there. *Where are my manners?'*

'James, it's Camilla that's come for the interview, not her boyfriend,' I said, feeling slightly exasperated. Not for the first time, I wondered if I had the strength for James' antics.

'Hello, you must be Tara,' announced Camilla, removing her helmet and giving me a smile. 'Sorry for the entrance. My car is in for a service, so my brother Lewis brought me here. Please excuse my flat helmet hair,' she added, fluffing it back into place.

I liked her instantly.

'Ah, your *brother,* even better,' James exclaimed, his eyes practically raping the poor man. 'Your brother must come in and wait for you, I absolutely insist. I'm more than happy to keep him company. You don't mind, do you Tara?' said James, as he pulled Camilla's brother past me.

'Well, I, erm… yeah I…' I stammered. *The little bastard, that's the last thing I want! Why does he always put me into awkward situations like this?'*

'Marvellous, magnificent. That's settled then. In you both pop. Come along…' James said over his shoulder, already halfway into the Salon with Lewis in tow.

'Laura, I need you… I need you right now please!' I called into the staffroom where she had disappeared to use the computer. Meanwhile I glared at James with gritted teeth as he ignored me.

'My my… what a beautiful big thing you have parked there Mister… err… err…' said James, planting himself in front of Lewis in his most provocative pose.

'Lewis. My name's Lewis,' he smiled.

Glancing over nervously, I could see Lewis looked amused by the exchange, but luckily not too phased.

'Yep, she's a Ducati 998 S,' he went on.

'How does it feel to have something so big and throbbing between your legs?' asked James. 'Is it as wide as it looks? I'd just love to take a ride on it. By the look of it, I might be a little sore afterwards, but I'm sure I can take it.'

'James - can you take Lewis into the staffroom, please?' I tried to stay calm and professional, but by now I was fuming with him. I didn't want him to blow my chance of getting decent staff because of his ridiculous flirting.

'Sorry, Tara, I can see it's inconvenient for me to stay,' said Lewis, turning to me apologetically. 'Shall I pop back and pick Camilla up after the interview? How long do you think you'll be? An hour?'

Great. Now I look like a total bitch as well as a loon.

'No, no it's fine, I just wasn't expecting… erm…' Then I dried up. I didn't know what else to say. It had been a while since I had spoken to anyone outside my close-knit group of family and friends. Why did the first person have to be an Adonis on a motorbike? I was too scared to even make eye contact, but strangely, he looked vaguely familiar.

I turned back to James, 'James, make some drinks please, while Laura and I have a chat with Camilla. And James, behave yourself, please…'

'Don't worry, Tara darling, Lewis is in safe hands with me,' James said, sounding very sensible (even though his facial expression said otherwise).

Forcing myself to focus on the here-and-now, I politely smiled at Lewis, but I still wouldn't allow my eyes to meet with his.

Laura and I sat down with Camilla. The interview lasted much longer than I wanted it to, but Laura being Laura and a complete 'jobs worth' went through every detail of Camilla's CV, then insisted that Camilla cut and blow-dry my hair. I really didn't want her to, as I still had bald patches in my hair where I'd pulled out some of my extensions. All I knew was my hair needed a break and so did I. Meanwhile, all I could hear was James laughing and giggling in the staffroom. It was very distracting.

As Camilla fussed around with my hair, I half-heartedly asked her what she would advise if I were a client.

'She could do with a really short, classic hair style,' interrupted Laura, 'no more of that porn star bleached mass… but of course, Tara,' she said, back-peddling, 'you know it's completely up to you.'

'Laura!' I hissed completely irritated whilst desperately trying to smooth my voice down. 'I know I'm in the bloody menopause, but does my hair *have to look* a siren stating that?'

'You *can't* be in the menopause,' Camilla said in shock, searching my pale face, 'you're way too young!'

'Thank you, Camilla,' I said, smiling in spite of myself, 'it's a very rare genetic disorder.' I added.

'No, it's not a rare genetic disorder – it's part of life, remember?' Laura shot back, shaking her head. 'We *don't do* denial anymore, do we? We embrace it, don't we?'

I couldn't believe Laura; she was now slowly nodding her head at me like I was an imbecile.

'I love short, sassy hairstyles,' broke in Camilla, changing the subject fast to prevent an impending assault, 'especially with a beautiful face like yours. You really could take it.'

'Can I hide a little of my face?' I pleaded. 'That's all I ask. I don't care about anything else.'

'No hiding anything,' insisted Laura, shaking her head at me.

Laura and Camilla began pulling out magazines as I sat and waited impatiently.

'How about this one?' asked Camilla, her finger poised over a picture. 'It's perfect for your face shape, short, yet still very edgy and youthful, with a long, peek-a-boo fringe that you can tuck behind your ears, or it can fall sexily over one eye.'

'As long as it covers some of my face, that's fine.' I said, accepting the picture and giving Laura a stern look.

'We could also dip-dye the fringe area in a soft ash to complement your natural, strawberry blonde tones,' she continued, confidently passing the magazine over to Laura.

'Oh yes,' chimed in Laura, nodding in agreement, 'very Gwyneth Paltrow from Sliding Doors.'

Just a few months ago, if anyone had come near my hair with a pair of scissors, I would have had a seizure.

They could tint it black for all I care; I just want to get it over and done with, I thought. But the last thing I needed was to make a bad impression on Camilla, so I plastered on a fake smile.

I already knew I wanted to hire her. She was perfect. She had years of experience and had just the right personality. Plus, she had managed a Salon earlier on in her career before she'd taken a year out to travel.

The whole interview and styling took an hour and a half. Poor Lewis must have been desperate to escape.

'Wow, you look great,' James announced as I entered the staffroom to let Lewis know the interview was over.

I glanced shyly over at Lewis and then looked away quickly. He was staring at me, open-mouthed. *Jesus, he must be thinking what a freakin' freak I am.* How humiliating. James was oblivious to it all, of course.

'Lewis likes stroking little furry things Tara, don't you, Lewis?' James giggled.

'Well, I guess you could put it like that,' laughed Lewis, grabbing his helmet.

'Can I have a little stroke of your helmet before you go please Lewis?' wheedled James outrageously.

Lewis laughed and pretended to knock James over the head with the bike helmet. 'I've been trying to keep you away from my 'helmet' for the last 90 minutes,' he said, 'I'm not going to give in now!'

I laughed nervously as I showed Lewis back into the main Salon. I then held out my hand to shake Camilla's.

Laura butted in: 'Thank you so much for coming in, Camilla. We will let you know in due course if you've been a successful candidate for the position.'

'Camilla - you've got the job.' I announced, cutting Laura off. 'You can start Monday. It's *my* Salon and I want you working here.'

'Tara!' Laura interjected sharply. 'We haven't discussed this. We need to see other applicants. Don't make any rash decisions...'

'Well, I think this arrangement is just perfect,' broke in James, whilst never once taking his eyes off Lewis' crotch. 'I can't think of anyone else I'd rather be working with.'

'What do you think, Camilla? You up for working here?' I asked, ignoring James, who was fastly becoming the annoying local queer pet.

'Wow, thank you so much. I really wasn't expecting to be offered a job so quickly. I would love to take the job! I promise you won't regret hiring me. Monday would be perfect.'

'Monday it is,' I said, wearily shaking both their hands and smiling as Camilla and Lewis left the Salon.

Laura didn't say a word - she didn't have to, her face was etched in complete disapproval.

'Laura,' I pleaded, 'please don't be angry with me, I need to start making my own decisions soon - you're not going to be around forever and I am grateful for everything you have done for me, honestly.'

'She's perfect,' Laura admitted, giving me a quick hug. 'Your hair looks the best I've ever seen it. You look ten years younger!'

'Really?' that had made my day.

'My - my,' sighed James, lustfully tossing back his precious mane of hair while frantically fanning himself with a magazine. 'You can't help but enjoy the view, can you? That man's sooo hot. He's *the* image of Bradley Cooper. And those green eyes were just... intoxicating.'

'I didn't even notice.' I shrugged, bitterly disappointed that the only decent piece of eye-candy I've seen in ages appears to bat for the other side.

After they left, I was feeling utterly exhausted from the morning's events. There were other applicants coming for the Beautician's post, but I really felt as though I'd had enough already.

'Laura, I'm so tired. I want to go home. I really can't cope with another makeover or interview.' I sighed shaking my head.

I stood, rubbing my tired eyes. Suddenly I heard Siobhan's voice bellowing through the Salon.

'Captain!' Siobhan saluted over to Laura, clicking her heels. 'Mission accomplished. I have found the missing Caucasian.'

Trailing in behind Siobhan was - Jackie! I was so pleased to see her! I leapt forward and hugged her as hard as I could before I burst into floods of tears. This was the one person on the planet who I knew for a fact was feeling much the same as I was.

'Tara, can I have my old job back please?' asked Jackie, wearing a huge grin with watering eyes.

'Yes… yes…! I couldn't think of anyone I would rather hire than you!'

That was it. The torrent of tears started again.

'I just had to get away, Tara. Well, until those two idiots were out of the picture at least.'

'I always warned you, Tara,' James snarled, 'Jayde was good for nothing.'

'They've both buggered off to Marbs,' Jackie announced, making a face, 'good riddance to them both.'

'Marbella?' I repeated, totally gob-smacked. 'Oh Jackie, I'm so, so sorry.' I shook my head, exhaling a deep breath of sadness.

'O-M-G,' snorted James dismissively, 'how utterly boring. Now, if you had said he took her to New York… or let's say… the Cayman Islands, or Miami, or even… Actually – Jayde, in Miami? I think not.' James began roaring with laughter. 'She wouldn't be allowed entry!'

'James!' I snapped. 'Please, have a little decorum.'

'Jackie, you look, - well… wonderful.' I stood back and examined her, shaking my head in wonder.

'Jackie?' James paused, cocking his head to one side. 'Have we had a little fun - with a wind tunnel?'

'Yep, I've had every lift you can think of,' she said defiantly lifting her hair-line to show minimal scars, 'Sheila added some Botox, fillers and a new skin care range and that *idiot* has paid for it all. By the time I've finished with his bank account they will both be sleeping on the beach. He's not even bothered seeing, or contacting, his own children. I think he deserves to suffer for a good while yet.'

'Go Jackie!' squealed James in complete awe. 'Whatever you're on Jaks, can you give some to Tara?'

'Come on Tara,' said Jackie giving me another hug, 'let's get the kettle on, you and I have got lots to catch up on!'

CHAPTER SEVENTEEN

[Three months later]…

'UGHH. I'm so bored,' sighed James dramatically. 'Nothing exciting ever happens around here anymore. I've even run out of horrible things to say now Jayde has gone. Tara - come on - the Salon is quiet and you've been talking about getting setup on this dating website for ages now. So let's get to it.'

'I haven't been saying that, *you've* been saying it!' I said, desperately wracking my brains for another topic that might divert James from his near-constant mantra about getting me back on the saddle. 'I'm really not sure if I'm ready. Apart from anything else, I still can't understand how my love life ended up like this. You know, where my so-called *friends* think it is okay to publicly discuss me having to go on a poxy website to find romance.'

'*Come on,* it's free to sign up,' said James enthusiastically, ignoring my protests (as always). 'The best way to get over a man is to get under another one! Your lady-garden must need tending to by now. There's only so much a Rampant Rabbit and some AA batteries can do. Trust me on that one.'

'Well…' I began, doubtfully. To be honest, I was running out of excuses. 'Okay.' I sighed.

'Right then. So we're doing it! Marvellous. Camilla, can you 'wo-man' the phone? Tara and I are off to get some tending sorted for a particular garden of hers.'

With that, James began to hustle me towards the computer in the staffroom.

James began to tap in information like a man possessed. I had never seen anyone type so fast; I guess he was racing through it before I could change my mind. In a matter of seconds, James had uploaded my best (photo-shopped) pictures. Then, as he got to the bit about height, age and interests I began to feel a rising sense of panic.

'Right, Tara. What are you looking for?'

'Hmmm. I don't know really.'

'A pretty boy? Tall? Thin? Gorgeous hair? Cute bum?' James turned to look at me, one eyebrow raised quizzically, his face full of expectation.

'James, this is *supposed* to be in aid of getting a man for *me*, and a real man too. We are not looking for a gay play thing for *you.*'

'Sorry, just trying to help.'

James looked a little crest-fallen and for a few moments I felt bad for snapping at him. Then I realised it was just an act. In a nanosecond he was back, pounding away at the keyboard again.

Let's see. I thought to myself, 'okay; seeking a knight in shining Armani, with washboard abs. Must be into sports, preferably rugby, with a northern accent, 6ft plus. Weaklings need not apply. In fact, if you're not remotely like Travis, don't apply.'

James swung around in his chair, glaring at me.

'What now?' I asked sharply.

'Tara, he may have been 6ft and incredibly strong with a *huge* bent dong, but mentally, he was incredibly weak and broke your heart. We are going to find you someone new, someone better. So tell me, what is it exactly that you look for in a man?'

'Okay, I want someone kind and gentle,' I said slowly, doing my very best to get into the swing of things. *Maybe if I thought about Travis and then just listed everything he wasn't.* 'Someone with a good kind soul. Above all, they must have excellent communication skills and be consistent.'

'Shall we put in, "no pecs, no sex"?' asked James, tapping away on the computer, utterly ignoring my more romantic aspirations. Sighing, my mind flashed back to Travis' perfectly sculpted body.

'Actually no, there are more important things,' I countered, as I pushed the painful, familiar image out of my head.

'Erm okay,' James said with a puzzled face, 'but you don't want to end up with a sack of lard do you? Just imagine Jayde with testicles. Not pretty is it?'

'Oh James, just put what you want, I'll leave it to you!' I huffed stamping out of the office.

Hold on, I thought, in alarm as I inadvertently began gnawing at my hand. *I must be out of my tiny mind leaving my dating destiny in James' hands.* My mind skittered around nervously. I had a terrible feeling that I had just made a humongous mistake.

Two hours passed and James was still in the staffroom. To take my mind off what he could possibly be doing to me, I started to go through the pile of receipts in the till. Takings were down again. Although I felt determined to pull the business back up to where it once was, it wasn't easy. Every time we got anywhere, we were always knocked back by some unexpected cost or a sudden downturn in business for no discernible reason. My train of thought was abruptly interrupted as a squealing noise filled the Salon.

'OH-MY-GOD. OH-MY-GOD. OH-MY-GOD!' James squawked, running into the main Salon on his tiptoes, his arms flapping wildly in the air.

'Darling. You have *ten* potential gardeners looking to get their fingers green into your lady-garden. How fabulous, darling!'

'Shhhhh,' I blushed, quickly raising my hands to my face in shock. I couldn't help it though, I was curious. 'Really?'

'*Yes*!' he screamed like a schoolgirl. 'Come and have a look!'

I walked over to the staffroom with Jackie and Camilla close behind me. They had tried to stay out of it, but like me, they couldn't resist checking out the fruits of James' labor.

With all of the staff looking over my shoulder, I opened the first email.

No. 1:

> Hey you look so juicy!
> If you were a bogey, I'd pick you first. lol.
> I'm so into older women, fancy having a toy-boy?
>
> [...]

'Eww! Yuck!' I slapped my hand over my mouth in disgust and deleted him before reading the rest.

No. 2:

Hi,

First... you are so hot! Deffo a solid 8!!!
I came across your profile and thought 'boom,' there she is... so thought I'd drop you a message.

I know it's forward of me but as my mum said, 'live for the moment' SO... I was wondering if I could take you for dinner in town next Thursday? Will have to be between 6 & 8 p.m if you're around, as I'll need my mum to drop me off and pick me up before she goes to bingo.

Unless you are heading my way? I don't mind if you want to pick me up? How about I let you choose where we go? Or, how about we all go to bingo together?

I look forward to hearing from you!

Larry

No. 3:

Hello

Neville here, I'm 45. I'm an IT Support Manager from Norwich.

I'm recently single after my wife left me for the decorator I hired to do our kitchen. He did a great job, but I don't think I will be recommending him.

I'm looking to make new friends and start dating again, so I wondered if you would like to come to mine for dinner one evening?

Now the wife has gone and taken everything, (apart from our four children) money's a little limited, but I'm sure you would love them all when you meet them.

Honestly, I could probably do with a hand at bath time anyway! Sunday's are homework days, but if I had a lady to help that would ease my life considerably. So if you're free let me know?

Anyway, I will stop jabbering. Hopefully you'll reply and we can arrange a day.

Anytime is good for me as I have a people carrier and can bring kids with me.

Look forward to hearing from you.

Neville

It wasn't a good start. After that disappointment, I scanned each email quickly. If it didn't catch my eye immediately, it was deleted. Amongst the emails, there were just two that stood out. One from someone called Jack and another from a guy called Luke. James and I agreed they were the only two worth a response.

Finally, alone in the staffroom, I began composing my reply emails.

Dear Jack,

I hope to find you well?

[Delete.]

Hey Jack,
Thank you for looking at my profile…

[Delete.]

'FOR FUCK'S SAKE!!!!!! I don't know what the fuck to
write! I just need a shag!'

[Send.]

'Shit!' I hissed. 'Shit! shit! shit!' I had accidentally clicked
the wrong button.

I was just about to give up and throw myself in front of a
bus, when I heard a pinging sound from the computer…

'Your message cannot be sent as it contains explicit
content.'

'Oh, thank God!' I flopped back in my chair, trying to
regain my nerves. I started typing again with much more care. I
sent a simple, carefree email to both Luke and Jack.

My replies seemed to do the trick. After a lot of back-and-
forth emailing, over a few days, I arranged dates with both of
them. I was slightly put off by the fact Luke always took a lot
longer to respond than his love rival - and, when he did email,
his replies were always very short and sharp. I was wary of
another Travis-type scenario, but Luke's good looks kept him
in the game (just).

Jack was the first of the pair to ask for my mobile number. The email landed while I was working and James, being nosey, took charge and emailed him my number without even mentioning it to me. Within a few minutes, I received an email back from him, with his number on it and a promise of a phone call later that day. I was cross with James because I worried things were moving faster than I could cope with, but I *was* secretly pleased. If I was left to my own devices, I'm sure I would have dithered and delayed so much that by the time I met up with one of these guys - I'd have been ready for my care home.

To prepare myself for the phone call, I went back through Jack's emails, (after all, I didn't want to confuse him with Luke and say something stupid). Jack's picture was that of a very handsome and distinguished man. He was quite a few years older than me, but he did have a bit of a George Clooney look going on. His description stated he was 5ft 11, with brown eyes and hair with an athletic build. Under 'Interests' he'd put that he liked fine dining and was heavily into motor racing. *Maybe I could do with someone a bit older and wiser*, I thought, as I nervously waited for him to call me.

A few hours later, he rang. I nervously cleared my throat and scuttled off to take the call in private, away from the giggles and screams of my excitable employees. Jack sounded incredibly posh. In fact, his voice sounded like that of royalty. To my surprise, I found his voice incredibly arousing, but also slightly intimidating. I giggled to myself - I really was watching my P's and Q's and putting on what Katie would call my 'telephone voice'.

After a long chat, Jack and I seemed to be getting on well. He asked if I'd like to meet up that weekend and I really couldn't see why not. In fact, I felt almost ready to meet someone new after all.

Yes, I still felt fragile on the inside - some days worse than others, but these days, sometimes an hour or two would pass before Travis even entered my head.

I gave Jack my address, even though the website had said it wasn't the wisest thing to do. He had insisted on picking me up (and quite frankly, I was enjoying the fact that a man was actually going out of his way for me).

My nerves were shot to bits for the next few days and I couldn't concentrate on anything. On more than one occasion, I keyed in a text to cancel our date, but at the last moment, I didn't press send.

I didn't sleep at all the night before and on the morning of the date itself I was no good to anyone. I don't think I had ever been so pleased to hear my front door open and a familiar banter as my two best friends crashed in.

'We're here!' shouted Siobhan and James as they ran up the stairs after letting themselves in.

'Come on, come on,' I ushered. As they tumbled into the room they were greeted with the sight of me standing in the centre of the room in odd shoes, a skirt and a chunky jumper; all worn in a crumpled lump over a fitted dress. In my hand I held an assortment of other garments. 'I don't know what to wear and he's picking me up in forty minutes!'

'Right Tara - calm down,' ordered James, sounding unusually focused. 'Let's start with that makeup.'

'I've already done my makeup James,' I faltered, 'oh my God, do I look that bad? I threw the other clothes I was holding onto the floor.

'Darling, *I'm* wearing more makeup than you,' said James gently. 'No worries, let's just touch it up a bit. Well, a lot.'

'I don't want to go, I won't be ready,' I moaned sulkily. 'I've changed my mind. I'm going to cancel.'

'You will in yer arse!' Siobhan said sternly, poking her head out from inside my wardrobe where she had been fumbling around for the past few minutes. 'You're going. I won't hear anything different from you. Of course - if you really don't want to go, can I take your place? I could do with a good shag.'

'Now now, Siobhan,' said James, sounding cross and shaking a large blusher brush at her. 'That's *not* helping.'

'Ah sure, I'm only playing with you. Don't worry, I'll find you something to wear.'

'I would go with the sexy, classy look,' James advised with a knowing pout. 'A long dress with a vicious slit up the side to show off some leg, and a nice bit of cleavage on display.'

'Fuck that, you big fairy,' snorted Siobhan. 'We're trying to get her some cock.'

Siobhan stood back to observe a pile of clothes she'd dug out of my wardrobe. 'I'm thinking mini-skirt... no - just a thick belt, stockings, suspenders and some nipple tassels if it is cold out like.'

'Siobhan,' interrupted James, 'remember what Tara has just been through. If she's going to go dressed like a hooker, she's going like a high-class one. Isn't that right, Tara?'

'I think you should wear this one.' Siobhan said, giving us both a raunchy look, 'it's feckin' gorgeous.'

The dress was one of my favourites; rich, deep, lilac satin to the knee, adorned with sequins, incredibly low cut, back and front, and very fitted. It was utterly sexy, yet elegant at the same time. However, it was the sort of dress that required a lot of confidence and attitude to wear - and I felt that I was severely lacking in both.

'James, what do you think?' I asked, unsure, as I pulled the dress on and smoothed it down.

'Wow,' gasped James, looking genuinely impressed. 'Perfect... Oh, your phone is ringing, I'll get it for you... Hello?... Oh, she's a little bit busy at the moment, can I take a message?... Ahh you're early and you're outside?... Okay, I'll let her know.'

'WHAT!? He's outside? He's here? Shit! He's 15 minutes early!' I said in a panic.

'Feck this for a game of soldiers, I'm going out for a look!' said Siobhan, making a run for the door.

'Not without me you're not!' shouted James, as they both abandoned me. I watched them shoulder-to-shoulder, battling out of the bedroom door, each trying to get down the stairs first. It would have been funny if I wasn't so sick with nerves.

'Err... guys?... Well I guess I'm wearing this dress then,' I said to the now empty room.

After quickly smoothing down my hair, I threw some heels on, grabbed my pashmina and bag and nervously headed downstairs. I cautiously went over to the window and pulled the blinds apart. Horrified, I looked out to find Siobhan straddling the bonnet of his car. Meanwhile, James was leaning into his open car window, deep in conversation while simultaneously doing his trademark seductive hair flick.

'SHIT!' I shouted, quickly moving away from the window. *The feckers! They're supposed to be on my side. What on earth is he going to think of me?*

'Oh. My. God.' Said James, looking rather flushed as he dramatically flung open the front door. 'He's gorgeous. He's perfect. He's driving an Aston. And I love him already. Sadly, I've already tested the waters and unfortunately he's 100 % straight. Just thought I would check for you darling. Now go on - go on - get out there before Siobhan eats him alive.'

A thought flashed across my mind that I wished it was Travis that was picking me up, but I quickly dismissed it. I knew it was time to move on. I didn't have long to dwell on it because in the next second, part two of the comedy duo crashed through the door.

'Feckin hell,' Siobhan gasped, pulling her skirt down. 'Go get him girl! He's feckin' ripe and ready for the picking that one. But keep off his bonnet it chafes like a bastard. Now remember; if you can't be good... be good *at* it.'

Taking one last look at me, Siobhan continued; 'Come here to me - your best assets need a bit of plumping and pumping.'

With that, Siobhan grabbed my boobs and hoisted them up and together before the duo shoved me out the door.

The date with Jack was very pleasant. He was a perfect gentleman and really good company. His good looks even took my breath away and I will admit our good night kiss lingered slightly longer than it should have done. But, that was as far as it went. There was one big problem with Jack - he wasn't Travis.

'Laura is right - maybe I do need to wait a while,' I said, looking at James and Siobhan as I nursed a coffee in the Salon. Bless them, I could tell they were trying to be on their best behaviour when all they really wanted to do was ask me if Jack and I had shagged.

'But, you're gonna see him again, right?' wheedled James. 'He is exceptionally gorgeous.'

'I don't know… he's gone to Germany for a month on business,' I said, with a shrug. 'Maybe I should just leave the dating game for a while.'

'Bloody nonsense,' scoffed Siobhan. 'You've got to throw your arse deeper into the dating game. Not literally of course, although I rather like a bit of back garden allotment tending meself.'

'Siobhan! Can you *please* stop bringing that up? I just want to forget all about that night.'

'You're just out of practise, you need to get back on the saddle. And fast!' added Siobhan urgently.

'A shag a day will keep the weeds at bay,' chorused James, strutting around like a bloody peacock.

'*A-shag-with-a-stud-and-a-roll-in-the-mud*,' sang Siobhan in her lowest bass voice.

'God, you two!' I groaned, 'I'm not some twenty-year-old, sex starved nymph!'

'But having a few good rounds of some damn fine rodgering will help cure you,' James said.

'Yeah, just get in, sit down, hold on and shut up,' stated Siobhan animatedly. 'It's easy - I do it all the time, yeah-baby-yeah,' her voice now going all-American as she playfully grabbed James' hips and began gyrating into his bum.

'You need some good old sex-ercising - at least daily,' shouted James, greeting Siobhan's exaggerated sexual thrusts with a crazy howl and slapping her thigh as she pretended to mount him from behind.

'Oh Gawd, but what if I start having a hot flush? That's hardly attractive.' I was putting any obstacle in the way I could think of.

'Women don't have hot flushes,' gasped James horrified. 'They have *power surges.*'

'Oh… James,' I said, reaching over to give him a hug in-between his thrusting, 'what a lovely way to put it. That's so sweet.'

'Anyway,' added James clicking his tongue, 'there's nothing wrong with looking like a menopausal Barbie.'

'Oh, thanks James… I think.'

'You know, Tara, my mattress does get rather a lot of action - and if it could talk…' sniggered James, 'mine would be sick of me.'

'If my mattress could talk… it would be mute,' I confessed in a sulky tone.

I have no idea how they persuaded me to do it, but in the end I was so fed up with their constant badgering that I agreed to try dates with at least five other men. They gave me a month to complete the challenge - we agreed that if it didn't work out I'd either try Jack again or give it up for a while. If I agreed to their terms, they agreed to stop hounding me. It wasn't a brilliant deal, but I could see it was the best I was going to get.

The only problem was - even though I had a few dates lined up, setting up five in one month was chaos. In the end, I got so confused with all their names, ages and interests that I had no alternative but to set up a spreadsheet. It must have been my inner-schoolgirl, but I have to confess I rather enjoyed designing my colour-coded spreadsheet and filling in the details like a sticker book. Filling it in certainly helped me to get through the following month:

TARA'S DATING SPREADSHEET

Name	Jack
Age:	55
Height:	5'11"
Zinger/Minger:	Zinger!
Job:	Racing Driver
Overall rating:	9/10
Notes:	Kissed like a dream, gave me goose bumps. Sadly, gone to Germany for a while.

Name	Charlie
Age:	39
Height:	3'2" (ish)
Zinger/Minger:	Minger
Job:	Oompa Loompa
Overall rating:	10/10 for his manor/castle, -10/10 for him.
Notes:	Despite the incredible abode, my imagination couldn't bypass the lack of height and far-from-symmetrical face. Plus, our nether-regions wouldn't fit together well... I have to stay true to myself, after all.

Name	Steve
Age:	36
Height:	5'11"
Zinger/Minger:	Zinger
Job:	Unknown
Overall rating:	2/10
Notes:	Gorgeous, but then pushed the pay terminal to me to pay for dinner. I thought he was joking and pushed it back to him. He pushed it back to me, the waiter got confused, so did I. I paid. Bastard.

Name	Zak
Age:	42 (allegedly)
Height:	6'1" (allegedly)
Zinger/Minger:	Zinger (based on his profile picture)
Job:	"Surgeon" (I doubt it)
Overall rating:	(Unknown)
Notes:	Cancelled on our first meeting – I gave him a gentle warning. I refuse to be mucked about. Now I'm even more desperate to meet this elusive gobshite.

Name	Troy
Age:	38
Height:	6'0"
Zinger/Minger:	Minger (in person)
Job:	Unknown. Probably on the dole though.
Overall rating:	-99/10
Notes:	Spent the evening discussing his 4 ex wives and 7 children. I yawned so much I got lockjaw several times.

Name	Omar
Age:	30
Height:	6'2"
Zinger/Minger:	Zinger
Job:	Porn Star
Overall rating:	1/10
Notes:	Arrived tanned and waxed within an inch of his life. Was buffed and wearing the tightest pair of skinny jeans (enhanced the lunchbox he was concealing in his pants). Date consisted of him detailing the "ins" and "outs" of his daily schedule... by that I mean the number of women he was "in" and "out" of on a daily basis. I have passed his number to James.

By the end of the month, I was still no clearer on the dating game. I hated to admit it, but it seemed like Laura might have actually been right. Those dates weren't doing me any good either. I was definitely going back on a rollercoaster of emotions and started to feel wounded all over again.

The dating game seemed too confusing. I felt myself becoming very agitated by all the weirdos. Then, there's all that effort; getting ready with such high expectations, only to be very disappointed more often than not. I really didn't know what I was looking for, which didn't help. Deep down, I knew it was because Travis was still parked in the back seat of my head. I would never have admitted it to Laura, but I still had my moments where I emotionally unclipped his seat belt and bought him to the front of my mind. All I found myself doing was comparing the guys I had been on dates with to Travis.

After dating my five agreed, I decided to give the internet dating malarkey a miss. I decided to contact Jack and tell him that I just wasn't ready. As I sat in the Salon reception trying to work out the best way to do it and whether dumping someone by text was just too cruel, Camilla wandered over.

'You know, Tara, my brother's really got the hot's for you!'

'That's sweet,' I smiled, trying not to sound too dismissive. Privately I thought *that is all I need, a guy who swings between both ways. I mean, at his age, really you would think he would know by now.*

'Lewis has been dying to ask you out for a date, but I said it was too soon,' Camilla pressed on, 'I told him to wait - you know, well… after what had happened to you.'

I looked up at her with a frown, wondering how to approach this one tactfully.

'Look, Camilla, it is really sweet of you to try and match-make, but I just can't do a complicated person right now. Your brother is utterly gorgeous, yes, but I want a man who likes women.'

'But, you do think he's cute though, right?' Camilla looked confused.

Oh God, where is this going? Did Lewis want to sample me to finally decide which he preferred, men or women?

'He's not stopped talking about you, since the day you hitched a lift on the back of his bike. Do you remember, that day you left your bag in the bank? He said it was like having a little angel wrapped around him.'

'Really?' I asked, casting my mind back to that day. It was quite a thrill sitting on that bike, come to think of it. 'That's so sweet, but I think he's more suited to, err, James?'

'Why James?' Camilla was now looking even more baffled.

I sighed hard. Didn't she even know her brother was gay? Was I going to be the one who would have to break the news to her? I hated giving bad news. It was almost worse than receiving bad news.

'Tara, you don't think my brother's a poof do you?' she began, her mouth curling into a smile, which was followed by a roar of laughter. 'He's as straight as they come. Oh my God, that's hilarious. Wait till I tell Lewis.'

'But James said… James told me… he likes stroking furry… oh *shit*.'

'That's because he's a vet!' Camilla added, doubled up with laughter.

'James, when you're finished with your client, can I have a word, please?' I called over my shoulder. Turning back to

Camilla, I wanted the ground to swallow me up. 'I'm really sorry Camilla, please don't tell him I thought that.'

'Okay, I won't tell him, but only on one condition. You have to go on a date with him!'

CHAPTER EIGHTEEN

[Text from Mum]

So I hear that Lewis is a dentist, can u ask him about my denture that keeps falling out? Well done anyway. So much better than a coach driver. Xx

[Text from Laura]

Have fun tomorrow. Just relax and be your lovely self x

[Text from James]

Please video him in action ;-) ;-) :-)

[Text from Siobhan]

Don't be having sex with him on the first date, wait till he asks for a threesome and call me, pronto!!

The night before my date with Lewis, I began to get cold feet. I must have drafted at least 20 messages to cancel, but in the end I didn't send any. I just couldn't. *Perhaps I'll feel better in the morning*, I told myself.

Leading up to the date, I was practically sick with nerves. I actually had to do some of Lickarse's breathing exercises when I heard the roar of Lewis' bike approaching my street. *Come on,* I warned myself as I straightened my t-shirt, pulled up my skinny jeans and opened the door.

'Morning, Tara,' said Lewis, removing his helmet, smoothing down his surfer-style, sun-kissed hair and pecking both of my cheeks.

'Hey, Lewis,' I said, breaking into a wide smile. *Why on earth had I been feeling this way? He is so nice and so goddamn hot, standing there clad in full biker leathers. Phwar!*

'Ready for our little adventure then?' he asked, handing me over a pair of leather trousers and a biker jacket.

'Yes… I think so. Where is it we're actually going again?' I asked, desperately trying to sound enthusiastic, as I eyed the bike wear suspiciously.

'It's a surprise,' he insisted.

I suddenly became very hesitant about the entire date. In a moment of panic, I involuntarily began blurting, 'Look… Lewis. I don't know how to put this… but can we *just* be friends? It's just that… well, I don't know if I'm ready yet.'

Lewis looked at me with his bright green eyes sparkling against his tanned face. 'Ready for what exactly?' he asked with an undeterred cheeky grin.

I felt my face flush. *Cocky sod, he knows exactly what I mean.*

'Ready for… well… I don't know,' I floundered. *Actually, that's a good point; what is it exactly I'm not ready for?*

'Shall we go then? Personally, I think you'll have a great time. But, you're under no obligation whatsoever to enjoy it. I won't even ask for one of your beautiful smiles. Scout's honour.' he said, holding up three gloved fingers.

'Hmm… Okay then. But do I *really* have to put this lot on?' I questioned, cocking my nose up at the pile of leather in my arms. They felt so damn heavy. *God knows if they will fit me. And doesn't leather put at least ten pounds on your behind?*

'I just didn't realise that we were going out on the bike. I thought we could...' I stopped short, seeing the spark of disappointment in Lewis' face. *God, I'm such a miserable bitch.*

'I have a little picnic ready, with Champagne. It's all in a cool-box on the bike waiting to go,' Lewis said, having recovered. 'It'll be fun.'

Before I could change my mind, I excused myself and ran upstairs to change into the leathers, leaving Lewis standing downstairs in the hallway. Privately, I was chiding myself. I knew I needed to make more of an effort. I'm sure part of the problem was that the leathers reminded me of my shameful experience with that poxy catsuit.

'Err, Lewis...' I shouted down the stairs. 'How easy are these to get on? I mean, do I need talc or something?'

'Err, no – I don't think so. The guy in the shop said if they don't fit you, we could return them for a different size. Are they too small?'

Even if they were too small, there was no way on this earth I would admit it. Grim-faced, I slipped my jeans off and started to put the leather trousers on one foot at a time, wobbling off-balance. I fell into my bedside table, sending myself and a lamp flying to the floor with an almighty crash.

'Tara! Are you okay?' Lewis shouted, running up the stairs.

'... I'm okay! Please don't come up!' I shrieked, horrified by the thought of him seeing me like this and with my trousers half on.

Too late, there was Lewis standing in the doorway of my bedroom. I grabbed the leathers and held them tight against me, my hand held out like grounded traffic policewoman in a vain bid to stop him in his tracks.

'Sorry – are you alright?!' he asked, shielding his eyes from my modesty. 'I thought… you might need a hand.'

'Oh really?' I laughed, pulling my leathers on and heaving myself up from the floor. I playfully shooed Lewis down the stairs, both of us still laughing.

'Tara,' Lewis shouted back as he clattered down the stairs, 'I know this is forward, but purple is most definitely your colour!'

I laughed out loud as I firmly closed my bedroom door. *Bloody cheek. My underwear is pink.*

… Underwear… Ann Summers… Bingo! I knew I'd seen Lewis before; he was the guy in the queue trying to buy underwear the day I got taken hostage in that gobbling catsuit! *What a small world,* I thought.

Within moments of composing myself, we were roaring up my street on the back of Lewis' Ducati.

As I molded my body around Lewis and rested my helmet on his back, I suddenly realised I felt totally relaxed around this man; even though we'd only known each other a short time (and the fact we were on the back of a terrifying motorbike). Somehow, it just felt right.

Before I knew it, we were thundering out of the city and swishing around corners on country roads. I closed my eyes tight and screamed at the adrenaline-fuelled, heady mixture of delight and fear rolled into one. After a while, Lewis signalled and turned off the road into a picturesque, lush, green field laden with bright red poppies.

'Phew,' I exhaled as I removed my helmet. After that incredible journey, I couldn't help but smile. Then I had a proper look at the breathtaking setting and smiled even more.

'Wow!' I shook my head in awe at just how amazing everything was right at that moment. I wondered if I would ever feel this good again. For a start, my heart was a long way from reaching its normal rhythm. Totally speechless, I clutched my chest.

'It's so good to see you smiling,' said Lewis looking almost proud, 'you have such a lovely smile.'

Blushing, I caressed the warm leather seat of the gleaming motorbike. 'I've got to get me one of these – it's such a rush!'

As Lewis unloaded the cool box from the bike and carefully laid things out on an old-fashioned picnic rug, I stood and took in the wonderful, calming views surrounding us. I suddenly felt weepy (not in an I'm-going-to kill-myself kind of weepy, but more of a today-I'm-glad-to-be-alive weepy).

'Are you okay?' asked Lewis gently. I suppressed my tears and turned to face him as he handed me a glass of Champagne. There was a look of concern etched over his face.

'Yes, I'm fine,' I nodded breathing in the country air, forcing a smile to make up for my soppiness. 'It's just so nice here. I can sometimes get a little emotional when I see things of beauty, sorry.' I blabbed.

Lewis politely ignored my moment of weakness and held out a bottle of water for himself.

'You're not drinking Champagne with me?' I asked.

'I don't drink and drive,' smiled Lewis as he knelt down and picked a poppy from the wild field, 'and especially when I'm carrying such precious cargo.'

'Well, you certainly score points for that corny line,' I smirked, 'I have to be honest with you, Lewis… I *was* going to cancel our date this morning… but now I'm so glad I didn't.'

'Well, I'm glad you didn't either,' he said, beaming. He then gently placed the beautiful red poppy into the side of my hair, pecked my nose and began quoting;

'Just living is not enough… one must have sunshine, freedom, and a little flower.' [– Hans Christian Andersen.]

'Wow… that's beautiful. It's so true and so poignant right now.'

Desperate to impress Lewis with an equally mind-blowing quote of my own; I stood, gormlessly, waiting for my brain to engage, looking up to the cloudless-sky for inspiration. *Nope. Nothing up there. Bugger. Come on brain, engage, engage!* I linked my hands behind my back (just as I had seen Laura do so often) and began pacing up and down in deep thought.

'Sorry… It takes time to kick-start this thing,' I said, tapping at my head with the empty Champagne glass. 'It's not that I'm not clever,' I added, recalling one of Laura's sessions with me, 'it's just… I'm more of a creative, rather than an academic person.'

'That's fine. Relax, please,' insisted Lewis, smiling and rubbing my arm tenderly. 'This isn't a competition.'

I waved a finger in the air, indicating I had an impending brain wave. 'Wait – I've got it!' I squealed, causing Lewis to startle.

Be prepared to be impressed, I thought, thanking God for sending this Eureka moment.

'A woman carries her clothes, but it's the shoe that carries the woman' [– Christian Louboutin]

Right back at you! I thought smugly.

'See, that's what I *lov*... err... what I *like* about you, Tara. You're smart, but also cute and innocent. You're... wonderful.'

Lewis was beaming, not in a *Christ-she's-dim* sort of way, but rather with a look of genuine affection. Laura may be a total lickarse, I thought, but she'd certainly done a fine job at getting my brain to engage.

I smiled bashfully, fingering the delicate flower in my hair, almost swooning. I changed the subject to draw attention away from my reddening face.

'Wow. There's not another soul around for miles. It feels strange for a city girl like me. Mind you, I could get used to it; it's just *so* calm.' I said, taking in every drop of the freedom I felt. 'Have you seen that gorgeous house over there? It's huge! And with all this beautiful, quiet land around it. Can you think of a more idyllic setting for a home?'

'Do you like it?' Lewis asked, casually chugging on his bottle of water.

'Who wouldn't?' I asked rhetorically, still stunned by the beauty of the backdrop.

'Good. Well, I've had that house for a few years now. I guess I must have been thinking ahead. I'd always thought it would be amazing to have my home and veterinary surgery here.'

'...You *own*... *all* of this?' I said, swinging around to face him. I needed to check whether he was just teasing me. I could tell by his face he wasn't. *Jesus.* I was gob-smacked. 'What, you even own those *huge* trees over there?'

'Sure do,' he smiled.

I handed over my empty glass to be refilled. Maybe I did fancy him more than I realised. He had such a lovely outlook on life. I loved the wild freedom of the motorbike and the place he had picked for his home and surgery.

Suddenly I eyed him with a whole different viewpoint. This was indeed a man to be taken seriously, very seriously. As a matter-of-fact, *I could end up being a vet's wife* I thought. *I wonder if he has letters after his name? Or before his name? Is he classed as a doctor? He must be, I thought, he's a vet... But would I be able to use those letters or his title with my name? Would that then make me...*

'... Lewis,' I began, as casually as possible, 'your surname - is it the same as Camilla's?'

'Yeah, we're both Copeland's, why do you ask?' Questioned Lewis, while tinkering with the strap of my helmet.

'Nothing, I was just wondering.'

Hmmm. Mrs. Tara Copeland. Mrs. Dr. Tara Copeland. Surely if we were to marry... I would get the Dr. title?

Oh stop it! Here I go again. I mean, why bother staying grounded when I can manufacture yet another crazy dream in my mind. That's the old Tara, raising her stupid ugly head. Clearly my brain matter was shrinking again.

I must not think this way, I must not become obsessive. I must not be delusional. 'Good, well done, I thought to myself, triumphantly. *I'm at least recognising the signs of delusional behaviour. It's all about the 'Zen,'* I began humming to myself.

'I was wrong this morning,' said Lewis, interrupting my thoughts. 'I shouldn't have come upstairs whilst you were changing. I don't know what came over me; I just panicked because I thought you had hurt yourself.'

'It's okay,' I blushed.

'No. I was completely out of order. It's been a while since, you know, I've been in the dating game.' He said, finally placing my helmet down on the handlebars of his motorbike.

'You're forgiven - but don't do it again,' I warned, wagging my finger playfully.

'Time is most definitely a great healer. I never thought I would get over my ex Fiancée.' He announced, standing closer to me.

'Fiancée?' I stepped back, feeling a stab of jealousy coming out of nowhere. 'I didn't know that you had been engaged.' So that's what he was doing in Ann Summers - buying *her* underwear.

'Yeah,' sighed Lewis with a slight nod, 'I thought she was *the one*,' he added, shrugging his shoulders. 'I couldn't have been more wrong.'

I certainly knew how that felt, as I reflected and considered my own emotional meltdown. Just the mere mention or thought of Travis and *her*, together with their baby, left a very bitter taste in my mouth.

'I caught her in bed with my so-called "best buddy"' he continued quietly.

'Oh my god,' I huffed shaking my head, 'that's just awful, losing your fiancée *and* your best friend. How on earth did you get through that?' I asked, stroking his delicious, strong doctor's hand and thinking *maybe* the *Big-Man upstairs* had been trying to pair us two together in Ann summers, even back then.

'I got myself a new girl,' he added, his face breaking into a grin. 'The quickest way to get over someone is to get on top of someone else.'

'Oh really?' I snapped, tossing his disgusting hand away and feeling my emotional balance swaying low. *Bloody bastard.* I huffed under my breath as my stomach clenched in total disappointment. *They're all the same! And to think, just a few minutes ago I wanted to be his wife! No sir-ee, not-in-a-million - he's a gobshite, just like all the rest.* And, quite frankly, I didn't fancy putting my hand up a horses arse anyway, no matter how much the doctor's gloves could stretch!

'Her name's Thumper and she's over there…' he added sharply, sensing my repulsion, while frantically pointing at his Ducati bike.

Lewis picked my hand back up and kissed it tenderly. *And so he should, for scaring me like that,* I thought as relief washed over me.

'Perhaps there's no such thing as *the one,*' I said. 'Perhaps, it's all just wishful thinking.'

I was suddenly feeling very philosophical and hoped he would argue the point with me.

Lewis remained silent. All I could hear was Lewis taking in a deep lung-filling breath as he squeezed my hand tight. I exhaled sharply and then held my breath as I dared to ask the next question.

'Do you still think about her?'

'Who?' asked Lewis with a sexy grin as he slid his thumb playfully around my palm.

Okay, I get it. Keep calm. He is saying his ex is history. Maybe Lewis and I have more in common than I realised.

'That was then,' added Lewis studying my face intently, 'this is now. And I'm rather enjoying the now.'

I fluttered my lashes and closed my eyes; giving off pouty, sexy signals that it was okay for him to kiss me.

He didn't.

Instead, he lay back on the blanket and stretched his arms up behind his head. Dizzy from the Champagne and disappointed that my pouty signal failed, I clumsily laid down beside him.

'Has Camilla told you what happened to me?' I asked, still feeling emboldened by the alcohol. I was almost positive that James would have filled her in; giving every tiny, dreadful detail. I had to tell Lewis the truth.

But before Lewis could answer, I blurted out the worst; 'I can't have children. I left it too late.' Choking on my words, I gulped back the emotion.

'Oh… well, my animals are my babies. That's plenty enough for me.'

Before I realised what I was doing, I dived on top of him and began kissing him. Instantly, the two of us were locked into a passionate embrace, tearing and fumbling at each others zips and layers of thick leather that were separating our quivering flesh. Around and around the grass we rolled, ripping off clothing and gasping for each other.

One moment Lewis was on top of me - then I was on top of him, fumbling and biting each other wildly as our tongues danced into each other's mouths. God, I wanted him so badly.

'This is all I have wanted to do since the day I met you,' he breathed hoarsely in my ear. 'I just want to look after you, hold you in my arms and keep you safe.'

His eyes were now searching my face for clues, or perhaps permission to take me. I nodded silently as he swooped in again, kissing me recklessly. Condom, no condom, we didn't care - and it didn't matter. Everything inside me stirred, awakening eager, wild lust. I couldn't help myself. It felt so good to be with him. All the crap that we had both endured in the past seemingly fell away. I hugged him tight, breathing in his beautiful scent, pulling him into me as I clambered on top of him and rocked my semi naked body gently against his.

'Tara,' he moaned staring intently at me. 'You're *the one.*'

'Sshh,' I smiled bravely, placing my fingers over his beautiful full lips, feeling the sturdiness of his beautiful body beneath mine.

'You're perfect,' whispered Lewis, as I gathered my hip rocking pace, easing his throbbing love-muscle into me slowly.

'Ahh… Tara… stop… it's been so long… I'm going to cum.'

'Then cum,' I added triumphantly, staring at his blonde hair, splayed around him like a halo. *Clearly, another message from the Big-Man himself.*

'No, ladies first,' he groaned hoarsely, desperately trying to hold on.

Not on your life. I thought to myself, holding it back. There's no way. *Not after my last nappy-requiring orgasm. No, mine can wait till we're both in the bedroom later. And anyway, it would make me far too emotional.* I wasn't quite ready to go there, not yet.

'Tara,' cursed Lewis in a husky tone, 'I can't hold on… please cum with me.'

'I am Lewis - I am,' I yelled, totally lost in him and I was; not in body, but certainly in my mind.

I cupped his beautiful square jaw, encouraging and comforting him, as his body trembled and shook; draining itself into mine.

As we lay there afterwards, absorbing the aftershocks, I couldn't help but think about how I felt. I was happy, yes, and satisfied, absolutely. *Yay!* (my days of waiting for the washing machine to vibrate on that particular cycle are over). Well, they will be later when I get in his bedroom. But there was something else. I felt calm, relaxed and safe. I knew instinctively this man would never hurt me.

I poured myself yet another glass of bubbly to celebrate.

'I know this is kind of sudden and I don't want to frighten you off,' announced Lewis clearing his throat and sitting up.

'What?' I asked nervously, raising my chin up to the sun and placing my hand over his tanned, taunt six-pack.

'Look, I'm just gonna say it. You don't have to say anything, but I've been busting a gut to say something all afternoon.'

Instantly I froze, everything flashing through my head like a whirlwind. *Please don't tell me you're bi-sexual, or worse still, that you do want babies and this was all a big mistake. Or,* I thought, my heart pounding, *that he wants to ask me to marry him?*

Panicked, I dismissed the glass and reached over to the bottle of Champagne and poured it down my throat.

'Tara,' said Lewis, clearing his throat again.

'Yes,' I hummed to myself, willing him to say whatever it was (and quickly). The latter of my thoughts would be just so perfect (marriage), but knowing my luck it would be the first of my thoughts (bi-sexual).

'I… err… love… your hair… short.'

'What?' I spat in horror, 'You were building up to say *that?*' I huffed. I felt like all the air within my lungs had been punctured. I mean, really? All that build-up… for that crock of shite!

'Tara…'

That could give a woman of my age, with my rare-genetic-disorder, a stroke or a heart attack. *What a custard launcher. I wouldn't look at him - and why the feck should I?*

'Tara…'

'What?!' I huffed, sulking and still refusing to make eye contact as I stumbled around, pulling my clothes back on in temper.

'I want you to remember this moment,' he said thoughtfully, breathing in hard. 'This is *our* special place.'

'Not sure what's so special about it,' I pouted folding my arms in protest, trying to steady myself.

'I was joking earlier, about your hair, I mean err… I love your hair, what I mean is… please don't get frightened… it's just that… I think I have fallen deeply and madly in love with you.'

Well that statement certainly grabbed my drunken attention! Unable to keep a lid on his excitement he pulled me down to him and kissed me again, I could feel a single teardrop snake down my cheek. I felt the warmth of his love exploding in my mouth as he kissed me again.

'Say it again,' I begged. 'Say it *again.*'

'I love you, Tara Ryan!' he shouted out to the world as he tenderly scooped me up and swung me round.

And at that moment, I think I really loved him too.

Like a crazy pair of kids we held hands, running wildly through the poppies, disappearing among them as we made passionate love all over again. Only this time I didn't hold back- well, I'm sure the poppies needed a good watering anyway.

I'm not sure how long we lay there after that. It was certainly getting dark by the time we began to think about moving. I was starting to feel cold.

'I can see why you love this place,' I said tentatively, breaking the silence.

'It's amazing, isn't it? I come here when I need to think - or sometimes when I *don't* want to think. I love the journey over on Thumper, I feel as though I can go as far as I want, as fast as I want. The rush can be so surreal, sliding around switchback corners with thousand-foot drops; my palms sweating, fingers clenching, muscles tightening.'

I could see he had drifted off. I really didn't mind though. I already loved that faraway look in his eyes. I loved his free spirit and sense of adventure.

'Sorry... am I boring you?' he said, looking worried as he snapped back to the here-and-now.

'Not at all,' I said, as I started pulling on my leathers.

'Today was special, wasn't it?' said Lewis, grinning.

It was. It was like a fairytale. *Girl meets hot boy of her dreams and they live happily ever after.* Sorted.

As we walked back to the motorbike, I felt like I was walking on air. Finally, *finally,* it had all come good. I had met someone who genuinely liked me for me, after all, he'd seen me at my worst, no fake-tan, no hair extensions, no flashy clothing and yet, he told me he loved me. I already knew he would never ever mess me about or let me down.

I watched Lewis gathering up the last bits from our picnic site and couldn't help grinning at him. *You soppy loon,* I chided myself. I think I had just had one of the best days of my life.

I heard the familiar ping of my mobile going off. *That's probably James or Siobhan wanting the dirty details,* I thought. It took me a while to locate it under all the usual debris of my bag. When I finally managed to dig it out, I could see a text from a number I didn't have saved.

[Text from (Unrecognised)]

Hi Tara, hope you're good. It turned out the baby wasn't mine. I still think about you every day. I need to make things up to you. Please will you meet me?

Travis x

… TO BE CONTINUED …

Keep up with Tara's next move:

'Like' Fur Coat No Knickers on Facebook:

facebook.com/FurCoatNoKnickersTheBook

Follow the trend on Twitter:

#FurCoatNoKnickers

Lightning Source UK Ltd.
Milton Keynes UK
UKOW02f0854130815

256878UK00004B/50/P